Bad Blood

Luke Deckard

Copyright © Luke Deckard 2024.

The right of Luke Deckard to be identified as the author of this work has been asserted by him in accordance with the Copyright, Designs and Patents Act, 1988.

First published in 2024 by Sharpe Books.

For Claire and Lana.

BAD BLOOD

1

LONDON 1922

Yellow smog choked the city as I exited Tottenham Court Road Underground. The day was a fight, and I didn't win. It was a cold, wet Monday evening in the middle of December, and I lusted over the idea of putting my feet up and sipping a warm coffee. I was everything a Private Investigator shouldn't be: tired, dishevelled, and cranky. Since 6am, I had been on a tail job, looking for a runaway teenager. The kid heard I was looking for him and went home before I could find him, so his family decided my time wasn't worth reimbursing. A day wasted, and my wallet was lighter than it ought to be; all I wanted was quiet and warmth.

The corner of Oxford Street and Tottenham Court Road bustled with double-decker buses, cabs, and horse-drawn carriages, and the pavement heaved with heavy foot traffic. London was decorated with tinsel and lights and glittered with Christmas festivities. The shops, restaurants, and theatres blinked with loud neon lights. Bright young things basked in it all, seeking carefree fun.

Making my way up Tottenham Court Road, a spotty-faced newsboy outside the Court Picture House shouted the big headline: "Treasury's To Scrap War Grants! European Immigrants To Repatriate." I picked up a paper to see what it was about but got distracted by an ad for Selfridges. Their big window display was reported as a 'must see.' I cringed. Henry Selfridge's bombardment of American consumerism in Britain made my skin crawl. It was like a faux remedy to make people forget the twenty million dead. It was empty showmanship fuelled by American arrogance: 'Give me your money; it'll sort your problems.' I once heard someone say, 'The Devil came from America,' and maybe it was true. I bought the paper and went on my way with it tucked under my arm.

I turned down Percy Street, where I rented a second-floor flat

LUKE DECKARD

that doubled as an office. It was nothing fancy, the front room I made into an office to meet clients with a bed in the back. There was no doorman or a lift. Just barely affordable rent as long as work remained steady. My services weren't steep, which allowed a steady cash flow to keep a roof over my head and to act as my own boss. After the war, I swore I'd never work for anyone else again.

My relief to be home abruptly ended. In my pigeonhole was a coloured postcard. It featured Lady Liberty and said, 'WELCOME TO NEW YORK'—the mere sight of her made me queasy, like all things American had done since France. There's something about watching your friends get blown into hamburger meat that leaves a guy disillusioned with the Land of the *Free*.

On the back, chicken-scratch handwriting said: *I'm in London. We need to speak ASAP. Contact me at the Corinthian Hotel. Room 405. Dad.*

"Shit." I crumpled the postcard in my hand. The note hit like a sucker punch. We hadn't spoken for nearly a decade, a choice neither of us regretted, or so I thought. So why the hell was he here? Did I even want to know after all these years?

I took my throbbing feet upstairs.

Outside my door, I removed the matchstick wedged between the door and the frame—a cheap but efficient burglar system. Inside, I threw the crushed postcard and newspaper on the desk. The paper knocked over a framed photograph. I cursed and rushed to pick it up—the glass had cracked, and I sunk inside. The black-and-white image was of Tim Powell, me, and a few other buddies taken in France during the war on a rare day when hell needed a rest. We sat in the middle of a field on abandoned armchairs. Jackson and Bill were reading a letter from Jackson's wife—she had written some naughty things, and the two were giggling like schoolboys over it. Tim looked at the camera. He was smiling and reaching for a bottle of wine. I raised my tin cup to salute the cameraman. I put the broken image down. Dad being in London meant I was returning to war.

I shed my coat and hat and paced the room, deciding whether to call Dad. I was happy with the way things were, well and truly out of each other's lives. He manipulated the majority of my childhood, I wasn't going to let him do that to me now. The electric heater buzzed, and Marion Harris's sultry voice played on the gramophone. A thought kept nagging at me: the fact Dad was in London meant that whatever his reason was for being here was serious. It had to be. If I didn't call, chances are he would show up anyway. Why stretch it out any longer than it should be?

I stood over the telephone, reluctant to pick it up, like a modern Pandora's box.

Sitting in my creaky desk chair, I lifted the receiver and wrapped the stiff cord around my hand as I waited to be connected first to the hotel and then to Dad's room.

"Room 405?"

The sound of Dad's hoarse voice over the crackly line stopped my heart for a moment, and I forgot to speak.

"Logan?" he asked. "Is that you?"

"Dad." I eventually said.

"Heh. Quite the surprise, eh?"

"You could say that."

"I need to see you, son. Tonight. Can you meet me?"

"Dad, what is this?"

"I can't discuss it over the phone."

"Can't or won't?"

"Logan, come to the hotel or let me take you to dinner. Somewhere discrete."

"Discrete? Dad, I've been out all day and am exhausted. Talk to me now."

"Son," he paused, "it's urgent." His voice lowered. "I need your help."

"With what?" I asked.

"Retrieving an item in Edinburgh."

"*Edinburgh?*" I spat. There was a pause.

"Son, it's life or death."

"What have you done?"

"Dammit, Logan. Let's talk in person, please. You know this

isn't easy asking for your help. I'll pay you, of course. Consider me a client."

"Dad—"

"Logan, I know after all these years I have no right to ask for your help, but I can't trust anyone else. I'm in over my head, son. *They've* threatened to hurt your mother."

"Mom? Who threatened you?"

"Dratted... Not over the phone, son. Please, meet me."

As a boy, I never saw Dad act desperate. Now, his voice was drenched in it.

My body shivered, but not from the cold. A typical job wouldn't feel like this. The bad blood didn't matter, just the blood—call it primal or supernatural, but I knew I had to help him even if it went against my instincts.

Before I said anything more, he spoke.

"Did you tell anyone I was here?" His inflexion went up.

"No, I literally just got home," I huffed.

"Someone's at the door." He sounded concerned.

"It's probably hotel staff."

"I told them not to disturb me." Dad's voice shook.

"Ignore it," I said.

"Hold on, son."

"No, wait. Dad. Dad?"

He put the phone down. Through the static, I heard a crash. Dad yelped. There were muffled voices at first, but his voice became clearer as he neared the phone. He was doing it for my benefit. Dad said: "I swear I'll get it. That's why I'm here. You got to believe me." There was a struggle."Logan!"

The line went dead.

2

At the Corinthian Hotel, I beat on Dad's door.

My mind raced. What kind of trouble was he in? Back in Chicago, he had been close to the Lombardo family. Drugs, racketeering, prostitution, you name it, they ran it, and he laundered the money through his church. My dad, the preacher. A spiritual pillar of the community and a money cleaner for the Mafia. When I became a Pinkerton detective, I avoided any job that might've led me to Dad. Despite our differences, I could never have done that to Mom.

I continued beating the door and calling out, but there was no answer.

I tried the handle—locked, naturally. I got out my pick and started on it. Within seconds, it clicked, and the door opened.

The room was dark. I reached into my coat and pulled my Colt M1911 from the shoulder holster. I cocked it as I glided over the soft carpet. I ran my hand over the wall, feeling the cool, smooth wallpaper until I found the brass light switch and flicked it up.

Lying on the green honeycomb-patterned floor, between the bed and seating area, was a fat man in a mustard-brown suit well-tailored to an egg-shaped frame. Next to his head was a pillow. His face was bloody. From the bend of his left knee, I knew it was broken—like someone had smashed it with a hammer or the butt of a gun.

I fell beside the man to check his vitals, but I froze. It took me a second, but I recognised the face—it was Dad. He had a jawline the last time I saw him. Now, it was lost beneath layers of fat. His hairline was now nothing but grey wisps. This wasn't the man I remembered. He looked like he went into a funhouse, and the wide-mirror version came out.

I tried to rouse him, but he didn't move. There were red strangulation marks on his thick neck. I felt for a pulse but couldn't find one. I took his wrist—his hands were bloody, and his fingers were grotesquely bent in unnatural directions, broken, with the fingernails peeled off. Whoever did this masked Dad's screams with the pillow. It was still wet with blood, saliva, and sweat.

I opened his eyelids—Nothing. I put my finger under his nose. I couldn't tell if he was breathing. I smacked his cheeks to stir him. Then, I began to perform chest compressions.

"Come on, Dad!" I pressed one-two-three. No response. One-two-three. My version of Dad's life flashed in my mind—the birthdays, Christmases, Thanksgivings, taking my brother Eli and me to see the White Sox and eating hot dogs, ice cream, and catching foul balls. Dad's monstrous snoring. His anger at my refusal to go to seminary.

"Don't die. Don't you do it." One-two-three. Pause. One-two-three.

Buried memories of death were pushed to the front of my mind with each compression—muddy trenches, carcasses of men and horses, bombs ripping my friends to shreds, and losing my best friend, Tim.

Dad suddenly coughed, and I jolted back. His eyes opened and rolled around. He was dazed but clinging to life. My mouth went dry, and my face felt flushed. There was a sharp pain in my chest, and my heart raced like a derby horse. "Not now, not now." I knew what was coming. Tim Powell's ghost stood next to Dad, the way I hated to remember my war buddy: his pale white face, dead-alive eyes, tatty, torn and bloody uniform, and a bullet hole in his forehead.

Blood roared in my ears as my ghost watched me. My eyes welled. The room blurred out of focus, and my vision tunnelled on Tim. I crawled away and clamoured towards the toilet. My head spun, and my knees shook. I plopped down on the porcelain toilet seat in the bathroom and tried to breathe. I could barely fill my lungs. My shaking hand took out the half-empty bottle of Winslow's Soothing Syrup from my trouser pocket, and I poured it down my throat. The bitter taste sent a chill through me, but the morphine was euphoric. They say enough of it will kill a baby—every time I took it, I asked: how much will kill a man?

I told myself to pull it together—Dad was dying, and there I was, crippled by my ghost.

Within moments, the Winslow's soothed my anxiety like a mother's lullaby. I stumbled out of the toilet and avoided looking at myself in the mirror. I rarely liked my reflection, but least of all, after moments like that. It's the shame—the shame of being messed up in the head, the shame of needing a drug to cope, and the fear that I can't control these episodes.

I called for a doctor, and then I knelt beside Dad. His chest moved up and down slightly.

"Dad, it's Logan. I'm here." I cupped his chubby face and tried to get him to look at me. "You're going to be okay. The doc is on his way."

His mouth moved, but talking was difficult. His eyes were barely open.

"Relax, Dad."

He grunted. His bloodshot eyes bulged. He had something to say, but the pain made him delirious. I leaned in close to ease his strain.

"Her... life... in d-danger..." Dad's raspy voice said. "They'll kill her... 'cause of me..." His eyes began to shut.

"Kill who? Are you talking about Mom? Dad, who did this?"

His eyes shut. I gently smacked his cheeks, and his eyes reopened.

He coughed, and a little blood came out of his mouth. "H-hat... h-at..."

His brown fedora was on the floor by the two-seater sofa. I grabbed it.

"Inside." His face twisted with pain. "Find her. Get it..." He winched with pain.

On the inside of the hat, hidden behind the flap, I found a folded piece of paper with an address scrawled: *Greta Matas: 7 Queen Street, Edinburgh.*

"Dad, who is this woman? Get what?" I needed him to speak clearly, but that wasn't going to happen.

As he faded again, he said, "Don't let them... kill Greta..."

LUKE DECKARD

3

Dad was rushed to St Thomas' Hospital opposite the Houses of Parliament. I gave a statement to a disinterested cop with a large moustache—when I asked if someone could call Edinburgh police to check on Greta Matas, the side-eyed look told me it wouldn't be followed up quickly. The copper didn't care to be told what to do by an American private investigator.

When he finished with me, I waited for a doctor to tell me about Dad.

I was sitting there, for I don't know how long, alone with my thoughts. How would Dad explain this to Mom? No way she knew that he was here, and if she did, what he was doing. Really doing. That wasn't much of an epiphany. Dad was a two-faced man, skilled at purporting to be righteous in front of his little congregation but also a master liar—a handy prowess most ministers have. What lie would he concoct to explain this mess? He'd undoubtedly expect me to cover for him as I did as a kid.

The ammonia stench of the hospital faded, and I was transported back to my childhood, to my little Chicago suburb, that the summer I first lied to protect my father.

I was eight. I ran to the church to hide from my brother Eli and his friends, who wanted to stuff a frog down my trousers. I rushed inside and shut the door, holding it closed with all my strength, waiting for them to beat on it. My heart was in my ears. When the pulsing in my head stopped, I heard a yelp. It was inside the church. I pushed off the door and walked through the sanctuary towards the back, where Dad's office was.

I could hear grunts and fleshy smacks from Dad's office. It sounded like someone was getting beaten up.

His office door was ajar—I peered inside, and my gut sank.

My Sunday school teacher, Miss Grace, was bent over the desk. She was naked. Dad, standing behind her, still wore his shirt, but his trousers were dropped. Miss Grace's hands lay flat on the desk, and her nails dug into the leather surface. Red blotches covered

BAD BLOOD

her milk-white skin.

"Yes... Faster..." she ordered.

Dad smacked her ass-cheeks.

I watched them, curious and confused. It took me a couple of seconds to register what was happening, but I knew it couldn't be right from the outset. Dad naked with a woman who wasn't Mom? I had no answers. I was young and stupid in the ways of sex. Despite the horror, I was caught up by the sight of a naked woman, a beautiful one. Miss Grace was a pretty, blonde woman.

"Faster... Faster, Danny. Yes, das it," she said.

Dad grabbed a handful of her long blonde hair and yanked her head back. The two groaned. I watched her breasts being squeezed by Dad's meaty, hairy hands.

"Logan!" Dad's eyes locked on me—they were wide. He'd been caught.

Miss Grace's eyes shot to the door. "Oh, God!" She pushed back into Dad and covered her breasts. "Deal with him!"

I bolted out of the church.

It didn't happen... It didn't happen... I told myself. That isn't what married people do. How could he? The Bible says that's wrong... people don't do that... But he did it? Do I tell Mom? Do I tell my brother? What was Dad going to do to me?

I leaned on the lamppost outside our house, and the world spun. My face was wet with sweat and tears. I ran inside. A chicken was roasting in the oven. I cried and hugged Mom. I couldn't tell her what I saw. She told me to 'man up' and that 'boys don't cry.'

The next morning, Dad told me to walk with him to the church. He brought me into his office and sat me down. I could see the marks in the leather from my Sunday school teacher's nails. He looked across his desk at me and asked if I had said anything to Mom. I said no. He said good and that what I saw must be kept between us *men*. He said if I told Mom, she wouldn't love me anymore.

When he finished, he gave me a new baseball glove and told me to go play.

The whole thing made me feel sick. I wanted to tell my brother,

Eli, but I never dared.

I covered enough of his lies in my youth. I wouldn't do it this time. No matter how badly it broke her heart, Mom had a right to know. But before that, *I* needed to know what the hell was going on.

"Mr Logan Bishop?"

I was back in the hospital. A mousy-looking nurse with a small mouth approached me. She told me Dad was unconscious and on heavy medication. He needed surgery on the shattered knee, and he might lose his pinky and ring finger because the breaks were so bad. By the look in her motherly eyes, I knew she was more concerned than she let on, so I asked: will he die? She just said, "It's not looking good, I'm afraid."

A waiting game to see if he would pull through meant the chances of us having a clear-the-air chat went straight to nil. The nurse put her hand on my shoulder and told me to go home and get some rest. I nodded and left the hospital.

It was cold and quiet at 2am. I walked across Westminster Bridge towards the Houses of Parliament with my hands stuffed in my coat pockets and the collar of my coat flipped up to fight the wind. From my pocket, I removed the note hidden inside Dad's hat. *Greta Matas: 7 Queen Street, Edinburgh.* Whoever she was, a target had been put on her, and it was somehow connected to what happened to Dad. The nurse said to get some rest. That wasn't going to happen. Not with this woman's life at risk—the only person who could explain this mess.

BAD BLOOD

4

I walked back to Percy Street, repeating the same four questions: who was after Dad? Who was Greta Matas? Why was her life in danger? And What did I need to get?

Hiking the stairs to my office, I felt used. I hadn't even had a proper conversation with Dad, and the grime was all over me. I already felt manipulated, a forced accomplice in his sin, just like when I was a boy. I remembered when I snuck into a bar in downtown Chicago at sixteen—one of those stupid things you do to impress a girl. The place was called Charlie's. It was the talk of the town—hard drinks, dark corners, and good jazz bands. I paid the guy at the door to forget my age. Halfway through the night, through the smoke and dim lights, I saw Dad at a corner table with a ginger woman draped over him and two dark-haired Lombardos with girls in their arms. I told my date we had to go; I didn't know what Dad would do if he caught me there; his deception didn't matter. Dad told Mom he would be at a Methodist preacher conference in Indianapolis for the weekend. Before I could get out with my lady friend, an arm wrapped around my shoulder—It was him. He pulled me aside, wrapped his arm around my neck and spoke into my ear. He said he needed a break and would be home tomorrow. He said he'd keep my secret if I kept his, and if I didn't, he'd have me expelled from school. Dad slapped twenty dollars in my hand and pushed me away. Secrets and lies were the only bond we had. Now, he wanted Greta Matas to be another one of our dark secrets.

Outside my door, I rummaged through my pocket for my key but stopped before putting it in the hole. The door was ajar.

My gun was quick and ready as I gingerly pressed the door open. I flicked the dolly switch, and the amber light illuminated the room.

The office had been tossed. The desk and filing cabinets had been pried open and searched. Papers, reports, photographs and photo negatives were scattered over the floor like confetti. The bookcase was in disarray. All my instincts told me the same men who clobbered Dad did this. What nagged at me, though, was *why* trash my place? What did they think I had? Did they think Dad left the unknown something with me? Then it dawned on me—I had an address for Greta Matas, and that's what they were after. They had no idea Dad kept it hidden in his hat.

My grip tightened on the gun as I moved through the kitchenette towards the toilet. Both were empty. Lastly, I crept towards the box room and kicked the door open. The door smacked the wall and swung back at me, bouncing off my shoulder as I charged in. I switched the light on and scanned the room down the barrel. Empty. I was alone.

Back in the office, I fell into the desk chair and rubbed my tired face.

Whatever was going on, not only was Greta Matas's life in danger, but so was mine, and there wasn't time to wait for Dad to recover to know why. Whatever she had that Dad needed created a target on her back. Whether I wanted to or not, I had to do something. The coppers were in no rush to contact Greta Matas, and the last thing I needed was another soul weighing down on my conscience.

I was going to Edinburgh. The quickest way would be the 10am train.

BAD BLOOD

5

Four hundred miles of cold steel track were between me and some much-needed truths. My hot breath fogged the window as the Scotch Express prepared to depart. Two old-world relics with milky white skin and a musty odour joined me in my compartment. On the platform, travellers moved through steam and stepped around the mounds of luggage. I'd checked for anyone who didn't belong—anyone who might be looking for me.

That was easier said than done. What did it mean to look like you didn't belong? I was looking for anyone *looking,* which I had done since I left my office earlier that morning. The thing about London, it's a jungle. You can be prey, stalked for miles, and have no idea. But I was careful. I didn't take a direct route to the station and before I boarded the train, I also took a gamble and sent Greta Matas a telegram. It said Daniel Bishop had been hurt and that I was coming to discuss an urgent matter regarding the item he had sent. I added that others were looking for her and to be careful until I arrived—that I'd be there either that evening or the next morning. That was all I could do.

The conductor blew his whistle, and the train hissed. Newspaper and sweet-sellers tempted passengers through the windows with a last-minute purchase—a Cadbury's chocolate bar would hit the spot, but my pudgy stomach said no. I had packed on a few pounds since the war. I barely liked my reflection as it was. Why make it worse? Besides, I had already wolfed down a sausage bun with a fried egg and had two cups of bitter coffee.

It took no time at all for London and the soot-covered buildings to disappear. The train rocked as it pulled out of the station and into a grey unknown. A fog lingered above frosty fields, as we cut through the countryside, and a dead fox lay frozen stiff on the side of the tracks.

Dead things stirred memories in me. I began to wade through them. Most stunk like an overflowing garbage bin of soured and rotten fragments. My last argument with Dad surfaced. At seventeen, he gave me an ultimatum: I go to seminary or move out, and my allowance would be stopped. My brother Eli, the golden child, had gone into stocks and made big money. A strategic move made by Dad, who, as a well-known minister, rubbed shoulders with wealthy people and politicians; some of the worst society had to offer. Dad loved it, but the pressure was on me to continue the legacy of a Bishop preacher, like his father and his father before him. Real biblical bullshit. The decision wasn't hard: I moved out and was cut off. Seminary wasn't for me. Dad called me a 'disgrace of a son' and said to never talk to him again. I called him a hypocrite and a lying sack of shit.

My thoughts were interrupted by the old man across from me. He violently hacked phlegm into a hanky. The old woman beside him didn't seem to mind and continued to knit. I got up and went for a walk to clear my thoughts.

Hours later, I sat in a packed dining car with other second-class travellers. A merry Scottish burr and a thick cloud of cigarette smoke consumed the car. The lights flickered as the train clanked over the tracks. It was pitch-black outside, but the journey was almost over. A half-eaten ham sandwich lay on my plate. The bread was stale, and the sharp mustard stung my nostrils. The meat was tough and dry. This second-class meal had nothing on suppers in the trenches: a tin of bully beef and a single swig of dark rum. This was five stars by comparison.

A sweet, peanut-and-raisin smell curled under my nose as I picked at the dry sandwich. It came from the two men with shellacked hair who sat catty-corner to me. I hadn't noticed them come in. One wore a dark grey suit, and the other, a preppy-looking fella, wore a brown pin-stripe suit with spats. I knew the scent well: Lucky Strike cigarettes. My war buddy Tim smoked Lucky Strikes relentlessly… until his death. The smell, that damn smell, dredged up *the* memory I tried to bury.

My mind slipped back in time to that day on the battlefield. I heard blood-curdling screams, as loud and as real as if they were in the carriage. Dying screams and the rattle of gunfire pierced the air. The sky burned red. Tim and I held our positions, looking to snipe Germans. A Lucky Strike tucked behind his right ear. Without warning, a bomb went off and threw us. Dust and dirt covered me, and my ears rang. The world was muffled and black. I could hear Tim in the blackness. He groaned in pain. I found him half-buried under blood-soaked earth, rock, and twisted steel. His body was shredded like pulled pork. He wept for his mother. His fear-filled eyes begged me to save him. I did the only thing I could… I reached for my gun.

I came out of the memory, staring at the half-eaten sandwich. I re-buried the intruding thoughts in the endless graveyard in my mind.

That's why so few of us talk about the war; it was a mass slaughter. We came back heroes, well, some of us. But if we spoke honestly about the fear, panic, degraded existence, and total mercilessness—no one would think us heroes—just soulless mercenaries.

Two teardrops landed on the table and exploded. I crushed my eyes shut and inhaled as I pushed Tim and the hate I had for myself to the back of my mind. I stamped out any more tears with my fingers and hoped no one watched.

"Are you all right, lamb?"

I lowered my hand; the tips of my fingers were damp.

A beautiful Scottish woman stood over me with concerned eyes. She had an athletic build and Titian hair, which plunged over her left shoulder. Her features were soft and round, her eyes were hazel, and her skin freckly. A navy dress clung to her figure with precision. It came into a modest V on her neck, and a white stripe rounded her waist. A crocodile-skin clutch was tucked under her arm.

"Yes…" I cleared my throat. "I am. Thank you."

The greasy-haired men smoking Lucky Strikes between their thick, wet lips eyed her like slobbering dogs in heat.

"You seemed a little… Well, I'm not sure. Distant." She didn't want to say broken, but I knew that's what she was thinking.

"The mustard made my eyes water." I smiled.

Her white teeth bit down on her red bottom lip. Concern faded from her face, and her eyes sparkled. I was caught in the allure of her. I realised I was staring like a smitten idiot. I shot up from the chair. "Thank you, though," I said. "For…" I didn't know what to thank her for. "Checking."

Her cheeks turned pinkish-red, the same as mine felt. "My pleasure."

The look on her face said, 'Ask me to stay, have a drink, and get to know me.' At least, that's what I hoped.

"Well, good evening…" She looked around the car for a seat.

"Do you want me?" The words sputtered and tumbled out of my mouth. "I mean, my table? You can have it."

A smile stretched across her beautiful face.

"You'd leave me to drink alone?"

"No. No, I would be happy to have a drink with you."

"Well, that would be impossible," she said.

"Why?" My smile receded, and my excitement sank.

"Because I don't drink with strangers."

I extended my hand. "I'm Logan Bishop."

"Harriet Napier." We shook. Her skin was soft, and her grip firm and confident. "Well, seeing as we are no longer strangers, however strange we may be, I'd love a drink." She sat down, and I fetched some drinks.

I sipped Bell's whisky, which tasted like piss and gasoline. Harriet Napier claimed the gin and tonic was good. The preppy guy wearing spats struggled to take his eyes off her profile. He met my eye line and winked. I ignored him.

Harriet pulled a cigarette and silver lighter from her clutch.

"Allow me," I said.

She handed me the lighter and placed the cigarette between her full lips. We leaned towards each other, and I lit her up.

With the burning cigarette dangling between her fingers, she asked: "Are you Canadian?"

"No, American."

"Aye, of course. I should have known. You have that American swagger; I like it. I would love to visit America one day."

"Where would you go, Miss Napier?"

"Oi, enough with the formalities, you silly man!" A cutesy, stern expression formed on her face. "My friends call me Harry. I'll call you Logan unless you have a nickname?"

"Logan is just fine."

She smirked while she sucked on her cigarette. "Boston, that's where I'd go," she added after exhaling. "Ever been?"

"A couple of times. It's a nice city. I'd imagine you'd make a stronger impression on it than on you."

"Cheeky boy." She tapped the ash off the end of her cigarette into the tray. "So, Logan, what are you doing in Edinburgh? Is it business?"

"Why do you assume business?"

"No one holidays there in summer, let alone the winter—unless they're crazy."

"What if I enjoy the cold?"

"Do you?"

"I love it."

"You are absolutely barking then!"

"Maybe." I smiled. "But I'm here on personal business." I hid behind my whisky. The last thing I wanted to do was sour the mood with shop talk about my dad's business. "What about you?"

"It's home. How long will you stay?"

"Not sure. Depends."

"Then what? Back to America?"

"London. I'm one of those dirty immigrants."

"You don't look dirty to me."

"Cause I bathe."

We laughed and blushed. She stamped out the remains of her cigarette.

"Were you in London?" I asked.

"Aye. For a few weeks."

"Doing what?"

"Working. Have you heard of Edwin Walter? The author? No? I'm surprised. He wrote the book, *Blue Eyes*."

"I don't recall it, sorry."

"Unbelievable." Harry giggled. "You must have had your pretty little head in the sand to miss it. There was a West End play last spring." She waited for me to remember, but I didn't. Her smile grew bigger and bigger. Harry continued, "I can't believe you, Logan. Anyway, I'm Edwin's secretary. We were in London to pitch his new book to his publisher."

"Don't tell me he's in first class, and you're stuck with the likes of me?" I asked.

"Ha, no. He travelled back up to Edinburgh before me. Even so, I don't like to travel in first class. It's far less interesting."

"I agree. So, what's the new book about?"

"Doesn't matter. The idea was turned down. Now, he is writing a country house mystery set during a dinner party. It will be good. They're very trendy right now. Each guest has a nefarious secret that comes out after the murder of the house chef. And the twists are... Conan Doyle, Christie, eat your hearts out! You must read it when it is out, Logan. It will be big. I could even get you a signed copy."

"I'll keep an eye out for it," I lied. "So, have you always worked for Edwin Walter?"

A shadow passed over Harry's face for a fraction of a second. "Heavens no. To tell you the truth, I used to work at Jenners—it's the big department store on Princes Street. I sold perfume. I hated it."

"How'd you meet Edwin Walter?"

"Unexpectedly. I like to paint. I would often go to the gallery to practise, and one day, he saw me. He liked my work so much that he commissioned two paintings from me. I felt as excited as the lass in that Henry James novel... Oh, what was her name?"

"Noémie from *The American*."

"That's it! Noémie. I guess a bit like her, Edwin changed my life. He told me I had too much talent to be selling perfume and that I could work for him and paint. But enough about me. What do you do, Logan? No, wait, let me guess. Are you in sales?"

"God, no! Do I look like a salesman?"

"My brother is in sales..."

"Oh. Well, there's nothing wrong with being in sales… I just…"
"I'm pulling your leg, lamb. I don't have a brother."
"Lucky you."

Her laugh was charming. She tucked her hair behind her ear and ran her red-tipped fingers down her pale, freckled neck.

She continued: "Only you have a delightful smile, which you have put to good use like a salesman."

"Is that so?" I chuckled. "Well, I'm no salesman, I'm a private investigator."

"A private investigator? Rubbish." She stopped smiling for a moment. "You're serious?"

"I didn't have cards made for kicks."

Harry's red nails glinted as she held my business card.

"I've never met a private investigator before."

"Happy to be your first."

"I bet you are." Harry put the card down. "I must say, Logan, you don't strike me as the type."

"Why's that?"

"You don't seem tall enough."

"Lucky there isn't a height restriction, huh?"

The train staff interrupted us to announce our arrival into Edinburgh Waverley and that the dining car would close soon.

Harry finished off her drink. "I better collect my things."

"Shame, I enjoyed this," I said.

"Aye, me too. Why don't you walk me out of the station?"

"And after that?"

Harry smiled.

6

The pasty old couple eyed me as I entered the compartment. It stunk of stale farts. The old man made a noticeable effort to avert my gaze, but the woman didn't. I took my trunk down from the overhead compartment. The woman wouldn't stop staring.

"Something wrong?" I asked.

"Well…" The woman stared.

The old man ignored me and gave his wife side-eyes as if to tell her to shut her mouth.

I faced them. The man sat up straight. His saggy old eyes widened as if me looking him up and down was an assault.

"What's going on? You're looking at me like I have shit on my face."

The old woman glanced into the corridor, then turned back to me and said: "Just thought ye should know—"

"Dinnae get involved!" the man spat.

"We have tae," she snapped, and then to me: "We went for a wee walk, and when we came back, a young man was going through your suitcase. When he saw us, he charged right out."

"Christ."

"We told the inspector, laddie," she finished.

I opened my trunk—someone had rummaged through it, but nothing was missing. Whatever this guy was after, I didn't have it. I shut the case. In my mind, I revisited the dining car. The two greasy-haired men smoking Lucky Strikes. Their eyes were on me the whole time. The one with spats eyed Harry. My gut sank—was she a distraction? Was, is, that her aim?

"What did he look like?" I said, turning back to the couple.

"A young man," she said.

"Was he fat, skinny, what?" I pressed.

"Naw, he wasn't fat."

"What colour was his hair? What was he wearing?" I pushed.

"I dinnae know. A dark coat and hat. We didnae see his face too well."

"That's incredibly unhelpful, thank you." I shook my head, took my trunk, and left.

It had to be the men who beat up my old man. I hadn't lost them like I thought. They were after Greta's address, which I had tucked safely in my trouser pocket.

I was on high alert when I found Harry. She was wrapped in a mink coat and smiled at me.

The train pulled into the station.

"I thought you'd forgotten about me," she said.

"Not a chance."

I eyed her, looking for a tell that she wasn't who she claimed to be. As passengers started to crowd behind us, I peered over my shoulder, looking for the men in the dining car. They were nowhere in sight. I glanced at Harry. Was it a coincidence I met her? I didn't want to believe Harry was involved with it.

"Is everything all right?" she asked.

"I hope so."

She squinted and said: "Logan?"

I smiled and said, "It's nothing, I promise."

The train stopped, and we stepped out.

Harry chatted away, carefree. She said things about Edinburgh that I couldn't take in. My attention was on the disembarking travellers behind us; I was followed. Turning around, I nearly collided with a boy wearing a flat cap, fingerless gloves, and a placard advertising Waverley Market's Grand Circus and Winter Carnival.

"Oi! Watch yersel, eh!" the boy said.

Harry laughed. "He told you, huh?"

Even I had to laugh at the little punk's boldness.

Outside, we came onto Waverley Bridge. I drank in my first view of the two-faced city. To my right, Princes Street's commercial glow illuminated New Town. It buzzed with life. Bodies, cars, and trams moved like spectres in the swirling golden fog. The light wells in Waverley Gardens glowed amber, like fire pits, and the elegant North British Hotel beamed. It was a Mecca for the wealthy.

LUKE DECKARD

To my left, Old Town was darker, jagged, and meaner, like looking into the eyes of a snarling old dog. The local breweries and coal depot soured the air with a sulphuric stench.

My teeth chattered. Of all places, why couldn't Greta Matas be in a beach town in southern France?

"Don't you like the cold?" Harry grinned.

"I did… I do, but this is…" I shivered and shook my head. "I mean, we have cold winters in Chicago, but I guess it's been a while since I've suffered them."

"Logan…" Harry hesitated. "There's a cocktail bar nearby… if you're interested."

I scanned the area for watchful eyes. Dad's attackers, Greta Matas's would-be killers, the ones who ransacked my trunk and office, were out there. And as much as I wanted to say yes to Harry, I couldn't be entirely sure she wasn't somehow connected. And if by some miracle she wasn't, then I didn't want to put her in danger.

I said, "Harry, really, I want to, but I can't."

"Oh. Okay." Her eyes dimmed with disappointment.

"What about in a day or two?" I asked.

"Maybe. Which hotel are you staying at?"

To tell her or not? Maybe it was reckless, but I said: "The Palace Hotel, on Princes Street. How about I call you tomorrow?"

She hesitated, and I wondered if I had just given myself away.

"I'll call you."

"I am sorry," I said.

She smiled. "Goodnight, Logan."

Harry got into a cab that drove towards the Old Town. I was disappointed, but my focus needed to be on Greta Matas, and I felt time was running out.

BAD BLOOD

7

Along Princes Street, a row of cabs sat with steamed windows in the thin fog. A motley crew of commuters waited for a tram outside the North British. The Baltic air bit at my cheeks and made my eyes water. The tram to Leith, to Greta Matas, was on the other side of the road. I went to cross over but stopped.

The man in spats from the dining car stood under the amber street lights on the other side. He watched me through the hazy fog like a starved dog eyeing a raw steak. I pretended to check the tram times among the cluster of commuters—Spatty carried on a few paces, then stopped. Behind me was his friend—the man in grey from the dining car. But that meant a third faceless man who rummaged my trunk was out there too.

They didn't know where to find Greta Matas and needed me. I needed to lose my stalkers.

Grey Man buried his right hand in his coat pocket, and a Lucky Strike burned between his lips. I sized him—six feet two, broad shoulders, approximately 180-190 pounds, and looked like he could handle himself. Spatty was maybe five feet nine, lankier, and built more like a runner. They were trying to corner me.

I stepped into a payphone and faked a call. Grey Man lingered within earshot, inhaling his Lucky Strike. Spatty, across the street, just watched.

I spoke loudly into the dead phone: "Greta, it's Logan. Tonight's no good. Yeah, don't worry. Stay low for a few days. Okay. I'll be in touch." I slammed the phone down.

Grey Man signalled with a nod to Spatty, but he couldn't cross the road. Trams on either side honked and pushed along Princes Street, their front lights beaming off the fog. As the waiting travellers began to shuffle, I yanked the phone booth door open just as the trams blocked the view for Spatty, and I darted around the corner and made my way over a bridge. I headed towards the snarling beast of Old Town.

Briskly, I walked up the road and peered over my shoulder. Grey Man tailed me at a moderate but determined pace—intimidation, to say I was prey. His friend wasn't with him. Maybe Spatty planned to cut me off somewhere. My limited knowledge of the city was my disadvantage, but I hoped it was mutual.

After *The Scotsman* building, I made a right onto High Street. There were fewer lights and long, deep shadows that way. It was starkly quiet compared to New Town, and I wasn't confident this gave me any advantage. The few visible public houses were the only signs of life, except for a few dim lights inside the mostly dark tenements. If I wanted safety in numbers, that would've been down the hill on Princes Street. I clocked every dark street, wynd, and close, expecting Spatty or the third man to dart out.

Ahead was St Giles' Cathedral. My tail didn't try to gain. He just kept a steady pace. The clap of my stalker's shoes echoed between the buildings. It was time to ditch him.

I darted down a pitch-black close and stopped after making a sharp left where stairs led into a court lit by a gas lamp. At the corner, I crouched and waited.

Running feet came down the close. I shot up and swung my trunk around, clubbing my stalker in the face. He flew back and hit the ground with a meaty smack. His gun flew out of his hand, clanking on the path. I picked him up and pushed him against the cold stone wall. I could just make out his face in the darkness of the close. He was dazed; blood trickled from his right nostril. I pushed my Colt deep under the man's chin.

"Who are you? What is this?" He didn't respond—I had knocked him out cold.

Bang!

I threw the man down and ducked around the corner. The gunshot dulled my hearing. I peered around the corner. In the close entrance was Spatty.

Bang!

A bit of wall shattered near my head. Before any more shots went off, police whistles ripped through the air. Frightened shouts echoed in the Royal Mile. I grabbed my trunk and ran down the meandering closes and lost myself in their darkness.

***

After an hour of lying low, I checked into the Palace Hotel. The clerk described my room as cosy. Cosy is British for cheap and small, both of which I manage well. And the clerk was right. The room was narrow, with a double bed that consumed most of the floor space. A small desk and chair were against one wall, with a wardrobe and a tiny safe against another. And there was a small toilet.

The room was too warm. I dropped my trunk on the bed, then I turned the hissing radiator off and cracked open the window. My body ached, and I was dishevelled from running and avoiding the main roads for a while, but I'd lost Spatty and Grey, and I barely felt the cold. My gut told me I'd bought myself some time—so long as Harry wasn't really working for them. And if she were, I'd be ready.

I sat at the desk, dismantled my gun, and cleaned it. I wasn't taking any chances.

Sitting there, brushing the barrel, I created a mental profile of the two men: both were white, had no facial hair, and had dark eyebrows. How they fit into the picture, I couldn't say. Only Dad could. All I knew was that I needed some sleep because I had to find Greta first thing in the morning.

8

I fell into a sea of black and surfaced into a nightmare… *"I will show you fear in a handful of dust,"* a dark voice said as I surveyed a dry wasteland from a tight foxhole with a German's head in my scope—sweat stung my eyes, and my finger pressed a trigger: pop-pop, kick-back, and the Jerry dropped like a rag doll, but beyond the dead body white lights flashed, flares streaked across the reddened night sky and the Four Horsemen rode into a swirl of black cloud as the earth erupted. I fell, and chunks of dirt and iron rained down; dust and smoke engulfed the world and groans carried on the wind as I crawled out of the foxhole, over rubble and dead men: *"Maw-maw. Uh wan' muh maw-maw,"* Tim muttered, and I called: *"Where are you? Man, talk to me."* Tim was half-buried under debris—dirt and blackish-red blood caked to him and a hole the size of a half dollar in his cheek, which had exposed broken teeth and a tongue like minced beef, and his face, neck, and hands were seared and a metal rod had cut his belly and his insides had spilled out from the gash, and there was a bloody stump where Tim's leg should have been; he was frantic and the convulsions and the fear of death seized him while his amber eyes begged for life to be put back inside and I lied, *"Tim, it's okay,"* and he cried: *"Maw-maw, I love you, maw-maw,"* and I gripped my gun and said, *"Don't make me do this again…"* The earth quaked and screams and gunfire rumbled over the ground and I dropped to my knees and sank into the mud beside Tim, as Death, drenched in black, rose over the battlefield, like a spectral giant, and all souls were harvested inside Death's cloak and the black, empty face of the Reaper locked onto me and Tim, and then moved towards us. Tim continued to convulse. Pop-pop. Smoke rose from the muzzle in my hand. Tim lied motionless, and blood and brains oozed out of the hole, and a shriek crippled me—

I awoke drenched in sweat. My body trembled, and my lungs ached, desperate for air. Swinging my legs off the bed, I sat up and buried my face in my hands. Tears streamed down my cheeks. The memory of Tim lingered. It had been weeks since I had an attack this severe, and I hated myself for it. I felt weak. I knew what I needed—the Winslow's.

Shaking, I dug through my coat for the tiny bottle—it wasn't there. I tore through my trunk, sifting through clothes, bullet clips, a razor, and shaving powder. Nothing. Hot panic surged through me. I gripped the edges of the trunk, digging my fingers into the leather. Every goddamned thing except *that* was there. I had been so tired and hurried when I packed that I left the bottles in London. My heart pounded in my chest; my head felt hot and dizzy. I growled and heaved the trunk across the room. Its insides exploded across the floor as it smashed into the wardrobe with a thud and fell with a bang to the floor.

I went to the cracked-open window and curled into a foetal position under it, with my eyes shut tight. Icy air blew in, and goosebumps rose on my arms. I rocked back and forth, feeling hot, cold, and shaky. I took a pillow and howled into it, begging the moment to end. The only thing stopping me from getting my gun was telling myself I had to help Greta; I had to get past this.

LUKE DECKARD

9

Daylight outlined the edges of the curtains. I sat against the headboard, my knees pressed to my chin, and a tremor crawled down my arm to my fingertips. The ticking clock on the wall was a pulsing reminder that I was losing time. Each minute crippled in bed was a minute closer to those gangsters finding Greta or me. I prayed Spatty and his pal were as crippled as me—maybe even the police nabbed them after that shoot-out.

Before I could do anything about Greta, I needed to get my hands on more Winslow's. I also needed food. First, I devoured a slice of dry toast and a boiled egg at the hotel restaurant. Second, I asked the clerk if I had any messages—I didn't. Harry hadn't been in touch, but I couldn't say that surprised me. Third, I went to a drugstore on Princes Street and picked up three bottles of Winslow's.

The air was cold, the sky was grey, and my mood was like charcoal soup. Outside the drugstore, trams squeaked along the tracks. I swigged the Winslow's. The bitterness gave me a chill and steadied my remaining nerves. I wondered if I'd ever find peace without that shit.

I hopped onto a tram headed towards Leith and found a stiff window seat in the back. Through the dirty window, I scanned Old Town's Gothic spires and towers; each erupted from the stone like they were carved from the dead volcanic crags. The tram turned left off Princes Street, and the city's mood changed. This part of town descended into slums. The people had sullen and haggard faces and walked like the damned going to the noose.

Queen Street was a slum near the dockyards. The houses, if you could call them homes, were uneven, dilapidated, and layered with soot. The plaster façades had gashes, and the stone beneath was exposed. Some windows were cracked, and others were boarded up. The gutters stunk of urine and rotten garbage. The dive into poverty was stark outside of the New Town. What business did my dad have with someone living here?

BAD BLOOD

Number seven was a first-floor flat accessed via a short, weathered concrete stair. I knocked on the door, and bits of peeling green paint fell with each hit.

After a minute, the door swung open. A woman with deep elevens between her brows glared at me. Her greasy strawberry-blonde hair was in a messy bun, with loose strands going in all directions. She wore a light-pink dress sprinkled with tiny white flowers and a cobalt cardigan that moths had eaten.

A boy, maybe five or six, with a dirty face and hair like a used mop, stood beside her. He was too thin. I smiled and waved at the boy. His big eyes stared at me. I turned my attention to the woman.

"Greta Matas?" I asked.

"No." She shook her head. "What you want?" she asked in a thick European accent.

"I'm looking for Miss Matas. Is this her address?"

"She gone. Like I tell other man."

"What other man?"

"She gone. I know nothing. Okay. You go, now." Her grey eyes were scared. She wanted to shut the door.

"Please, ma'am. Who was this man?" I pressed.

The boy started climbing his mother like a bear cub climbs a tree. She peeled him off with an air of exhaustion and spoke to him in a language that sounded like the Ruskies I met during the war. She put him down, and the boy vanished around the corner.

The woman turned back to me. "I know nothing. You go. You go." She started to shut the door.

"Ma'am, wait." My foot blocked the door. "I'm an investigator. My name is Logan Bishop."

"You police?"

"No." I reached for my wallet and flashed my ID. "I'm a private investigator. Greta Matas is in trouble. Can we talk?"

She hesitated. I offered her a pound note from my wallet. She eyed it like a starved child outside a bakery window. She looked between me and the cash, deciding on what to do. She took the cash.

Inside, my breath clouded in front of me. It felt colder inside than out. The flat consisted of a short corridor with one bedroom and a lounge and kitchen. Black and green mould grew on walls with large cracks and peeled wallpaper. In the lounge, I noticed a half-burnt chair in the fireplace. This was no way to live. This was not what I fought for in France.

She took me into the kitchen. A pot rattled on the stovetop. The dirty-feet-like stench of boiled cabbage curled under my nose.

"I make you tea, then talk," she said. "You sit." She pointed at the table pushed against the wall. A few letters lay on the surface, and my telegram was on top. The woman plopped two used tea bags into the only mugs she owned, filled them with lukewarm water, brought them over and sat.

"Thank you." I placed my notebook on the table.

"No sugar, no milk," she said. Embarrassment flashed across her tired face.

"I don't take it anyway." I smiled. "What's your name?"

"Mary."

"Mary…?"

"Palvienė."

"Are you married?" I asked.

"Yes."

"Is Mr Palvienė at work?"

"He is gone." She didn't want to say more than that.

"Mrs Palvienė, I sent that telegram." She eyed it. "Did Miss Matas read it?"

She shook her head. "I see her end of November, the twenty-first or twenty-second and no more."

"So she's been gone about three weeks?"

She nodded and took a sip of tea.

"Do you know where she went?" I asked.

"She no tell me where or why. She just go." Mary Palvienė shrugged.

"The other man looking for her, who was he? Was that yesterday or today?"

She ran her finger over the chipped rim of the teacup and then said: "No. Last week. He say he is her friend. Say she not at work for a month. He ask me why. I say I know nothing."

"So, Greta disappeared three weeks ago, but a week or two prior, she hadn't been at work?"

Mary nodded.

"What was Greta's job?"

"She clean rooms at big hotel by the station. What you call it?"

"A chambermaid at the North British?"

"Yes."

"Did you have any idea Greta wasn't working?"

"No. She leave in morning like she go to work, and come home like she there."

"Did the man give you his name?" I asked.

She thought for a moment. "Gabriel, like the angel. He is no angel. When I say she not here he say I hide her and he come in shouting her name and upsetting the children. When he cannot find her he leaves."

A loud thud came from one of the bedrooms. The little boy began to cry. Mary Palvienė's tired face sank. "You wait." She ran into the room and started to soothe a crying child.

I sipped the tea and immediately spat it back into the mug—it tasted like dirty water. The bad tea was worth it, though, to learn that Spatty and his friend hadn't been there.

Mary returned with the boy in her arms. His eyes were watery, and his face was red. She sat and plopped him on her lap, gently bouncing him.

"Mrs Palvienė, did Miss Matas ever mention Daniel Bishop?"

"No. You say Matas. Her name Matienė."

"What's the difference?"

"She is married."

"Where's her husband?"

"He die many years back in Lithuania before she come to Scotland."

"She's Lithuanian?" I clarified.

Mary nodded.

"As are you?"

"Yes. But people don't think Greta is. She sounds like you."

"Like me? She speaks English well?" I asked.

"Yes. She talks like you. She helped my English, little bit."

"Mrs Palvienė, did Greta ever hint that she was in trouble?"

She played with her son's hair, considering what to say next. Then said: "Greta and her son Petras have big fight before she leave."

"What about?"

"A man. I think Gabriel. I come home, and Petras is here. They shout at each other, and Petras tells her, 'You no trust him.' They stop when they see me, and Petras run out. I ask Greta why they fight, but she keep it to herself."

"Where is her son, Petras?"

"Barley Grange—with many Lithuanians at the coal mine. Davies Colliery, it called."

I wrote that down. "Does he know she's missing?"

Mary shrugged. "I no tell him."

"What about the police? Did you tell them Greta went missing?"

"Police do nothing for people like us."

"Greta is connected to some dangerous men, Mrs Palvienė. I worry they might come here looking for her. That's why I sent the telegram. Greta might've run away because she's afraid of something. Do you know anyone she might've spoken to or seen before she left?"

Holding her boy tightly, she said: "You think someone will harm her?"

"I do. That's why I need your help."

"Will they harm us?"

"No, you'll be safe. They just want Greta."

The boy in her arms squirmed, and she let him go. He ran off into the lounge.

Mary stared at the ceiling. "It was a Sunday when I know she gone. Saturday she has midday meal, at Mrs Mears'. A Scottish woman. She live on Cables Wynd. She rents rooms to Lithuanians. Greta rent a room until my husband go to war, then she live with me."

"Does your husband know Greta very well?"

Mary sank with sadness. "You cannot speak to him. Jokūbas not in the country."

"Where is he?"

"Vilnius. The British Government no allow him to return after war. They tell us, 'no proof, no proof!' He is no Bolshevik. It stupid." Grief wrinkled her face. She held in tears.

"I'm sorry to hear that."

"No one sorry enough to bring him home. It no matter. We go back to Lithuania in the new year to be with him."

"You're being repatriated?" I said, remembering the headline I read back in London.

She didn't understand.

"The government is paying to send you back to Lithuania?" I rephrased.

She nodded. "Many leave now. Many women have no husbands, no money, we afford little. We no live. The government takes grants, telling us we Communists. They wrong."

I understood her frustration. But there was little I could do other than say how sorry I was. Then I asked, "Has Greta left anything?"

"You wait," she instructed.

Mary went into the single bedroom and returned with an old black leather suitcase. It was worn and cracked, and the leather peeled. Mary placed it on the kitchen table. "Greta leave this. I pack up her things and put them in here. Maybe it help you."

I stood and opened the case. My eyes locked with the glass eyes of a yellow stuffed bear. Tied to its arm was a tag: *To Greta, From Daniel.*

"When did Greta get this?" I asked, holding the bear up.

"I find it in the front room behind sofa."

"Hidden?"

Mary shrugged.

The last thing Dad said: Get *it* back—he couldn't have meant the bear?

I scanned the rest of the items for clues. There were a few stray pieces of clothing: a shawl and a pair of white socks. An empty bottle of perfume. A bent photograph of two men—both square-jawed, broad-shouldered, good-looking fellas with bright smiles. Mary said they were Greta's cousins who used to live in Edinburgh. She lived with them before the war, then moved in with Mrs Mears. Her cousins never came home. They died in the war. There was a Communist Labour Party of Scotland brochure signed by John Maclean. Greta met him in Glasgow when she participated in the Red Clyde protests. Lithuanian literature included a Lithuanian Communist Party magazine, a newspaper with the name *Žmonių Balsas,* and a pamphlet for the Lithuanian Working Women's Association, dated November 1922.

"Greta's a communist?"

Mary eyed the literature with disgust. She and Greta were clearly on opposite sides of the political spectrum. "You take her stuff, yes? I no want it."

"Yeah, thanks. Do you have a photograph of Greta?"

Mary said no.

"Can you describe her?"

"Taller than you, thin, and pretty. Yellow hair, blue eyes."

There was another loud clunk in the front room. Mary shot up from her chair. Her son had knocked something over. He ran into the kitchen and jumped into his mother's arms. She huffed.

"That is all I can tell you. You leave, now, yes? My son need me, and I have chores."

I smiled at the tired woman. "You've been helpful. Here." I gave her five pounds. She thought I gave her too much, but I assured her I didn't. I figured she needed it more than me. I gave her my card and wrote *Palace Hotel* on the back. "If you remember or find anything, contact me here. And if anyone else comes looking for her, don't let them in. Don't tell them anything."

I knew I had scared her by the look in her eyes. "Yes. Yes," and she shooed me out into the cold, like a dog with mange.

BAD BLOOD

10

I took the suitcase with Greta Matas's belongings to my hotel. There were still no messages from Harry. Checking was merely a fool's hope. And the clerk said no one had come in asking for me. If Spatty and Grey Man were with her, they were taking their time. Maybe my suspicion was wrong, and Harry wasn't with them, or so I hoped. In my room, I placed Greta's weathered case on the bed. A faded G M was on the side, where she had inscribed her initials at some point. I snapped it open and itemised everything. The clothing, a couple of faded and hole-ridden dresses and blouses, went into a pile. There was an empty bottle of Palmer's Apple Leaves Perfume. The label was scuffed and faded. I lifted the lid and inhaled—the scent took me back to when I was a young boy, reminding me of my mother. Every Sunday, she put on the very same perfume before we went to church. I wondered if she still did that. I placed the bottle next to the clothes. The photo of Greta's cousins gave me nothing. I wished one of them were alive and here. Even if one had lived, I thought, there's no telling if the British Government would've let them back into the country, like Mary Palvienė's husband. I removed the communist and Lithuanian literature last.

Standing over the bed, I picked up the bear and held the tag.

It didn't make sense to me. Why would Dad send it? This couldn't possibly be the thing he wanted to get back. No one would kill a man for a damned stuffed bear. Right?

That's when I noticed something odd—the seam stitching. The left was a thick white thread, while the right was a thin golden yellow that matched the fur. That had been impossible to see in Mary Palvienė's dark home. Now, it was plain as day. I squeezed the bear's stomach and felt something hard inside its guts. A box. The bear's glass eyes looked anxious now. He and I knew what needed to happen.

I flipped open my pocket knife and went to work. The first incision started at the top of the left seam and went straight down—cotton intestines spilt out. The operation was crude but effective. I reached inside and removed the hard object.

A blue velvet ring box with a note rubber-banded around it was in my hand. I ripped the band off and put the message to one side. The box opened with a snap. Inside was a stunning ring. It had a lush, blueish-green emerald in the centre. The stone was surrounded by tiny bright white diamonds on a glowing gold band. The year 1874 had been engraved on the bottom of the ring. There were no scuffs or chips—the preservation was pristine.

I put the ring down and unfolded the note. Once again, I was looking at my old man's recognisable handwriting, which read: *Consider us even.*

"What the hell does that mean?" I said to myself.

I needed to know more about this ring.

Consider us even. The ring was a payment; but for what? Get *it*, Dad said in the Corinthian Hotel. The ring. Spatty and the Grey Man were after the ring, but they didn't know where it or Greta was, so they wanted me. They needed me to take them to Greta. Knowing what they did to my old man, what would Spatty do to her if he found her and she *didn't* have the ring? The thought sent a chill down my spine.

Pacing the room, I thought through what I knew.

Greta Matas disappeared three weeks ago. My eyes went to the emerald ring. She expected that ring, or, at least, some form of payment from Dad—so why did she leave without it? Unless she never realised what was inside the bear? Otherwise, why leave it? That line of thought was a dead end.

I reclined in the desk chair. For whatever reason, Greta didn't tell Mary Palvienė why she needed to leave. That came as a shock to Greta's co-worker, Gabriel. So, who was she confiding in? I wanted to speak to Gabriel and get his side of things. Her son, Petras, too. Maybe there was something in their argument? Maybe he could tell me who the man was he didn't want his mother to trust. Was it Dad, Gabriel, or someone else?

I rifled through the communist literature, looking for notes in margins, underlined events, and anything that might give me a

BAD BLOOD

little more about Greta. The magazines were well-read and bent, but nothing in them helped me. I thumbed through the Lithuanian Working Women's pamphlet dated November. The thing was in English. A woman named Rūta Kanaitė led a discussion on women's pay rights in Lithuania and Britain and discussed the recent announcement about the war-grant termination for Lithuanians. That was causing waves through this community. I opened the newspaper, *Žmonių Balsas*. It was useless to me—the paper was in Lithuanian, and I didn't, and still don't, speak it. So I tossed it and rose.

Something on the bed caught my eye. A piece of paper had dislodged from between the pages of *Žmonių Balsas*. To my relief, it was in English. The handwriting was smooth and steady. The letter read:

Nov 6th.

Dear Greta,

A family in New Town is looking for a nanny. They are happy to hire you regardless of losing your job at the North British. They trust my word, but they want to meet you first. Please meet me the day after tomorrow at Žmonių Balsas, and I will take you to meet the family.

Rūta Kanaitė.

The November date at the top stood out to me. The letter was written during the weeks Greta supposedly worked at the North British Hotel but wasn't. Now, I knew why: she was let go.

"Kanaitė," I said to myself. I looked at the Lithuanian Working Woman's pamphlet—there she was. There were no contact details. No head office or postal address was listed. I searched the Lithuanian newspaper—on the back, I found: Lee House on St Mary's Wynd. I scanned my Edinburgh map. St Mary's Wynd was in the Cowgate area in Old Town. Whomever Rūta was, she had information that Mary Palvienė did not. I hoped Rūta Kanaitė could shed some light on where Greta went.

It was 3pm, and daylight was running out. My head was groggy from travelling the day before. I decided to wait until the morning before I trekked to the coal mine at Barley Grange to interview Petras. Instead, I grabbed the ring and decided I'd have it appraised and then pay a visit to *Žmonių Balsas*.

BAD BLOOD

11

As I stepped out of the hotel, it started to snow. The wind battered the pedestrians. I pulled my hat low, raised my collar, and pushed against the flurries. The hotel concierge said there was a jeweller on George Street. What I found out: the emerald in the ring was Russian-cut. The man behind the counter asked where I got it. I said at an auction. When I asked how much it was worth, he said a gut-churning £1000 at a rough guess, but maybe more. I took the ring and left before any more questions were asked.

I had a death grip on the ring box inside my pocket as I made my way back to the hotel, where I put it in the hotel room safe before venturing back out to the Lithuanian newspaper. No way would I walk around town with a ring like that in my pocket.

I mulled over the ring the entire walk. Where the hell did Dad get it? Russian jewels had been circulating since the Revolution, but Greta was a poor Bolshevik Lithuanian living in an Edinburgh slum. What business did Dad have giving her the ring? Last I knew, he was firmly in bed with the local mobs in Chicago. The split-second thought that he ditched the mob for Bolshevism made me laugh. That was too hard to believe—he didn't bleed Red; he bled Stars and Stripes and the Holy Word. Americans and Brits saw Red shadows everywhere, and here I was, possibly seeing them where they didn't belong. Or was I just telling myself that? For all I knew, Spatty and the Grey Man were Reds. Had Dad turned?

St Mary's Wynd had a dusting of white powder. Several second-hand clothing shops lined the narrow street. The best items were in the window: a suit, a dark-brown dress, women's and men's hats and shoes, and cheap glass jewellery. In one of the windows, I spotted a ring that wasn't too dissimilar to the emerald ring.

I entered Lee House. It smelt damp. A business list displayed a solicitor, an accountant, a nanny recruitment agency and *Žmonių Balsas*. The Lithuanian magazine was on the lower ground floor down a dimly lit corridor. The door had cracked frosted glass and

LUKE DECKARD

Žmonių Balsas in bold black letters. It was dark inside. A sign on the door handle, written in English and Lithuanian, read: *Back Saturday*.

A temporary, but nevertheless, dead end.

That left me three days to chase other leads before looking into Rūta Kanaitė.

I trekked back to New Town, tired, hungry and annoyed that my leads weren't paying off. As I came around the corner onto Princes Street, I saw my path had taken me to the North British Hotel—Greta's former place of employment.

"What the hell."

I went inside, hoping for answers.

It was bright and warm and smelled like vanilla and lavender. The doorman and bellhops wore crisp red jackets. The concierge, a ferret-like man with a pencil-thin moustache, sat at a cream-coloured French desk and spoke with a lanky woman in a Dalmatian fur coat. The guests were no cheap affair. All were well-groomed, expensively dressed, and sparkled with jewellery. Every shoe, except mine, glimmered on the marble floor. My gumshoes were a heresy.

The clerk's wavy brown hair was cut into a fashionable bob and parted down the middle of her moon face. She was attractive and wore little make-up. When she smiled, she flashed a canine snaggletooth—that somehow made her look more endearing. Her long black dress was loose on her thin frame but pulled in at her waist by a thin black belt with a round silver buckle.

"Hello, sir, checking in?" her voice chirped.

"Afraid not, ma'am. My name is Logan Bishop, I'm a private investigator." I flashed my ID. Her face morphed from hospitable to concerned. "What's the name of the manager?"

"That would be Mr Gordon Connell," she said.

"I need to speak with Mr Connell about a sensitive matter. Could you take me to him?"

She went pale. "I'm sorry? Mr Connell isn't tae be disturbed."

"I'm sure he's not, but I've travelled a long way, Miss?"

"Webster, Denise Webster."

BAD BLOOD

"Miss Webster." I smiled. "Here's the thing, there's a problem with one of his employees that I'm sure he doesn't want to escalate to front page news, so it's in his best interest to speak with me."

I didn't want to be pushy with her, but it worked. She disappeared through a door behind her. When she returned, she had refreshed her lipstick.

"This way, Mr Bishop."

I followed her down a narrow corridor.

"Have you worked here long, Miss Webster?" I asked.

"Two years in April," she confirmed. "You're American, Aye?"

"Guilty."

"Who's in trouble?" Miss Webster asked.

"I can't say," I replied. She looked disappointed.

"Sorry, that must be terribly improper."

"Aye," I said. She giggled.

At the end of the hall, we came to a door with G. Connell on a gold plate.

Denise opened the door. "Mr Connell, this is Detective Bishop."

"Private Investigator," I corrected.

"Sorry," she said.

"Mr Bishop, come in." Mr Connell arose from behind a dark oak desk with a red leather top. He was tall and wiry with grey bushy sideburns and an arched nose a sniper could hit from two hundred yards. His charcoal three-piece suit was a dashing Gieves and Hawkes of Savile Row.

"Afternoon, Mr Connell. Thank you for meeting me." We shook hands.

"Not at all. Thank you, Denise."

She flashed a smile at me before leaving.

"Please sit, Mr Bishop."

He waved at the two armchairs facing the desk.

"Thank you."

"Smoke?" Connell opened a box of cigars.

"No, I don't smoke. But don't stop on my account."

"Aye, for the better. My doctor tells me to stop, but I enjoy it too much."

LUKE DECKARD

Connell chopped off the cigar tip, then wetted the end with his tongue before lighting it between his lips.

With the cigar between his teeth, he said: "Miss Webster says that there's a problem with one of my employees?"

"Yes, Greta Matas—"

"Heaven's sake, not this again." Connell tensed, his lips tightened around the smouldering cigar. "Like I told your friends, I've nothing to say."

"Were other Americans here asking about her?"

"Aye, last night." His face wrinkled with annoyance.

"I'm not with them, what did they say?"

"They wanted to know where to find her." He huffed and shook his head. "Mr Bishop, I'll tell you as I told them, Miss Greta was an irrelevant member of staff whom I dismissed. I'm afraid there is nothing further I can, or will, discuss." Mr Connell stamped his cigar out. "So let's not waste any more time, hm?"

"Mr Connell, I have good reason to believe her life is in danger. And those Americans are that danger."

"Mr Bishop, that is not my concern. I suggest you speak with your compatriots."

I needed to deflate the tension in the room and try to appeal to his heartstrings.

"Mr Connell, I'm not here to stir trouble. I'm trying to figure some stuff out. Mrs Matas went missing after she was let go. All I'd like is to speak with a few members of your staff. Greta's supervisor and a man named Gabriel, I don't know where he works in the hotel."

"Absolutely not, Mr Bishop. The matter is resolved. I'm sorry, but I cannot waste any more time on this; I've said all I can. Now, if you will excuse me," he waved towards the door, "Good day."

"Listen…"

"If you do not leave, I will have the hotel detective escort you out like I did the others." Connell pressed a buzzer on his desk.

"Calm down, pal. I'm gone."

I stormed out, feeling dejected. So Greta had lost her job. Whatever Greta did to get fired had Connell's panties in a twist and his mouth shut tight. He wanted nothing to do with her now. Rūta was helping her, Dad had sent her an emerald ring, and the gangsters were still on her and my trail. I didn't like that they had been to the hotel. How much closer were they to finding her than me?

At the front desk, Denise smiled and said, "Done so soon, Mr Bishop?"

We both leaned on the counter and faced each other.

"Miss Webster…"

"Denise, please."

"Denise."

"Yes?" Her eyes smiled like half-moons.

"Do you know an ex-employee named Greta Matas?"

She pushed off the counter as the excitement drained from her face.

"Heh, that's not what I thought you were going tae ask me."

"What did you think I was going to ask?"

"Something more exciting…" A smile flickered. "But I don't know her. Why? Is she the lass in trouble?"

"She was dismissed, sounds scandalous. Happened about five weeks ago. Connell wouldn't say why he let her go. That doesn't ring a bell?"

"Afraid not. Why didn't Mr Connell tell you?"

"Denise, do you fancy making some extra dough?" I asked, ignoring her question.

"What do you mean?" Suspicion swirled in her eyes.

"Find out why Connell let her go, and find out if a man named Gabriel works here. I hear he's something of an imposing guy. I'll make it worth your trouble."

"Mr Connell will have my neck if he finds out—"

"Make sure he doesn't. Besides…" I rubbed my index finger and thumb together.

Intrigue washed her face. "How much?"

"Five dollars if the information is good. Two for the initial trouble."

"Dollars?"

"Pounds, an old habit."

I placed the money on the counter. Denise glanced out of the corners of her eyes—no one noticed us. She laid her hand on the money and slipped it into her stocking.

"It'll cost more than that," Denise replied.

"You want to bargain?" I held down a laugh.

"Add a drink and a wee dance with me tomorrow night, and I'm your lass." Denise tempered a smile.

"I don't dance as well as I drink, but we have a deal."

"That's braw." Her face beamed. "I'll see what I can find out for you. Meet me in front of the Palais, in Fountainbridge at 9.30pm."

"I'll see you there," I said and left.

Back at the Palace Hotel, there were still no messages from Harry. Why I kept checking, I'm not sure. Maybe I liked having my hopes dashed. Denise was cute, but she wasn't Harry. I didn't want a date, just information.

I used the telephone in the lobby and called St Thomas' Hospital in London to check on Dad. If he was well enough, I wanted someone to get him on the phone and answer some questions. Help me understand what this mess was about. But I didn't get far. No one at the hospital could answer my questions about his current state. The man I spoke with said he could have a doctor call me back, so I gave him the number to the hotel. I told the front desk that I was expecting a call and would be in the restaurant for the next hour or two.

My hunger pains felt like they were eating my insides. I wolfed down roast ham and potatoes and greens. Two hours later, I went to the front desk. Dad's doctor had called and left a message for me. It said: *Mr Bishop. There is bad news. Your father suffered a heart attack yesterday morning. He's in a coma. I'm not certain if he'll pull through. Advise you return to London ASAP.*

I felt dizzy as blood rushed to my head. I don't recall what I did next, I just remember being in my room, lying in bed, thinking about death. The last family funeral I attended was my grandpa's and my granny's before that. I didn't cry at their funerals. I waited until I was home and hid in the bathroom. No one could see me there. I learned my lesson years ago when my cat died and Eli, my brother, laughed at me, and Mom scolded me: "Men don't cry, Logan." There's a lot that grown men do that everyone tries to say we *don't*. Crying is just one of them. I imagined Dad's tombstone next to my grandparents'—an arched slab of limestone and a mound of dirt littered with yellow, brown and orange flowers. I shut my eyes, and a tear fell—if Dad didn't recover, we'd never make peace. You can't bury the hatchet with a dead man. After the war, countless sought forgiveness and reconciliation from tombstones, but few found it. If he died, all I would have left is Greta. If she was dead, the legacy of my relationship with Dad would be: failure. I didn't want that. I already had enough for a lifetime.

LUKE DECKARD

12

At 8.30am I got the train from Waverley to Barley Grange. I headed to the colliery to speak with Greta Matas's son, Petras. Dad, on death's door or not, I had to continue. A few passengers were on the train, one being a fresh-faced man, maybe twenty-four or twenty-five, wearing a tan wide-brimmed hat and brown coat. He passed a handful of perfectly empty seats to sit a couple of rows behind me. I probably wouldn't have noticed it had he not made awkward eye contact and nodded at me. I considered moving cars, but I shook it off. Ever since I got to Edinburgh, I had been on guard waiting for Spatty and the Grey Man, but the kid didn't strike me as a threat.

Stepping off the train at Barley Grange, the pale winter sun was lost behind inky clouds. The pungent stench of burnt coal and oil soured the air. I asked the stationmaster for directions to the Davies Colliery. He told me I'd find it about a ten-minute walk outside the village. On my way, I stopped at a bakery and bought a sweet bun with raisins from a fat baker. I couldn't tell if she spoke English or Scottish Gaelic or if she just spoke gibberish.

Leaving the bakery, I noticed the young man who sat behind me on the train lingering across the street. He was in front of the grocers, smoking a cigarette. Was he following me?

I took a bite of the bun and watched the kid for a moment. He didn't pay me any attention. The dry bun clung to the roof of my mouth. My tongue wrestled to peel it off so I could swallow. The thing needed to be drenched in melted butter. It wasn't worth the struggle, so I tossed it into a slushy gutter and two desperate pigeons shot down to peck at it. The kid across the street just stood there smoking, looking back and forth like he was waiting for someone, so I went on.

As I walked through the snowy, grey village, the bells in the clock tower chimed. The hairs on the back of my neck stood. Checking over my shoulder, I noticed the kid had followed me. He was now on my side of the street, several yards behind. He smoked and walked slowly with his hands in his pockets. I recalled what

BAD BLOOD

the two old folks said on the train—a young man had rummaged through my case. Was it him?

I wasn't going to do anything without provocation. If I grabbed the kid and was wrong, that could land me in trouble, and I didn't care for that. I squatted and pretended to tie my shoe. I kept the kid in my peripheral vision. He approached but didn't so much as look at me as he passed and made a right down the next road. I rose, peered around the corner, and watched him until he disappeared into the church at the end of the lane.

I shook off the worry that I had been followed and found Davies Colliery about ten minutes later. The stack spat up charcoal smoke as if from the Underworld, and mechanical grumbles churned. The headframe ground, the wheels and the conveyor belt squeaked. A clanky train full of coal departed the depot.

Outside the mineshaft, three boys in grubby clothes smoked cigarettes and tossed stones at jars on top of a barrel. A dwarfish old man with a pot belly and a cane shouted at them to stop, and they ran off towards the miners' village, which was a bleak mesh of grey structures.

I found the office.

A woman with curly sandy hair sat at a typewriter. She must have been nineteen or twenty. The clicking of keys stopped as I approached, and she glanced up from her work and smiled. Her youthful face had a few stubborn spots of acne. She wore a grey cardigan over a brown dress, and a silver cross hung around her thin neck like a shackle. Her nameplate read Robin Rankin. Behind her was an office with the words Manager—Donald Yonge on the door.

She said: "Morning, sir, can I help you." Only it sounded like: "Mornin', sir, can ah help ye?"

"I'm Logan Bishop; I'm a private investigator. I need to speak with one of the miners."

Her head tilted. "What's the name of the miner?"

"Petras Matas or Matienė."

She studied me carefully. "What do you want with him?"

I flashed my ID. "That's my business."

Just then, a boxy bald man, stuffed into his three-piece suit with a close-trimmed ginger beard, emerged from the office. He reminded me of an out-of-shape Irish boxer I once met in Chicago.

"Mr Yonge, I presume?" I said.

"Aye." We shook hands. "And you are?"

"Logan Bishop, private investigator."

"He's here 'bout Peter Mathews, sir," Robin said with a shaky voice. She saw me look at her confusedly. "Peter Mathews is Petras," Robin clarified and stood.

"Why two names?"

Robin said, "He went by Peter Mathews... it was easier."

"For who?" I said.

"Immigrant workers," Yonge said, "Too many of them have funny names, most end in 'ski' and aren't worth the trouble pronouncing."

"Doesn't matter if it's their name, huh?" I said.

"What do you want with Mathews?" Yonge asked.

"To speak with him about his mother; she's missing."

Yonge stuffed his thick hands into his pockets. "Mr Bishop, Mathews is not here. But, if you find him, give him to the police."

"Police?"

Robin's eyes danced between Donald Yonge and me as she chewed on the inside of her cheek.

Yonge continued, "Mathews is a murderer!"

"What?"

"Aye. He murdered our coal-weigher, Tom Clackman, two days ago and hasn't been seen since." Yonge shook his round, red, head and rocked on the balls of his feet. "He took an axe to the man's head like some mindless savage." Yonge peered over at Robin, who looked like she could throw up. "Forgive my vulgarity, lassie."

"Excuse me, please," Robin said. "I'm going to step outside for a smoke." She rushed out with her coat.

"Poor thing is quite distraught over the matter," Yonge added. "It's not uncommon to lose a man down in the mine, but murder? It's unholy."

"Why would Petras kill... Mr Clackman, you say?" I pressed.

Yonge shifted his eyes and then perched on Robin's desk. "Well, before Mathews's morning shift, the day of the killin', the two got into a nasty dispute about wages." Yonge rolled his eyes. "It was utter nonsense. Miners toss rocks into the carts to make them heavier. Well, I don't pay for rock, Mr Bishop. I pay for coal. And Tom told the Pole that. All the men know it. Well, Tom then heard the lad was stealing and selling coal, and he confronted the lad at his accommodation. That's when the damn kid killed Tom." Yonge shook his thick head.

"Mr Clackman went on his own?" I asked.

"Aye."

"You find the stolen coal?"

"Nah. Must be long gone," said Yonge.

"Hm. Petras, does he live alone?"

"Ha! No one lives alone here," Yonge said.

"Was anyone in the house when Clackman arrived?"

"No. The others were on a shift."

"Did you know Clackman was going to confront Petras alone?"

"Had I known, I'd have gone with him. Why he went alone, I don't know. Foolish man."

"Do the police have any leads?"

"Last I heard, the lad might've headed to Edinburgh, but he could easily have gone to Glasgow. The Pole is probably stowed away on a boat and is halfway to somewhere else."

"He's not a Pole," I said. "He's Lithuanian."

"Makes no difference to me."

"It should. Mr Yonge, I want to speak with Petras's roommates."

"I won't pull anyone out of the mine for a chat, Mr Bishop. Time is coal, and coal is money."

"Are they on a shift?"

Yonge grunted as he pushed himself off the desk. He went to the window and called for Robin.

She returned, her cheeks red from the cold and stinking of fresh tobacco.

"Are the lads Peter lived with on or off shift?" Yonge asked.

Robin picked up the telephone and spoke to someone. She hung up: "They don't finish until eight tonight."

"There are, Mr Bishop," Yonge said. "You are welcome to

discuss it with any of my employees after their shifts."

I checked the time—staying would clash with my date with Denise Webster. I didn't see the point in cancelling that to chat with a few miners who might not know a thing about Petras or Greta.

Instead, I asked: "Could I look at Petras's lodging?"

"No one's meant to go in until it's cleaned," Robin said.

Yonge nodded. "The police searched the place thoroughly, laddie, so I don't know what you think you'll find."

"No offence to your local coppers, but they might've missed something."

Mr Yonge flashed a chubby grin at me. "Have it your way, pal. I'm off to the city. Robin can escort you, Mr Bishop." Looking at Robin, he said: "But don't take long. And let Mr Bishop go in alone, aye? It is no sight for a lass."

Frustration burned in her eyes. She opened a drawer, and keys jangled.

Robin led the way to Petras's lodge in silence. Her arms folded against the cold, and her eyes kept straight ahead. This was clearly the last thing on earth she wanted to do.

The miners' village was nothing but dirt, rock, and monotony: no bushes, trees, or grass. The path was muddy, and brown slush and dirty snow lingered in the gutters. We passed tired-faced men and a frail-looking woman who was shaking a water pipe with one hand and holding a bucket under the spout. I heard her say, "the water's fuckin' frozen!"

The destitution was depressing. The people who worked to provide the country with the fuel for power lived in such squalor… it didn't seem right.

I turned to Robin, curious to learn what she knew about the murder: "So Petras killed Clackman because of a wage dispute?"

"Something like that."

"What does that mean?" I asked.

"Nothing."

"It means something," I said.

"What Mr Yonge didnae tell you was that Mr Clackman was accused of skimming wages."

"Accused by whom? Petras?"

She nodded. "And others."

I knew the scam. Miners are paid by weight, and the weigher adjusts the weight logs.

"What about unions?" I asked. "Did they not step in?"

"They refused."

"What about this stolen coal?"

"A load of pish. Anyway, this is the house."

Robin went to unlock a sad-looking door to a sad-looking dwelling.

She went to insert the skeleton key but dropped it. We both bent to fetch it, but I got to it first. She stepped back, and I opened the door.

Apprehension was on her face as she looked into the darkness.

"Stay out here," I said.

I stepped inside. I held down a gag—the front room was rank. It stunk of slaughter and stale blood mixed with musty dampness. My stomach went into knots. Dirty dishes were piled in the sink, and plates with breadcrumbs and mice droppings littered the table. The tin bathtub in the corner had grimy water with a thick yellow film on the surface.

A large crimson and rusty stain clung to the floorboards. Hundreds of brownish-red drops peppered the walls and the mantel, even a few I spotted on the ceiling.

Fear and hatred lingered in the house like a spectre.

Robin stood beside me. She was engrossed by the scene. She gulped and breathed hard out of her nose.

"Your boss said not to come in…"

"So what…"

"Suit yourself."

Robin cleared her throat. Her body swayed as she stared at the remnants of savagery.

"Are you okay?" I reached out to hold her arm.

"Get away."

I pulled back. Her eyelashes glistened with tears, and she rushed out, hiding her face.

I let her be and looked around.

LUKE DECKARD

The stink of decay choked the front room. I pitied the souls who had to clean this up.

Three sets of bunk beds, a wardrobe, and a dresser lined the walls of the bedroom. The personal belongings of the other miners had been removed. I found nothing but a dead moth in the dresser and more mouse shit in the closet.

I lifted the mattresses—a sour, dusty stench wafted off each bed. I inspected each for holes where Petras might've hidden something. I had no luck there, either.

I didn't know what I expected to find. A letter, maybe? A journal? Something that the police missed.

I nearly gave up when I noticed that under the third frame were scratch marks from where the legs had been dragged. One of the floorboards had marks like someone had pulled it up. I scooted the bed away from the wall and took out my knife. The blade went between the boards, and I tried to lift it, but it was nailed down. The nails had a loose grip and were pried out easily with my fingertips. I lifted the board and found a rusty coffee tin. Inside was a carton of Woodbine cigarettes with the initials P M written in pencil. There was something inside the carton. I found three unsmoked cigarettes and a folded slip of lined paper. A shadow passed in front of the window—Robin peeked in. We made eye contact, and then she ducked out of view.

A list in Lithuanian was written on the paper. On the other side of the page, Ivy House was written in childish handwriting in English. The page and carton went into my pocket. I put the tin, floorboard, and bed back.

Outside, Robin smoked a cigarette. Her body shook, but not from the cold. Her eyes and the tip of her nose were red. She'd been crying.

"You okay?"

"Fine."

"Listen, does Ivy House ring any bells?"

"Doesnae mean a thing to me." She threw her cigarette on the ground. "Are you done? I have work tae do." She marched off with folded arms.

"I guess I am."

13

The Barley Grange police station was a dinky cop shop.

A man with a droopy face and silver hair sat behind a desk. His name was Constable McDonald. He surveyed me with seasoned eyes. I introduced myself, said I had come from the mine, and had questions about the murder. He offered me a seat.

"The colliery murder, Mr Bishop, that's nasty stuff," Constable McDonald said. "Never in my life have I seen such Godless brutality." He tutted and shook his head. "What's your interest?"

"The kid, Petras, I guess he's called Peter Mathews, is a person of interest in my investigation. His mother went missing, and I wanted to know if he'd been arrested yet."

"Aha. The lad hasnae been arrested, as far as I know. His mam's missing, you say? He a suspect?"

"No, not at this stage. I just want to talk to him. When you searched his accommodation, did you find any letters or a diary, perhaps?"

"Letters or a diary?" McDonald spat a laugh. "Mr Bishop, I'd be surprised if any fellas in that mine could string the alphabet together, especially in that lad's house. No more than a lick of English spoken, let alone writing. Illiterate, the whole lot."

The list of Petras's in my pocket said otherwise.

"You don't have to speak English to know how to write, Constable."

The grin on his face faded. "No, I suppose not. But in my experience, them foreigners at the colliery aren't well educated. It's why so many of them cause trouble. Now, we gathered up the lad's belongings, but there wasnae anything interesting. Dirty clothes, pair of worn shoes."

"Hm. Can I see it?"

"Not got it. Chucked it. Wasnae any use."

"Good God," I muttered. Before I turned to leave, I asked: "Does Ivy House mean anything to you? Is it a local place or somewhere in Edinburgh?"

LUKE DECKARD

"Ivy House? No place around here with that name. Maybe in the city. Sorry."

"Well, thanks for your time."

***

The train took me back to Edinburgh. It was almost empty. Robin hung in my mind for some reason. She was like a hedgehog—cute but prickly. She didn't want to be told what to do. Her protest at Yonge's instructions told me she had a little rebel in her blood. Except she picked the wrong time to be rebellious, she was jarred by the scene. She felt the hate, same as I.

Yonge wasn't willing to go any further than to call the issue with Thomas Clackman and Petras a dispute. Why did he leave out the part about the potential wage skimming? Miners have been the butt of corporate greed since forever. Shit accommodation, stripped of names, and robbed of pay—I'd be tempted to kill a man doing me over like that.

Then there was Ivy House. Someone had to know where it was. But without Petras finding out would take time. My hope was that Denise Webster or Rūta Kanaitė could lead me somewhere promising in my hunt for Greta. Mary Palvienė also mentioned Mrs Mears on Cables Wynd. The job wasn't entirely hopeless; I hadn't dried up all my leads, but I didn't feel lucky. I knew next to nothing... like playing a game of chess blindfolded. Dad, a fallen king, Greta, an elusive queen; and me, a scrambling rook, avoiding the gangsters who also wanted Greta and the emerald ring.

My attention turned behind me. Out of the corner of my eye, I spotted a figure in a tan hat watching from the connecting carriage. As I fully twisted to look, he walked away.

I recognised the wide-brimmed hat. It was the kid who took the same train to Barley Grange and whom I suspected of following me through town.

I had a tail, and I needed to sort him.

I got up, took the Colt from its holster, and went to the back of the carriage. Peering through the window, the man now sat and read a newspaper. There was no one in his carriage and no sign of a ticket collector. I went through and walked past him. It was the same person. This must've been the one who rummaged through my suitcase while Spatty and Grey Man watched me in the dining car, I told myself as I continued into the next carriage, pretending not to notice him. Once through, I ducked into the immediate seat on the right and waited.

Two minutes went by before the door opened.

The young man emerged, I grabbed the door and slammed it into him. He yelped. I released the door, took him by the shirt, and then threw him forward. His head bounced off the back of a seat, and he tumbled to the floor, face down. A Smith and Wesson dropped out of his pocket and slid away. He scrambled to get up, but I slammed my foot into the middle of his back. He cried. I went down, digging my knee into his spine and got his gun. I put it in my pocket.

The train approached Edinburgh; Arthur's Seat filled the window.

I picked the kid up and looked him in the eyes.

"What the hell is going on? I said.

"I ain't telling you nothing," he said.

He spat in my face and then tried to surprise me by swinging a blade at my belly. I jolted back, and he missed me by centimetres. I threw a lead hook and bashed him behind the left ear. That knocked him out cold, and he tumbled into the seat. I threw his knife and gun out of a window into a field with red-haired cows. Patting him down, I found a wad of American money in his pocket but no identification.

I heard a door shut. In the carriage behind, I could see the ticket collector coming. I wasn't going to hang around and explain myself.

The train pulled into Waverley, and the kid was still out. I ditched him and moved on before the collector came through. Before the train stopped, I wanted to be as close to the front as possible. I made it through three carriages and then exited.

I walked towards the barriers. A jolt of fight or flight went through me—I spotted Spatty and Grey Man, whose nose was bruised from where I hit him with my trunk that night he followed me.

They scanned the crowd—no doubt looking for their friend and me.

I darted out of their line of vision and into an empty waiting room. My heart thudded, and I tried to think of a way to get past them.

I crouched down to remain out of sight. I peered through the window. Spatty walked down the platform towards the waiting room. He stopped outside, his back to me. Hunched, I scrambled to the other side of the waiting room and slipped out the other door. I kept low on the other side, pretending to play with my laces but keeping my eyes on him. Spatty twisted and turned his head.

A sharp whistle caught his attention. He rushed to the young man in the wide-brimmed hat. He was disoriented and moving slowly, holding his head. The two men argued—Spatty pressed his finger multiple times into the young man's chest. He was getting a good grilling for losing me. I grinned. The young guy gave a *sorry, don't kill me* look. Together, they stormed to where the Grey Man waited.

A train arrived on the platform where I was standing. I waited as travellers disembarked, and then I hid amongst them. A North British bellboy in a red jacket pushed a trolley heaving with luggage towards the elevators that led into the hotel. Trailing behind was a couple, with a boy holding onto the mother's hand.

I walked with the trolley as a shield from the three men, and I went with it into the elevator.

"Oi, sir, this lift is full," the bellboy huffed.

"Hey, pal, my boss is out there... I can't let him see me... he thinks I'm out of town." I slipped him a crown.

"Oh, aye." He winked.

"Press in, press in," the bellboy told the couple with a child.

The elevator door shut.

14

That night, the red neon glow of the Palais de Danse sign bathed me. I shivered in the cold as I waited for Denise. Music filtered into the street: muffled thuds of drums and crashes of cymbals, the wail of brass and the thump of a double bass. It sounded like *Jazz Me Blues* by the Original Dixieland Band. The atmosphere outside was charged with a winter's equivalent of spring fever. Couples cuddled and stole kisses in the queue. Most of them looked like they were ten years my junior. I didn't really belong at a young person's dance hall, but this was the hand I was dealt tonight.

Thinking over the afternoon's events, I figured that for Spatty and co to have followed me, they must still not know where Greta Matas is. They got as far as the hotel, and that was it. Of course how they found me, I wasn't sure. Maybe it was Harry? Or maybe they just spotted me on the street. Nevertheless, they tailed me because I had a better chance of finding her. I had to make sure I didn't lead them to her. Not that I was any closer to finding her myself. The slip of paper I took from Petras's hidden tin wasn't getting me anywhere. I spent the afternoon looking through the address book and questioning the operator about Ivy House. There was no such house in all of Edinburgh. Only Petras could clarify it for me, and he was long gone.

"Logan!" Denise approached. Two bells hung from the garter on her left calf, so each time she stepped, everyone knew—a damn odd bit of fashion. Her eyes and mouth smiled. Underneath her open coat, a peach-sequin dress shimmered. Her nails and scent matched.

She greeted me with a kiss on the cheek.

"You clean up well," she said. I wore a clean shirt under my blue tweed suit. I even had my tan Oxfords polished.

"You look like a dream."

Inside, we got glasses of red wine and found the last available table on the balcony. Below, the dance floor had at least three hundred people crammed together—the humid air was a blend of alcohol, sweat, and perfumes. The band played upbeat numbers. The hot stage lights beamed off the musicians' sweaty faces as they dominated their instruments. The music was fast and chaotic, and dancers One-Stepped, did the Foxtrot, Duck Waddle, and whatever goofy wiggle they could that didn't have a silly name.

Denise scanned the crowd with a determined look.

I raised my glass: "Cheers."

"Cheers."

The glasses clinked. I brought mine to my mouth.

"No, wait," she cried. I lowered the wine. "When you cheers, you look the other person in the eyes while you drink. Otherwise, it means seven years of bad… you know… sex."

"And we wouldn't want that, would we?"

"No, we wouldn't, Mr Detective."

"Cheers," we said in unison, our eyes staying locked as we drank.

"I should be angry with you," Denise said with a smile.

"Oh?"

"Mr Connell had a proper go at me after you left. He saw us talking. Luckily he didn't see you give me money. He said if you ever come back tae the hotel, the house detective is tae boot you out. Mr Connell says you're a troublemaker. But I like troublemakers."

"I don't see myself as a troublemaker; it's just trouble keeps me in business."

She grinned and moved her eyes back to the crowd. Her face lit up.

"Someone down there you know?" I asked.

"Oh, no. Just looks fun." She took a gulp of wine.

"So, Greta?" I pressed.

"Oh, settle down, Mr Detective. Dance with me! That was our agreement."

We found our way onto the dance floor. Denise placed her hand on my abdomen as we danced. Like an electric shock, I tensed and sucked in my gut.

The frills of her peach dress swished and beat against me. She spun and then pushed her body into me—I smelt the wine on her hot breath.

Her playful eyes gazed up at me. She took my face and kissed me.

We broke apart, and she smiled. Her boldness was thrilling. She looked past me for a moment. My grip on her waist tightened, and she kissed me again. Her hands wrapped around my neck, and her tongue plunged deep into my mouth. We sank into each other.

A force tore Denise away from me, and a thick hand jerked me back. I fell into the crowd, who then shoved me back towards a bald man. His face was red as a cherry, and he breathed like an angry bull.

"You looking tae get torn into, mate?" He pointed a meaty finger at me.

Dancers watched us.

"Al! Stop!" Denise shouted.

"What do you think you're doing?" I straightened myself and stepped closer to Al.

"Youse better explain." He waved his finger at Denise and me.

"Are you blind? I'm on a date," she said.

He turned to me and laughed. "With this git? I'll cut your fuckin' tadger off if you dinnae get the hell off my lassie."

"Al, stop this!" Denise pleaded.

"I'll no be pit on, Dee. You're my lass."

"Your lass? You said you didn't want a thing to do with me, remember? Said you wouldn't leave your bitch of a wife for me."

He stepped towards her. I stepped in between them.

"You need to back off, pal," I ordered.

He pushed me with the tips of his thick fingers.

"Al, don't start!" Denise cried.

I stared Al down and said: "If you know what's good for you, you'll turn around and leave."

He grinned a yellow, crooked-toothed grin and then swung. I ducked and lunged out of the way. Moving behind him, I pinched the nerve in his shoulder—he roared.

Al threw his body weight into me, and we stumbled into two

men who shoved us forward. I lost Al for a moment.

First, I saw the fist. Then felt it smash into my ribcage.

I threw my arms up and blocked the incoming hits to my face. My abdomen absorbed a punch. An opening formed, and I shot my fist across his face. It rattled him. Next, I one-two'd him. He grabbed my lapels and crashed his head against mine. Through the buzz and delirium, I tried to long-knee him. He clobbered me in the head. I fell face down.

With one hand, he pressed my face against the sticky dance floor, and with the other, he pounded my kidneys. "You are a dead man!"

Adrenaline surged, numbing the pain, and my vision went red. Memories of strangling a bloody-faced Jerry in a muddy trench flashed in my mind. Sinking a blade into his throat. I was back in that moment—I refused to die.

The next thing I knew, two hulking bouncers pulled me off Al. He was under me, bloody slobber around his mouth. He lay on his back and rocked in pain. His front teeth were broken. As the bouncers dragged me away, the crowd filled in, blocking Al from my view.

I was thrown out a back door and rolled into a row of waste bins. Two giant rats with fat bellies squeaked and fled the scene.

"Don't let us catch you in here again!"

The door slammed shut. My heart thumped so hard I thought it might explode. I sat on the ground and tried to calm down. "Shit!"

I stood and brushed myself down.

I walked to the front of the Palais, and my right hand shook. I took a swig of Winslow's, and my body eased. I had been played. Denise set this up. A crowd of smokers stared at my dishevelled state. I fixed my tie and tucked my shirt back in, but the suit needed cleaning. It was wet and bloody.

Denise searched for me out front. She had our jackets draped over her arm and my hat in her hand. She spotted me and ran over.

"Are you okay, Logan?"

"No thanks to you." I yanked my coat and hat from her.

She cupped my face in her hands. "I didn't expect him tae do that." She examined my red hands. "Oh, Lord." She held them there. Let me clean you up. My flat is nearby."

"I think you've done enough tonight."

"Excuse me?" She stepped back. "I didn't mean for that tae happen! Damn you, Logan. Guess it doesn't matter that I jeopardised my job for you! Here, here… if you're going to be so ungrateful." She reached into her purse and got a piece of paper. Tears streamed down her face as she smashed it into my coat pocket. "That's what you used me for."

"I didn't use you; I hired you." I tasted blood in my mouth and turned and spat. I wiped my face with my sleeve. Neither of us spoke for a moment. "I didn't mean to snap. Just, what the hell was that, Denise?"

She wiped tears from her eyes and looked away a second, then retook my hand: "Please, let me clean this up. I want tae make it up tae you. I'll tell you what I found out."

15

Denise lived in a trashy studio on the third floor of a run-down tenement. The stink of mildew was everywhere. A single bed with a sunken mattress and ruffled covers was on one side of the room. The pillows were thin, like folded cardboard. An ashtray with cigarette butts sat next to the bed on the floor. On the other side was a messy kitchenette. A couple of chipped dishes, several empty wine bottles and a sack of potatoes were on the counter.

Denise took my coat and hat and told me to sit at the beat-up table in the middle of the room.

I kept my hands in my lap; I didn't care to touch anything. The kettle boiled, and she rummaged under the sink for her first aid kit.

"Where is it?" She removed bottles of bleach and wine. "Where the hell is the kit?"

"Forget it. I want to talk about Greta, Denise."

"One moment. I have it here somewhere."

She kicked a bottle, and, like dominoes, the cluster toppled. Denise growled and fell back on her butt, and sobbed. The bells on her garter jingled as she cried like a frustrated toddler.

I ached, but I got up and knelt beside her like a parent with a distraught child. I placed my hand on her shoulder. I held her for a few minutes.

"Come on, get up," I encouraged.

Denise calmed down. I helped her up. Make-up smeared over her face as she wiped her eyes.

Denise boiled more water on the electric hotplate and found the first aid kit. I washed my hands in the sink with a worn bar of soap. The water turned pinkish as my blood washed down the drain with the suds. Minutes later, we sat at the table with cups of black tea, a towel and rubbing alcohol.

My body was stiff from the fight, and I cracked my neck and back. Denise began to clean my hands with alcohol. I bit the inside of my lip to mask the sting.

"Denise…" She looked up at me. Her eyes were watery. "Talk

to me about Greta."

She sniffed and said: "Someone caught her stealing jewellery from a guest's room during a clean." Denise smirked. "It's not exciting gossip when a chambermaid is fired for stealing, especially when it's a Pole."

"She's Lithuanian," I corrected.

"It's all the same. And we know what they're all like," she said casually.

"Sorry, what? What are they like?"

"Don't be daft, like you trust them? We've got too many immigrants taking our jobs."

"I am an immigrant."

"Not the same, Logan, now, here…" She wanted to dry me.

I took my hand away and dried it myself. "We're all people trying to get by, Denise." I dumped the towel on the table.

"Yes. I just think some should get by in their own country. Most of them here don't speak English. It's not right."

"Can say the same thing about some of you Scots."

"Ugh, don't be like that. You know what I'm saying."

"Whatever. Get back to Greta. Who did she steal from?"

"Strangely, the lass in charge of the chambermaids wouldn't tell me. Said it wasn't my business."

"So Connell's covering it up?"

Denise shrugged.

"What about Gabriel?"

"He's a cook in the hotel's kitchen. He wouldn't talk about Greta. Told me to mind my business."

"Well, at least I know where to find him."

"Don't let Mr Connell see you." There was a pause. "Hey, Logan?" Denise took my tender hand. "I'm sorry about tonight… really." Her eyes tried too hard to convince me.

"You said you didn't expect Al to do that. It was all a ploy to make him jealous."

Denise backed away and folded her arms. I let the silence linger between us.

"You don't understand, Logan."

"Correct. I don't understand why you didn't just tell me."

"You'll think I'm a foolish lass; my mam says I am. Maybe she's right." Denise rose and crossed the room. She didn't seem sure where to go and ended up sitting on the bed, picking at the sequins on her dress. "Al is married tae a proper rough bird with terrible, yellow teeth. Perhaps if she bought false teeth, she might be decent, but she doesn't look after herself. Al came back from France and found a wreck of a wife. Those war years weren't easy for any of us, and Lord knows now isn't easier... but for him tae come home tae that? It's cruel. She doesn't satisfy him. I do. Did. And I wanted him back. You miss a person when they're gone or when you can't have them."

I felt bad for her, so I went and sat beside her. "Good people mess up, Denise. They fall in love with the wrong people, too. Learning from these bad relationships is how we move forward; otherwise... you're stuck in a cycle."

"I never learn," she said, wallowing in self-pity.

"I hope you will because I don't like being used, Denise."

She frowned. For a moment, I thought she may cry again, but she didn't.

She took my hands and looked them over.

"You must be sore?"

I laughed. "I am. All over."

She brought my hand to her mouth and kissed it.

"Denise."

She kissed another spot.

"Wait, Denise."

She climbed on top and straddled me, cupping my face in her cold hands. "You have nice eyes." She began to kiss my cheek and neck.

I held her waist. "Let's not do this, Denise," I whispered.

She kissed harder, rubbing herself against me.

"Denise, please."

Her thighs tightened around me. "It's okay, Logan," she whispered.

"Denise, I don't want to do this."

BAD BLOOD

Her waist continued to move on me, and she wouldn't get up. I started to get hard, but I didn't want to.

I pulled my head back. "Denise. I want to stop." My voice was stern. My body was tense.

"Just let it happen, Logan. You can do whatever you want with me." She pulled at my belt buckle. "I want to make this night better…"

"No, stop it, Denise…" I pushed myself up, and she fell off. I shot for the door.

"Fuck you, Logan. Fucking leave. You're a fucking dog."

I put on my coat and hat. "You used me once tonight… that's enough." I reached for my wallet. "Here. For your services." I walked over and handed her the agreed payment.

She shot up and shoved my hand away. "Don't pay me like I'm a whore!"

"Then don't act like one."

She slapped my face. Afraid, she jumped back, expecting me to react.

"I don't hit women, Denise." I threw the money on the floor. "You did the job. Shut up and take the money."

I stormed out into the dark. All I wanted was to lower myself into a hot bath and wash away the filth from the night. My lingering question was, why was no one willing to say who Greta stole from? I had the feeling Mr Connell was hiding much more than I realised about Greta's termination.

16

At 6am, someone pounded on the door. I growled, fumbled to turn on the bedside lamp, threw the duvet off and pulled on my robe with considerable pain.

I shuffled to the door and rubbed my lower back.

"Logan, are you there? I need to talk to you, lamb," a woman called from the other side.

Half-asleep, I thought it sounded like Denise.

I opened the door to a surprise.

"Harry!"

She had bloodshot eyes and a forlorn face under her black cloche hat. She wore a leopard-print coat and held a crocodile-skin bag. I looked up and down the hall. She was alone. No Spatty, kid, or Grey Man was out there. But I couldn't shake the coincidence of her arrival after losing those thugs on my way back from the mine.

"Where have you been?" she demanded. "Don't you check your messages?"

"There weren't any from you. If you're just here to grill me, I'm going back to bed. I'm sore enough as it is."

Harry sagged. "No. Logan, goodness, forgive me. I'm out of sorts. I called late, and the clerk said you were out. I hoped you'd check your messages when you got in and call me."

"Well, I didn't. What are you doing here?" I stifled a yawn.

"I need help. May I come in?"

I threw another look down the corridor. Still empty.

"Sure." I waved Harry inside. "Sorry for the mess."

I scrambled to pick up clothes strewn on the floor. My pale legs flashed from behind my robe as I shoved my stuff back into the trunk on the floor.

Bending stretched my tense muscles and cracked my lower back.

Harry stood in the middle of the room, uncertain of where to go.

"Please sit. Oh, dammit…" I removed Greta's suitcase from the chair. The whole scene was like a Charlie Chaplin act. I decided to put some clothes on before we started any serious talk.

BAD BLOOD

I perched on the edge of the messy bed in my trousers and undershirt. My socks were in my hand.

"What's going on?"

"Logan, my employer, Edwin Walter, has a problem. He wants to hire you."

"Me? Why?"

"I recommended you," Harry said.

"What kinda trouble is he in?"

"The night we met, I was robbed."

I paused, half-putting a sock on. "My God, are you okay?"

She nodded unconvincingly.

"Was it an American?" I asked. My thought was maybe the kid had followed Harry while Spatty and Grey Man followed me.

"American? No, I mean, I don't know. I think it was a Scottish man. Two of them."

"Two?" That blew a hole in my theory. "What happened?"

"Edwin's manuscript was taken. They ambushed me on my way home. One man held me against the wall while the other rummaged through my suitcase." I could see faint scratch marks on Harry's left cheek that she'd tried to mask with powder. "Once they got Edwin's work, they ran off." Harry lifted her glassy eyes to the ceiling. "This is my fault." She rubbed her temples.

"Harry, this isn't your fault."

"It is. Lord, I should've known better." Her brow creased. "I shouldn't have taken that way home so late at night. If I hadn't…"

"Where were you?" I asked. It was a foolish question. It's not like I would know.

"Castle Wynd stairs. I was walking back to New Town… oh God."

Harry buried her face in her hands.

"What's happened?" I pressed.

She looked up at me. "Edwin is being extorted for the document's safe return."

"And he wants me for the exchange?"

"Yes. He wants private help. Edinburgh is thin on private investigators, and he doesn't trust the police."

"His book, you said, was a mystery novel. Why is Mr Walter willing to play ball for something so trivial?"

Her head hung a moment.

"No, that's what he's working on next. The book stolen was a tell-all memoir his publisher refused to publish. It exposes dark secrets of many high-profile individuals."

"What kind of secrets?"

Harry puffed out her cheeks. "Long-standing affairs, back-door deals, the hypocrisy and corruption in Edinburgh's elite. It damned local MPs, tycoons, and artists. Edwin's publisher in London will not touch it, so he agreed to twist it into a mystery novel. Wrap the truth inside the lie of fiction. I had everything in my case on the way back to Edinburgh. The rejected manuscript, the notes, all of it."

"And your boss is afraid if he doesn't buy it back, everything he wrote about will be leaked, and he'll get in trouble?"

"That's correct. His publisher said he wouldn't risk a scandal either, so if this gets out, it could end Edwin's career if the papers get a hold of it. Logan, Edwin is willing to compensate you handsomely."

Harry removed an envelope from her bag and handed it to me. "This is just for a consultation. He wants you to know he's serious."

Inside was one hundred pounds.

"When's the handover meant to take place?"

"Tonight, at 11pm."

"Jeez. That's cutting it fine." I spat. "What was he going to do if you couldn't find me?"

"I said I'd go."

"When does Edwin Walter want to meet?"

"Now."

I looked Harry over. This could very well be a trap if I left with her. Dump a load of money in my lap, make me think there's an urgent problem, then get the shit beat out of me by these goons hunting Greta. Then again, if all they wanted was the ring, maybe I should just give it up in the hope they'd leave Greta alone.

However, these guys didn't seem to be the type to leave loose ends. And the ring was my biggest bargaining chip. I weighed up the risk. The idea of confronting these guys intrigued me.

"Logan, we need to go."

"Harry."

Tears streamed down her face.

"Forget it." She went for the door.

"Wait," I said. She stared at me. Something inside said she was being honest. There was still another day before I could visit the Lithuanian newspaper and see about Rūta's involvement with Greta. Trap or not, for the money, I would risk trusting Harry. "I'll come."

17

There was still a good hour or so before any hint of daylight, but the city was awakening. Slow-moving people dragged their feet under the flickering street lights and through the cold morning fog. A cab drove us through the grids of New Town; I kept waiting for the twist. For Harry to reveal her connection to Spatty and Mr Grey. But she sat quiet during the short ride.

We ended up in Stockbridge and stopped outside 21 Danube Street—a three-level terraced house with tall windows. Two leopard statues guarded the footpath to the front door with snarled expressions. If Harry were walking me into a trap, it was a lavish one.

Harry told the driver to wait for me and handed him a payment.

The entrance hall was L-shaped and wide. The floors and trim were polished cherrywood, and the walls were a pastel-green paper with a floral pattern in gold leaf. The house screamed money and status. Mounted to the wall, in a gilded frame, was an oil painting of Cleopatra. The queen lounged on a barge as it sailed along the Nile. Her white dress was transparent against her brown skin; her curves were teased beneath the thin cloth as she held a golden wine goblet while servants presented bowls of fruit and others fanned her.

"I painted it," Harry said.

"I'm impressed." I pushed my hat up a little more and noticed a stylised H in the bottom right corner.

"Thanks." A smile flickered on her face.

We discarded our coats and my hat. Harry's cream slacks hugged her waist, and her slim black jumper was tucked into them. She replaced her leopard-print coat with a white cardigan that consumed her.

"This way." She pushed the sleeves up to keep her hands out.

My hand was ready to draw my gun if needed.

We walked into a well-furnished pastel-blue lounge with a blue Chesterfield sofa and armchairs around a marble fireplace. Behind the couch was a faux globe. The top was open, and an assortment of dark spirits was displayed. Pencil sketches of Paris, London, and Edinburgh dotted the walls. Harry's stylised H was on each of them. Her skills were professional.

A door at the far end of the room was ajar. Harry knocked as she opened it.

"Harry, darling?" A desperate voice answered.

Edwin Walter sat behind an oak desk in a high-backed armchair made of stag antlers, like some wannabe woodland king. Behind him, a set of antlers was mounted on the dark green wall, just above his head, like a crown. The two chairs in front of the desk were also made of stag antlers, with more sharp edges than any chair needed. They were lower than his chair. It didn't take much to guess why.

Edwin Walter was a greying man with close-cut hair and a pushbroom moustache that hid his upper lip. He had a narrow head and a weak jawline. His grey eyes had no joy, and purple circles sagged under them. He wore a brown cardigan with wooden buttons and a white shirt, undone at the top. A tuft of white hair poked out. A tumbler filled with whisky was beside a near-empty bottle of Highland Park.

"Edwin, this is Logan Bishop," Harry said.

My alertness dropped, and relief began to wash over me. This wasn't a ruse. Harry wasn't connected to the goons who were after Greta. She was genuine. The only genuine person, next to Mary, I had met since I arrived.

"Morning," I said and approached the desk.

Edwin Walter checked his wristwatch. "Yes, I suppose it is."

He remained seated for a moment before he finished the dram: "Thank you, Harriet, for collecting the detective. Let us speak alone. Do sit Mr Bishop," he said to me.

"Oh, right... of course," Harry stammered. "I'll be outside."

Like a child reluctant to go to their room, Harry left.

I eased into the pointy antler chair.

"My nerves are terrible tonight. Drink?" He held up his crystal tumbler.

"No, thank you."

He poured a bit more whisky.

"Thank you for coming, Mr Bishop, and at such an unwelcoming hour." He stood, pushed his chair in and started to pace behind his desk, holding his drink. "What are your affiliations with the police?"

"I have no. I am a free agent."

"Good. What's your professional background, Mr Bishop? You're American. Did you fight in the war?"

"Yes. I was a sniper." He waited for me to continue. "Back in the States, I worked for the Pinkerton Detective Agency out of Chicago. I busted mobsters, was involved in several successful manhunts, an operation to stop a train robbery, and averted an assassination attempt on a prominent political figure. How's that for a background check?"

"Aye." He grinned, the whisky glass spun in his hand. "Are you armed?"

I opened my jacket and showed off the Colt. Lust for justice filled his eyes.

"First things first. I do not want the authorities involved," Edwin affirmed, "and I want complete discretion and full confidentiality."

"My card says privacy, fidelity, and accuracy guaranteed. I won't do anything illegal, so don't ask me to. However, you forfeit the right to confidentiality if you are guilty of illegal activity. I'm no lawyer, and I'm not going down for someone else's crimes."

"Aye. That seems fair. I assure you, I'm not the one doing anything illegal."

"Good."

"What is your fee, Mr Bishop?"

"It varies. Let's discuss the job first. Harry gave me the background to your predicament."

Edwin Walter froze.

"Harriet had no business telling you the details before we had a formal agreement…"

"I wouldn't come until she told me what was up. I don't get out of bed at 6am without a good explanation."

"Hm." Edwin Walter swigged the rest of his whisky. The crystal pinged when it re-connected with the desk. He continued. "The manuscript and all my notes were stolen from Harriet, that is right."

"What about the carbon copies?"

The distressed author tried to mask his frustration, but the tightness around his mouth gave him away.

"Harriet brought the manuscript from London. Yes, I have a carbon copy here." Edwin Walter laid his hand on a polished wooden box on his desk. It was locked. "That's not the problem. In London, I presented the manuscript to my publisher. Needless to say, he did not have the guts to go forward with the book. Published, it would've been a wildfire. Gossip is a powerful tool, you understand. Still, my publisher feared libel suits. He felt that I made too many claims about people with too much power. Maybe he's right. I was told a book like mine could be career-destroying for him and for me."

"If you wanted the information out anyway, why does it matter if the thieves leak it?" I asked.

"Because it needs to be done on my terms!"

"Do you have the proof to back up your claims?"

Edwin Walter said: "That would be telling, wouldn't it?"

"I think it's worth telling."

He took a deep breath and then said: "Over the years, I have acquired pieces of information. A secret lover letter here, a gambling habit there, back-door deals. Still, that is not good enough for my publisher and won't stay a lawsuit. Therefore, I ceded to my publisher and proposed a rewrite. He gave me a month to transform my work into a flamboyant mystery novel set around a dinner party in a remote mansion in the Shetlands. The same exposure, of sorts, would be masked in fiction. Now, the very thing I wanted to release is being used against me."

"And the publisher won't have your back if the stolen book leaks."

"Precisely. I was on the phone with my publisher yesterday after

LUKE DECKARD

I received the ransom letter. He said if it comes out, they will cut ties with me, and my work will be relegated to trash rags, if that."

I asked: "Have you considered the thief is someone you wrote about?"

"No."

"No? How do you know someone didn't find out what you were up to and wanted to stop it, and now they want to hurt you for it."

"Only three people knew about the book." Edwin offered a condescending grin and sat down. "Me, Harriet, and my publisher. If it were someone whom I wrote about, they wouldn't return it. They'd burn it or, better yet, sue me. Whoever robbed Harriet is not aware of what they have. All they believe is that they possess a famous writer's unpublished manuscript and want to use it as a cheap way to get rich."

"What's the demand?"

Edwin read from a note on his desk: "Pay £2,000 for the manuscript's return. Have the ginger lass bring the money to Calton Hill alone at 11pm on Friday. No police! The exchange will happen behind the Dugald Monument."

I pulled the letter up to my nose and sniffed it. It smelt of some kind of incense.

I said: "This could be the start of a long game of milking you for money, Mr Walter. Their entire scheme might be to bleed you dry financially. My advice is not to pay. Call their bluff and catch them when they make a mistake—people like this always do when someone doesn't play their game—"

"I will pay, Mr Bishop!" Edwin barked. "The legal implications, the press, losing my publisher... it is unthinkable. I do not expect a man of your stature to understand. Nor is this job paying you to."

I put the note on the desk, and I stood.

"Good luck, Mr Walter." I turned to leave.

"Where are you going?" he moaned.

"Harry dragged me out of bed at 6am, and now you have insulted me? I'm not your man."

"Please, wait..." Edwin Walter came round the desk with his hand up in surrender. "I am exhausted, Mr Bishop." He took me by the shoulders. "That was rude of me to say. Please help me?"

"This job will cost you," I said.

"Fine."

"A lot," I said.

Edwin straightened his posture.

"How much?"

"One hundred for expenses and a further three hundred for the job."

"Money is no issue."

"Well, you seem to be the man with a plan," I said. "So what do you want from me?"

I could've squeezed more juice from his lemons, but I didn't want to lower myself to becoming an extortionist.

We sat again.

"I want Harriet to deliver the money as requested. I want you to observe the transaction and only intervene if Harriet is in danger. When the transaction is complete, follow the man, get my money, and bring him back to me. I want to look my blackmailer in the eyes."

"Has Harry agreed?"

"Harriet, come in, darling," Edwin called.

She was quick through the door. Edwin came around the front of the desk, and the three of us stood in a triangle.

He explained the plan, and Harry drank it in. Maybe it was his storytelling skills or the smoky tone of his Scottish accent, but she looked enraptured by him. Like a devoted daughter eager to make her daddy happy. She reminded me of how my brother, Eli, stared at Dad whenever he gave orders. Unwavering devotion. When Edwin finished, he said: "What do you say?" He sandwiched her hand between his. "Will you do it, darling?" His wedding band glinted as his thumb stroked the top of her hand.

Harry glanced at me. My eyes told her to say no. Her's said she had to do it. Edwin held down a smirk.

"I'll do it."

18

Edwin Walter paid me the hundred in cash for expenses, and I wrote him a receipt for the job. He thanked me and then decided to try to sleep.

Harry led me to the front door.

A woman wearing a green velvet dressing gown glided down the stairs. She looked at Harry and me for half a second while I put my coat and hat on. Her features were delicate, and she had a narrow neck. Her thick, black hair, with streaks of attractive grey, was pulled back into a ponytail. Something about her reminded me of the actress Maude Adams.

Without any acknowledgement, she disappeared into the lounge.

I turned to Harry. "Mrs Walter?"

"Francine, yes." Harry opened the front door, and a gust of frigid air rushed in.

"Seems friendly. What does she think about all this?"

"You'd have to ask her," Harry whispered. "I don't know if Edwin has told her yet."

Harry's tone had an unmistakable air of animosity, but I didn't care to explore it.

I stepped onto the landing. Harry folded her arms around herself and tried to keep warm. The cab driver was asleep, his head pressed against the steamy window.

"Logan?" Harry came closer to me.

"Yes?" I closed the gap between us a little more.

"Thank you for agreeing to help Edwin."

"About that. Are you sure you're doing the right thing?"

"What do you mean?"

"One misstep, you could end up hurt—"

"Edwin needs my help, Logan."

"I understand, but…"

Harry looked away and flared her nostrils. She steamed like a bull.

"There's too much at stake, Logan."

"For him... not you."

"For me too, Logan."

"How?"

"My job, my home..."

"Your home?"

"I live here with the Walters. I owe this to Edwin. He has done so much for me. I have to do this."

"Harry—"

"Logan, please. Don't press the matter. The cab will take you back to the hotel."

She started to go back inside.

My hands went up in surrender: "I just don't want you to take any unnecessary risks."

Harry turned and looked at me: "What's life without risk? Logan, I can do this."

"I believe you. Listen, all this early excitement has stirred up my appetite. What do you say to some breakfast? Make up for that drink we haven't had yet. We can talk through the details about tonight."

Harry smiled a moment, then glanced back at the open door.

"I shouldn't now."

"There're a lot of things we shouldn't do." Her smile faded, and her eyes were serious. I put my hands into my coat pockets. "Or do you mean you shouldn't go with me?"

Harry hesitated. "Now that you're employed by Edwin, that complicates things."

I swallowed her words like razor blades. "Right, okay. Never mind, Miss Napier."

"I'm sorry," she called.

"Don't be." I threw the words over my shoulder and approached the cab. I tapped on the cabbie's window. He jumped awake and turned the engine on.

"Logan—" She made a few non-committal steps towards me.

"Good luck tonight. You know the plan." I shut the cab door, "Drive," I ordered.

The cab set off, leaving Harry standing on the pavement.

"Where to, sir?" he asked.

My watch read 7.40am. I had lost my appetite.

Given that I had the whole day to kill before I needed to stake out Calton Hill, and I couldn't follow up on Rūta Kanaitė until the next day, there was still one or two stones that I could look under in the meantime: Mary Palvienė had given me the name Mrs Mears.

"Cables Wynd," I told the driver.

19

The cab stopped at the top of Cables Wynd.

"Far as I go," the driver said. "It's down that way." He pointed with his head.

I got out and walked up Cables Wynd, between towering greystone tenements. The whole area stunk of sewage. Trash littered the gutters of this slum. Two dirty-faced children squatted over a dead cat in the middle of the cobbled street. They poked it with a wooden spoon.

I knocked on the door Mary Palvienė said Greta Matas had once lived behind and where she ate lunch on Saturdays.

A woman with a narrow face and wrinkled neck answered. She wore a plain grey dress that matched her thin hair and pale skin. She had boils on her face, like a fairy-tale hag, and her left eye was lazy. She looked like a real-life modernist painting.

"Afternoon, ma'am. I'm Logan Bishop. I'm looking for Mrs Mears."

"Aye, that's me; how can I help you?"

"I'm a private investigator. I spoke with Mary Palvienė, who said…"

"Sonny, I cannae understand that accent of yours. Gonna need you tae speak slower, aye?"

"My apologies, Mrs Mears," I replied slowly, like a record at half-speed. "Mary Palvienė," I made an effort to enunciate my words, "said Greta Matas used to live here and that you two ate lunch together on Saturdays?"

"Greta?" But she pronounced it more like Greetuh. "Aye, she lived here. Greta was a good tenant. Never missed a meal. Of course, I havnae seen her in weeks."

"That's why I'm here. She's missing."

"Missing?" She searched her mind as if the answer was in there, but she shook her head when she realised it wasn't. "What happened?"

"That's what I'm trying to figure out. I'd like to ask you some questions about her."

LUKE DECKARD

Just then, a skinny fella, about twenty, screeched his bicycle to a halt. I stepped back, half thinking he was going to crash into me.

"Oi, slow down, Henrikas!" Mrs Mears ordered.

"Sorry, Mrs Mears." Henrikas hopped off the bike and set it against the dirty façade. He eyed me a moment while he adjusted his flat cap.

He nodded, then squeezed past Mrs Mears and disappeared into the house. She shook her head at him. Then she turned to me. "You said you have questions for me, sonny? Well, it's too cold tae be talkin' out here."

We sat in the lounge. The floor space was taken up with dark, bulky Victorian furniture. To my relief, a healthy fire crackled and warmed me. A partition separated us from the dining room. From the other side, I could hear the clicking of a plate and the slurp of someone eating.

I told Mrs Mears an edited version of events: Greta was fired and left without a word, and her son is no longer at the mine. I mentioned Greta's interest in communism, which made her grey, narrow face even greyer and narrower, and her wrinkled mouth dropped open.

"A Bolshevik? I would'a never imagined. Three weeks you say she's been missin'?"

I nodded. "Mrs Palvienė noticed Greta wasn't home on the following Sunday. Did she have lunch with you on the Saturday?"

"Aye, she did. But Greta didnae give us the impression that anything was wrong. She was, she seemed very happy. But thinkin' about it all now, she did say she wouldnae be coming to lunch for a while. Somethin' about the hotel changing her shifts." Mrs Mears paused. "Funny thing is, Mr Bishop, I coulda swore I saw her no' a few days later in Portobello. I was seein' my sister there when I spotted Greta with a very handsome young man."

I inched forward in my chair. "What were they doing?"

"Gettin' intae a cab."

"Do you have any idea who this man is?"

"Fraid no'. He was very handsome, though. Nicely dressed, in all."

"Mrs Palvienė mentioned that Greta was friendly with some of your tenants. Do you think they might know this man?"

Mrs Mears turned towards the dining room, stretching her turkey neck. "Henrikas knows Greta. The other tenants who knew her have moved on. Many of 'em went tae America, others back tae the Continent. About the only options left for 'em these days. But I tell you, Mr Bishop, I'd rather have a building full of Poles and Lithuanians than Scots. Most reliable tenants I ever had."

"Yeah, that's great," I said flatly. "Can you bring Henrikas in?"

Mrs Mears called for Henrikas, and he came through the partition, eager to know what was up.

She asked: "You hear from Greta lately, sonny?"

His face was blank, and his mouth formed the shape of an O. "No."

I said, "You sure?"

"I am." He folded his arms.

"You are, *sir*," Mrs Mears corrected him.

"Sir."

"Mrs Mears saw Greta in Portobello a few weeks ago with a well-dressed man. Any idea who that was?" I asked.

He hesitated and thought. "No, I don't think I do."

"Mr Bishop tells me Greta is missing. You sometimes see her son, Petras. Has he said anythin' tae you?"

Something registered in his eyes, but Henrikas said: "I haven't seen him in a long time, Mrs Mears." There was a beat. Henrikas said, "Sorry. Uh, I have to go. I have deliveries to make."

"Be home for dinner, aye," she ordered.

"Yes, Mrs Mears."

Henrikas gave me a side-eyed look before he rushed out. The kid knew something. I wanted to catch him.

"Well, thank you for your time, Mrs Mears," I said. "If you speak to your other tenants and they know something, you can reach me at the Palace Hotel."

She walked me to the door.

I wanted to get out and speak to Henrikas, but Mrs Mears kept talking.

"I hope you find her, Mr Bishop. Would hate for somethin' nasty tae happen tae a sweet woman like that. She never seemed to be dealt a winning hand. I was hopin' that handsome lad was a change in the wind for her."

She opened the front door. Henrikas was pedalling away. I wouldn't catch him now. I turned back to Mrs Mears. "What do you mean, never dealt a winning hand?"

"No husband, raisin' that son of hers alone, losin' cousins in the war. She's a lassie who deserves some good fortune but has not had any. But you'll tell me if you find her, aye?" Her grey eyes looked sad.

I said I would, thanked her, and left. I walked up Cables Wynd, watching my feet and feeling disheartened. Finding Greta had become a nightmare. It could've been made easier had Dad just told me what the hell was going on, but that was never his style. He kept the family in the dark. It used to eat Mom up. I remember listening to their arguments through the heating vents in the house. Men came to the house late at night and had conversations with Dad. Mom wanted to know why, but he'd never tell. She'd find wads of money stashed in the house, and he refused to explain where it came from. Look where his secrets got him. Look where they got me.

Around the corner, to my surprise, Henrikas leaned against the building beside his bicycle and smoked a cigarette.

"Oi, sir," he said.

I stuffed my hands in my pockets. "You waiting for me?"

"I was thinking I might have information for you." A wry smile formed on his smug face.

"What's that then?"

Henrikas tossed the cigarette to the ground. "What will you give me?"

"My attention…"

He shook his head.

"This isn't a negotiation, kid." I walked off.

"One pound," he called, coming up alongside me, wheeling his bike.

I stopped and stared at him. He chewed the inside of his lip. I took out a shilling. "Tell me what you know first. I'll determine if it's worth more."

BAD BLOOD

He adjusted his hat as he said: "Well, I might know something Mrs Mears don't."

"What?"

"On the Sunday, a week after Greta came tae lunch, I saw her." He turned his head in the direction of the road. "That way. I remember because I shouted tae say hello and waved, but she didn't notice. She was in a hurry. I shouted again, but nothing. She just rushed into Marsh Travel on Leith Walk."

"And the other time?"

"A few days later. I saw her collecting something from a locker at Waverley Station."

"Did you talk to her?"

He nodded. "She was surprised. I asked how she was; she said fine. She said she had to go because she was getting on a train. I asked where—she just smiled and said to take care of myself."

"Why didn't you tell me this back there?"

"I wasn't sure if I should. And I didn't want tae upset Mrs Mears. That's why I was waiting for you here…"

"Well, isn't Mrs Mears lucky to have someone like you around? Do you remember which locker she used?"

"Twelve, yeah, I think it was. So about that pound?"

"A shilling will do for now." I handed it to him.

"You said a pound."

"No, you did." I walked off. "If you remember anything else, I'm at the Palace Hotel. You can work your way up to a pound." I paused. "Speaking of that, you hear from Petras?"

The boy looked surprised. "Nah, not talked in a while, like I said."

"If you do, I want to chat with him. That'll earn more than a pound."

"Why don't you go see him? You know, at the coal mine where he works."

"Because he's no longer there."

"Oh. Well, I've really got deliveries to make."

Henrikas hopped on his bike and peddled off.

I went to Marsh Travel.

83

20

Marsh Travel stood between an optician and an undertaker. Gold lettering on the glass offered bespoke holidays in Europe, Africa, Australia, the United States, and Canada. Inside, a stout man sat behind the single desk. He wore a red corduroy jacket that was one size too big, a blue shirt, and maroon corduroy trousers. A ledger lay before him, and a tray filled with pamphlets was to his right. The cover text read: *Your Next Adventure*.

"Hello, sir." He rose and extended his hand. Black and red ink stained his fingers. "I'm Mr Green. How can I help you?"

"About two or three weeks ago, a woman came in here." I held up my ID. He gave it an edgy look. "She might've purchased a trip through you."

"A woman, you say? A bunch come in here daydreaming about getaways. Which one are you looking for?" Mr Green clasped his hands and laughed.

"A tall blonde woman, very slim, with blue eyes. Accented, Eastern European, but speaks English well."

"Her name?"

"Greta Matas."

He shot a split-second look at his ledger.

I continued: "She would've come in about three Sundays ago."

"No. She doesn't ring a bell."

"Maybe you can look." I eyed the ledger.

"Right. Heh, heh, of course, let me check." He looked down at the ledger to scan his bookings. He shook his head after he flipped a few pages, giving them a half-glance. "No, no one by that name here. I'm sorry." He looked up at me. He shut the ledger and sat back.

"You sure?" I asked.

"Yes, sir.?"

"Well, someone saw her enter this shop."

He smiled. "People come and go here all the time, heh, heh. I can't remember them all. Do you have a picture of this woman?"

"No."

"Shame." His eyes shifted, and then he asked: "Why are you looking for this woman anyway?"

"She's missing."

"Is that so? Oof, I'm sorry that I can't help you."

I pushed my hat up. "Yeah, sure."

I left and hopped on a tram back to New Town. I didn't believe Mr. Green. He knew something about Greta Matas but didn't want to tell me.

Greta must've known that she was in danger. She had to. It was why she didn't wait around for Dad's payment. That would explain why she tried to steal from the hotel—she was desperate for money to get out of town. Whether she knew Spatty was coming after her, I couldn't say. Or was her reason for fleeing unrelated? Perhaps she ran because of what happened at the hotel. She was hardly living in the lap of luxury—maybe she stole because she just wanted out. And she ran because she feared prosecution—like her son. Was this man Mrs Mears saw her with some form of escape... or worse?

There was one person I could talk to—I hoped he had something I could go on.

21

Denise was behind the front desk at the North British. Her eyes were bright, and her smile was broad as she chatted to the concierge with a pencil-thin moustache. Her smile dropped when she saw me. The concierge eyed me like he wanted to do something about me. I ignored them both. I wanted nothing more to do with the kind of person Denise was. I figured it wouldn't be long before she became a headline for the wrong reasons.

I went to the kitchen to find *Gabriel*. I pushed through the double doors. The temperature rose, and the noise level increased. The prep and line cooks prepared meats, sautéed vegetables, and filled meat pies. Sizzles, pops, chops, and metallic clanks played to a rhythm. A dish-washer at the far end was up to his elbows in suds. Soapy water drained down his rubber apron.

The aromas made my stomach growl. A plate of sausage and tattie scones sat on a counter, ready to be delivered. My stomach screamed: FEED ME. I grabbed the triangular tattie and ate it.

"Excuse me," I said to a thin prep cook as he filled the meat pies.

He turned to me with a tired expression. "You're no' allowed tae be back here."

"I'm not a guest. I'm looking for Gabriel." I flashed my ID at him. He checked it and then rolled his eyes at the tattie scone in my other hand.

"Need another tattie!" he shouted, and then, "He's there—and dinnae take any more food, aye?" The pie-man pointed at a husky fella in his early fifties with large, jutting ears, wearing a white shirt and dirty apron. His sleeves were rolled up over meaty biceps, and the serrated knife in his chunky hand sliced through a plump tomato. I understood what Mary Palvienė meant—he didn't look like an angel, he looked like muscle for hire.

"Gabriel?" He looked at me, tomato guts dripping off the knife. "I'm Logan Bishop. I want to ask you some questions." He studied my ID. The massacred tomato brought the murder scene in Davies Colliery and the image of Petras crushing Tom Clackman's head to the front of my mind.

"What do you want?"

"Greta Matienė."

The point of the blade aimed in my direction. "I have nothing tae say."

"Don't believe you, bud," I said. "I'm trying to find her. Like you, when you stormed Mary Palvienė's house, scaring her half to death. So why don't we talk somewhere quieter?"

His cold, steel eyes surveyed me. Gabriel wiped both sides of the blade on his apron before returning the knife to a holder.

"Back in twenty," he called out to the kitchen.

Gabriel and I stood outside the delivery door next to the sour-smelling barrels of food waste. He dragged on a roll-up he took from his pocket. The bitter cold didn't faze his thick, exposed arms. Part of a tattoo poked out from under the sleeve, but I couldn't make it out at first.

"So go on then," Gabriel said. Smoke blew out his nostrils.

"When did you see Greta last?"

"The day after she were sacked. Only I didnae know she'd been booted at the time. And nothin' since." He wanted to sound tough and look tough, but his exterior couldn't hide the sadness in his eyes. No matter how hard-boiled you wanna be, the eyes give it away.

I didn't say anything. The roll-up hung between his wrinkled lips. He flicked the ash. "I didn't mean tae frighten the lassie and her kiddie. I just wanted tae know where Greta was."

"Why were you so desperate to find her?"

He shrugged and sucked on the roll-up.

I said: "The way you rushed into that house makes me wonder: did she leave because she was frightened of you? Maybe you found out she was seeing some posh guy? It pissed you off."

"What kind'a savage do you take me for? Eh?" Gabriel puffed his chest out like an ape and stepped towards me. I didn't move.

I said: "Sometimes things happen between a man and a woman, and the woman needs to leave."

Gabriel inched closer still, with rage in his eyes. "I never hurt her, do you understand me?" His thick finger pressed into the centre of my chest. I studied his face. Beneath the frustration, there was immense pain and sadness. He was a man unable to express his grief in any other way than aggression. "I had nothin tae do with her leavin'. I dinnae know about this other man neither."

I put my hands in my pocket and nodded at him.

The tattoo beneath his sleeve became exposed—in the centre was a five-point star with an infantry horn underneath and foliage on the sides.

"Cameronians." I pointed at the tattoo with my eyes. "Rifle boys."

Gabriel glanced at his arm and nodded. He eased back.

"I was a sniper," I said.

"No' much respect for your kind."

"We did our job, like everyone else."

"Aye." Gabriel filled his chest with air and then let it all out.

"What happened between you two?" I asked.

"I didn't hurt Greta. I've had enough violence. Understand that. Yeah, I loved her, but she didnae love me back. We had a thing for a couple of months, and then she ended it." The memories flashed behind his eyes. "After she stopped comin' tae work I went tae see her. I was worried, yeah. First, I thought the lassie was lyin' when she told me Greta had left. Was a proper surprise, that, her going and not sayin' a thing. Thought Greta was just tryin' tae avoid me, so I pushed my way in… I was wrong."

"Was Greta in trouble?"

"How dae you mean?" He stuffed his thick hands into his pockets.

"She's a Bolshevik."

He nodded, a little ashamed of it.

"You're not?"

"Nah. And honestly, mate, I dinnae know how much of one she was. More just somethin' she was interested in."

"Did that ever get her into trouble with the police?"

He stared past me and explored his memories.

"Nah." He stopped and thought more. "But, I dunno." I waited.

BAD BLOOD

Gabriel looked at the door. "I need tae get back tae work…"

"Paint a quick picture, man."

He sighed. "Maybe the Bolshevik stuff, or maybe no. The few months we were together, she was, like, hot-tempered. Wouldnae tell me why. I figure maybe money. We're all bothered about that, eh? Then she goes and ends things, then she up and leaves, and I'm none the wiser for it." Gabriel shrugged.

"The rumour is that she was fired for stealing. Any truth to that?"

"Pure lies, mate…" Gabriel scoffed. "Greta ain't got a dishonest bone in her."

"You sure about that?" I asked. He glared at me. I could tell he was trying to work out how much he believed it himself. "If she's not a thief, what happened then?"

"No one really knows. Or those who do won't say." He hesitated. "But I heard this posh lassie from London walked in on Greta takin' her jewels. Some overpriced glass, I bet. But I don't buy it. Greta weren't no thief, like I say. I did hear some gossip that the lassie kicked off, and ordered Mr Connell tae get rid of Greta."

"The police weren't called?"

"Nah. But Connell got rid of Greta. And anytime someone tried tae find out more, we was told it weren't our business."

"Who is this woman?" I asked.

"No one'll say."

"Connell kept it a secret?"

"He's a coward, right."

"Did you ask Greta's friends where she went?"

He looked ashamed. "We were together long, mate, and we kept it private. There isnae much acceptance between the Catholics and Protestants. And you ain't goin' find many who accept mixed couples, like what we were. If you're with a foreigner or coloured person, makes stuff hard. I'm not saying that's how it should be, just the way it is."

"Life's a bitch. What about Petras, Greta's son? Did you think to ask him?"

Gabriel gave me a *get real* look. "Naw. Only saw him once.

Wouldnae know where tae find him if I tried anyhow."

There was nothing more to get from the big sad man.

"Right," I said, "I'm staying at the Palace Hotel; if you learn who this woman is who has Connell by the balls or if you remember anything else Greta said or did that might be helpful, contact me. I'm not leaving town till I get something."

He nodded.

"Mr Bishop!"

The shout startled both Gabriel and me.

Standing in the service entrance was Mr Connell, and next to him was a stout man, in a suit, with a smashed face—the hotel detective. Denise must've ratted me out. Bitch.

"You. Back to work," Connell ordered Gabriel.

Gabriel raised his eyebrows at me and walked back inside.

Mr Connell and the hotel detective stood in front of me. "If you come in here and harass my staff once more, I'll have you arrested. Show Bishop out, Jimmy."

The hotel detective slugged me in the gut.

22

It was dark and cold as I climbed up the steep incline of Calton Hill. The wind whipped and roared in my ears as I neared the top of the incline. I was glad to take a pause on Greta Matas. That afternoon, when I left the hotel with an ache in my gut, I went to my hotel and slept the pain off. The bread and tomato soup dinner sat nicely in my belly. My gut was still a bit sore from the hotel detective slugging me. Connell wanted to make sure I stayed away. Something told me the story Gabriel and Denise fed me about Greta's dismissal didn't warrant the action Connell had taken… something else had happened. And I would find out what sooner or later.

I adjusted the shoulder holster, loosening the buckle two notches to fit better with my thick jumper as I neared the top of the hill. I broke into a light sweat. My calf muscles felt it—I hadn't stopped walking uphill since I arrived in Edinburgh. Every road seemed to be at a thirty-degree or ninety-degree angle. It was exhausting.

At the top of the hill, a yellow hue lingered over the medieval city, and the clock face of the North British was like a miniature moon above Princes Street. A cylindrical Greek-style monument stood against the Edinburgh skyline. It was the Dugald Monument where the transaction would take place.

Behind me, the Observatory House had no signs of life. Further out, the blackness was incredible—Arthur's Seat was out there somewhere. The lights from incoming ships moved across the water down by the docks.

I had forty minutes before the handover, so I looked around the Dugald Monument—no one was hiding behind it. I went around the Observatory House; no one was there either.

I positioned myself in a thicket facing the monument. The chilly air attacked me through my trench coat and jumper. The wait reminded me of the days and nights in the trenches, cold and damp and hungry, with men waiting to be dead. Or the gruelling times scouting German machine-gun nests. Still, it beat being holed up in a rat-infested dugout. And Edwin Walter's fat payment was a nice reassurance. For whatever reason, I started to enjoy this little distraction from Greta, Dad, and the ring.

I removed an open Cadbury's bar from my pocket and let a square of chocolate melt on my tongue.

Sitting in the bushes getting fat on chocolate, Harry's rejection that morning nagged me. It made me feel like I was guilty of impropriety. What was complicated? Had I misread her on the train? Did I invent the sparks between us? I didn't think I had.

Another square of chocolate went into my mouth. I stuffed the rest into my pocket and resolved to stop acting like some lovesick asshole.

The crunch of pebbles underfoot pricked my ears. An orange glow from a cigarette shone against the blackness. I took the Colt from the holster and hovered my thumb over the safety.

The figure appeared to be a man. He wore a bowler and a long coat and held some kind of packet. A woody aroma came off the cigarette, and the orange glow reflected off glasses. He did as I had: poked around the back of the Greek-style monument, then around the dark house. I went undetected in the thicket.

Next, he walked north-east, around the observatory hill, and vanished.

I loosened the hold on the Colt and waited.

Footsteps returned from the direction he last went.

It wasn't him. It was Harry. It was showtime.

She wore a long dark coat, but the bright-red band on her cloche hat stood out. She held a briefcase in her left hand: Edwin's ransom.

Her confident stride stopped just shy of the monument. She froze, hesitating.

"You can turn around and go home if you want, Harry," I whispered.

She pushed forward and stepped around the back of the monument. A butterfly circus kicked off in my stomach.

Next, the dark figure returned, this time from the direction of the medieval-like tower that, for all I knew, housed a princess. I switched off the safety and tracked the character down the barrel of the Colt.

He disappeared behind the monument.

The wind howled. Trees rustled and creaked. The minutes moved like hours, and I bubbled with anticipation. I expected to hear a scream, a shot, something—I heard nothing.

Two minutes. Come on, come on, come on, what are they doing?

Four minutes. This was taking too long. I'd give them one more minute.

Five minutes.

The man emerged with Edwin's briefcase in hand. He hurried along the path and made a sharp turn to descend towards the road.

No sign of Harry.

I scrambled out of the thicket, the blood rushing in my ears, and raced around the monument.

"Harry," I whispered.

She sat against the iron bars of the fence with her knees pressed up to her chest. She wasn't moving, and her head hung. I crouched and grabbed her by the shoulders.

She jolted and yelped. I covered her mouth. She squirmed for a second.

"Shh! Shh! It's me, Logan. It's okay. Be quiet." She eased. I removed my hand. "Are you hurt?"

"Logan!" She embraced me. Her face was wet with tears. "He handcuffed me to the fence while he checked the money… I thought he was going to kill me…"

"Did he hurt you?"

"No. I'm all right. I have Edwin's papers." A thick packet lay on the ground beside her.

"Drink this. It'll help the nerves." I gave her my bottle of Winslow's. "I'm going after that guy."

I started down the path after the man. He neared the bottom.

I moved quickly and kept close to the darker edges. My foot scooted over a patch of ice, and I braced myself against the wall. The man paused and turned. I held still, watching him. He felt my presence and sped down the steps. I aimed my Colt, but he ducked around the corner. I flew down after him.

I came out at Waterloo Place. Ahead and across the road, he rushed towards the New Town. He looked back and did a double-take.

He spotted me and began to run. A rattling truck passed and blocked him from my view for a split second. He disappeared, and I felt Edwin's fat payment disappear with him.

I darted into the middle of the road. He wasn't holding onto the truck—was he inside?

I spun around, confused. Then I noticed the dark archway into Old Calton Burial Ground. The iron gate was open; I went into darkness with the Colt in hand.

23

I stalked up the dark, shallow steps and hugged the left wall. There was a haunting stillness as I emerged at the top. On either side of the gravel path were seas of tombstones, crosses, and monuments. Ahead was an eighty- or ninety-foot obelisk. In the southwest corner, a cylindrical structure stood silhouetted against the city's light below. Close by it was a monument to Abe Lincoln and the Scots who fought for the Union in the US Civil War—this was the last place I expected to find my kin.

I crouched behind tombstones as I moved forward. Pebbles and dead leaves crunched under me as I approached the obelisk.

There was no sign or sound of the man.

The path broke into a T—dark mausoleums lined both routes. None of them had doors or roofs, making each a perfect hiding place and pinning him almost impossible.

I stopped and tried to listen for movement. The only sounds on the frigid air were the rustle of leaves, squeaks and clicks of trains from Waverley Station and the coal depot down the hill.

Something moved in the darkness behind Honest Abe, and I jumped out of sight to the other side of the path and moved along the outer wall of a mausoleum.

I spied on Abe with the Colt ready. The man wouldn't get away.

I stepped around the front of a mausoleum and darted inside for cover.

A banshee's screech ripped through the night air.

"Christ!" A hot jolt of fright went through me. Something, no some*one* was underneath my foot. I leapt back and spun around, aiming my Colt at the ground.

"Ye comin' in here tae fuck wi me? Ah'll gut ye!"

A drunken hobo had a bony grip on my leg. I tried to jerk him off. Then I felt his mouth clamp down on my calf.

"Get off me!"

I kicked to free myself of the lunatic and smacked the butt of the Colt on his matted head until he let go and crawled away, hissing in pain.

I stumbled out of the mausoleum in time to see a figure bolt through the graveyard. I darted around the tombstones after the man. I tackled him as he neared the ledge that dropped a few feet to the path. He smelt of spices, a bit like hash but floral. His face smashed into the cold, hard earth. Edwin Walter's suitcase and his hat went over the side. His arm swung back at me, and I dodged the blade in his hand—he cut my coat sleeve but didn't reach my skin. I grabbed his hand a twisted it. There was a cracking sound. He screamed. The knife fell. The man swung his other elbow around and cracked me in the face. My head went fuzzy as blood and saliva mixed in my mouth. He ran, but I reached out and grabbed his coat tail. I was dazed, and I couldn't find my gun. I yanked his coat, and he pulled forward, slipped out, and went over the ledge.

Still unsteady from the blow, I got to my feet and scanned the ground—I found my gun and went after him, clutching his coat.

Out on the main road, I couldn't see him anywhere.

My neck was sore, and my leg stung from the homeless man's bite, but I searched Princes Street and trolled the area around Waverley Station. I asked the doorman at the North British if a man without a coat but holding a briefcase came in—he didn't. I tried a few other hotels along Princes Street, but no luck.

Once I accepted that I had screwed up, I returned to my hotel. I cleaned up the bite on my leg and drank whisky in my room. I looked through the man's coat for something to identify him. There was nothing. I went downstairs and called my client. It didn't matter to me that it was 1am, I needed to move quickly with his money in the wind.

A woman answered.

"Logan? Where are you?" Harry's voice was frantic.

"Harry, I need to talk to Edwin… I lost the guy… I fucking lost him. He…"

"Logan? Logan, I need you to come over, quick."

"What's wrong?"

"It's Edwin…"

24

Harry opened the front door. Her face was in shadow. The light inside haloed her fiery hair.

"Logan!" Her embrace felt like a tackle. "Thank God you're here." The side of her face pressed to mine. My nose was buried in her lavender-scented hair.

"What happened?" I asked.

Her hold tightened.

"Edwin's dead."

"Dead! How?"

She broke away and took my hands. Hers were clammy.

"Logan, he's been..." Harry paused, her eyes welled. "Someone cut his throat." Her hand clutched her neck. She bit her red lip, and her wet eyes stared into the distance. "I found him on the office floor—Christ, it was horrible."

I embraced her. When she pulled away, I asked: "Where is Mrs Walter? Is she hurt?"

"No, Fran was at a dinner party tonight. I arrived maybe ten or fifteen minutes before her. But that's not all, Logan. The papers in the packet are blank. We didn't get Edwin's manuscript back."

"Didn't you verify the documents during the handover?" I rubbed my brow, my head hurt.

"This isn't my fault, Logan! You followed him. Where'd he go?"

"Calm down. I didn't say it was your fault."

"Logan, there's something else..."

"What?"

"Miss Napier?"

Harry jumped. A blond inspector with close-together eyes and V-shaped facial features stood in the doorway.

"Who is this?" he asked.

I stepped towards him. "Logan Bishop."

"Aye. The private detective Mr Walter hired."

"That's right, Mr..."

LUKE DECKARD

"Inspector David Joy." He held his eyes on me. "We should talk."

A meat wagon pulled up outside the house. Neighbours peered through curtains and shutters to observe.

"This way." Inspector Joy waved us inside. He paused and stopped Harry. "Just Mr Bishop, please, Miss Napier." She looked at me as if to say, *don't leave*. I nodded at her not to worry.

Joy paused in the lounge doorway—Fran sat on the sofa with an older man in a black suit. He was trim, with a well-groomed salt and pepper beard. A scar on his right cheek disrupted the whiskers like a river in a forest. Fran sat near him in a pea-green party dress and white elbow-length gloves. Her hair was done up in a high bun with curls on either side of her face.

"DCI McLean, the wagon is here," Inspector Joy said.

"Thank you, Inspector," DCI McLean returned.

Inspector Joy and I entered the dining room and sat at the end of a long cherrywood table. We both took out our notepads. His pencil was sharpened to near extinction. Mine had a few good grinds left.

We went through the simple details. Name: Logan Bishop. Address 9 Percy Street, London W1. Nationality: American. Been in the UK since September 1919. Been a PI since December that same year. Worked for the Pinkerton Detective Agency in Chicago before I went to war. I told him I had no prior connection to the Walters and met Miss Napier on the train. She contacted me a few days after the theft and ransom note.

He then asked about the robbery and the ransom.

I told Inspector Joy what Edwin Walter and Harry had told me. She had returned from London following a meeting with his publisher. A few men came out of nowhere and ambushed Harry, taking Walter's manuscript. Walter's publisher wasn't happy with the manuscript, fearful the contents might encourage libel suits. With the papers stolen and Walter's publisher uneasy about the book as it was, a leak could severely damage his career. He wasn't willing to risk that, so he wanted to pay to retrieve everything. The V's on Inspector Joy's devilish face deepened as I spoke.

"So," I continued, "Mr Walter hired me to help get the document back and find out who it was that had stolen the book." I produced the receipt. Joy's arched eyebrow looked sharp enough to cut glass.

"What can you tell me about Walter's stolen book?"

"He had written a memoir of sorts. It put high-profile individuals in a bad light. A tell-all kind of book, I guess. The publisher wasn't willing to risk releasing it. But Walter figured if any of the people he wrote about were behind the theft, they wouldn't extort him for the book's return. A sound argument, from a certain point of view."

Inspector Joy tapped the pencil on the paper. I gave him everything, and he didn't seem happy about it. "Did Mr Walter tell you whom he wrote about, Mr Bishop?"

"No. That wasn't part of my job."

Inspector Joy sat back. "Did Mr Walter have proof to back up whatever claims he made in this book?"

"He said he had pieces of information and a carbon copy in his desk."

"He did?" Inspector Joy's face lit.

"Yes, in a box on his desk."

Inspector Joy's face dipped.

"It was stolen?" I said. I didn't get a response. I added: "Edwin didn't go into specifics, but Harry must know, or Mrs Walter, what and who he wrote about. Certainly, his publisher does."

Joy adjusted himself in his seat. He didn't engage with what I said. "Mr Bishop, why did you not suggest Edwin Walter bring the matter to the police?"

"No offence, but you don't pay my bills. Mr Walter wanted independent help, and he's entitled to that. And that's what he paid for. All I did was do my job. It was his choice to come to you, not my responsibility."

"Simple as that, mmm?"

"Simple as that," I said.

"And this exchange took place tonight?" Inspector Joy asked.

I ran him through the Calton Hill events. I described the

extortionist as male, tall, fast, and wearing glasses, a long coat, and a bowler.

"And you followed him?"

"I tried. I chased him into the cemetery, and… he tried to stab me and got a solid hit to my head," I showed the cut in the arm of my coat, "then he got away."

Inspector Joy watched me a moment. Putting down his pencil, he said: "Mr Bishop, I don't need you playing a wannabe Sherlock Holmes and twisting a moustache at our investigations."

"Poirot is the one with a moustache, not Holmes."

"I don't care. We don't need a cheap PI causing more trouble than already done."

"Inspector, you're acting like I'm keeping something from you when I'm trying to help."

Inspector Joy gave me a blank stare.

"Mr Bishop, I have a dead body and a grieving widow. This could've been averted had you persuaded your client to come to us, the proper authorities. You didn't, and now a man is dead."

"Are we done?" I asked.

Joy sat back in his chair.

"For now."

Joy called Harry back in. I wanted to ask her about the stolen carbon copy, but there wasn't time. I waited in the corridor, staring at the painting of Cleopatra, wishing I was one of her servants. I took a quick swig of Winslow's, partly to steady myself and let the bitter taste wake me up.

Three police officers, DCI McLean, and a bald police surgeon stood in the lounge. Fran Walter wasn't around. I overheard the police surgeon say the stab wound killed Edwin. DCI McLean said it looked like a break-in gone wrong. Then he thanked his colleague. Two officers and the surgeon left. Edwin's body had been taken while I was with Joy.

DCI McLean spotted me looking at the painting.

"Hullo? Who are you?"

"Logan Bishop, sir. I am the private investigator Mr Walter hired. I was just in with Inspector Joy."

"Aye. You were with Mr Walter this morning?"

"Yes."

"Tell me, do you recognise this?"

He held up a golden chain laced with red gems.

"No, I don't."

"Certain?"

"Very."

"Did Edwin mention having difficulties he was having with any particular people?"

"I'm afraid he didn't."

"Hm." He went into the dining room without another word and interrupted Inspector Joy. He asked the same question to Harry about the chain.

"I... I don't, no," Harry stammered—another thing the police don't like, a stammerer.

"You don't know?" McLean pressed.

"No, as in no, I've never seen that in my life."

"Not on Mr Walter? Or Mrs?"

"I said I don't recognise it," Harry snapped.

"Did you find that with the body?" Inspector Joy asked.

McLean grunted.

"Have they gone?" A mousy voice came from behind.

I turned; Mrs Walter was on the step behind me.

"Uh, they're in the dining room."

"I mean, is Edwin's body gone?"

"Oh, yes..."

"Good."

Mrs Walter looked drained. She shifted her eyes as she tried to think of what to do and say next. But McLean barrelled down the corridor before she had to make a decision.

"Fran," his voice had softened as he approached, "could you identify something for me?"

"Yes, I can try."

She came off the bottom step, and McLean showed her the chain. Her eyes narrowed, and she looked at the floor momentarily and said, "Uh, no, no, I don't recognise it, sorry."

"Very well. We'll take this, and we have the blank manuscript." DCI McLean turned his head towards the dining room. Inspector Joy came out with Harry in tow.

"We're finished for now," Joy said. To Mrs Walter he said, "I'll keep you abreast of our developments."

"Very well, Inspector," Mrs Walter replied.

Inspector Joy felt my eyes on him.

"Mr Bishop," he began. "Don't leave Edinburgh. I may have a few more questions."

"Okay."

His right eye twitched at me. Then Mrs Walter saw McLean and Joy out.

McLean stepped out first. Joy patted Mrs Walter on the arm. "It'll be okay, Fran," he said. She smiled at him.

Harry whispered: "Come to my room."

25

Harry's pastel-blue room was expansive, with high ceilings and smelt of lavender and rose. Oak and chestnut furniture lined the walls. A large desk with a typewriter was littered with papers, pens and ink jars. An easel, tucked into a corner, had the muddy beginnings of a painting on the canvas.

Harry sat on a low bench facing the tall, arched vanity table mirror. Before her were crystal and glass bottles of perfumes, creams and powders in silver and ceramic tubs, mascara, and nail polishes.

She patted the seat as an invitation, and I took it. She rested her head on my shoulder, and I wrapped my arm around her. She cried for I don't know how long.

Her hands covered her face. I squeezed her and dispensed the usual platitudes. "Don't worry, it'll be okay. The police will find the person who did this."

She said, "It's like a part of me is missing. It's unbearable—it doesn't feel real." There was a pause. "Inspector Joy is only interested in what Edwin knew about the people he wrote about. He raided Edwin's office, looking for information. He's callous." Harry huffed and sat up. Her nimble fingers plunged into her hair, and she scratched her scalp.

"He's trying to find a murderer, Harry. He said the carbon copy was stolen?"

"He kept asking me about that... like he thinks I know where it is."

"What did you tell him?"

"There's nothing to tell him," she huffed.

"Did you give him the names of people that Edwin wrote about?"

Her hands fell into her lap.

"I'm so tired and shaken by all this, I don't even remember what I had for breakfast, let alone the details of that book..."

"You must know, Harry? Joy suspects that whoever killed

Walter knows about the book. Joy is an ass, but he's probably right. If Walter planned to humiliate and expose people in the book and someone found out..." I shook my head. "Come on."

"Don't you do that."

"What?"

"Don't blame Edwin for what's happened."

"Who else is to blame?"

"Jesus, Logan, I didn't bring you up here for this." She rose and stood by her desk, her hands planted on her waist.

"Harry, I'm sorry." I approached her.

"I want to be alone now." She turned her back to me.

"Harry..."

"I said, I want to be alone. Go. Now. Please."

I held down a growl, and I left, shaking my head.

Downstairs, I tried to open the front door, but the deadbolt stopped me, and I looked around for a key without success. I was just about to go back up and ask Harry for help when someone said:

"Where are you going?"

The voice came from the lounge.

Fran Walter sat cross-legged in the corner of the sofa and leaned into the tall arm. She clutched a pillow in her lap. Her posture straightened when she saw me. An empty tumbler with a wet inside sat on the coffee table before her.

"Sorry, I need a key to get out."

"Mr Bishop, I wasn't aware you were still here. Forgive me."

She threw the pillow aside and dried her eyes with a yellow hanky. Mrs Walter still wore the green dress, but the gloves had been abandoned, like her shoes—she now wore house slippers.

"Nothing to forgive. I didn't mean to disturb you, Mrs Walter."

She sniffled and clutched the hanky in her hand. "Fran. Call me Fran. I've been called Mrs Walter all night, and I'm tired of it."

"Formality does grate after a while, huh?"

"Were you upstairs with her?" Fran asked.

"Harry? Yes."

"No time wasted."

"Pardon?" I said.

"Nothing."

The silence was awkward. I didn't quite know how to respond. I tucked my hands into my coat pocket and said: "She's upset."

Fran Walter nodded. "We all are. Sit with me, Mr Bishop." She waved at the armchair across from her.

I sat down while Fran picked up a silver cigarette case with a stylised 'W' from the side table.

"Here." I offered my lighter. She leaned forward and ignited the cigarette.

"Smoke?" She offered me the case.

"I don't smoke."

"But you carry a lighter?"

"They're useful," I said, putting it back in my pocket.

She returned the case to the side table.

"I don't do it often," Fran admitted. "To tell you the truth, I think it's unattractive when women smoke." A hypocritical smile formed. She exhaled, and a cloud hung around her. Fran, in her green dress with immaculate hair and a strong, beautiful face, in this elegant room, was the image the Piccadilly ad agencies lusted after. I'd snap a picture and sell it to them if I had a camera. She'd sell millions of cigarettes.

She took another long drag and then blew more smoke. "What are you thinking, Mr Bishop?"

"I'm too tired to think. The last twenty-four hours are a blur."

Fran chuckled and said: "For a man too tired to think, your eyes tell me otherwise."

"I guess we're a couple of contradictions then."

"I like a thinking man," Fran said and inhaled again. "I never knew what Edwin thought. He wrote all those books, plays, and short stories. He was happy to tell the world what he thought, but with me, it was like there was nothing in his head for me. Does that make any sense?"

"Reminds me of my parents back in Chicago. My dad only talked to my mom when he wanted something. I don't recall them ever having a conversation just for fun."

LUKE DECKARD

"I suppose that's the nature of marriage. Are you thirsty? I'm having another."

I declined the offer.

Fran placed the smouldering cigarette in the crystal tray on the side table, took the empty glass, and went behind the sofa to the globe. She poured herself a generous portion of Dalmore. Fran drained the glass dry in two quick gulps. She hovered over the globe, lost in deep thought. She pulled at the gold chain around her neck, and a locket emerged from underneath. She began to stroke it.

Standing there, she clicked the locket open and gazed at the inside. "My two sons…" she said.

"You have kids?"

"Had."

"I'm sorry. Is that why there are no photos of them in the house?"

Fran lifted her eyebrow and pursed her lips. "Edwin removed the pictures after their deaths. He didn't like the reminder." Fran poured another drink. This one she sipped. "Do you know how many Scots died in the war? 134,712. Why couldn't that number be shy by two." She shut the locket and let it hang below her pea-green neckline. Her eyes glossed over.

"May I see them? Your sons."

Fran almost smiled. She abandoned her drink and came over and unlatched the gold chain. She perched on the side of the chair, her face near mine. Dalmore and cigarette-stained breath washed over me.

"The one on the right is John, my first. He was in the Navy. Phillip was in the army, in the Black Watch."

The two men were handsome and young. Bright and naive, like many of us who went into that bloodbath. Phillip took after Fran, but John looked more like a mixture of his parents.

"Brave young men," I said.

I returned the locket, and she rose, giving it another look before she shut it. "They were."

She latched the locket around her neck and returned to the sofa.

BAD BLOOD

"We received a letter from a man once," she continued, "his name was Cecil something. He said John saved his life... my boy. My wee John. Did you write to anyone, Mr Bishop?"

I nodded.

"What was his name?"

"It's not... I don't talk about it."

"The Egyptians say we all die two deaths. The day our bodies die and the day when the last person remembers us dies. Remember my sons, and I'll remember your friend."

"Tim, Tim Powell," I said. "He was a good kid from Indiana. A little foolhardy, at times, but every bit worth his salt." The moment of his death replayed in my mind: the explosion, Tim on the ground bleeding out and crying for his mother, and me easing his pain and fear with a quick bullet and wanting to turn the gun on myself after.

"Edwin wasn't a brave man." Fran sounded distant.

"No?"

"No. Edwin thought his stories were brave. Antagonism isn't bravery." Fran had another sip of Dalmore. Each sip loosened her tongue a little more. "He liked to shame people in his stories. I stopped reading his work years ago because of it. No wonder someone stole his book. I told him that one day, he would reap what he sowed. That man." She finished off her drink. "Has Edwin paid you, Mr Bishop?"

"He paid my expenses, but I can't accept more—I didn't complete the job. Tonight was a disaster."

"If it's all the same, I want to pay you. How much are you owed?"

"No, I don't feel comfortable accepting payment—"

"You'll tell me, Mr Bishop."

I was quiet for a moment. Fran wasn't going to negotiate.

"Three hundred was our agreement," I said.

Fran went to the bureau and rummaged through the drawers. She opened a wallet and displayed a wad of cash. "One, two, three, four..." She put the money in front of me.

"Fran, that is more than we agreed."

"Take it." Fran waved the bills. "Just, please don't speak of these events with anyone—none of it, ever. Edwin put you in unnecessary danger tonight, and look what good that did to him. I want all this behind me now."

I put three hundred in my jacket and left the rest on the coffee table. "Thank you, Fran. You have my word; I won't discuss this case with anyone." She looked nervous. She wanted me to take the money, but I didn't like being paid off. It's funny what the rich think money will buy.

An awkward silence lingered. Then the telephone rang.

"Excuse me." She answered it. "Hello? I'm okay. No, not now. The... A private detective is here. No, he's just leaving. Yes. Goodbye."

"A call at this hour?" I asked as she walked back over to the sofa.

"Hm? Oh, uh, it was my neighbour. Well, I should retire, Mr Bishop. Thank you for sitting with me."

"You're welcome."

I rose, and Fran showed me to the door, and she said, "Mr Bishop. I thank you for your discretion."

"Anytime."

BAD BLOOD

26

It was around 10am when I woke up. Four short hours of sleep that felt more like a fifteen-minute nap. Part of me wished I had never met Harry on the train. Nothing had gone my way since I left London, and I was getting tired of it. I needed a win. As much as I wanted to rest, there was no time. I was down to my last two leads on Greta, the Lithuanian magazine and speaking to Rūta Kanaitė, but I needed a good meal first. I devoured mince and tatties—which was some slop of beefy gravy and carrots sided with mashed potatoes. It looked like shit on a plate but tasted delicious.

The previous night's events were stuck in my mind as much as I didn't want them to be. I didn't like failing at a job and how things ended with Harry, in particular. Edwin's murder investigation felt like a complication I didn't need or want right now. And Inspector Joy and his stupid devil face annoyed me. The last thing I needed was a cop who hated me on my tail while I searched for Greta, particularly when her son, Petras, was wanted for murder. In my experience, give someone a badge and an ounce of authority; if they don't like you, they'll do whatever possible to hurt you.

I dragged my attention back to Greta. What did I know so far?

Aside from her communist interest, she was let go from the hotel for stealing, paid a visit to Marsh Travel, where she may or may not have bought a trip, and was last seen by Henrikas at Waverley Station, where she boarded an unknown train to somewhere—if she boarded at all.

Mr Green at Marsh Travel gave me the feeling he was withholding information, which was something else for me to explore. Did he know where she went? Was he covering her tracks? Did she pay him off? I wanted to get answers from Rūta Kanaitė before I started retracing steps.

I left the hotel to walk to *Žmonių Balsas*. That was something I enjoyed about Edinburgh. For a city, most places worth going were within walking distance. As I flipped up my collar and headed up Princes Street, someone shouted: "Logan Bishop!" I stopped and turned on my heel. Harry approached me. She wore a red cloche hat, and her leopard-print coat swished as she jogged over to me.

"Hi," she said with some reluctance.

"Harry... what's going on?"

Her freckled cheeks were blotchy from the cold. Her eyes were red, and dark circles clung under them. Yet she was beautiful, smelt good, and dressed well. To look at her, you'd have no idea the ordeal she went through the last night. That was her armour.

"I wanted to see you," she said.

"What for?" My tone was sharp and my face tight with annoyance.

She cocked her head. "You know, forget it."

Harry turned. The hurt in her eyes made me feel bad.

"No, wait."

She faced me. "If you're gonna be like that..."

"I'm sorry," I said. "Hell of a night, you know?"

"Wasn't the best, was it?" She said, easing a little.

"No." I shook my head.

"Well, I wanted to return this." She held up the Winslow's I gave her on Calton Hill. "Tastes revolting, you know. I can't believe we give that to babies." She half-smiled.

"Yeah, it's terrible stuff." I took the little bottle and dropped it into my pocket.

For a moment, we looked anywhere but at each other like a couple of bashful children. We both waited for the other to speak. Her hands fidgeted at her sides, I dug into my pockets.

We spoke at the same time.

"Listen, I—"

"Logan—"

"Sorry, after you," I ceded.

Harry thought for a moment and then said, "I wanted to ask you to check something for me."

"What?"

BAD BLOOD

By the look in her eyes, I knew what was coming, and I didn't much like it.

"Logan, I don't think it's a coincidence that Fran came home just after me."

"Fran wasn't dressed to kill," I said.

"Then I think she planned it."

"What, go to the party, come home, kill Edwin, dispose of the carbon copy manuscript, leave, and come back just after you?"

"Maybe. I don't know."

"For a start, that's a hell of a contrivance. Murder is rarely so mechanical unless you're reading some crummy mystery novel. But *why* would she kill her husband?"

"They had an awful relationship, Logan. Totally loveless. They hadn't shared a bed in years. All they did was argue, argue, argue."

"What did they argue about?"

She hesitated. "His writing, her spending, their sons. Logan, I'm probably wrong. I hope that I am. I only want to know if she was at the party last night. I want you to find out."

"What about the missing carbon copy?" I said. "Was Edwin writing about his wife?"

She hesitated, "No, he wouldn't do that. But he writes about her friends."

"Harry, why don't you tell Inspector Joy or that other guy, McLean was it?"

"I want to be certain before I do anything official."

I understood where she was coming from. Joy, in particular, didn't seem like a man you could reason with, McLean, maybe. But it's a hell of a risk bringing an accusation against your boss's wife.

"I can't believe I'm even asking you to do this." Harry smiled nervously.

"It's OK."

"These last few days have been…" Her eyes widened, searching for the right words. "I don't know how to describe it…"

"Horrible?"

"Yes." She laughed nervously but stopped, embarrassed by it.

"Laughter is good, don't worry."

She looked relieved.

"I've never experienced anything like this—I mean, of course I haven't. This isn't normal."

"Not for most," I admitted.

"After you left last night, I realised you must deal with this stuff day in and day out, and I started to wonder: how do you remain sane in such chaos? The more I thought about Fran and that party and you, the more I understood. You don't sugar-coat. It's straight to an explanation, to the facts, to know where you stand. You weren't cruel when you blamed Edwin—it's true, it was his fault, and I didn't want to hear it. And that's it; the only way for you to remain stable is to hold on to some aspect of truth."

"What are you doing, Harry?"

"Last night, I didn't understand you. But you didn't understand me either. Understanding is a two-way street, and neither of us was going the right way."

"True. Like when you suddenly felt you couldn't spend time with me after Walter hired me."

Harry stepped closer to me, biting her bottom lip. Her lavender perfume curled under my nose.

"I'm sorry about that…" She placed her hand on my forearm. "I was confused. Too much was going on at once. I want us to start over."

"Because you want to hire me."

"No. Well, yes. It's not that straightforward. Logan, I just need to know if Fran was really at the party, and you're the only person I can trust with this right now. You won't bullshit me. Tell me you'll do it, if only for my peace of mind. The suspicion is too much to handle. Here." Harry held forty pounds in her hand. "It's all I have."

I looked at the time—it was already 11am. I had no idea how long it would take at *Žmonių Balsas*, but it didn't seem unreasonable to think I couldn't also look into this for Harry. Maybe I was a sucker for her pretty face. Maybe my motivation was shallow. I don't know. I wanted to believe her. I also wanted to believe that maybe there was something between us, which possibly made me ignorant, or foolish.

"Keep your money," I said. "Where was this party?"

A look of relief eased her tense face, and then a smile formed. "25 Palmerston Place. Hosted by the Wrights." Harry then told me how to find the address. It wasn't far—about a ten-minute walk up Princes Street, then a right somewhere.

"I'll look into this as soon as I can, but I've got some other business to see to first."

"Oh, Logan!" She hugged me. "How can I thank you, Logan?"

"Have dinner with me tonight?" I said.

Harry smiled. I caught it and smiled back.

"Okay."

"Except, I don't know anywhere nice in this town."

Harry thought. "Meet me at Cafe Royal at seven."

"It's not a dance hall, is it?"

"Lord, no." Harry laughed and gave me a perplexed look.

"Okay, good. And tell you what I find out."

Harry took my hands and kissed my cheek. Her lips were warm and soft.

"See you later, lamb," she whispered into my ear before kissing it.

"You bet."

27

I walked down the dimly lit corridor to the door with *Žmonių Balsas* in black letters on it. I lightly tapped the cracked frosted glass and said, "Hello?"

"Hello, yes?" someone responded. "Come in." The man's Eastern European accent was mellow, and his English was confident.

The hinges creaked as I opened the door.

Grey indirect light poured into the office from a dirty window.

Sitting at the cluttered table of papers, pens, jars of ink, two typewriters, and a candlestick telephone was a small man with a tuft of grey on top of his bald head. Silver pince-nez rested on his nose, and he wore a thick grey cardigan over a white shirt and black tie. He eyed me with suspicion.

The grimy walls of the narrow office were lined with dusty filing cabinets and a printing press. Hung on the dank walls, with peeling wallpaper, were elegant, hand-carved wooden frames displaying pamphlets with the titles *Aušra, Apžvalga*, and *Valstietis*. I couldn't even pretend to pronounce them in my head, let alone understand what they meant. It hit me how easy it was to get by, just about anywhere, by speaking English, and I wondered how hard it must've been for people like Mary Palvienė who knew so little.

The man rose from the chair and hiked up his loose tweed trousers.

"Hello, what can I do for you?"

"Hello, I'm Logan Bishop. I'm looking for the editor."

"That would be me. Darius Lanka. How may I help you, Mr Bishop?"

"I'm looking for a woman named Rūta Kanaitė. Do you know her?"

He adjusted his pince-nez. "What's your interest?"

I showed him my ID, he glanced at it.

"A few weeks ago, Rūta Kanaitė planned to meet a woman here

and take her to a job interview. That woman is missing. I'd like to speak with Rūta if you can arrange an introduction. I will compensate you for the efforts."

His dark eyes surveyed me.

He paused for a beat. "A missing *Lithuanian* woman?" Lanka's suspicion morphed into curiosity.

"Yes."

He crossed his arms and held his chin with his forefinger and thumb. He stretched his face as he said, "Won't you sit, Mr Bishop?" He waved at the table, and we pulled up chairs. Lanka leaned forward, putting both arms on the table. "This missing woman you speak of. What's the story?"

"She worked for a hotel, lost her job, and then left without telling her friends or family—no explanation. What I do know is that she's in trouble."

"When was this meeting with Rūta arranged for?"

"About three weeks ago."

"Hm, yes, that does ring some bells. What kind of trouble do you think she is in?"

"I'm not sure. She's connected to a man, an American, who was recently hospitalised after a brutal attack in London. This man has dealings with bad people and, for some reason, gave this woman an item of significant value. Now, these men who put the guy in the hospital are looking for her."

"Troublesome news, indeed." He paused. "Gone for three weeks, you say?"

"Yes."

"We haven't placed any help ads in two months."

"Help ads?"

"People wanting help locating a missing loved one. They started because of the wars, but the repatriation has spurred renewed interest. Many lost souls yet to be found."

"Wars?"

"Yes. Thirty thousand were taken by the international war and two and a half thousand by the war for our independence; loved ones wishing and praying to find someone either stuck in Russia,

Lithuania, or Germany or simply to know if they were dead. What is the name of the woman you're looking for?"

"I was told her name was Matas. But I discovered her real name is Matienė."

Lanka smiled. "Ah, yes, of course. Spellings differ between men and women in Lithuania, like the French."

"I guess English is for simpletons."

He chuckled. "I will make a call."

He picked up the telephone.

Lanka's entire conversation was rapid and in Lithuanian. I picked up a word or two: Greta Matienė, Logan Bishop, something that sounded like a private detective. I looked over at the pamphlets on the wall and then at the old man—Lanka was a long-suffering freedom fighter in a dingy Edinburgh basement still pumping out literature.

I rose and walked around the table while he spoke on the phone to take a closer look at the framed pamphlets. They were beaten up, old, wrinkled, and dirty—just like how I felt.

Darius Lanka hung up and approached me.

"If you can be patient, Mr Bishop, I should get a call back shortly."

"Sure. I can hang around. What are these?" I asked.

Lanka peered over the top of his pince-nez. "Ah, papers I used to write for. My first publications were in each one of those."

"In Lithuania?" I asked.

"Yes, that's right."

"What do they mean?"

Pointing, he said: "Aušra means Dawn. Apžvalga, The Review, and Valstietis means Peasant."

"Subtle, huh? Are you a communist?"

Darius Lanka laughed. "No, my boy. No. Not many Lithuanians are."

"Greta Matas is…" I produced the Lithuanian Communist Party tracts. He took them. "This was hers."

Lanka scanned them and tutted.

Giving them back, he said: "Mr Bishop, what do you know

about Lithuania?"

"Not a thing, really."

"What do you know about communism?"

"It's a joke."

He laughed.

Looking at the pamphlets, he said: "The Russians attempted and failed to establish a communist Government in my country. And, despite the British Government's fears, we are not a communist people any more than your fellow Americans, Mr Bishop. You are American, no? I thought so. I'll tell you why. Lithuania is an agricultural nation. The land is our source of wealth, and we value the right to own and produce from the land. Communism prohibits such ideas as land ownership. You will not find many Lithuanians willing to deny their right to own what brings them wealth, stability, and security. It was no surprise that Lithuania's first communist government fell quickly. But it breaks my heart to see my fellow people being taken in by this." He waved the pamphlet.

"You sound like most Americans, Mr Lanka. But still, some Lithuanians subscribe."

"Yes, there are radicals—there will always be some who believe my country's future ought to be shaped by socialism, as is the same in America and Britain."

"We live in an ideological wasteland if you ask me."

"I am inclined to agree with your sentiment."

Lanka said: "Most of those were written before you were born, no doubt. You seem like a young man." I smiled at that. "I wrote these back when Russia waged a cultural war against Lithuanian customs, our language, and our Catholic devotion. Of course, it's not much different here in Britain. Well, at least we're not forced to be British." He laughed. "That is better than Russian."

"What do you mean?"

"It's why so many of us left Lithuania. Escaped the Russification—to save our lives. Our language was illegal, and so was our literature. Imagine if tomorrow, Mr Bishop, English was illegal and you had to learn, oh, I don't know... Welsh or Scottish Gaelic. And if you spoke, wrote, or worshipped in English, you could face criminal charges? Do you think God discriminates against language?" He shook his head.

"I wouldn't know. So these pamphlets were bootlegged?"

"Yes. We had to bootleg our writing, like you Americans bootleg your liquor." Darius Lanka grinned. "It was a push-back at the Russians. My friends and I would write these pamphlets and smuggle them across the borders. When a friend of mine, Jonas, was arrested by the Russians, I knew I'd never see him again and that I needed to get out. Or I would have been arrested too—likely imprisoned or killed. I ended up here, in Edinburgh. Of course, the Scots don't want us here any more than the Russians."

The telephone rang. Mr Lanka darted to answer it. He spoke in Lithuanian. His face looked stern, his brow creased as he listened and then replied with spitfire dialogue. A minute later, he hung up.

"Miss Kanatiė is interested in speaking with you, Mr Bishop," he said. "I will take you to her now."

28

Lanka took me to Doris's Tea Rooms, a creaky joint somewhere between Cowgate and Grassmarket. The style inside was vulgar—rickety chairs and tables and loud red and gold Victorian wallpaper. I sipped a coffee that tasted burnt, and Darius Lanka swirled a biscuit in his milky tea. The only thing missing was Rūta Kanaitė. The clock on the wall read midday.

"How long is she going to be?" I asked.

"She will be here soon. Patience, Mr Bishop."

I liked Lanka. He had a calming personality, and I decided to test my budding trust in the old man.

"Could you look something over? I think it's in Lithuanian, and I'm curious to know what it says."

I handed him the slip of paper I recovered from Petras's rooms back at Davies Colliery.

He glanced up at me over his glasses and half-smiled. "It's a to-do list."

"You're joking," I said.

He pointed at the words.

"Wash clothes. Drain bathtub. Get carrots and potatoes. And well, you can read that."

"Does Ivy House mean anything to you?" I asked. "If it's in Edinburgh, it's well hidden and not publicly listed."

"I am unfamiliar with the name Ivy House, Mr Bishop."

"You can call me Logan if you like."

He nodded and chomped down on his soggy tea biscuit.

"Ah, she's here," he said and dabbed his mouth.

We rose.

Rūta Kanaitė entered. She was tall and bony, with light-brown hair. Her face was gaunt, and her nose arched. Under a beige coat, she wore a woman's grey suit with a teal V-neck sweater underneath. She was even taller up close—at least six foot one, a good two to three inches on me.

She greeted Lanka with a kiss on both cheeks. I got nervous

she'd do the same to me. I never mastered the art of the European greeting. They spoke in Lithuanian to each other for a moment.

Lanka turned to me: "This is the private investigator, Mr Logan Bishop. Mr Bishop, this is Miss Rūta Kanaitė."

Rūta craned her head and smiled—I couldn't help noticing that her left front tooth was grey.

"Hello, Mr Bishop. It is nice to meet you." Her accent was similar to Lanka's. We shook hands, and I was relieved to avoid the greeting kiss manoeuvre.

"Thank you for meeting with me, Miss Kanaitė."

"What would you like to drink, Rūta?" asked Lanka as he helped her out of her coat, which she put on the back of her chair.

"Earl Grey, please. Thank you."

He darted to the counter, and we sat.

"I understand you are looking for Greta Matienė," Rūta said, right to the point.

"I am, yes. Greta left your letter behind when she disappeared."

I produced it, and Rūta's long fingers gingerly held the paper, and she read it.

Rūta said: "Darius tells me she has been missing for three weeks?"

"That's right. I hoped you had information on her whereabouts."

Lanka returned. "Your tea will be a moment."

"I'm afraid I don't know where she went," Rūta said.

"Miss Kanaitė," I continued, "someone has to know something. How does no one in her social circles have the slightest idea? What's going on with her?"

"You think I am lying to you, Mr Bishop?" She tried to hold down her nostril flares. Lanka froze, holding his tea midway between the table and his mouth.

"Here's what I know. Something's made her run. Some ruthless men are looking for Greta. And it's all connected to an emerald ring sent to her—a Russian-cut emerald ring. Bad things are on the heels of it. The men after it have already put my... put a man in the hospital. They've also tried to get me a few times since I got to town. I can't say if they just want the ring or Greta as well. I also don't know who they are, but I know Greta is a Bolshevik." I produced the tract I showed Lanka. "Maybe her sympathies are the reason she's disappeared? Maybe that's why no one will tell me what the hell is going on with her, but I'm here to make sure she doesn't end up dead... if she's not already."

Rūta sat like a statue with her hands in her lap. A waitress placed Rūta's tea on the table, but she didn't touch it.

"Look," I continued, "the police watch suspected communists. I'm not naive about what happens with them or immigrants the government finds troublesome."

"What do *you* know of the troubles of immigrants?" Rūta challenged.

"I am one," I said.

"You're American," Rūta replied.

"And?"

"You don't count."

"Oh, well, sorry I'm not immigrant enough for you, sweetheart. But I'm the only immigrant interested in finding Greta. The only one who wants to ensure she's safe and alive."

"Mr Bishop, I do not discount you," Rūta defended. "But..."

"Bullshit. You just did. You've put me into a box of others. The same thing the Scots and the British, in general, do to you and any other immigrant they fear. You think they don't do the same to me? I'm a yank. Forever an outsider. I'm no nobleman with refined taste and a good education that opens doors. I'm a poor kid from a Chicago suburb, and the Brits can smell the lower class on me. I'm a grunt worker. You and I aren't so different—we're both the 'us' in the them versus us. From where I sit, if we're not all equal, none of us are, Miss Kanaitė. I don't care about Greta's nationality, who she's slept with, or her politics. I want to find her because I want the truth."

Rūta's face turned red.

"Settle down, Mr Bishop," Darius said.

The two Lithuanians angrily muttered in their native tongue, and then Rūta glared at me.

"I can't help you." Rūta rose.

LUKE DECKARD

"Can't or won't?" I said.

"Pick one," she said, walking off.

"Miss Kanaitė—"

"This is over." She was through the door, coat in hand.

I shot a look at Lanka, who sat there like a shy child.

"Hell." I pushed out from the table.

"Logan, wait," Lanka called, but I ignored him.

"Miss Kanaitė! Hey!" I followed her through the cold. She walked and buttoned her coat. "I didn't mean to offend."

"Our conversation is over, Mr Bishop. You accuse me of lying and misleading. You raise your voice at me. I will not have that." Her pace quickened.

"Will you stop walking for one damn moment?"

I caught up and stopped in front of her. She looked down at me with narrowed eyes and fists clenched at her sides.

"I'm sorry. My reaction was hot," I said. "I'd chalk it up to being a blunt American, but the truth is I'm frustrated. Every rock I've turned over has led me nowhere. I need your help. I need to know where Greta went."

"Why is this woman so important to you? There is more to it than what you are telling me."

I hesitated a moment. She began to move around me. "It's my dad," I admitted. Rūta turned to me, and after a beat, I continued. "He came to London wanting my help. He wanted me stop some men from killing her. I don't know why and can't ask him either; he's the man lying in a hospital bed in London in a coma after some men beat the life outta him. It's all to do with the ring. The men in Edinburgh right now looking for her. They are a nasty lot, and they might do the same thing to her that they did to my dad. Especially if they find her and she doesn't have the ring. I can't sit around knowing she could be killed and do nothing. But I also need her to make sense of all this."

"Is everything all right?" Lanka approached.

Rūta studied my face. Darius watched us. Then she said: "Yes, Darius. It was a misunderstanding. Let's go back inside. I will tell you what I know."

BAD BLOOD

We sat back inside the tea room, and Rūta began to tell me about Greta Matienė.

She met Greta in 1916 when she joined the Lithuanian Working Women's Association. For the same reasons all women like her do, Greta was looking for community and solidarity. She didn't feel accepted by the locals, by the Scots. Being an immigrant and a woman was not easy. She was discriminated against at her job—being an immigrant, she was paid less than Scotswomen. The Lithuanian Working Women's Association fought for her, and she fought for them. Championing her sisters' rights here and at home. She took an interest in Bolshevism through a couple of radicals in the group, but she never did anything more than hand out tracts and attend protests. Rūta didn't believe Greta was of any interest to the police. There were too many other people of interest, but she wouldn't tell me who they were.

"Greta just wanted to be happy," Rūta continued. "Life had not been kind to her. Her husband abandoned her for another woman when she was pregnant, her cousins died in the war—"

"Wait, Mary Palvienė, the woman Greta lived with, told me Greta's husband died in Lithuania, not that he abandoned her for another woman."

"I can only tell you what I was told, Mr Bishop. Perhaps Mrs Palvienė misremembered. Perhaps Greta was not honest with her. We think we want the truth until we have it in our hands, and it's nastier than we imagined."

"I guess it's easier to be ignorant."

"It is," Lanka chimed in.

"When did you see her last?" I asked.

"She came to me a few days after she lost her job. She was worried about finding new employment since she was let go from the hotel without references."

"Is it true she was let go for messing with a guest's jewels?" I asked.

Rūta glanced at Lanka.

"No, Mr Bishop." Rūta frowned. She hesitated, then said: "Greta was caught in bed with a young man by his mother."

"Who?"

"Greta wouldn't say. She was too afraid to say but told me what happened. Greta said the man's mother entered the room and found them together. The mother was enraged but wanted to avoid the scandal—according to Greta, this man is engaged to the daughter of a powerful man. Greta was accused of seducing this woman's son; she had Greta dismissed and ensured the hotel kept it quiet."

I thought back to Mr Connell. That was why he wouldn't discuss Greta with me. Both Denise and Gabriel had been fed a lie—Greta didn't steal any jewels.

"That's why you tried to help her," I said.

"Yes. I found a nanny position for her, but she didn't turn up the day she agreed to meet me and the family. I sent her a telegram but she didn't reply."

"Something spooked her," I said, more to myself than to Lanka and Rūta.

"But what?" Rūta wondered.

"Only she can tell me. One more thing. In Leith, she went to a travel agent days before she went missing: Marsh Travel."

"Marsh Travel?" Rūta turned pale.

"Mr Bishop, are you certain?" Lanka said.

"Someone saw Greta go inside. That same person ran into her at Waverley Station a few days later, where she said she was going away. The man at Marsh Travel said he knew nothing, but I don't believe him."

Something stirred in Rūta's mind. She knew something.

"Mr Bishop, we may speak in a few days."

"What's going on? What aren't you telling me?"

"Mr Bishop, please be patient or forego my help."

I turned to Lanka, then back to Rūta.

"Two days then."

BAD BLOOD

29

I left Doris's Tea Rooms just after three o'clock that afternoon. It was getting dark as I walked through Old Town. Darius Lanka said to return to the paper the day after the next. I knew I needed to check out Marsh Travel again, but I also needed to wait for Rūta Kanaitė. She knew something about that place, and it made me uneasy.

As I climbed a steep, narrow close, my calves burned, and I mulled over events. The more Greta's story unravelled, the more questions I had. What I knew now, the father of Petras abandoned her—so why did she tell Mary Palvienė that he died in Lithuania? She wasn't dismissed from the hotel for stealing—she was caught sleeping with an engaged rich boy whose mother threw her weight around. Who is this woman Mr Connell is protecting? Was that man the same one Mrs Mears saw Greta with in Portobello? If so, Greta's disappearance might not have anything to do with whatever mess she and my father were in. The only comforting thought was that Spatty and his pals wouldn't have it any easier if I had this much trouble pinning Greta down. Or so I hoped.

It started to snow as I walked up Princes Street. I decided to check out Palmerston Place for Harry before we had dinner. But before that, I ducked into my hotel, used a payphone, and called St Thomas' Hospital. It had been a few days since I checked in on my old man. He was still vegetated, and I was urged to see him and say my goodbyes. I said I couldn't, and I hung up.

Outside, I leaned against the building. I felt hollow. There were no happy memories of Dad to seek out, no matter how hard I tried. It was like looking at moving figures through frosted glass. Everything happy was too distant to come to me, if those memories even existed. All I had stored up were nightmares. Him beating my ass raw with his belt after the White Sox game because I spilt mustard on my shirt. Not speaking to me for months after he found out I had been seeing a black girl. If he died, I didn't know what I'd feel. Sadness? Regret? Relief? I had avoided these questions since I left London. All I could think, the Devil was dying.

"Mr Bishop…"

A red Rolls Royce was throttling in the street. From the back seat, a square-faced man with coppery hair looked at me.

"Yeah?" I asked.

The back door opened. "Get in. I'd like a word." The man had an English accent. It stood out after days of listening to Scots.

"Do I have a choice?" I asked.

"Of course," the man said. "But if you walk away, then you'll miss out on making a lot of money."

The man scooted over, and I climbed in.

The Rolls took off, and I got a better look at the man sitting in the corner of the seat with his legs crossed. He wore a pin-striped suit and smelled of cinnamon aftershave and cigarettes.

"You know my name, sir," I said, "but you've not told me yours."

A slimy lawyer-y smile stretched across his wide blockish face. "My name is Stan White. I suppose you know why I'm here?"

"Enlighten me, Stanley," I said.

His smile receded.

"It has come to my client's attention that you are investigating the incident that transpired with a certain chambermaid at a certain hotel. Whom are you working for?"

"Can't tell you that, Stanley," I said.

"Come now, Mr Bishop." Stan White chuckled. "My client wants to know what they want."

"Well, I'm not gonna tell you," I said. "Why don't you just come out and tell me what *your client* wants?"

"Ultimately, for you to stop poking around the hotel. The incident is delicate. My client does not want the ordeal to grow out of proportion and become public knowledge. It was a private family matter, you understand. They will pay you handsomely if you will back down from your investigation and leave it alone."

I smiled. "Sorry, that's not gonna happen, Stanley. But I'd consider dropping it if I could have a conversation with your client."

"That is out of the question."

"Then I'm afraid we're done."

"We will pay you five thousand pounds to walk away."

"You can't buy me," I said.

"Everyone can be bought, Mr Bishop."

"Information is my currency." I paused. "Unless your client can tell me where the *chambermaid* is, we have nothing more to discuss."

"They couldn't possibly say where she is."

"You ran her out of town, didn't you?"

"Mr Bishop, we are not thugs." He laughed.

"No, you're worse; you're a lawyer. Your client took that chambermaid's livelihood because *she* was too worried about *her* reputation."

"It's not so black and white, Mr Bishop."

"Well, let me tell you what is—I don't care how much money you throw at me, I won't take it." I smacked the roof of the Rolls. "Driver, stop the car. I'm getting out."

"Mr Bishop, I urge you to drop this matter."

"And if I don't?"

"It would be a shame if the Home Office decided your residence status in Britain became problematic. One phone call from my client to the Home Secretary could make your life here very difficult."

"We're done."

I opened the car door as the driver turned off of Princes Street. He slammed the brakes, and a car behind swerved to avoid rear-ending us. I got out.

"You're making a mistake, Mr Bishop," the lawyer said.

"No. You did," I said and then slammed the car door shut.

30

I watched the Rolls speed off and make a right on the next road. My hands shook—I hadn't expected his threat to get to me, but it did. I took a hit of Winslow's. Whatever I was doing was ruffling feathers and I didn't plan on stopping. I had stumbled upon a sex scandal that now risked my status in the country, all to find out what the hell had happened to Greta Matas and keep her out of harm's way from the goons who beat up my dad. Everything was murky, and it was hard to see clear connections. Motives were all over the place.

I made my way to Palmerston Place and continued up Atholl Place.

"Where are you, Greta?" I muttered to myself. "What did those people do to you?" Of course, I didn't know who 'those people' were yet. But Mr Connell knew something. He must've tipped off the woman who got Greta dismissed. There was no chance I'd go ask Denise for any more help. Gabriel, on the other hand—sure.

My feet stopped outside 25 Palmerston Place. The end-of-terrace house was a beautiful five-level sandstone mansion with a spiked iron fence guarding the deep trench around the front and side. I pressed the bell under the tall arched entrance, and the dongs echoed inside.

A dark-skinned woman opened the door. She was middle-aged, with her black wavy hair pulled back into a tight bun. She wore a flattering green dress with a brown cardigan.

"Hello, sir?"

"Afternoon, miss. My name is Logan Bishop. I'm a private investigator. I'm looking for Mr John Wright. Is he available?"

"May I ask why?" the woman asked.

"I need to ask him a few questions about the party he hosted recently."

"Unfortunately, Mr and Mrs Wright don't take unexpected visitors."

"I'm not a visitor, miss. I'm an investigator. Tell them this is about the murder of Edwin Walter."

She pulled back a little. "One moment, sir. Please wait here."

She brought me into the closed-off entryway and disappeared into the house.

On a stand next to the door was a guest book. I flipped the pages to the night of the party and spotted names I recognised: Fran Walter and David Joy. Inspector Joy's name was above Mrs Walter's. So he was at the party with her. Before I could tear the page out, the housekeeper returned.

"Mr and Mrs Wright will see you, Mr Bishop. Follow me."

The foyer had white marble floors partly covered by a Persian rug and a domed stained-glass ceiling with a mural of dark blue skies and yellow stars. Each level of the house looked out onto the foyer. The trim and stairs were dark polished oak, and every wall was adorned with pretentious portraits of young and old white men and women from the 16th, 17th, and 18th centuries.

I followed the housekeeper up a set of stairs with a thick red runner—it gave the impression of a waterfall of blood.

She led me into a well-furnished lounge on the first floor. It was littered with china bric-a-brac and landscape paintings. A man and a woman drank tea at a small table where a card game had been abandoned.

The man looked to be in his early fifties. He was thin with greying hair and wore tan slacks and a thick cream jumper. The woman, maybe in her forties, had strawberry-blonde hair and a tennis player's build. She wore a brown tweed skirt, thick cream stockings, and a teal jumper.

"This is Mr Bishop," the housekeeper introduced.

"Thank you, Lizzy," Mr Wright said. She left the room.

"Afternoon, Mr and Mrs Wright." I removed my hat. "I appreciate you taking the time to see me."

I approached the couple who now stood.

"Mr Bishop," Mr Wright continued, straightening his jumper. "How can we help you?"

"I wanted to ask about your recent party."

Mrs Wright asked, "What does that have to do with Edwin

Walter?"

"Hopefully, nothing."

"Why don't we sit?" Mr Wright offered.

The couple took their teas to a pair of armchairs by a lit fireplace. I sunk into a two-seater sofa facing them and continued, "Mrs Walter attended your party?"

"That's correct," Mr Wright said.

"Did you notice anything unusual about her?"

"I don't think so," Mr Wright said.

I turned to Mrs Wright. "Ma'am?"

She looked up from her teacup and then up at me.

"Not that I can recall."

"Is this about Francine?" asked Mr Wright.

"I'm just getting an idea of where people were that night. Was Edwin invited?"

The couple tensed and looked at each other. Mr Wright then said, "No, we only extended the invitation to Fran."

"Why?"

"Frankly, no one likes Edwin," Mrs Wright admitted.

"Doris," Mr Wright chided.

"It's no secret, John."

He looked irritated at her.

I asked: "Why does no one like him?"

Mrs Wright continued, "We never knew what piece of conversation would end up in his stories. No one wanted to be around him for fear of what he'd write next. So, we don't... didn't invite him."

"And Fran was happy to attend events without him?"

"Aye," Mr Wright said. "Fran is an old friend of ours. She's always welcome here. Why should she suffer because of her husband's nuisances?"

"Would you say Mr and Mrs Walter were in love?" I asked.

"That's not our place to say," Mr Wright said.

"She put up with him, John," Mrs Wright said. She looked at me. "She might've loved him once. Now, I don't think so."

Mr Wright glared at his wife.

"Right. How late was Fran here?"

Mrs Wright chuckled. "We weren't sitting on the door, checking the time; we were entertaining."

"Approximately then," I said.

Mrs Wright squinted. "I think Fran was here until about eleven."

"You're certain of this, Mrs Wright?" I asked.

The floor in the corridor creaked, and Mr Wright shot his eyes to the door and then back to me.

"We are sure." Mr Wright spoke for his wife. The two nodded. "Mr Bishop, I'm growing uncomfortable with these questions despite my wife's openness. You are wrong if you think Fran had anything to do with Edwin's death. If you think anyone at our party knows what happened, again, you are wrong. No one here that night would kill the man over his stories, mind. Sue him, certainly."

"No one's accusing anyone. As I said, I wanted to confirm movement on the night."

"And you have," Mr Wright said. Mrs Wright eyed him and half-smiled. It looked forced. "Now, if you'll excuse us, we must be getting on."

We rose. "Don't trouble yourself. I'll show myself out. Thank you, again, for your time."

Leaving the room, I spotted the housekeeper's head vanishing down the stairs in the hall. Down in the foyer, she was busying herself with a ficus plant in the corner.

"Beautiful house," I said.

"Yes, it is, sir." Lizzy smiled. It was sweet. She faced me, clasping her hands in front.

"Do you always eavesdrop on conversations?" I whispered.

Lizzy's eyes widened.

"Sir, I…" She backed away, uneasy.

"You're not in trouble. The story they told me, was it true?"

Lizzy nodded. But her eyes gave her away.

"But it's not the whole story?"

"I don't know, sir," Lizzy whispered. "Please, forgive me. It's not my place."

LUKE DECKARD

"I won't tell them, Lizzy. I need the truth."

"No, I don't know anything. I'm sorry. Please." She waved towards the door.

I took a five-pound note from my wallet. "Tell me what you know, and it's yours."

She glanced upstairs and then said: "Come out here."

Lizzy shut us out of earshot in the cold entryway.

"Something did happen, but Mr and Mrs Wright don't know. Or I think they don't know."

She reached for the money.

"What's that?" I pulled it back.

She glanced over her shoulder a moment.

She moved closer and spoke in a low voice: "During the night, I went up to the top floor for a moment's peace when I heard voices in one of the rooms. I saw Mrs Walter and Mr Joy in each other's arms. Kissing. But Mrs Walter broke away suddenly. She might've heard me. She said she was worried they'd be caught. Mr Joy sounded irritated and asked Mrs Walter what was wrong. Naturally, I was curious, as anyone would be. So I listened. Mrs Walter said something about her husband finding a letter about a man named Harry. That's when Mr Joy said, 'It's either him or me'. I don't know what Mrs Walter said next, I didn't hear. She was crying then, but Mr Joy was angry and said: 'Edwin is always creating messes, and it needs to stop... He doesn't deserve you'. I could hear him stomping towards the door, so I ducked into another room. Mrs Walter was alone and crying. I raced downstairs in time to see Mr Joy leave the party."

"What time was this?"

"It was around nine-thirty."

"And Fran, she was here all night?"

"She was. Her mood brightened after that."

I handed her the five pounds.

"Don't tell anyone else what you saw. And keep this between us," I said. I reached for the guest book and tore out the page with Fran Walter and Inspector Joy's signatures. Lizzy gasped.

I left and headed back to Princes Street.

BAD BLOOD

That was some revelation. Joy went to the party and was seen kissing Fran. They got into an argument, and he left. Then he just happened to get the call about Edwin's death and was dogged about the information inside Edwin's book and where the materials were that he supposedly possessed. He tore the office apart. What was he after? What does Edwin have on Joy, and did Joy want him out of the way to be with Fran?

I needed to know where he went after the party. But I didn't know what to tell Harry at dinner. I suddenly realised my nice suit wasn't so nice. It was covered in filth and blood after my date with Denise that ended in a brawl with Al, and being thrown in the gutter out the back—so I headed to Jenners to see what I could find before I met Harry.

31

I left the hotel for the Cafe Royal to meet Harry. The cold night air burned my clean-shaven cheeks. The peachy scent of the new cologne, Mitsouko, I'd picked up at Jenners, kicked up in the wind. I wasn't sure why I went and got the cologne, to be honest. I just thought it'd make a nice touch to the evening. I wore a new grey suit off the rack, too. My clothes had taken a good beating since I arrived in Edinburgh. The suit was a decent fit. The jacket sleeves were a hair too long, but I still looked sharp.

Cafe Royal was tucked away just off Princes Street. It was busy. The island bar was encircled by drinkers decked out in flashy and expensive clothes. Others lounged in comfortable-looking leather booths.

The host told me Harry hadn't arrived and then raised an eyebrow at my tan Oxfords. The leather on the sides had scuffs from being thrown out of the dance hall the other day. Even a good polish couldn't get them out. But my feet would be under a table, so who would notice, I figured, especially in the dim light offered by the establishment? I guess this guy.

He walked me through the dining room. On the walls were stained-glass depictions of hunters and expansive and intricately painted tile portraits of historical men who I ought to know but didn't. The elegant coffered ceilings, brasswork, and polished dark-wood features felt late Victorian.

Sitting at the table waiting, my nose itched. I glanced at the woman across from me, weighed down in diamonds. Her perfume smelled of mothballs and fruitcake, which undoubtedly cost more than I make in a month. She chomped on squid. The man with her wore pearl cufflinks and a Freemason pinky ring. He slurped oysters. This wasn't the kind of place where I belonged. I preferred a smoky cocktail bar with a pretty woman behind a microphone and a whisky sour in my hand. This was all too Old-World for my liking.

I thought about Harry and what I should tell her about Inspector

BAD BLOOD

Joy and Mrs Walter. I tried to play the devil's advocate with myself. What did it matter if they saw each other behind Walter's back? Their argument at the party didn't make Inspector Joy a killer. Even so, I didn't have enough information to accuse him, an inspector—and one who dislikes me—of murdering his lover's husband. I remembered how Mrs Walter spoke about her husband the other night in the lounge. Married by legal obligation, nothing more. Walter had done away with pictures of his boys, and angered his wife's friends with his stories—it was not a surprise she sought solace in another man's arms. I understood why anyone stuck in Joy's situation might get angry. Just, was he mad enough to kill?

Harry arrived. She wore a nicely fitted wood-green dress with a leafy hairpin in her Titian locks. She smiled, and her red velvet lips contrasted with her bright teeth. I had to keep telling myself that a woman like this was only out with a guy like me because she hired me. I hadn't forgotten her rejection the other day. As much as I wanted to entertain notions of romance, I knew hoping for it was a bad idea.

I shot up and pulled her chair out.

"Hello, lamb," she said. The oyster slurper next to us gave Harry a once-over. Thou shalt not covet.

Harry's eyes turned into lovely half-moons as her smile widened. Her red mouth kissed my cheeks, and in return, I planted an awkward kiss on her. I inhaled her lavender perfume.

"You smell nice, Logan," Harry added.

"So do you. And you look lovely."

Harry's cheeks blushed, and she bit her bottom lip, smiling. There she was again—that same flirty woman from the train. For a while, I forgot that I was there to discuss Fran Walter at all.

We drank red wine, nibbled on chicken liver pâté and haggis fritters, and talked about fun-nothings like a couple of people without any troubles in our lives.

"So we should just get this out of the way," I finally said. "I paid a visit to the Wrights," I added, spreading pâté over a cracker.

"I'm nervous to know," Harry said, piercing haggis with her fork.

I sipped more wine and then said: "Mrs Walter was at the party all night, Harry. Both Mr and Mrs Wright confirmed that she was acting normally. I don't think she had anything to do with his murder." My gut told me to keep Joy out of this conversation.

"Honestly, I don't know what I was thinking." She hung her head and shook it. "I overreacted this morning. Of course, she didn't do it. I just miss Edwin so much, Logan. I went looking for monsters, and Fran was the obvious one. What a bad idea that was." She rolled her eyes. "If Fran knew what I asked of you, well, thank God she doesn't. I've had a constant headache since this all began." Harry put the wine glass to her lips and drank more. "If Fran were to kill anyone, it would be me." Harry smiled.

"Why do you say that?"

"Oh, doesn't matter."

"Come on."

"She doesn't like me much." There was something in Harry's eyes—a thought she didn't want to share.

"What happened between you two?"

"Nothing happened. She never liked me." Harry played with her food, glancing up at me while she spoke: "Fran treated me like some beggar Edwin had brought home. She used to call me 'The Stray'."

"That's cold," I said.

"I didn't come from Edwin and Fran's world. I was a poor shopgirl from Leith with no family. Fran didn't like Edwin hiring me and didn't like me living in her son's bedroom. I didn't belong in their world of fancy parties and nice things. It was worse in the early days. Eventually, Fran learned to be civil with me—but only just. I still can't believe what happened."

"Losing Walter has been hard for you."

Harry pushed haggis around her plate.

"He was good to me." Harry smiled sadly. "I know he frustrated other people, but he didn't deserve to be murdered." Harry sighed. "You know, I saw a lone magpie the day he died. I didn't say, 'Hello, Mr Magpie'. I should have."

"Why?"

"It's bad luck. If you don't say hello to a magpie, it means sorrow will follow."

"Well, I doubt that has anything to do with what happened." I cracked a smile.

"I don't know, Logan." After a moment's pause, Harry said, "Inspector Joy came around again today."

"What for?"

"Not sure. He was at the house when I got back from seeing you. He and Fran were going through Edwin's office and looking through his papers for the lawyer. I don't know why she needed Joy for that, but I could tell Fran had been crying. I've never seen her cry, Logan, or look sad. There's no time to grieve when lawyers get involved."

"It's odd that Inspector Joy was there, no?"

"The two have known each other for years. And Fran won't ask me for help. Probably for the best, too, I can't go into Edwin's office. I can barely live in the house. His smell clings to everything." She paused. "Fran won't know you went asking about her at the Wrights, will she? I'll be humiliated. I want the whole thing dropped, please."

"Even if they tell her, they'll never know you asked me to do it."

"Thank God."

Our next course arrived. I decided not to say anything about Joy. A cop at the scene covering up his murder, it felt too easy, to cliche. And I didn't know enough about Joy or Fran's relationship to jump to murder. At least no yet. Harry tucked into Highland venison, and I devoured vinegar-drenched golden battered haddock and chips. My gut was appeased, like a damn holy sacrifice to the gods. There were a few moments of silence. Harry's mind was preoccupied as she chewed.

Harry gingerly sliced her meat and asked, "Do you think people who talk to the dead—Mediums—can really do it?"

"No, I don't."

"Do you think it's possible?"

"No."

"Edwin believed in it. Fran doesn't know this, but he communed with his son, John, after he died. But he couldn't with Phillip, as much as he tried. Logan, I might try it." Harry's eyes were desperate and grief-filled. "Maybe he could tell me who killed him."

"The Scottish obsession with ghosts and fairies is silly. The people who do that are cons."

"Some are. But I don't think they *all* are. So you don't believe in life after death? In God?"

"There are days I find it hard to believe there's a god of any kind," I said. "What happens when we die is anyone's guess."

"I know there's something after this life." Harry leaned forward and looked me right in the eyes. "If I tell you, promise not to laugh?" I nodded. "When I was a wee girl, I saw the ghost of my gran. She was sitting in the rocker in our lounge, where she would knit. She looked up at me and smiled. I ran out of the room to get my mum and show her, but when we came back, Gran was gone. I can see you think I'm loopy. I swear to you, she was there."

"Harry, I don't know what you saw."

"My gran."

"Maybe you did." I didn't care to argue about it. Who was I to say what she saw was real or not? My beliefs don't have to be others' beliefs and vice versa. Besides, coping with existence by believing in some afterlife is probably healthier than my habit. I could feel the Winslow's in my trouser pocket. At least Harry's ghosts don't haunt her.

The conversation moved on. We downed another bottle of wine like our mouths were bottomless drains and ate dessert. After that, we drank a few cocktails. I told Harry about a few jobs I did with the Pinkertons, and she told me about some of the outrageous parties she attended with Edwin. She moved the conversation on to family. Harry asked if I ever wanted to return to the States and if I had family there. I said I wasn't interested in returning, but I had family in Chicago and Indiana—I just wasn't close with them. That made her sad.

"I miss my family," she said. "My mum died when I was a wee girl. She had tuberculosis. It was hard to watch her go. It was harder on my dad. He died a few years after Mum. There was an accident at the dockyard where he worked. He fell into the harbour and drowned. I would give anything to hold them again." Harry caught a tear and shook off her memories. "I'm always like this when I drink too much." She laughed. "Let's talk about happier things, Logan."

We drank a little more and talked nonsense a little while longer before we decided it was time to leave Cafe Royal.

We walked through New Town arm-in-arm and as straight as we could. The cold air sobered me some. There was something beautifully eerie about wandering through the Gothic city covered in snow. We went past the Scottish National Gallery and stopped to look over Princes Street Gardens. We leaned on the wall and faced Waverley Station and the North British Hotel. A light fog had rolled through the snow-covered city.

"This would make a lovely painting," Harry said.

She smiled at me. She was beautiful. We faced each other. Her smile flickered. Against my better judgment, I took her in my arms and kissed her. Harry wrapped her arms around the back of my neck and held on tightly. Then harry's face felt wet as we kissed. Without warning, she broke away.

"Harry? What's the matter? Why are you crying?"

"Why did you make me do that?" Her words stung.

"I didn't mean to upset you... I'm sorry."

"I have to go. I can't do this, Logan."

Harry walked off.

I reached out and took her hand. "Harry, what's wrong?"

"Let me go."

I did. "Harry?"

Harry's face scrunched with sadness and guilt.

"This was a mistake, Logan. Goodnight."

She marched off. I tried to keep pace as we headed towards Princes Street.

"Harry, what's going on? I don't understand," I begged, like a sap.

"I don't need you to understand, okay? You've done enough!

We're through."

We both ran across Princes Street. Harry ignored me. She jumped into the cab, and it drove off, leaving me stranded and confused on the pavement. My neck felt warm, and my skin tingled.

A tremor suddenly inched up my arm. I reached for the Winslow's inside my trouser pocket and refused to succumb to the attack. I gulped the syrup. I leaned against a building and stared at the sky. It was dark and cloudy. The bitter cold nipped at my face. I had no idea what the hell just happened. The bottle of Winslow's was empty. The shakes weren't gone, and my mood wasn't improved. I threw it into the gutter where I felt like I belonged, but for reasons I couldn't understand.

"Awfy cauld," a petite girl engulfed in a brown woollen coat said to me. "Yer lookin' lonely." She exaggerated a shiver.

The Winslow's steadied me. I was in no mood for this.

The girl must have been eighteen, twenty tops. Her features were sharp, and her cheeks sunken. Her mousey hair was stringy. A prostitute. She batted her dark eyelashes at me. Her lipstick was overdone to fill out her small lips— a girl playing a woman.

"Dae ye no' want tae keep a lass warm for a bit?" Her fingers brushed my arm. "What dae ye say?" She stepped closer.

"I said, I'm not interested." I walked off.

"Fuckin' poof," she chided. I stopped and looked at her. She ran off.

I went back to the hotel alone.

32

The next morning, I woke angry and confused. Confused because of what happened with Harry. I didn't know what I had done, but I felt awful all the same. I felt slimy. She made me feel like I had taken advantage. Had I? And I was angry because of a dream that night. Two men were dragging me onto a boat, deporting me back to America. I gripped a rail as they forced me up the ramp. I wouldn't let go, and they yanked on me. I wanted to run back down the dock and get away. I didn't want to leave. I didn't want to go back. All my struggles to free myself were futile. The next thing I knew, an axe chopped my hands off, and I was taken aboard. I knew where the dream came from—the jackass lawyer who threatened me the day before. I felt like I was losing, and now my dreams knew it, too.

I needed to return to the North British, but the hangover had to wear off first. So I rested a bit longer and then ate. By the afternoon, I felt alive enough to get some answers.

Denise was behind the front desk at the hotel. She gave me a frightful look.

"Connell in?" I asked.

"Yes, but—Logan. Logan!"

I stormed past her and down the corridor to his office.

"What are you doing!" Denise shouted behind me.

"Getting answers."

I swung Connell's door open and entered.

"Good heavens!" Connell jumped behind his desk. His lanky figure shot up from the chair. "What's the meaning of this? What are you doing here?"

"I want the truth about Greta Matienė."

Denise flew in behind me. "I'm sorry, Mr Connell, he just... he wouldn't stop."

"I got a guy at *The Scotsman* ready to put a story to print unless you talk," I bluffed.

He tried to read my face. "Leave us," Connell ordered Denise.

She frowned at me and slammed the door.

"What do you think you know, Mr Bishop?" Connell planted his fists on the desk.

"Well, I had a lovely chat with a lawyer yesterday who threatened me. Seems no one here wants the truth to get out. Greta wasn't fired for stealing jewels. She was caught having sex with a guest. Here's the thing: I don't respond well to threats. If the lawyers aren't called off, and you don't clarify some stuff for me, the story as I know it comes out… names and all. Including you."

Connell's face tightened. We stared at each other until it became uncomfortable for him.

"I hate Americans."

"I hate cowards," I said.

"Yes, all right, it's true." I half-expected Connell to see through the simple lies. He buckled. "You should know," he continued, "I regret what happened to Greta, but what could I do? Do you understand the authority the Clarks wield? Lady Clark's husband has a financial stake in this hotel. If she wants a blind eye turned to her son's misbehaviour, it will happen, you understand. She was furious when she found Ian and Greta in bed; she accused her of coercing Ian. Maybe she did. She's a beautiful woman."

"So she's automatically the villainess?"

"No, that's not what I mean, Mr Bishop." He huffed. "Lady Clark made it clear that if the situation was not put right, the hotel, and by extension, me, would be sorry."

"So you saved yourself," I said.

"My hands were tied, Mr Bishop. Greta had to go. It was the only solution."

"You could've let your own head roll."

"Yes, and she would have hired someone else who would've fired Greta."

"So the story of the jewels became the cover, in case anyone asked."

Mr Connell nodded slightly. His eyes were loaded with shame.

"You threw an innocent woman out of a job because some rich cow told you to." I shook my head.

BAD BLOOD

"I know how it sounds…"

"It sounds like you're a coward," I said.

"Have you found her?" Connell asked. "Is she well?"

"Her blood is on your hands."

He gulped. "She's dead?"

I didn't say anything.

"You must understand," Connell protested. "I tried to find another solution. There was none. Lady Clark made sure no reference could be given to Greta. Maybe Ian reached her, I don't know."

"Reached her? What do you mean?"

"You don't know?" He shook his head. "No point in keeping it a secret, you know everything else. He contacted me days later and told me to give her back her job. I said no. So he told me to financially compensate her. I asked if his mother approved, and he said it didn't matter. He wanted Greta taken care of. I knew he was doing it behind his mother's back." This slowed things down in my head for a hot second. Connell continued: "I told him no and ended it there."

I reached down and grabbed his address book.

"Mr Bishop!" He jolted up and grabbed my wrist.

"Sit down," I ordered. He did. I flipped through his book until I found the Clarks. The only address details were for Mr and Mrs Clark, not Ian, the son. I took the card. They lived at 5 Barkston Gardens, Kensington, London. I pocketed the card and said, "Tell the Clarks to back off. Don't mess with me, Connell," then I stormed out of the office.

Outside, I ducked into a payphone on Prince's Street.

"Five Barkston Gardens," a woman's voice answered. I assumed it was a servant girl from the Cockney accent and high-pitched tone.

"Put Lady Clark on," I demanded.

"I beg your pardon! Who's calling?"

"Logan Bishop. Tell her we talk now, or I will tell everyone what I know about Ian and what happened at the North British Hotel."

"Hold, please." The girl rushed off. It wasn't long before a new voice came on.

"This is Lady Clark, who is this?" The woman's voice dripped with the smug poshness you'd expect of a Kensington resident.

"This is Logan Bishop. I know about your son, Ian, sleeping with the chambermaid at the North British. I know you forced Connell to fire her. You sent your slimy lawyers after me. I'm calling to tell you to back off. Otherwise, the full story will come out in the papers tomorrow."

"You think you can power-play me, Mr Bishop?"

"Did you know your son went behind your back to Connell to get Greta's job reinstated?"

Lady Clark went quiet. I waited.

"What do you want?" she said. "I have tried to give you money to drop this matter."

"I don't want your dirty money, lady. I want to know what you did to Greta. She went missing after your power-play at the hotel."

"I had nothing to do with that!" Lady Clark said.

"What about that son of yours?"

She hesitated. "He… he doesn't either. Mr Bishop, what can I do to get you to stop prying into my family?"

"First of all, you threaten me again, I'll share the story," I lied. "Second, if I find out you're lying and you had something to do with her disappearance, I'll bring your entire family down."

I slammed the phone back onto its cradle.

BAD BLOOD

33

I walked through Waverley Rooftop Gardens. Crowds filtered into the Waverley Market Carnival for cheap fun. Untangling Greta's story wasn't getting easier. It was four o'clock, and my shadow stretched under the street lights. I thought back to what Mrs Mears saw. Greta was with a posh man in Portobello. Was it Ian Clark or Lady Clark's lawyers? That would've been between Henrikas seeing her at Marsh Travel and later at Waverley Station. Did Ian send her somewhere? Did Lady Clark? Everything pointed back to those few days. I wondered if Rūta was going to shed any light or if I needed to go banging on the door of Marsh Travel one more time. I decided I'd go back to my hotel and call Darius Lanka. Maybe Rūta had been in touch.

I approached the Palace Picture House. Outside the cinema sat a wino begging for change. A couple scoffed at him as they came out. He wasn't the kind of tragedy they wanted to see. They wanted thought-provoking dramatics or Buster Keaton comedies… not reality. Not a real guy in a ratty and stained—by God knows what—Royal Fusiliers jacket. Nor his half-marred face and stump leg. Since the war ended, it had become far too easy to ignore the broken images that cluttered the streets. But those of us who carried the scars couldn't.

I dropped half a crown into the wounded soldier's hat. He mumbled, "Bless you." I didn't feel blessed as I entered the Palace Hotel.

Inside, I was met with a surprise. Harry sat in the foyer. I stood in place for a moment. Two suitcases were on either side of her armchair, and a white leather handbag was in her lap. She didn't look mad; she looked broken. She saw me, and I approached her.

"What's this?" I eyed the bags.

"Can we get a drink?" She rose. By her tone, it wasn't a question.

***

We sat in a curved booth in the hotel restaurant. I had a double Black Label, and Harry stared into a glass of cherry brandy.

"What's going on?" I asked. "Is this about last night?"

"No, it's about Fran…"

She yanked her hat off and threw it down on the bench. Her Titian locks were dishevelled.

"Talk to me, Harry."

"The twat kicked me out of the house." Her face looked pale and confused. "She told me with Edwin gone I am no longer needed and that his passing feels like a natural conclusion to my living and working arrangements. Logan, does she know about the Wrights?"

"There's no way she knows you sent me," I said. "What happened?"

"Well, of course, I brought up Edwin's unpublished papers, short stories, letters, et cetera and told Fran we could organise them and publish collections. Believe me, Logan, it's years' worth of work! And let me just say, Fran doesn't understand his catalogue as I do. But the bitch said no. She has no intention of publishing Edwin's remaining works. This just kills him all over again, Logan." Harry shook her head and took a generous gulp of brandy. "She didn't like me pushing the matter, which ended in us getting hot-headed with each other. She told me to leave. That she won't live under the same roof as me one more day. I told her I had no place to go and little money, so she wrote me a cheque—enough to keep me going for six months—and ordered me out. I rushed and packed my cases, and… here I am."

"I don't know what to say. I'm sorry."

"I hate that woman, Logan. I hate her so much. She wants everything associated with Edwin out of her life. That's why she won't publish any more of his work. You know, I'm glad. I'm glad I'm gone. I am." She attacked the brandy. Some of it missed her mouth, and she wiped it away. "I don't know where I'll go. I haven't had time to think." Harry deflated. "I stormed out of the house with no idea where to go, and I found myself here waiting for you. Which I know is silly with how last night ended."

I laid my hand over hers and squeezed. She gave me a sad smile.

"I am sorry about Fran. And I'm sorry about last night."

"Logan, it's not… I wanted to kiss you. That's what made me

sad."

"I don't understand."

"I don't expect you to. You didn't do anything wrong, just know that."

It didn't matter what she said; I still felt in the wrong. She started to cry, and I scooted around to hold her. After a few minutes, she stopped. Harry's smile lost some of its sadness as we looked at each other.

"You're a good man, Logan." Harry stroked my cheek and then pressed her wet face into mine, and we kissed.

We pulled away and grinned at each other like a couple of kids.

"God, I'm such a mess," she said, fussing with her hair. "Logan, may I freshen up in your room?"

I thought I should go call Darius Lanka, but looking at Harry, teary and broken, I told myself that call could wait a little bit.

"Yeah, come on."

I took Harry upstairs.

My bed was unmade, and the desktop was cluttered with Winslow's, Colt clips, a tin of beans, and a cluster of bullets. Clothes from the Calton Hill adventure hung over the desk chair and radiator, drying, and my trunk was open on the floor with my dirty suit inside.

"You tidied," she said with a mischievous look.

"I wasn't expecting guests."

I put her luggage down and shut the door. Harry stood in front of me.

"The washroom is there." I pointed. "Do you need a towel?"

"No." Harry stared at me. I looked into her hazel eyes. "I'm curious, Logan, how did you want the night to end?" The space between us narrowed. Her lavender perfume engulfed me. Her pink lips split apart, and a surge of nervous desire went through me.

"Oh, uh, well, I don't know… I suppose…"

"You suppose… what?"

"I didn't want it to end at all…"

"I'm here now."

We threw ourselves at each other and fell onto the bed.

34

"Is that how you wanted the night to end?" Harry said.

She looked at me with accomplished eyes. Our sweaty, naked bodies clung together on the bed. The blanket was on the floor, and the sheets had come off the mattress.

"That was the fantasy." I grinned. Her thumb brushed the smile on my face.

"What's the time?" Harry asked after a while of us just lying there.

"Going on 6.30." There was a pause. Her eyes became distant, and she furrowed her brow.

"What's wrong?"

"I need to find a place to live." Harry's concern evaporated some of the romance in the room.

"Hey." I tapped her chin. "Stay with me for now."

"Do you want me to stay?"

"I do." I smiled at her.

She kissed and hugged me.

"Is someone excited again?" She giggled.

"Don't start," we kissed, "what you can't," we kissed, "finish," I said.

She sat up. "Down boy... we have all night. Let's go out."

I checked the time and figured it would be too late to get anywhere with Darius if he was even at the office. I stroked Harry's face and said: "Where? This is your town, remember."

"Let's go to the Winter Carnival. I've been dying to go."

***

Waverley Market heaved with an excited crowd. Kids chirped and shouted. Groups applauded and cheered at whatever gimmick they watched. Pigs, baby cows, and horses grunted, huffed, and neighed. The air stank of manure and hot food.

Harry eyed the vendors selling toffee apples, Dundee cake slices, fudges, shortbread, and Scotch eggs and pies.

BAD BLOOD

We devoured a Scotch egg each and played balloon darts, ring toss, and the wheel of chance—but we didn't win any prizes. I bought a small portion of roasted cinnamon nuts for Harry. As I dug through my wallet, a photograph of Tim flashed between the business cards and pound notes. I tried to hide the image, feeling caught out.

"Is that your brother?" Harry commented as I paid the vendor.

"Not by blood," I said. "A war buddy."

"What's his name?"

My voice caught in my throat—I cleared it and said: "Tim."

"You fought together."

"Until the end."

"Where is he now?" Harry asked.

"In a field in France," I said.

"Oh, lamb, I'm sorry. I don't know what to say now."

The vendor handed her the greasy bag of nuts.

"There's nothing to say. It's in the past."

"It seems rather present for you."

"Heh. Let's enjoy the carnival."

Harry popped a few nuts into her mouth and smiled. "They're delicious! Have one," Harry said, trying to ease the tension. I crunched a few warm, sugary, cinnamon-coated nuts.

We past performing animals. Three sea lions were on a stage. They passed a large ball between them, and applause roared.

Harry said: "Oh, look! Come on…"

I followed her—people clustered in front of a wooden hut with a curtain over a doorway. The sign read *Rosie Brooks, The Fattest and Widest Woman Alive*.

"How fat do you think she is?" Another handful of nuts went into her mouth.

"Do you want to see this?"

"Yes, don't you?" Excitement rose in her voice.

"Er…"

Most people like the surprise of seeing little people, giant people, fat people, bearded women and so on at carnivals. I never did, still don't.

LUKE DECKARD

The showman burst on stage and roused the spectators. I stood with my hands in my pockets.

He asked a chubby man what he ate that day, and the man said, "Eggs and beans for breakfast, a meat pie and chips for lunch." The showman replied, "Rosie eats half a dozen scrambled eggs for breakfast with four Cumberland sausages and jam and scones. She may eat a whole roast chicken drenched in gravy with potatoes and mushy peas for dinner. And she'll have an entire Victoria sponge for dessert."

Gasps waved from front to back. Harry chewed and shook her head in awe.

The showman asked: "Are youse ready for Rosie Brooks, the Fattest and Widest Woman Alive!"

The people shouted, "Aye!"

The curtain was pulled back to reveal a fat woman on a chair. The whole scene was grotesque: the crowd gawked, snickered and sneered. Rosie Brooks smiled and waved like it was all normal. She pushed herself off the seat and held handles on either side of her. The showman informed us of her weight and dimensions. Rosie's red face wore a big grin. He brought a thin woman on stage and compared the two to more rumbles of bemusement.

"Can you believe that, Logan?" The brutal spectacle enraptured Harry.

"Sure. Let's walk around."

"But… Okay. Guess there's not much left to see here. Well, there's a lot to see." She giggled. I didn't.

We continued through the market, drank mulled cider, and watched an acrobatic troupe.

Harry asked: "Logan, how much longer will you be in Edinburgh?"

"I'm not sure. It's a trickier job than I anticipated."

"How so?"

"The woman I'm looking for hasn't been easy to find. But I have a few pathetic leads left to follow."

"I hope you don't leave anytime soon."

Harry stopped. A round, red velvet tent that looked like a

lampshade caught her attention. The name over the entry read: *Clairvoyant*. Harry's body seemed drawn to it. She broke the link with my arm and said: "Logan, I want to go in, will you come with me?"

"Oh, Harry…"

"Please. Indulge me."

My shoulders dropped, and I agreed. We went behind the veil. It was close, and there was a smell of spicy incense inside. It was familiar. The woody and floral notes hinted at memory. A flickering oil lamp hung overhead, bathing the tent in an atmospheric amber glow. Smoke swirled in the light. A thin man sat at a small table with a crystal ball in the centre. It was hard to see his face in the dim room.

The man asked us to sit. We did.

He looked normal enough—he wore a grey suit. His hair was shellacked. If you saw him on the street, he was just another plain-faced man in his forties. The only oddity was recent scratches on the right side of his face, which he'd covered up with women's cosmetics.

"Hello. Welcome." The clairvoyant's voice was like a smooth Scotch. "Would you like me tae read your palm? Foretell the future with my tarot cards? Or tell you if this is true love?" His eyes squinted—no doubt stinging from the ceaseless smoke that was choking me.

Harry looked at the showman like he held the answers to all her questions.

Harry replied: "I want to talk to someone. Someone who died."

"Ah, yes. Grief is heavy on you. I felt it as ye entered. Your loss was very recent, was it no'?"

"It was. Yes."

"And unexpected."

"Yes."

"Do you possess anything that belonged to the departed?"

"I do."

Harry took a blue Parker pen from her handbag. The clairvoyant held it and withdrew a pair of round spectacles to study it further.

LUKE DECKARD

The right arm on the specs was bent, and the right lens cracked. The man's right hand was wrapped up. My mind flashed back to Calton Burial Ground. The smell, the scratches, the injured hand.

"I know you," I said.

The clairvoyant turned to me.

"Logan?" Harry said.

The clairvoyant smiled: "I remember everyone I meet, I don't know your face, sir."

"I'm the guy who threw you to the ground at Calton Burial Ground."

I stared directly into the man's eyes. I knew his thoughts—escape.

"Logan, what is going on?" Harry asked.

"I'm taking you in," I said.

The man's eyes grew wide and wild. He flipped the table over, sending Harry and me onto the floor. She screamed. We rolled out of the tent and scrambled to our feet. The clairvoyant pushed his way through the crowds. I reached for my gun and chased after him.

35

The clairvoyant shoved people mercilessly out of his way and ducked between stalls. We did our best to keep him in sight. I wasn't going to lose him this time.

He went running through the petting pens, scaring the kids. The pigs and goats squealed and baaed and ran chaotically in all directions. Harry went around, and I followed behind the clairvoyant, charging through the pens, dodging the animals.

Coming out the other side, my foot got caught on a fence, and I fell. Harry helped me up. Ahead, the clairvoyant ran into a clown who was juggling balls. The cluster of children screamed as the clown went down. We were after him.

Frantically, the clairvoyant grabbed a couple of the balls and threw them at me and Harry. One whizzed past Harry's head. She shrieked. Another came right at me. I twisted, and it hit me in the shoulder. Another ball hit me. When I turned, I couldn't see him in the crowd.

"There!" Harry pointed. The clairvoyant pushed people out of his way and ducked inside the Hall of Mirrors.

"Come on," I said.

We charged past the confused carnival-goers. Kids and adults ran out of the Hall of Mirrors entrance, and the ticket collector tried to calm them down.

"Sir, the man who just ran in is wanted by the police. Where's the exit?" I asked.

"Around the back," he said.

"Get to the exit and wait for him," I ordered. "If he comes out before I get him, tackle him. I'll go in and try to flush him out."

The man didn't hesitate. He was off.

"What about me?" Harry asked.

"Stay here, guard the entrance. Shout if you see him!"

I dashed inside, my gun out and ready.

The corridor was dimly lit with flickering golden lights. The walls were painted with a forest scene. Ahead, there was a doorway with shiny silver tinsel hanging in front of it. I pushed through, and all around me were reflections of myself. I moved forward, determined, my grip tight on my gun. I could see a turn to the left. I went to follow it and jumped back. A man stood in front of me. I aimed, but before I fired, I realised I was staring at myself—the mirrors.

I spun around and moved forward a couple of steps. I froze. There was movement. A figure flashed across the faces of the mirrors. I tried to follow them with my gun, but it was hard to tell what were reflections and what was flesh and blood.

I moved into the next mirrored room.

"Stop!" I shouted.

The clairvoyant was ahead of me. He turned, a grin stretched across his face. He charged at me. I fired a shot, shattering a mirror. Suddenly, something shoved me. I collided with another mirror. My hat fell off, and a hand gripped my hair and smashed my head against the mirror's edge. The pain was sharp. I tumbled to the floor, dazed. My head spinning, I saw the clairvoyant running away. I tried to fumble my way after him. I had to pause and regain my composure.

I exited the hall, my heart pounding and my head aching. There was a small cut above my right eye. The ticket collector was slumped on the floor, propped against the Hall of Mirrors. His face winced with pain, clutching his arm. The upper part of the man's jacket was discoloured and wet. His hand was covered in blood. A couple of carnival-goers were standing around him.

"What happened?" I asked him.

"Guy came out. Tried tae stop him. He sliced me."

"Where did he go?"

"I dunno know. Ah, God, I need a doctor."

"One's on the way!" someone said behind me.

"Sir, look at me," I said. "Tell me which way he went!"

"I dunno know. Christ, this hurts."

"Sir, focus!"

"Ah. That way, I think. Back tae the front."

"Shit. Harry!"

BAD BLOOD

I raced round to the hall's entrance. Harry was gone.

Panicked, I asked if anyone saw the red-headed woman standing there. I got headshakes and confused looks. Harry and the clairvoyant were gone—lost in the sea of faces. I tried to look over the heads of the crowds, but I couldn't see a damned thing. I needed a better view.

Next to the Hall of Mirrors was a ring-toss game. Two kids and a young couple were attempting to toss rings around awkwardly positioned bottles. I climbed up on the counter, interrupting the game. They all shouted at me, and the carny running the stall tried to grab me. I kicked him, and he fell back, crashing into the bottles.

I scanned the carnival for Harry's Titian hair. I couldn't see her. My gut wrenched.

The carny grabbed at my legs. I shoved him off again.

"Logan!"

There. The clairvoyant had Harry. He was leading her out of the Princes Street exit.

I chased after the clairvoyant darting around pedestrians. Outside, He dragged Harry along by the arm towards Waverley Bridge. He glanced over his shoulder as he pulled Harry into the road. Horns honked, and brakes squealed. I skidded to a stop over a slick patch of pavement. A braking car clipped the clairvoyant, and he and Harry rolled across the tarmac. Traffic and bystanders stopped.

The driver that hit him got out and shouted obscenities at the clairvoyant as he pushed himself up. A woman raced over to help Harry. My eyes locked with the clairvoyant.

He grabbed Harry again, shoving the woman aside who'd come to help her. He wrapped an arm around Harry, constricting her left arm. She yelped as he put a switchblade to her throat.

"Back off!"

"Logan!" The blade pressed under her chin.

No one knew what to do. Pleads to release her were ignored.

I aimed the Colt at the man's head.

"I'll kill her!" His voice cracked with fear. "Do you want her blood on your hands?" He looked directly at me and backed away with Harry.

There was nothing I could do. If I shot and he moved, I might kill Harry. If I missed, he'd slash her throat, or a bullet might bounce off the bridge and hit someone else. I lowered the Colt.

"Logan. Help!"

I lowered my gun.

"Keep still," I told her.

The clairvoyant looked behind him, up towards the Old Town. He wasn't going to get away with Harry in tow. He threw her back into the road and took off. The crowd's attention fell on Harry, helping her up. I continued after him.

He ran up a steep road and then turned left up a dark close.

My legs ached from the hill and the steps, and I slowed down. We zigzagged with the path. My lungs tightened—deep breaths were impossible. The man zigzagged and went out of sight.

My heart pounded. I thought it might explode. My fitness wasn't what it was.

I came around the corner. Ahead, the man ran in a dead heat up a flight of stairs towards the exit on Royal Mile.

I stopped, unable to climb further, and aimed the Colt above—the shot cracked like thunder in the narrow close. The noise startled him—he lost his footing and fell forward, then slid down a couple of steps. It wasn't enough for me to gain. He got up, took off, and disappeared before I could get near.

I climbed the steps towards High Street. My chest hurt, my head ached, and the old wino bite stung.

Near the top, I spotted his cards on the ground with the image of a palm with an eye in the centre. I looked around to see where he went—the man was gone. I grabbed the cards and went back to get Harry.

36

Harry was still on Waverley Bridge, and traffic remained halted while a couple of police officers took statements from eyewitnesses. I limped down the hill towards her with a stitch in my side. She leaned against the bridge with her arms folded and face angled towards the ground.

"Harry."

Her head shot up, and she leapt forward and hugged me.

"Logan." Cupping my face, she said: "Are you okay?"

"I'm fine." I took her hands. They were cold and shaky.

"What happened to the man?" she asked.

"He got away. But he dropped this." I showed Harry the card.

"Oh my Lord, I know this design," Harry said.

"You do? Where from?"

"The Medium Edwin used to commune with his son. That is his card. Edwin's had it in his office. Logan?"

"Where did Edwin go to meet this guy?"

"In… in Old Town. Logan, we should tell the police."

"There's no time. He'll be on his way out of town within an hour or less. We gotta go now."

Harry's face lit with knowledge. "Follow me!"

We trekked back through Old Town over snowy streets. Harry led us past a Gothic church near the castle. It looked ripped out of some Grimm fairy tale, with its sky-piercing steeple. We veered left down a sloped road. The castle loomed high to our right. Harry paused at an entrance to a dark stairway leading down to Cowgate. The sign read Castle Wynd South. Her feet were glued to the pavement. She shivered, but not from the cold.

"I don't know what's wrong with me." A tear-stream shone on her pale, freckled face.

"This is where they robbed you of Edwin's manuscript."

"Yes."

"It's okay. I'm with you," I assured. We linked arms. "I won't let anyone hurt you this time." She wouldn't move. "Harry, I need you. We need to keep going if we're going to get the guy."

She nodded and took it one step at a time.

At the bottom, Harry led us through Grassmarket and past the White Hart Inn, where a trio of drunk Scotsmen sang a crude song about Catholics.

"This is it," Harry said.

We stood in the archway of Brown's Close. A gaslight danced and hissed above us, pouring a dim yellow glow. Three doors were on each side of the short, cobbled path. At the far end of the close, on the left, there was a narrow pitch-black tunnel.

"It's that one there." She pointed at the third door on the left.

We went in and crept towards the door. A soft light outlined the thick curtain. Frantic voices argued inside. I could only make out segments of their bickering.

A woman: "Were you followed, Clive?"

A man: "Naw, I lost 'em."

The woman: "Are you sure?"

The man: "Aye!"

The voices lowered to a dull murmur for a moment. Suddenly, the woman exploded: "You idiot, you did what with that blasted knife? Christ, this is a disaster. I wish you'd never had gone back to the cemetery to find it! You've mucked this up proper, Clive."

"What are you doing?" Harry scolded.

I had taken out my pick and fiddled with the lock.

"I'm going in."

The lock clicked, and the door came ajar.

"Stay hidden." I pointed my eyes at the tunnel.

I pushed the door open slowly and listened.

The entryway was lit by the light spilling in from the front room. I knocked over an umbrella and grabbed it before it fell, making a noose. I carefully propped it against the wall.

"What's that?" the woman said.

"Nothin', get a move on," said Clive.

I remained still for a couple of seconds while the two moved around in the front room.

I placed the umbrella down, left the door open, and got my gun.

BAD BLOOD

I crept to the edge of the door, gliding carefully over the floorboards, and spied around the corner—a strong wave of spiced incense and a hint of hash and opium hit my senses. The front room was filled with mystic objects. A round table was covered in a blue velvet cloth with gold frills. On top were a crystal ball and a statue of some pagan god with a goat's head and a male body. Above the mantel was a chalk sketch of the palm with an eye in the centre. On it were crystals, bones, and half-burnt candles with wax that trailed down the stems and stands and pooled on the mantel top.

A woman approached the roaring fireplace with a thick stack of papers in her hand. She had leathery skin, a small head with a pointy chin, and long yellow hair that went down to her back. She wore a black dress with white stars all over and a pink, transparent shawl. Clunky rings rattled on her fingers as she looked through the papers.

"What do we do with the manuscript?" She said.

Clive said, "It's no use to us now."

"No thanks tae you! Git the case with the money," she snarled over her shoulder.

Clive's returning footsteps made me duck away. He placed something on the table with a thud. I peered around again. His back was to me. He opened a suitcase full of Edwin Walter's money. The woman still cradled Edwin's manuscript.

She suddenly looked over and shrieked.

"Someone's there!" Her bony finger pointed at me.

I swung around the corner, pointing my gun. Clive dived at me. I sidestepped and took him by the arm. I twisted it around his back as I rammed my weapon into his thin neck.

The woman's eyes burned yellowly. She twitched and had the frantic look of someone high on drugs, which made her the most unpredictable person in the room.

"You're not getting this back," she said. "Unless you let him go."

She lowered the pages closer to the fire.

"Stop," I said.

Clive jerked—he slashed his blade at me. I swept his leg and sent him to the floor with a thud.

"If you get up, I'll shoot you," I told Clive the Clairvoyant. To the leathery woman, I said: "Hand me the pages, now."

She looked at Clive on the floor and made one step towards me. Then she threw the pages into the fire. The flames whooshed, eating the manuscript.

"No!" I shouted.

I raced to save them. The woman screamed and leapt aside. Clive tackled me to the floor before I could rescue the burning book from the flames. He tried to pry the Colt from me. I kneed him in the crotch and pushed him off. I reached for the papers, but there wasn't anything worth saving. It was all ash.

A crystal ball suddenly flew past my head and exploded in the fire, sending burning pieces of paper and ash into the air. The woman grabbed the suitcase and went to the door. I jumped back, hot ash pricked at my face.

As she fled, I shouted, "Stop!"

Rounding the door, an umbrella swung, smashing her in the face. She fell backwards with a shriek, dropping the suitcase. Harry stood in the doorway, eyes wide, breathing hard. The leathery woman writhed in pain, her face a bloody mess.

"You bitch!" Clive roared, going at Harry. I fired my gun, shattering the front window. That paralysed him, and he turned white as a ghost.

"We're gonna talk," I said. "Clive, pick the woman up and move over there. Harry, the briefcase."

Clive helped the woman up, wiping the blood away from her mouth and giving her a hanky to hold to her nose.

"You're going to walk me through how we got here," I said.

Clive and the leathery woman shared a look.

Clive the Clairvoyant, was something of a party trick throughout town. He said that at one party, about a year and a half ago, a man told him that he should speak to Edwin Walter—that he was grieving the death of his sons. The man thought it'd be funny if he pretended to channel them. The man paid Clive two hundred

BAD BLOOD

pounds for it. But Edwin, it seemed, had been taken in by it. So, every few months, he would come and see him. Clive knew Edwin was desperate to speak to both of his sons, but he would never channel them both in order to keep him coming back and paying for more sessions. A month ago, an Irishman came to see him. He knew Edwin visited regularly, and he threatened to bust the whole operation unless he did something for his employer… rob Edwin's new book. How this man knew about the book was a mystery. It took time to develop the plan, but Clive concocted the scheme with the leathery woman. The Irishman knew Edwin and Harry were discussing the memoir with Edwin's publisher in London. Clive and the leathery woman decided to rob them when they returned to Edinburgh.

"Who is this Irishman?"

"I don't know him. No names were given."

"Where did you take the book to?"

"I was told to leave it in a locker in the station at Waverley."

"What locker?"

Clive thought for a second. "Forty-two."

"So you came up with the plan to blackmail Walter, not the guy who hired you."

"Aye." Clive nodded. "When we stole the book, we found two copies."

I looked at Harry. "There was Edwin's copy and the publishers," she said.

The leathery woman beside Clive was fidgety. She didn't like him spilling the information.

"Was it you who murdered Edwin?" Harry exploded at the leathery woman. She rushed at the robbers sitting on the ground like she wanted to beat them with her bag. I grabbed her and held her back.

"Calm down. Calm down!" I ordered.

"You don't get it, Logan. Edwin trusted these liars! They pretended to speak with his son. You're a bunch of fucking frauds!"

"We didn't kill him!" the leathery woman shouted.

LUKE DECKARD

"Harry, please!" I said. She tried to compose herself.

The leathery woman said: "We had nothin' tae do with that you twit. Why would we kill him?"

I looked back at them. "Hell of a coincidence he's killed the same night you arranged the exchange," I said. "No, I don't buy that. You're not telling the whole story, are you? You were told to do it that night, weren't you? Whoever hired you wanted Edwin alone. That's why Harry was asked to bring the money. You were the decoy. A smokescreen. But the money…"

"We were told we could keep whatever we got…" Clive said.

"So they didn't care to blackmail Edwin for money," I said. I turned to Harry. I could see it in her eyes. She had Fran Walter back on her mind. I had Inspector Joy. I continued: "You were set up," I said. "You two will go down for the whole thing. Because you have the burnt papers there and the money there and no other person, no name, to pin it on."

"I will not go tae jail for this!" the leathery woman hissed. "No for you, Clive, not for nobody!"

"Well, that's where you're going. Edwin's murder will fall on you," I said.

Strapped to her leg was a blade. She grabbed it.

"There's no way out, lady," I said.

Her eyes were wild, and she hissed through her gritted teeth, "Aye, there is!"

In her fit, she drove a blade into her neck. Harry screamed and turned her face.

Clive shouted and gripped the blade. I told him to leave it, but he didn't listen and pulled it out. Blood flowed from the wound. The woman began to choke and shake. The redness seeped between Clive's fingers, staining his hand. In a minute, the leathery woman's convulsions stopped. She was dead.

Clive looked at me with hatred in his eyes. "What have you done? I'll fucking kill you both!"

He leapt up and tackled me onto the table. The force of our landing broke it, and we crashed on the floor. My gun fell out of my hand and landed by the fireplace. Clive was on top of me with

BAD BLOOD

the knife. His eyes were wild with fury. He brought the blade down, but I blocked it, holding his wrists. His entire body pressed down. My arms shook, trying to hold him off. The blade inched closer and closer to my chest. I couldn't stop it. Harry swooped in and struck Clive over the back with a fire poker as the silver tip began to press into my jacket. He winced and let up. I twisted the blade free and threw it. Just then, Clive spotted my gun, and he scrambled for it. He grabbed it and swung it at me. I dove at him and went for the gun. We struggled on the ground. Our sweaty hands fought over it. He went for the trigger. I tried to twist it from his grip. There was a bang. My gun had gone off.

37

Clive wasn't dead; I'd shot him through the shoulder.

Harry was shaken, and I was too. I nursed a bottle of Winslow's and fought off cold sweats. We stood outside in the freezing air. It had started to snow, and it was heavy; piling up to a few inches.

The police arrived.

First, a couple of beat cops, then more cops, including Inspector Joy and a police surgeon. Clive was rushed to the Royal Infirmary to be treated, and the woman went to a morgue.

"What the hell is going on?" Joy asked.

"We found your blackmailer," I said. "Sort of."

"It's the money." Harry handed Joy the briefcase with Edwin Walter's pay-off.

He looked at the contents and nodded, then he huffed and left us outside while he searched the house.

"You'd think he'd be grateful," I said.

"He's a git," Harry said.

When Joy came out, he had me searched. My gun was taken. He also found the empty bottle of Winslow's and a freshly opened one in my pocket.

"What the hell is this, Bishop?" He held the bottles up.

"Medication."

"Christ, it is. It's baby killer." Joy got in my face. "Let me smell your breath."

"Back off, pal." I pushed him off.

Joy pointed in my face: "Would you prefer it if I arrested you?"

I breathed in Joy's face. "Happy."

"Your breath stinks of it." Joy threw the empty bottle at me—it landed in the snow. "You have caused more problems than you're worth. You're a reckless son of a bitch off your nut on morphine medication. You lost Edwin's manuscript. Now, a woman is dead, and a man is shot. You have jeopardised my investigation for the last time. I should throw you in a cell."

"Fucking do it then," I said. "Do you think I want this mess?" I closed the gap between us. "Look at this." I motioned at the bloodstains on my coat. "This is why I take that medication. Did you fight in the war or not? How many times have you witnessed someone die? Huh? Watched life go out like a goddamn light switching off? Or witnessed a bullet shatter a man's head? Maybe for you, you can see that hell and go on as normal. I can't. I won't! That morphine shit is my only escape. Because let me tell you, my horrors never go away." Joy shook with anger. "What, you have nothing to say, huh? Fuck you, and fuck your judgement of me."

Joy grabbed me by the lapels and slammed me against the cold stone building. I took his wrists and squeezed.

"Watch how you speak to me, Bishop."

"Either arrest me or fuck off!"

"That's enough, Inspector Joy!" Harry shouted.

A crowd of cops had come out to see what the fuss was about.

Joy shoved me away; adrenaline surged through me. I wanted to rip his head off and punch my knuckles raw on him.

"Sir, is everythin' okay?" one of the officers asked.

"Aye. Get back to your work," he ordered. He pointed a finger in my face. "Explain yourselves, now."

I did. I stated how the incident on Calton Hill tipped me off when we met the Clairvoyant at the carnival. We confronted him, he ran—Joy was aware of the incident on Waverley Bridge. When I said Harry knew where he might go, the V's on Joy's face deepened. Joy asked how the man got shot, and a woman was stabbed in the throat. I was silent for a few seconds. The struggle with the clairvoyant repeated in my head—his grip on the Colt and coming down on me with the knife. Me jerking the gun, his gritted teeth and wild eyes. The flash. The boom. The crunch. The splatter of blood on my face.

"Bishop?" Joy snapped at me. I told him what happened and what the pair admitted to, but I didn't give away the locker information. I didn't trust Joy but knew he'd make life difficult for Harry and me if I played hardball.

"Mrs Napier," Joy's devilish face focused on her, "these were inside." He showed her the cards with the open palm and eye in their centre. "We found a card like this in Edwin's office the night he was murdered. I showed it to you. Yet you said you didn't recognise them."

I looked at Harry.

Harry held herself. "I didn't think it was relevant."

"That so? Or are you hiding something else? Like where the carbon copy went in Edwin's office."

Tears started to stream down her face. "I swear, I'm not. No."

"Then explain this!" Joy's voice echoed down the close.

Through her tears, she explained what I already knew. Edwin Walter didn't want anyone to know what he was doing.

"And what sort of relationship must you two have," Joy began, "for Edwin to entrust something so personal?"

Harry slapped him. "How dare you. I want to leave."

Joy grabbed Harry and yanked her towards him.

"You're not going anywhere until I'm done." Joy's eyes burned with rage.

"Hey!" I said. "She's been through hell tonight."

He glared at me and then shoved her away. His devilish eyes fixated on me. "This is the line in the sand, Bishop. Do you understand me? Two dead and connected to you, and I find you doped up…"

"I'm not doped up…" I said.

"I could hang this all on you if I wanted to," Joy said.

"Go ahead and try… maybe some of your secrets will come out in the process."

For a split second, he looked like a scared devil. Joy shoved my gun back at me. "Get the hell out of here."

We lumbered to the hotel down The Mound. The city was ready for bed, including the homeless. A haggard man walked along the bridge, using his cane for sight. His head was bent down, and his body bobbed back and forth. He held a doctor's bag and had a lunchbox strung around him. A silver tin can was tied to his breast through the buttonhole of his coat. A sign tucked under his arm read: *Blind, Can't Work, Need Money to Eat*.

I deposited a shilling into his tin can.

BAD BLOOD

Harry and I didn't speak. The only sound was the crunch of snow under our feet. I felt dirty—I wanted to scrub my skin with soap and sandpaper—make sure I got the blood off. As mad as I was at Inspector Joy, what dominated my mind was when the gun went off. Clive's face. The panic. The fear. It reminded me of Tim. I tried to stop thinking about it and see the world around me. But that didn't help.

At the hotel, I wanted to sleep. I wanted to sleep alone, but Harry was in my bed. She lay with her back to me. I think she was crying. I lay flat and stared at the ceiling. Neither of us had spoken, but I had plenty of questions for her. Why didn't she tell Joy about the clairvoyant? Joy got at something between Harry and Edwin; what he implied I suspected but had tried to ignore.

38

The next day, after we had bathed and gotten dressed, I realised it was after midday, and we still hadn't spoken. When I tried, she would say, "I don't want to talk right now." Now, Harry sat on the bed, powdering her face. She wore a pink cardigan over her tan dress. I sat at the desk, cleaning my gun and wondering what she was thinking. Asking myself, why hasn't she spoken to me? She wanted to stay with me last night; her nerves were bad. She shook most of the night—she had nightmares. I wanted to know things; I wanted to know what she knew and thought.

"Harry, we should talk."

She looked over her shoulder at me.

"Logan."

"I just want to know why you didn't tell Joy about the clairvoyant. If you recognised the card and knew Walter went there—this isn't the time to keep secrets. Joy is gunning for a suspect."

"What do you want me to say, Logan?"

"The truth."

"Fine. Yes, I lied to the inspector. Edwin is entitled to his privacy. He didn't want this out in the open. He didn't want people to know he was seeing a Medium. I didn't think it mattered. How was I supposed to know that it did? Why didn't you tell Joy about the locker with the other manuscript? Or about the Irishman whom the clairvoyant worked for?"

"Because… I don't trust Joy," I said.

"Well, maybe I don't either."

"What sort of relationship did you and Edwin Walter have?"

Harry's nostrils flared. "You're a bastard."

Harry took her coat and bag and stormed out of the room, slamming the door behind her. I deserved that.

I leaned back in the chair and buried my face in my palms.

Ten minutes later, there was a knock on the door. I thought it was Harry, having cooled off. It wasn't. It was a messenger with a note from Darius Lanka. Rūta Kanaitė wanted to meet. From the hotel's payphone, I called Lanka and told him I could see him anytime. He said to come to the office at four o'clock.

I decided there was enough time to go to Waverley Station and see if I could find out who rented locker forty-two in the last few weeks.

As I went through the lobby, I spotted two well-built men with eyes on me. They weren't Spatty or the Grey Man—they'd all but disappeared in the last few days. Maybe they realised Greta was an impossible task, at least I hoped. Still, who were these new guys? Had Lady Clark hired them? Or was this Joy keeping an eye on me?

I got my hat, coat, and Colt from my room and decided I needed to lose these guys downstairs. I figured the front would be the wrong way out, though the back might be watched too. Still, I took the service elevator and slipped out onto Rose Street North Lane and zigzagged my way to Waverley Station without any tails.

The station's elaborate, wood-panelled ticket office, which looked more like a wooden Victorian fortress, was in the centre of the ticket hall. Seven or eight teller windows went around it, and I approached one. The man on the other side had a sleepy face and pale skin. I flashed him my ID and said I needed information. He didn't seem to care much at all about who I was. I asked for the names of those who used locker forty-two.

"I can't give you that," he said.

"Get me the names, and I'll make it worth your while."

He looked around, worried someone had overheard. They hadn't.

"What's it worth tae you?"

"Five pounds."

He said, "Let's have it."

I laid it down, and then he retrieved the logbook.

To avoid looking suspicious, he started to tell me how much a locker would cost, a deposit for the key, and all that. While he did that, I scanned the pages and dates for the locker. One name stood out: Johnny Walker. I looked at the teller. He didn't seem phased.

The name was an obvious fake, but he didn't care.

"While you're at it," I said, "show me locker twelve, three weeks ago."

He flipped the pages. One name stood out: Mr Green. Green was the name of the man at Marsh Travel.

I thanked the guy and went straight to Darius Lanka. Darius and Rūta sat at the table in the dingy newsroom with a half-drunk bottle of red wine.

"Good afternoon, Mr Bishop," Darius said.

"Hello," Rūta said and raised her wine at me.

"Afternoon."

Rūta angled her gawky frame in my direction—she cradled the wine in her lap.

"I found a man with information. He wants me to take you to him to discuss Greta."

"No names, I take it?"

"No names," Rūta said.

***

I sat in the back of a small delivery van with Lanka in total darkness. The smell of leather, oils and petrol was overpowering. Rūta was in the cab with the driver and fresher air. Lanka assured me the trip wouldn't take long.

"Why won't you tell me where you're taking me?" I said.

I felt his hesitation in the darkness.

"What I will tell you, it is a member of the Lithuanian Communist Party."

"Not a friend of yours, then?"

"Hardly."

"So, a friend of Rūta's?"

"Don't judge her too harshly, though, Mr Bishop. Rūta is not a Bolshevik. She is a good woman. She doesn't identify with either side."

"What does that mean? She just toes the lines and goes with whoever wins?"

"Not at all, Mr Bishop. Don't let ignorance blind you. During the Great War, many Lithuanians didn't identify with either side, Russia or Germany. It made no difference to us. Both are our enemies. For us, you see, the war was an opportunity to nurture the idea of independence amongst the people. There is little honour in being conscripted but much honour in volunteering, you understand. Who won the war paled in comparison to us gaining our independence. There is a proverb, Mr Bishop, 'When two are fighting, the third wins'."

"I'll keep that in mind."

The van stopped.

"Put this on, Mr Bishop," he requested.

I reached out and found his hand and the hood he held.

"Stinks of onions," I said with it over my head.

He laughed. I didn't find it funny.

Lanka led me from the van and into a building. Then down a corridor and then a flight of stairs—the smell of dampness soaked through the hood—we had to be in a basement.

"Sit him there," Rūta said. "Give me a moment." Her feet clapped up the stairs as Lanka put me in a chair and then removed the bag. We were sat at a table. Stacks of pamphlets with the hammer and sickle painted on the front were in front of us—the same pamphlets with Greta's belongings. There were also stamps, trays of various-sized letter blocks and a box of chocolates. My tongue craved the chocolates, I hadn't eaten much all day.

Against the chipped walls were a couple of messy desks with crane lamps. Shelves were stuffed with crates of printing paper, bottles, jars, pens and tools. Two printing presses stood at either end of the room.

Lanka smiled, sat beside me, and said, "See, not too long, huh?"

"Sure." I wiped my face. The bag had the words *onions* in faded blue lettering. "An underground print shop, eh?"

Lanka nodded.

Footsteps came down the stairs. Rūta was followed by two men.

The first man was a little taller than me, thin-framed, with sunken cheeks, a large forehead and a receding hairline. I put him at forty-five. He wore a sharp blue tartan suit. His brogues shone even in that insufficiently lit room. The second man I knew. It was the stout man from Marsh Travel, Mr Green. I had been brought where I wanted to go. Mr Green wore the same red corduroy outfit but a white shirt this time. He recognised me.

"So much for the cloak and dagger," I said.

"Stand," Mr Green ordered me. Lanka and I both stood. Lanka went over next to Rūta, leaving me face to face with Mr Green, who said: "Lift your hand."

Mr Green removed my Colt, released the clip, and broke down the gun. Next, he felt around in my coat pockets, took my wallet, and looked inside. He removed the picture of Tim.

I grabbed his wrist and said: "Leave that alone."

Mr Green turned to the man in the blue tartan suit. I was on the verge of breaking his wrist.

"Leave it," the man in blue said. His accent was the Eastern European type I was becoming familiar with. Mr Green eased. I let him go, and he placed the wallet and the photograph on the table. Rūta and Lanka huddled together. The man in blue just smiled. Tension partially dissipated.

"So what do I call you?" I asked the man in blue.

"Names aren't necessary here, Mr Bishop."

"I take it his name isn't Green? Fine, I'll call you Mr Blue," I said. A wry smile grew on his face as he looked at his suit.

"As you wish."

"Okay, Mr Blue, let's talk about Greta Matienė."

39

"Mr Lanka, Miss Kanaitė, do you mind leaving us to talk?" Mr Blue asked. The two shared a look and then glanced at me. I nodded to tell them I'd be fine. They went up the stairs with Mr Green.

Mr Blue rose, went to a cabinet, and retrieved a bottle of red wine with no label and two glasses.

"Drink?"

"No."

He shrugged and poured himself a glass of wine. When he finished, he sat back in his chair, sniffed the wine, and let out an 'aw'. "So, Mr Bishop, Greta, Greta, Greta."

"What business did she have with you?" I asked.

"People come to me when they want something that they cannot have."

"Such as?"

"Money. Freedom."

"And what do you expect in return?" I asked.

"Not much. A favour here or there. Greta was in a particularly troubling situation."

"I know about the hotel."

He nodded. "An example of how the wealthy continue to control the lower classes. Cast them off like filthy rags."

"What did Greta want from you?"

"A fresh start," Mr Blue said.

"What does that mean? A new life?" I asked.

"Something like that."

"You forged new ID papers," I said.

He smirked.

"Like many Lithuanians now, she was afraid of being deported."

"And what did she have to do to get these papers?" I asked.

"All I asked of her was to make a delivery."

"Smuggle propaganda, you mean?"

"Propaganda, you call it? Is it wrong to spread a message of hope, Mr Bishop? I suppose you are an ardent capitalist. So, to question the status quo and offer an alternative is utter evil, hm? My party plans to revolutionise the world if the people allow it, and the people deserve the option of choice. They deserve to be free of the capitalist chains, you understand."

"The way I hear it, owning land is just a little bit too important in Lithuania for a real communist government to take over."

"Ha. You've been talking to Mr Lanka. He is bourgeois. Deluded, corrupted by capitalism. Hands so full that he can barely hold all he's got. He probably fed you stories about Lithuania's desire for freedom and independence. What Lanka won't tell you, my country's war for independence was nothing but imperialist—a treacherous defence of the capitalist machine. He's a blind fool."

"Life ain't fair, nor will it be under communism," I said.

Mr Blue shook his head at me. "So you succumb to what your democratic government gives you? America is fragile, as is Britain, Mr Bishop. The West is blinded by its greed, enslaved to it and without hope of emancipation. Does not every man deserve equal footing? Every man deserves freedom. Why should workers like Greta toil for the few to become wealthy? From each according to his ability, to each according to his needs, as Marx said."

"Who decides who needs what and how much?" I said. "You think you can recondition the entire human race? I've known people dumb as rocks with more money than they know what to do with. I've also known intelligent people with no money in the bank. Do you think the dumb-as-rocks people will give up their money to the intelligent man who could do more with it? Do you think the intelligent will give up their money to the poor, just to create equal footing? You're all insane."

"I can see that you, too, are blinded. Do you know how many wars have been fought in Lithuania since the end of 1918?"

"Not a clue."

"There have been three wars in Lithuania since the Great War ended. My people are in a tug of war between Russia, Germany, and Poland. Many of us are scattered between Britain and the

United States, scraping up a pathetic existence as second-class citizens. Seen as less than human. And, in the case of Britain, being removed because we are deemed unwanted and a drain on the economy. You will not see the same treatment with the Russian Jews. They seem to have the ability to procure military exceptions and avoid repatriation."

"Now you just sound racist."

Mr Blue lifted an eyebrow at me. "It is my people, Mr Bishop, who are singled out. No matter that our blood and sweat provide the comfortable reality for so many—with our men in British mines and factories."

"But it's not *just* your people, isn't it?"

"Many of them! And our daily existence is a ceaseless struggle for survival against the capitalist machine. What sort of life is this? Why should we not unite and create an equal working class?"

"Look, I'm not interested in your manifesto or who the government's current favourite is for persecution—I want to know where Greta is."

He took a drink of the wine.

"You Americans believe you are strong-willed individuals because you transformed a wilderness into a united nation. Fighting savages, beasts, and the elements—it's romantic. What you are, of course, is arrogant and stupid. Your whole country, just like Britain, is in desperate need of re-education. Greta was dedicated to this re-education."

"Where did you send her?"

"To America."

"Who was her contact?"

"Come now, Mr Bishop."

"Was it Daniel Bishop?"

He pressed his lips together and frowned. "No, I don't know this man."

"Where you sent her, does it have anything to do with someplace called Ivy House?"

"Once more, you know more than me. I am unfamiliar with Ivy House. All I know is where she was *meant* to go."

"Where?" I pressed.

"Chicago."

"Chicago?"

"Yes. She wanted to go there. She specifically asked me if she could, and as it happened, I needed a letter to be delivered there, and I trusted her."

"She went to the American communist party headquarters?"

"No. She never went," Mr Blue said.

"What?"

"She took the travel documents and money that were in the locker and was never seen or heard from again. She never got on the boat at Glasgow. She absconded. Or the police arrested her. I can't say for certain yet. Of course, I have had feelers, waiting for her to pop up somewhere, but so far, nothing. I would be very interested to know where she is too, Mr Bishop."

"So now you want to hire me?" I said.

"Maybe we can come to an arrangement."

"Maybe we can," I said. "You made her a new identity. Do you have a photograph of her?"

Mr Blue nodded. He pushed off the chair and went over to one of the desks. He opened a metal box sitting on top and rummaged through before returning with a photograph.

My hands went clammy as I looked the image over.

"This is Greta?" I clarified.

"It is."

The image was black and white, but you couldn't mistake Greta's bright-blonde locks. Her cheekbones were sharp, and her nose narrow. She was a beautiful woman. She was familiar.

"Mr Bishop?"

I stared at the image: "I know this woman."

40

The woman was Grace Matthews, my Sunday school teacher. The very woman I caught Dad fucking in his office when I was eight years old. Looking at her photograph, more of my childhood memories came back in detail.

Their affair went on for a few more months afterwards. They would get a hotel in town. Dad would tell me where to reach him in an emergency, and he'd give me money to call via a pay phone at the post office.

Miss Grace and I could barely look at each other at Sunday school.

She would stammer her way through lessons.

But after one lesson, something changed. She talked to the class about King David. How he was a man after God's own heart, whom God trusted and loved. But David also lusted over a woman who wasn't his wife. Her name was Bathsheba. David gave in to his lust and slept with Bathsheba, and she became pregnant. The problem was she was married. So David sent her husband, Uriah, to the front line to kill him off so that he could take Bathsheba for himself—hardly a role model. Grace said what David did was wrong, but God will always forgive us for our sins.

After that lesson, she asked me to stay and help tidy up the room. I felt obliged.

"How are you?" she asked as she tidied her desk, and I put the Bibles on the shelf.

"Fine."

"Do you need to talk?"

"No, miss."

I swept the floor and organised the chairs. When I finished, I went for the door.

"Logan…"

Miss Grace smoothed out the front of her long skirt as she walked towards me.

"It must be confusing for you, Logan, I know." She played with my hair. "One day, when you're older, it might make sense. I want you to know that you're a good boy."

She started to tear up, and she left.

Was I a good boy because I didn't tell on them? I never found out.

Miss Grace was gone. I never saw or heard about her again.

Miss Grace… Greta Matas.

Blood rushed in my ears. Mary Palvienė said Greta talked like me. She didn't mean well-spoken English, Christ; she meant her accent. Greta sounded American! I sat there in that communist print shop because Dad had sent me to pay off his former mistress. I wanted to return to London and shake him out of his coma. Mr Blue stared at me, expecting me to explain. What could I say? What should I say? I felt like a little boy all over again, powerless with the information. My eyes watered.

She was my Sunday school teacher who disappeared. My stomach turned. Petras was a kid. Seventeen or eighteen. Greta was pregnant when she arrived in Edinburgh. Her name is, or was, Grace and is Grace again.

It made sense, finally.

That was why no one here knew the truth about Petras's father. Mary Palvienė said he died in Lithuania. Rūta Kanaitė said he abandoned her. Gabriel said he abandoned her too. My dad sent Greta away; he abandoned her. He stayed with Mom and not her. I thought the emerald ring might've been some communist business between her and my dad or that she was blackmailing him. The emerald was penitence. That was how he would pay her off.

Petras was my half-brother. This was what Dad wanted to cover up. He knew it would ruin the family if his affair came out.

My head spun, like when I was a boy. I felt hot, used, and stupid.

I rose and walked away from the table. Mr Blue asked what was wrong. I ignored him and leaned forward, staring at the box of block letters. A's, B's, C's, Q's, R's, and S's, and every letter in between. My fists were planted on the table, and my stiff arms shook.

BAD BLOOD

"Goddammit!" I punched the table. The tray of letters bounced, and Mr Blue jumped.

I scooped up the pieces of my gun and snapped them together in a few seconds. I stuffed Greta's photograph into my pocket.

Mr Blue rose and said, "Mr Bishop. We have more to discuss."

"No, we don't."

He approached and reached for a pistol in his coat. I one-two'd him and punched him in the throat before he could do anything. He fell to the floor and coughed. I flipped open the box of chocolates and took a handful. His red face looked at me in horror and anger. I popped a chocolate into my mouth. I grabbed my wallet and Tim's picture and walked out into the night.

41

I didn't care to find Lanka or Rūta. It was late afternoon, and darkness descended on the city. I swallowed the chocolate with a gooey cherry core and took a hit of Winslow's as I stalked down an alley and came out onto the main road—it was Leith Walk, and there was the travel agency.

A tram heading for Princes Street approached, and I got on.

Greta wanted to go to Chicago. What did my old man really know? Did Dad come here to stop her from coming? So he got the emerald ring from somewhere he shouldn't have to pay Greta off? Spatty's gang followed Dad. Did they think he was skipping town and they wanted to make him pay? Now they were after Greta as further retribution?

What caused Greta to ditch her obligation to Mr Blue? It wasn't a scam; she wanted to go to Chicago for a reason. Why didn't she?

Something told me Petras had the answers I sought. I hadn't given much thought to him the last few days. Nor the fact that he was wanted for murder. He was now the only person left who might know where Greta was and what Ivy House was, and I hadn't a clue where he could be.

I dug out the photograph of Greta, of Miss Grace, from my pocket and stared at it. Her face was expressionless—like all ID photos. It dawned on me that that kid Henrikas saw her at Waverley—it was possible someone there might recognise the photo. That would have to wait until morning.

***

A message from St Thomas' Hospital had been left at the hotel. I called the hospital. I had to wait twenty minutes to get someone on the phone, but eventually, I did.

"Mr Bishop, this is Doctor Burr." His tone was sombre.

"He's dead," I said matter of factly.

There was a pause. "I'm very sorry, Mr Bishop… "

"When?"

"Yesterday night. We need to discuss the next steps."

He spoke, but I didn't listen. How would I tell the family? What would I tell Mom? How does one ship a body to America for burial?

"I'll be back soon," I said to the doctor, cutting him off.

I slammed the phone down and went back out into the cold. My feet took me to St Cuthbert's at the end of Princes Street. The church was empty. I sat alone in a pew. At the front of the church, in the chancel, was an altar with a cross and a stone-carved depiction of the Last Supper on the wall.

Dad was dead, and I was living. Here I was, looking for his mistress, wondering where Petras could be and if he was my half-brother. I struggled to explain to myself why I sat in a church to think this through. I grew up eager to get out of church, and here I was with no rational explanation. Call it primal, call it supernatural, I needed to be here, and I prayed for my father's soul. That surprised me—I didn't think I would care. I guess I did.

I lost a good hour in that church before I left. I even lit a candle for my old man.

I walked back. Part of me thought I should go back to London. Forget all this. But no, I wanted answers, not speculation. And there was no guarantee Spatty and co would give up—so going home wouldn't mean it was all over. I also wanted Greta to know that Dad was out of the picture. She needed to know that as badly as I needed to know that she was safe.

"Evening, Mr Bishop." DCI McLean stopped me outside the National Gallery. He was wrapped in a thick grey coat and wore leather gloves—the salt and pepper beard of his looked prickly like a porcupine.

"Evening, Mr McLean," I said.

"Where are you off to?" he asked.

"My hotel."

"Ah, the Palace." He made a point. "Mind if I walk with you? I'd like to have a little talk."

"Am I in trouble?" I asked.

He smiled and laughed. "Goodness, no." We started to walk

towards the hotel. "I hear you had a rough time with Inspector Joy last night."

"You might say that."

"Aye. He can be ferocious." McLean smirked. "He told me about the medication he found on you. Winslow's Soothing Syrup, I believe?"

"Is he going to make a deal of that?"

"He's tempted."

I grunted, then said: "I know what people think, but it's the only thing that keeps me from losing my mind."

"I understand that all too well." McLean's tone was soft. "A piece of advice, though? Relying on stuff like that will be the death of you. I've known very good men go down that road and, well, wean yourself off the poison before it's too late."

I paused a beat. "Why are you doing this?"

"Doing what?"

"This. What do you care about what I do?"

"I took the liberty to investigate you after we met at the Walters'. Believe it or not, obtaining information on London's only American PI is rather simple. A friend of mine in London knew about you. You did some work last year for that negro lawyer, a George Sutherland."

"Yeah, that's right. He's a good friend," I said.

"He's your only friend, as I understand it. I had the privilege of having a chat with him. He spoke very highly of you. He assured me I could trust you, which brings me to my question. Edwin Walter confided a great deal in Miss Napier, as I understand it. We are interested in what she might know but hasn't yet told us."

"That's what this is all about—you want me to find out what that might be?"

"This stolen memoir of his—I understand the book is still out there. A carbon copy was taken from Edwin's office and one of two taken from Ms Webster was destroyed last night."

"Seems that way."

"So you want the copies and you think Harry might know where they are?"

McLean stuffed his hands into his coat pockets and thought for a moment. "I knew Edwin Walter. He was a pain in the ass. But he was smart. The copies I'm not that interested in, neither is Joy. Edwin doesn't make accusations without evidence. I spoke to his publisher, and Edwin certainly had it, but the publisher won't divulge any of the details. We need the evidence if we're to find Edwin's killer, and I think Miss Napier might know where it is. I understand she's staying with you at your hotel?"

"Is it your men who have been lingering in the lobby?"

"Do you even have to ask?" McLean smiled.

"I guess not," I said.

"Joy has been through Edwin's house," he continued, "and we've gone through his safety deposit box at the bank. His lawyer doesn't have the proof either. But it's somewhere. Maybe she has it; maybe she knows where it is."

"Maybe she does."

"If you can look into this for me, I can ensure that Inspector Joy will not create any further issues for you. Considering what happened with Clive Roberts and the woman who killed herself, it's a good deal, aye?"

"So that's the play," I said.

"I like you, Mr Bishop. Think of this as me helping you. Joy is like a dog with a bone. He'll gnaw you in half and then bury you."

We stopped outside the hotel. The yellow lights spilled onto the pavement, and I watched a tram squeak past us. Headlights flashed in my eyes.

"Fine. I'll see what I can do."

"Whatever you find out, bring it to me personally. This is sensitive."

"You got it, chief," I said.

I left McLean outside and went into the hotel. My head was a mess, and I just wanted to sleep. I didn't want to think about Edwin Walter, Harry, Greta, Petras, or Dad.

Harry was in the room, sitting at the desk reading a publishing magazine.

"Where have you been?" she asked.

I didn't know what I could or should tell her. Or what I wanted to say to her. I just sat on the bed.

"What are you thinking?" she asked.

"I don't know. It's been a long day. Where have you been? You were pretty angry at me earlier."

"I had things to do. It helped me calm down."

"Sorry," I said.

"Logan, is something wrong? I mean, something besides what's going on with us?" She climbed into bed next to me. "Is it Joy? Should I be worried?"

"No. It's the job I'm on."

"You haven't told me much about it."

I decided to try talking. But I wasn't ready to bring up Edwin or McLean's request.

I caught her up on the case with Greta. Told her about my dad's arrival. That Greta was his mistress. I showed her Greta's picture and told Harry who Greta was and that her son was on the run, wanted for murder. I concluded with the news about Dad's death. "I'm lost right now, Harry. Lost in the dark. I have so many unanswered questions about her. What happened between her and my Dad? Did he get rid of her, or did he not know about her pregnancy? I mean, I keep going back and forth in my head over it. Could my old man be such a shit that he'd abandoned the woman carrying his child? I want to know her side of the story because, hell, I'm not getting anything from my dad's corpse. Not to mention Greta's son. I mean, shit, I come to Edinburgh and find out my very likely half-brother is on the run after killing a guy. Honestly, this is such a fucked-up situation."

"What will you do, Logan?"

"I'll try the station, show her picture around, see if that jogs anyone's memory."

"You looked stressed."

"I damned well am," I snapped.

She kissed me. At first, I felt reluctant, but the closeness and hope of relief took over. Slowly, we gave in to each other. We took off our clothes. I was inside her. She started to breathe harder as I kissed her wet lips. I whispered in her ear that she felt good. She looked me in the eyes and said, "Tell me you need me."

I hesitated.

"Tell me."

"Harry…"

She moved on me. "Don't stop. Say it. Say it, please. Say you need me."

I groaned: "I need you."

"More."

"I need you."

"I want to be on top," she said. She mounted me and told me to keep saying, 'I need you.' The more I said it, the faster she went and breathed harder. She dug her nails into me—the pain turned me off. She kept demanding that I tell her how much I needed her. She cupped my face and planted our foreheads together. Her face scrunched, and her mouth hung open. We came together, and she cried: "Yes! Eddie, yes!" Then her body went limp on top of me. I panted, staring at the ceiling with her head on my chest.

I felt sick. I couldn't speak. Eddie. *Eddie*. She had called out Edwin Walter's name. I waited for her to say something. To say how embarrassed she was. To say sorry. Nothing. She said nothing, as if she didn't know what she had done. For a moment, I questioned myself. Did I mishear? No, I didn't. I knew what I heard. Was she really clueless as to what she had done?

"Did that help?" Harry asked. She leaned on her elbow and looked at me. She smiled.

The room was sour with the smell of sex and lavender.

"Yeah."

She smiled wider. "You wore me out."

That was a lie. I'd done nothing. It was her thinking about Edwin that got her off. McLean was probably right about her. So might Joy be. I understood why she fucked me now. We both fell asleep to the stench of our corrupted sex. What a fucking awful day.

42

A knock on the door startled us awake. It was 5am.

"Who could that be?" Harry said, groggily. Then, "What are you doing down there?"

I was lying on the floor next to the bed. No blanket, no pillow. When I made the transition, I couldn't say.

The knocking continued. They were heavy, worried knocks.

"One moment," I shouted, lifting my body off the floor. "Put something on," I said to Harry. I was tired of her naked body.

Harry slipped into a dress—I could barely look at her. I pulled on my trousers and an undershirt.

I was mad about everything, and I regretted having sex with her. In my mind, I could see Harry's expression as she came and called me Edwin. It made me feel worse than shit. She wasn't even with *me* in that moment. I was used and discarded.

I opened the door, expecting Inspector Joy, McLean, even Lanka, Rūta or Mr Blue.

Instead, Gabriel was on the other side, with concerned eyes and bouncy feet. He smelled of spices and cooking oils.

"Do you have any clue what time it is!" I said.

"I'm sorry, but it's Greta's lad, Pete."

Gabriel paused, seeing Harry behind me. She had tied her hair up, reapplied lipstick, and sprayed a fresh dose of lavender to clean the air of our corrupted sex.

"I didnae mean tae interrupt. Shit. It's important."

"There's nothing to interrupt now. Come in. Gabriel, this is Harriet Napier."

"The pleasure is all mine, lassie." He removed his flat cap and nodded. His cheeks were red.

"Good to meet you, Gabriel."

Gabriel sat in the desk chair, I took the desktop, and Harry perched on the side of the messy bed—Gabriel shot a few glances at her legs.

"What's up with Petras?" I asked.

BAD BLOOD

Gabriel wagged his head. "Pete was outside the hotel, waitin' for me last night. This kid comes into the kitchen, a delivery boy, yeah. He gives me a note, says someone's out back, wantin' tae see me. I figured it was you, after what Connell was like, aye. So I went tae the delivery entrance, and there was Pete! The lad was in a proper grim state, like. He looked like a tramp…" Gabriel eyed the Woodbine carton on the desk. "Can ah smoke?"

"Fine," I said.

"Dae you mind, lassie?"

"Not at all," Harry said. "So what did Peter want?"

I gave Harry a side look. I didn't like her taking over the conversation. I didn't like her much at all right at that moment.

Gabriel lit a roll-up and then continued: "Money, what else?" Smoke poured out of Gabriel's mouth. "I told him I had none tae give. He looks like he's about the cry and begs me for help. Grabbing me by the arms and says he's got tae get out of the country but needs a little more dough tae do it. I've never seen desperation like that. And, I guess I saw Greta in the lad's face. Made me think she might be out there hungry and needin' money. Of course, I asked if he was in trouble. He says somethin' bad-like happened at the colliery, but wouldnae say what."

"Did he say where he'd been hiding?" I asked.

"He said he spent a few nights in Leith, but no more. Said time was short now—whatever that meant."

"Where is he now?" I asked.

"At my flat. The lad had some clothes that needed cleanin'. Told him he could do that at mine and sit tight for a few days, aye. That's why I'm here." Gabriel shrugged. He dragged the cigarette, and the glowing paper receded like dry grass during a California wildfire. He tapped the ash into the waste basket. "He's been told to stay put while I get money."

"Did you ask him about Greta?" I asked.

He hesitated: "I couldn't bring myself tae ask…"

"Did you tell him about me?"

"Aye. I told him you were tryin' tae find his mum. He wouldn't come here with me when I said he should talk tae you." Gabriel lowered his roll-up and waited for an answer. Ash fell to the floor.

"Did he say anything about the colliery incident?"

Gabriel shook his head.

"He's wanted for murder," I said.

Gabriel's face flushed. "You're talkin' mince."

"Whatever the hell that means, I'm not. He allegedly killed a man named Tom Clackman at the coal mine—that's why he's on the run."

"Shite." He threw the burning roll-up in the bin. Smoke rose from it.

"Goddammit, man, don't set my room on fire…"

"It's okay." Harry shot up from the bed and tossed a cup of water on the smoke. She stood in front of Gabriel. "Are you all right, lamb?"

Gabriel continued to process the information.

"Murder?" he said. "Hell. I cannae be involved with that." Gabriel stirred in the chair. "I cannae be harbouring no murderer. Shite, shite, shite."

"Give me your address, and I'll go deal with Petras. I need to speak to the kid before he's out of my reach."

"Should I come with you," Gabriel said.

"No. I got police shadows."

"What are you talking about, Logan?" Harry pressed.

"I noticed some guys watching me the other day. We can't all walk out the front together."

"I'm coming with you," Harry said.

"No, you're not," I told her.

"I'm not going to be stuck in here all morning while you're out. You forget, I know this city better than you."

Gabriel grinned. It's either funny or awkward to be a spectator when a couple argues.

I thought about the men downstairs—worst-case scenario, we would split to avoid them. At least I could make use of her.

"Fine. Gabriel, give me your key and address. I'll bring it to you later at the hotel."

43

Gabriel went to leave out front. Harry and I took the service elevator and went out the delivery entrance out back. She led us towards Playfair Steps. That's when I noticed our two tails. I told Harry one was behind us, and another followed parallel from The Mound. "They're going to corner us at the top, Harry."

"No, they won't."

We rushed up the steps and darted across the street up another flight of steps and down a dark passage. The two men followed behind.

We came out on Lawnmarket and made a sharp left down a close. Harry weaved us through a series of closes and narrow passages until we came back out on Lawnmarket, where we then ran across it, and down Fisher's Close.

Our legs and lungs were aching when we sauntered across George IV Bridge, but our tails were gone.

"Not bad," I said.

"Thanks." She smiled at me, fuelled with adrenaline. "That was fun. Is this what it's like for you?"

"Stuff like this loses its charm after a while," I said.

For a moment, in the glow of the street lights, I thought she looked beautiful, but her saying Edwin's name resurfaced and made me feel bad again.

Gabriel lived in a tenement on Potterrow. We went inside and crept through the dark as we descended the stairs to his basement flat.

The door creaked open, and I flicked the dolly switch. A dull yellow light bulb buzzed in the one-room flat. Whoever owned the building had chopped it up to maximise profit. A ceramic stove, a washstand, a bed, and a chest of drawers were crammed into this room. On the table were mugs and a half-drunk bottle of whisky, a loaf of bread, a hacked-at block of cheese, and some broken eggshells.

The one thing was missing: Petras.

"Dammit." I turned to Harry: "He's gone."

"Maybe he'll come back?"

"Without a key?"

A mouse ran across the dirty, crumby floor and vanished under the stove.

We looked around. I went over to the stove and hovered my palm above the hotplate. "It's warm," I said. The eggshells were wet. "Petras left recently."

"Why? Doesn't he trust Gabriel?" Harry asked.

"I don't know."

She stopped: "Ew, look at this." Harry stood at the washstand.

The bar of soap by the sink was black and grey, and dirt marks dotted the inside of the basin. Looking at a pile of discarded clothing at the base of the washstand, I lifted a shirt with my pencil; it was covered in coal stains. The same was true of the trousers—they were Petras's work clothes. I laid them out on the floor to examine them.

Harry squatted next to me, holding her hand over her mouth to filter the stench.

"This doesn't look right, Harry."

"What?"

"Petras is said to have axed a man to death, but look at the clothes. This, here, these spots of brownish-red are blood." I pointed to the left shoulder and the right side. "Except, there is a higher ratio of soot and dirt than bloodstain. I saw the murder scene when I visited the mine—it was macabre. The amount of blood spray on these clothes is too little. His clothes should be drenched."

I turned the shirt over—there was no blood on the back. I examined the trousers next: almost no spray at all.

"What does that mean?" Harry asked.

"Means Petras wasn't alone when Clackman was murdered. It also means he couldn't have been the killer."

"But he's on the run?"

"Doesn't make him guilty."

"Doesn't make him not, either."

"No, but it tells me something isn't right."

"Are you saying that because of what you know about his mother?"

"No. Well, I don't think so. Petras murdered Tom Clackman with a pick-axe to the head," I confirmed. "And it wasn't just one hit. There were many."

"Logan…"

"Think about it, Harry… and look." I waved my hand over the shirt. "Several blows. Have you ever cracked a head open?" I asked.

"No."

"Not a lot of blood."

"Maybe he wore a coat? Or a waistcoat?"

"No, it's on his shoulders. It would've been on the top front, at least if the middle of his torso were covered. So who swung that axe?"

"You tell me, Mr Detective."

"Investigator. And I don't know. I just know this doesn't look right."

I searched the pockets. They were empty. I examined the trouser legs. Empty too. I snatched a paper bag from the kitchen counter, bundled up the clothes, and then stuffed them inside it. The paper bag crinkled in my grip as I scanned the filthy room.

I pushed my hat up and scratched my brow. "Where did he go? Wait. A delivery boy. Shit, of course. That's what Gabriel said."

"What?" Harry pressed.

"Petras was in Leith. I know who I need to talk to."

44

I banged on Mrs Mears's front door. It was 7am. The sky was still dark, and the street lights would buzz for another hour. I thought about a Sherlock Holmes story I read as a kid. The detective said: *'It is a capital mistake to theorise before one has data. Insensibly one begins to twist facts to suit theories, instead of theories to suit facts.'* It was the most sensible thing Conan Doyle put in the mouth of Holmes. The blood told me a story: someone or something was in front of Petras to block the spray. He wasn't alone.

"Who is it?" Mrs Mears shouted through the door.

"Logan Bishop, ma'am."

The door opened. The old woman was in her dressing gown and a nightcap.

"I need to see Henrikas," I said.

"What is this about?"

"He's been in touch with Greta's son. Petras is in trouble, Mrs Mears. And Henrikas could be too."

Mrs Mears didn't hesitate. She led Harry and me upstairs to his room. She didn't knock. She just barged in and turned the light on.

"Wake up, Henrikas!" Her voice boomed in the small room.

Henrikas jumped up from his bed, dazed and confused.

"Hey kid, remember me?" I said.

"What's going on?" he stammered, half asleep.

"Time to earn that pound," I said. "Petras. Where is he?" I asked.

Mrs Mears and Harry stood behind me. Henrikas shivered in his single bed, half covered in a grey blanket.

"I don't know where he is. Why?"

"Cut the crap. You've been hiding him, haven't you? I know you helped him contact Gabriel at the North British."

"Henrikas, is that true?" roared Mrs Mears.

"Pete needed my help," Henrikas said. "I swear. He's scared. Needs money."

"What's he trying to do, Henrikas? If he wanted to get out of town, why is he hanging around?"

"He can't go."

"Why?"

Henrikas said: "I don't know, he wouldn't tell me."

"Tell me where he is," I said. "He's not with Gabriel anymore."

Henrikas hesitated.

"Kid, if you don't tell me, I'll get the police here to deal with you," I said.

"He said he was going to get money from that guy at the hotel who liked his mam. If he wouldn't help, he was going to see Mrs Palvienė. That's all I know. Really."

I looked at Mrs Mears. "He's all yours."

Harry and I left.

***

Mary Palvienė swung open the door—she wore the same tatty blue cardigan I met her in. The tired circles under her eyes were darker—the exhaustion on her face was indescribable and known only to mothers.

"Mrs Palvienė, I need to speak to Petras." My breath hung in front of me. She looked over my shoulder at Harry and then back at me.

"You wake the child with all this pounding and loud talking." She blinked faster than a hummingbird flapping its wings.

"I'm sorry. I wouldn't be here if it weren't urgent. He's here," I said. "Petras."

"No, no. Go. You go. You leave us alone. I want no more trouble." Mary pushed me like a child who needed to be sent home.

"The police, Mrs Palvienė, want Petras. It won't be long before they are knocking on your door, and I don't think that's something you want. Let me speak to him—I might be able to help."

"Please, ma'am," Harry added. "We want to help the boy."

"Who this?" Mary asked sharply.

"This is Harriet Napier. She's helping me," I said.

Mary thought a moment. She looked like she wouldn't let me in, but then she widened the door.

She tapped her knuckles on the bedroom door and went through, leaving Harry and me in the hallway. We could hear murmurs.

"Are you going to tell him?" Harry whispered. "That he's your brother?"

"God, I don't know."

"You should tell him. It might help."

"Just leave it alone," I snapped.

Harry scoffed.

Mary opened the door. Behind her was Petras Matas.

It was like looking at my dad as a young man. He had the same eyes and brows and caramel hair—before Dad lost it. He shared Dad's thin runner's build he used to have. He looked sleep-deprived and scared.

I tried to smile at the young man. Petras. Greta and Dad's son. My half-brother, there was no doubt in my mind. Looking at him, I felt like I knew him or, at least, understood him. Both of us had been rejected by the same man—our father, the Reverend Sinner.

He stood with shoulders slumped and hands stuffed in his pockets—timid, for a murderer, if he was one. His clothes, which were Gabriel's, were fresh but baggy.

"Let's sit in the lounge," I said.

In the drab room, Petras placed himself next to the mantel. An oil lamp flickered a menacing shadow over his face. Mary turned on a light next to the window and then sat on the sofa with Harry. I perched on the arm.

"Hold this?" I asked Harry and handed her the brown bag with Petras's clothes. She put it in her lap and grimaced.

Petras moved on the balls of his feet and chewed the inside of his cheek. He looked cornered and nervous.

"Petras," I started. "Have a seat and relax? I just want to talk."

His body stiffened, and he narrowed his eyes.

"I'll stand." His accent was Scottish. He leaned on the fireplace. The light from the oil lamp continued to dance on his face. He folded his arms. "Mary says you want to help me? You are the man Gabriel talked about?"

"I am." There was a pause where I didn't know which lane to

take with him. Which confession to go after. I started with the basics. "Petras, my name is Logan Bishop, and this is Harriet Napier. I came to Edinburgh to find your mother, Greta."

"What do you want with my ma?" he asked. His jaw tightened.

"Dangerous men after her—I want to make sure she's safe."

Petras looked to Mary, then to me.

"She not here. She safe."

"Is she at Ivy House?"

Petras didn't speak.

"Where is Ivy House?"

The look in his eyes told me he knew, but he said, "Never heard of it."

"Petras, I found it written on a piece of paper back in the colliery. It was in a tin box under your bunk."

He looked at Mary, then at me. "Why you here?"

"Petras, I'm here about your mother. Not about the mine."

The march of feet outside pulled the room's attention to the front door.

Thud-thud-thud.

"Police, open up!"

"You brought them here?" Petras screamed. "You are police!" He looked betrayed. He panicked and searched the room with frantic eyes, unsure of what to do or where to go.

"Calm down, Petras!" I said. "I can handle this."

"Mr Bishop is not police, Petras," Mary assured. She and Harry now stood.

"You lie." Petras pointed at Mary.

"No, no, Petras," Mary pleaded.

Thud-thud-thud.

"Open the door!" a police officer shouted.

Petras grabbed an iron poker from the stand in front of the fireplace.

"Get out of my way!" he ordered.

The police continued to beat at the door.

Mary's boy cried from across the hall.

Harry gave me a *what do we do?* look.

"Put it down, Petras," Mary begged. "My son, my son!"

"Mama! Mama!" Mary's little boy, Valdemaras, shouted as he raced into the room. Mary scooped him up and held him close—shielding his face from Petras.

I stood between the woman and Petras. Harry had the brown bag in hand.

"Shut yourself in the room with the children," I said. "Go!" The women ran across the hall and slammed a door shut.

"Petras, I didn't bring the cops. Let me deal with them." I stepped towards him—he swung at me—I jumped back.

Snap! The timber door frame cracked and began to splinter.

I reached for the Colt but stopped. I couldn't pull it on him.

"Get out of my way!" Petras ordered. He stepped towards me, swinging the poker.

"No, Petras," I said. "I can help you."

"Liar! You cannot help me!"

He slashed the air, and I dodged the swings.

Petras grabbed the lit oil lamp and threw it at me. I dodged it. But it hit the floor, and glass shattered, and the oil spilt. The carpet ignited, and flames feasted. Petras ran for the door. I tried to grab him; he swung the poker and hit my left side; pain tore through me. I stumbled and fell into the wall, groaning.

Petras darted into the kitchen. I heard glass shattering. He was going to try to slip out the window.

The front door crunched open the rest of the way, and two cops charged inside.

One shouted, "The kitchen, the window!" They stormed through. Petras screamed. Mary's boy cried. The fire was growing out of control. A police officer said: "Pull him through, pull him through!"

I took a pillow from the sofa and beat the flames. "Harry, get water! We have a fire," I called.

The flames crawled towards the sofa and spat at the wallpaper.

I grabbed one end of the rug, and as I yanked it, the sofa jumped. I did it again, and the rug came out from under the far legs. I folded the flames inside it. Heat beat against my face as the fire chewed and smoked through. I folded the rug once more and dragged it down the hallway—flames leapt out.

I ditched the burning rug in the gutter. A police van and a Ford Model T were outside. A man sat behind the steering wheel of the Ford and glared at me and the burning rug.

I ran back inside, and one of the two police officers ran out, shoving me aside. He yelled, "The boy got out the window!"

In the kitchen, the window was smashed. Petras was gone. He'd slipped out the broken window and disappeared into the early morning. I turned around and looked down the hallway—Inspector Joy was staring at me.

45

"What the hell is this?" I asked him, standing outside.

"I'm arresting a murderer," Joy said.

It hit me. "Gabriel? Your spooks at the hotel got him."

Inspector Joy nodded. "Aye." He gave me a snarky smile. "We picked Gabriel up as he left your hotel." I imagined Gabriel roughed up in an alley with Joy looming over him. "He quickly told us what we wanted to avoid going to jail. He told us what you were doing. One of my men kept a tail on you, we arrived at Cables Wynd just after you left. Had a lovely chat with Mrs Mears and a young man who told us you were here."

One of the officers interrupted us to say Petras and got away. Joy ordered the man to get after him.

"Where is he going, Bishop?" Joy asked.

"Hell, if I know. You've scared him off."

"Is soothing syrup surging through you, Bishop? Perhaps I should bring you in. Covering the tracks for a murderer."

"Dammit, Joy."

"You know, McLean isn't the only one to dig into your history, Bishop. From what I hear, life in America isn't easy for people with blue tickets." He paused to let that sink in. A surge of anger went through me. "Is that why you've stayed in Britain? Afraid to face your dishonour? I wonder how business would do if your story got out in the London papers…"

I got in his face: "You say one more goddamn thing…" Memories rapidly flashed in my mind like machine-gun fire: my superior officer calling Tim a coward after his death, accusing me of killing him, me punching him out, getting arrested, spending the night in jail, and being thrown out of the army.

"What? I told you not to fuck with my investigation. You brought this on yourself."

"What the hell do you want?"

"To do you a favour in exchange for one."

"A favour?" I spat. "What are you talking about?"

BAD BLOOD

The V's on Joy's face sharpened. "That ginger wench is hiding Edwin Walter's documents. I want them. You get them, and I won't release this."

Inspector Joy produced a photograph. Harry and Edwin were having sex with a woman whose face was out of view.

"That isn't—?"

"Real?" Joy grinned. "It is, Bishop. I found it in Edwin's desk. Miss Napier is a naughty lass. But you would know…"

"Damn you," I said.

"Careful."

"No, you be careful, Joy. Harry's not the only one with a secret lover. Or is that why you're so keen to get the documents and find the missing copies of Edwin's manuscript?"

"Are you slow or something, Bishop? You cannot threaten me. You have no power. So listen up—if you go to McLean, I'll release the image. Get the documents or the story of your blue ticket and the secret life of Edwin Walter and his mistress come out," he said. "You have three days." Standing in front of the car, he said: "Merry Christmas, Blue Ticket."

Inspector Joy got into the Ford Model T, revved the engine, and then sped off.

Inside, Harry looked after the mother and child. Both were in shock. The incident had scared them half to death. I left Harry to it and tried to put the front door back together. After thirty minutes, it was an approximation of fixed. Fresh daylight could still be seen through the cracks, but it shut and locked. The whole frame needed to be replaced, just like the rug and the wallpaper and their lives.

When I finished, we stood in the kitchen drinking weak tea.

"Mr Bishop?" Mary Palvienė asked.

"Petras got away," I said. "This is a mess."

Mary continued: "He is good boy. He tell me he not want this. He not want to run."

"Then why did he?" I said. "He's not helping himself out. Mrs Palvienė, did he say anything about Greta?"

"No, but he find two letters for Greta under sofa cushion. Petras showed me."

"What did they say?" I asked.

"My English is no good. I remember the name Daniel. Made me think of Daniel in the lion's den." Mary nodded. "The letters anger Petras."

"Who's Daniel?" Harry questioned.

"Daniel Bishop, my dad." I paused, anger boiled inside. "Dammit!" I shouted. The women jolted. "Sorry… I'm sorry. I was this close, this close to getting somewhere… and Joy… damn Joy."

"Logan, stop it!" Harry ordered. "This isn't the time or place."

"There's no bargaining with Joy, Harry."

"What are you talking about?"

I bit my lip. She was right. That wasn't the place. "Nothing. Mrs Palvienė, where are the letters?"

"I get them now."

Harry stood in front of me.

"What's going on?"

"This was all Joy. He got Gabriel to spill everything. But it's worse than that."

"Worse how?"

"Now's not the time for *that*."

Mary returned with the letters, and a grey woollen coat hung over her arm.

"Here." She handed them to me.

The first letter read:

Greta,

Do not contact me again. I owe you nothing. So don't you dare attempt to threaten me. Who would believe you after all these years? This is desperate and beneath you. I've done more than enough for you. I sent you to Edinburgh when you refused to get rid of it. I paid to give you a new life… what you did with it is not my problem. This matter has ended.

Dan.

The second letter:

BAD BLOOD

I intercepted the letter you wrote to my wife. How dare you threaten to come here. Do not come to Chicago. You will regret it. Stay where you are. I do not want to see you or discuss anything in person. This must stop. I will arrange a one-off payment and no more—do you understand? Do not contact me again. You will leave my family and me alone.
Dan.

Dad, you monster. The phrase 'get rid of it' stayed at the front of my mind. I dropped my head. I was right. The ring was to shut her up. He didn't want anyone to know about his affair, about his bastard child. But something went sour with the emerald ring he sent; he needed it back to stop the thugs, but he failed, and Greta never realised it was inside the bear before we went M.I.A. He wanted to pay her off, but he also didn't want her to be harmed.

"Petras's coat," Mary said. I shoved the letters into my pocket.

I rummaged through the pockets—the coat smelt of cigarettes, spices, and cooking oil—like Gabriel. The front pockets were empty, but inside the inner jacket pocket, I found a brown leather wallet. It was cracked and frayed. I undid the catch. Thirty pence was in the change compartment, and a note was in one of the flaps. It read:

I'll wait to hear from you and meet you as soon as you can.
Yours, Liepsnelė

"What's this?" I asked Mary. "Is this Lithuanian?" I pointed to *Liepsnelė*.

"It's a, uh, a girl he calls redbreast," she said.

"A lover," Harry proposed.

"Yes, a lady friend of his," Mary said.

"Who?" Harry asked.

Mary didn't know.

I said: "We need to find out."

46

Harry and I sat in the back of the tram going into New Town. The first place to look for Liepsnelė was the colliery. But I struggled to focus on that. Not only was Dad's infidelity eating at me, the photograph Joy showed me, and this threat loomed heavy on my mind. It lingered in my mind, and I couldn't decide if I should tell Harry what had happened or not. Did she know about the photograph? Or had Edwin taken it without her consent? The humiliation it would cause her if it leaked could be devastating.

I didn't like what I knew about Harry. I didn't much like Harry since she called out Edwin's name during sex without realising it. But I also didn't like Joy threatening to shame her either. No matter what I thought, it was Harry's life, Harry's business, and the public didn't deserve to know it unless she spilt it. That must've been what the man who wanted Edwin's manuscript thought. The urge to take out the person threatening him festered inside me like it had to have done for him. Joy knew my pressure point. I had avoided returning to America because of my blue ticket, and I didn't want anyone here to know about it.

I needed to get Joy off our backs before I could do anything more about Greta or Petras.

If I were Edwin, I'd have kept the materials close—in the house, in the office. McLean didn't know where they were. Joy or Fran don't either.

"What's wrong, Logan?" She placed her hand on my thigh.

"Nothing."

"You're a bad liar. What did you mean back there? Something worse has happened?"

I didn't know how to tell her what Joy had on her. And I didn't want to tell her what he had on me.

"Logan?"

I studied the freckles on her face and then said: "When we arrived in Edinburgh, why did you want to go out for a drink?"

"What does that have to do with anything?"

"Just tell me."

"Well, I mean... I don't know, because I thought we'd have fun together."

"Simple as that?"

"Does it need to be complicated?"

I laughed.

"What?" she pressed.

"Nothing."

"No, tell me, Logan."

I sat up. "I know why you cried the night we first kissed and why you ran off. You and Edwin were lovers."

Her eyes widened, and her neck tensed. She pretended to look confused, but she was caught. "I don't know what you're talking about."

"Harry. I saw a photograph..."

Her body pivoted towards me.

"What photograph?"

"Of you and Edwin in bed with another woman. Joy has it."

She sat forward, her hand covering her mouth. She was uneasy, looking around the tram for an escape. Harry jumped up and ran off the tram.

I followed. She marched up the street, not paying attention. Anyone in her way had to dodge her to avoid a collision. She braced herself against a building and threw up.

"Harry." I laid a hand on her back as she bent over and retched. When she stopped, her face was pale, and she was crying.

"How did he get that?"

"From Edwin's office," I said. "Must've been the day he and Fran went through everything."

"Fuck! What's he going to do?" Her voice was shaky.

"He wants Edwin's documents—whatever incriminating evidence he has got on the people he wrote about. He won't share the picture if we get it to him."

"How will he share it?" she asked.

"A story in the papers, the secret life of Edwin and his mistress. Or so he claims. Where are the documents, Harry?"

"God, I don't fucking have them, Logan! Get that into your head, okay?"

People on their early morning commutes eyed us as Harry shouted.

"He thinks you do, and he's not the only one."

"What?"

"McLean wants the docs too. He stopped me the other day to discuss it, but he's a friend. I think Edwin has dirt on Joy, and that's why Joy is desperate to get what Edwin has. That's why he's threatening us."

"Edwin didn't write about Joy. I would've known."

"That doesn't mean that Edwin didn't have something on him, though. Which Joy must think he does. But now we can't go to McLean—Joy knows he's spoken to me. We're up against it, Harry. You have to think, where would Edwin keep documents like that?"

"He never told me." Harry rubbed her face and growled.

"You have to think," I said.

"I can't!"

Frustration bubbled up inside of me. "What the hell was that all about anyway?" I blurted out. "You and Edwin? I mean, jeez, he's married."

"Like you've never slept with another man's wife?"

"No."

"Of course you'd say that."

"Did you not think how it might hurt Fran?"

"Fran? Fuck Fran. Get enlightened! Victorian values of propriety are just masks to hide who we are and what we want. We're bloody carnal beings. Logan, you can be with someone, be totally devoted to a person, but share affection with someone else."

"Carnal indulgence? Is that all we are?"

"God, stop overthinking, Logan. What does it matter what we are right now? Is carnal no good? Do we need to be more or less? I don't need to commit to one person, least of all to you. I should be free to explore whomever I want without persecution. Lust is natural; love is greedy. Lust is simple and clear. But you can't see that because you're like all men, you want to control me, control women."

"Anyone can justify their actions; fat, greedy men justified twenty million deaths. Controlling carnal impulse is the only damn thing that separates us from the beasts we evolved from. The fabric of society is undone."

"If you're going to judge me, fuck off. Otherwise, help me with this problem!"

I stuffed my hands in my pockets and turned my back on her. I looked up and down the road, at the cars and the trams.

"Fine," Harry said.

"We need to get inside the house and look around," I said.

I turned back to her. Harry hugged herself. Her face was red with anger and fear.

"Fran won't allow that," said Harry.

"Can you get her out of the house?"

"Possibly. I don't know. I'd have to think."

"Harry…"

"Logan, I need to be alone. Don't you need to give Gabriel his key?"

Harry walked on, and I let her go.

I went to the North British to find Gabriel. To tell the truth, I was glad to be alone. I didn't want to be around her. I needed space to think. I felt pulled in too many directions. Dad, Greta, Petras, the gangsters, and Joy. It was a wasteland I wanted to be free from. My hands shook, so I took a swig of Winslow's to steady myself. Putting it back in my pocket, I told myself I'd never be free.

I walked through the lobby of the North British, relieved Denise wasn't at the front desk. I was sick of her disillusionment and wanted to keep her out of my life.

I stuck my head into the kitchen. Gabriel slopped a watery brown substance into unbaked pie bases. He hadn't noticed me until I was on him. His face had bruises starting to form—Joy's men gave him a pounding. Another scoop went into a base; chunky squares of steak and potato sticking out of the water.

"Hey, fella," I said.

"Bishop. I was wonderin' about you."

"Here."

Gabriel wiped his hands on the yellow-and-brown-stained apron, and then I dropped the key into his expansive hand. He stuffed it into his pocket.

"I'm sorry... I messed up."

"What's done is done. Joy knows how to squeeze. I don't hold it against you."

He nodded and began to put the tops of the pies on, unsure what to say next.

"I wanted tae ask you somethin', Bishop. The story about Greta stealin' jewels—that's a sham?"

"Yeah. Connell covered up the truth."

Gabriel stopped pressing the crust and flared his nostrils.

"I want tae know what happened."

"The truth won't help you," I said.

"Tell me. I need tae know."

"She was sleeping with some rich boy named Ian Clark. His mother caught them, got upset, and got Greta dismissed."

Gabriel slammed his fist on the counter, making the pies and kitchen staff jump. He stormed off and went into the walk-in freezer.

I followed.

Gabriel sat on a box of fresh cod, a cigarette smouldered between his lips.

Gabriel dragged on the cigarette. He breathed out smoke and tapped ash onto the freezer floor. We stood in silence for a minute. Then he continued. "There were rumours, aye. People liked tae speculate. Pregnant... some of them said. But at her age, that made me laugh. Syphilis was another. Others said she was probably arrested for spreadin' her communist pamphlets." He sucked on the cigarette. When he pulled away, he gave it a nasty look. "I had tae buy these Woodbines. Gave my last few roll-ups tae Pete. I hate Woodbines." The cold nipped at my face. Gabriel was thinking—he wasn't done talking. He stomped on the cigarette as he stood and rubbed his cold ass. He swallowed down some bubbling emotions. "Greta didnae want tae be the wife of a hotel cook."Gabriel looked deflated. "What's happened tae Pete, then?"

"He ran away. The police didn't get him."

"Damn."

"Gabriel—"

"Bishop, I'm done, aye? I've got tae move on. There is no use in holdin' on tae dead things. Bury the dead and leave 'em buried." Gabriel huffed and sank. "I'm sorry, though 'bout telling the polis."

"Forget about it, pal. Gabriel..." I extended my hand. "Keep well."

"Aye. You too."

Outside, I rested on a bench in Waverley Rooftop Gardens. Across Princes Street, Jenners and Maule's department stores advertised Christmas gifts. That seemed odd since Scots don't celebrate Christmas. At least it wasn't an official holiday here. But that never stopped the capitalist machine.

I thought about the emerald ring locked in the hotel safe. I was lost in a labyrinth, and I was getting nowhere fast. Petras was my best and last option for information, but Joy's threats were disrupting my plans.

The muscles in my neck tensed. I cracked my neck. The pops ran down my spine.

A nice-looking mother and her well-fed son walked past me. The boy held a toy truck, and Mary and her son flashed in my mind. The smouldering rug in the gutter, the burn marks on the walls. Clumps of mud, from the police, in the corridor and kitchen. The broken door and the near-empty kitchen.

Merry-fucking-Christmas.

47

I knocked on Mary Palvienė's door. It wobbled on the hinges. She answered. Her face was tired and drained. Her eyes took in the bags in my hands, then moved beyond me to the chubby cab driver with more bags in his arms.

"I, uh, got you things," I said. "May I come in?"

"Where is that lady friend?"

"Not here."

"Oh." Mary looked disappointed. I wasn't. "Okay, come in."

The cabbie and I set the bags down in the kitchen. I tipped him and sent him on his way.

"Mr Bishop?" Mary stood in the kitchen doorway, Valdemaras, her boy, beside her. "What is this?" She came into the middle of the kitchen and surveyed the bags.

"I'm playing Santa," I said.

"What?"

I handed her a sack of potatoes and two dozen eggs from one bag.

The boy lingered in the kitchen doorway.

"Hi, pal." I waved at him.

He gave me a shy look.

I reached into the Jenners bag and took out a toy truck with a red ribbon wrapped around it.

Mary paused with the eggs in her hand and bit her lip.

"Do you like it?" I asked. He didn't move. The boy's big brown eyes turned to his mother. I glanced at Mary. She spoke in Lithuanian. "It's yours. Here you go." I extended my reach. His little hand took the truck, and a smile stretched across his face.

"Merry Christmas, kiddo," I said as he ran away into the lounge with the truck.

"Valdemaras," Mary said.

The boy came back and said: "Ačiū."

Mary translated, "That say thank you."

"You're welcome, bud."

Her eyes were glossy.

I said: "I, uh, well, I don't know what kids eat or like, other than milk." I removed jars of powdered milk and tinned vegetables. "I also got him this, I had a similar one as a kid." I handed Mary a stuffed golden bear with two glass eyes.

Mary held the bear, and her thumb followed the curve of its smile.

"This is for you…" I gave her a blue cardigan. "Tried to find one that matched the colour of that one… and I guessed your size. I hope it fits." She looked at the tatty one wrapped around her. "Blue is nice on you."

The bear went on the counter, and Mary took the cardigan.

"Mr Bishop…" She lifted the cardigan in front of her and brought it to herself. "Why do you do this?" Tears ran down her face.

I started to unpack the rest of the bags and pretended not to notice. I placed bags of flour and sugar on the counter, and more tins and jars of goods.

"It's Christmas."

I towered the tins of beans, peas, and corn.

"I can't repay this…"

"It's a gift." Her watery eyes watched me. There was a tingle in my throat. I coughed it out. "Here… help me put this stuff away."

When we finished, I took a bag of coal into the lounge.

Valdemaras sat on the floor, ran the truck back and forth, and made a vroom sound.

While the boy played behind me, I removed pieces of the burnt chair from the fireplace. I put coal and firewood in and ignited it. I doubted the room had been warm since summer.

Mary entered wearing her new cardigan. It fitted well, and she looked warm and happy. Her cheeks blushed. "Thank you, Mr Bishop." Her hands smoothed it out.

"You're welcome."

The fire warmed the room.

Mary sat on the sofa and buried her hands in her lap.

"You are kind man, Mr Bishop. All this…"

"Please, not another word."

"Mr Bishop? Do you think Greta is alive?"

"I hope so. I think Petras knows something."

"What put her in danger?"

"My dad."

Mary looked confused, but I wasn't going to explain. "Listen, something I wanted to ask you, did Greta ever mention the name Ian Clark to you?"

"No."

"Ah, never mind."

"I worry for Petras," Mary said.

"With good reason. Did he tell you what happened at the coal mine?"

She shook her head. "I tell you, Petras knocks on my door, tells me he needs to come in, he needs to eat. I feed him. He says he does not want to run away... but has to." She paused. "But why?" Mary's hands go up.

"BSHH!" Valdemaras crashed the toy truck into my shoe. He looked up at me and smiled, and I smiled back.

"Having fun, pal?"

Mary beamed at her happy child. She then moved over to the fireplace and warmed her hands.

"Can you remember anything else?" I asked.

"He want money."

"How much?"

"Thirteen pounds. I tell him I have no money. So he asked if he can sleep here a few nights until he goes somewhere else."

"Did he say where?"

"No."

"It doesn't cost thirteen pounds to get out of the country... A return trip, maybe, or the cost for two."

My stomach growled.

"You hungry?"

"I am."

"I make you food."

"That's a kind offer, but I need to go." I patted the boy on the head. "Dinner another time, Mrs Palvienė." Before I left, I handed her an envelope. Inside was a wad of Edwin Walter's case money I'd been paid. I said: "Hopefully, this'll do you some good," and I left.

48

I found my way back to the hotel. Joy's men were gone, which unsettled me. After breathing down my neck, why were they called off? The brainwork hurt my head, so instead of going to the room to sleep or deal with Harry, I went to the hotel bar and got lost in several glasses of Black Label. At one point, the barman said to stop trying to find the bottom of the glass.

I said: "I'm just trying to find some peace."

He said, "Focus on simple things."

I lifted my drink to him—"Easier said than done."

Downing my drink, I grumbled: "I can't connect nothing with nothing."

The drunker I got, the more unhappy I became.

The barman asked me if I was okay. I said: "Who is?"

I ordered another whisky and thought, hour after hour. I had been lost in the brown fog of my mind, with questions burning. Begging for answers—I had some, now. I knew who Greta was, and I knew why Dad had sent me. I had waded through the slushes of vice and vanity as a scavenger trudges through garbage along the Thames. My entire existence had become a scavenger of other people's filth. I stopped thinking and started talking to anyone who would listen, mostly the barman.

"Logan?"

Harry was at my side. Between the pursed lips, wrinkled brow, and narrowed eyes, I knew she wasn't happy—and I didn't care. I searched for a clock and forgot I had a watch in my pocket. Time had lost meaning at some point several whiskies ago.

"How long have you been here?" Harry pressed. "I've been waiting for you. We need to talk about Edwin."

Her calling me Edwin in bed jumped to the front of my mind. "I wanted to be alone and then got talking to…" I looked at the barman and squinted, "Chhh…"

"Carl," he confirmed.

"Carl! I've been making friends with Carl."

"Logan, you're soaked to the bone."

"Hey, you remember my name."

"What does that mean?"

"Join me... Harry." I looked at Carl. "Us... join us. I was telling Carl about France." I turned away from her and focused on the barman. Even in my drunken state, I could see the awkward tension on his face. I just ignored it. I continued my story. "So here I am, with two broken fingers and a bullet wound in my thigh, and me and seven soldiers charge the Germans with our bayonets. It was nasty shit, Carl. Hot pain shot through me as we raged forward. But I tell you, the feeling of a bayonet as it plunges into a Jerry's gut... rips your soul right out. And you know why? Because you realise that other guy thinks he's the good guy, and you're both just fucking pawns with permission to murder. War doesn't make heroes out of anyone. It just creates monsters and casualties."

"Logan..." Harry's hand rested on my shoulder. "Come upstairs."

"Sorry, Carl, I guess I gotta go." I rolled my eyes like a petulant child.

"S'all right, Mr Bishop. She'll take care of you."

"Don't count on it," I said.

Back in the room, Harry said: "Sit down and drink some water."

"Yes, nurse." I plopped down at the desk.

"I'm not your nurse."

"Cause I'm not Edwin?"

"Excuse me, Logan?" She towered over me.

"Funny, you always remember my name when you're mad at me."

"What the hell are you talking about? You know what, you're drunk, we'll talk when you're sober."

She made for the toilet, shaking her head.

"Let's talk now," I shouted. "Let's talk about how you called *his* name out in bed."

"You're a liar." The baffled look of surprise told me she really didn't know what she had done, and that just pissed me off more.

"Like hell I am! Have you ever had sex with someone, and they called someone else's name? Cause, boy, that stings. And you might not remember it, but it happened."

She stood in the bathroom doorway with tears running down her face.

I continued. "You don't give a shit, do you? Because all this is carnal indulgence. Completely meaningless. So you'll forgive me if I am a little upset that you called out a married man's name when I was inside you. You only fucked me the other night to play make-believe that I was Edwin."

"You're awful, Logan!"

"Maybe so. Maybe it's my fault. Maybe I'm old-fashioned when it comes to sex, but I try to avoid married women and threesomes. But at least I'm honest. I'm telling you because I don't know how or when else to do it."

"Logan... I..."

"Don't say you didn't mean it."

"I'm sorry."

I planted my elbow on the desk and stared at the paper bag on the floor at my feet. Then I looked at the chocolates I took from Mr Blue on the desk.

"Logan?" She made a few steps in my direction.

"Don't come near me. I don't wanna talk."

"Logan, let's talk, please," Harry's voice softened.

"I don't wanna."

"Don't be so immature about this, Logan."

"I'll be however the hell I wanna be, Harry. Why don't you go find some other sap to satisfy your fucking needs."

"You're a brute! I'm going to bed. You sleep on the floor."

49

I woke up with a hangover and a dry mouth, but not on the floor. I was in bed. Harry was awake and had water and tablets ready for me. I drank the water with the tablets. She perched on the side of the bed—the atmosphere was different. When I looked at her, there wasn't any attraction—and I got the feeling she didn't care much for me either. Last night was the point of no return that some relationships have. The problem was that we still had to work together.

"What do we do about Joy?" Harry asked.

"We get him what he wants," I said. My voice was hoarse. "We need to do it as quickly as we can. Once we find Edwin's documents, we can barter for the picture. You still think you can get Fran out of the house long enough for me to have a look around?"

"Yes, I think so."

"Okay." I took another drink of water. "Harry, about last night…"

"Don't, Logan. What's said is said. Let's get through this so we can move on."

"Fine."

***

I waited around the corner from the Walters' residence. Harry stood at the front door. She gestured emphatically with her hands as she talked to Mrs Walter, who wouldn't let her inside. The door shut on Harry, and she lowered her head. She glanced in my direction and waved at me to stay put. The door reopened, and Fran emerged. The two women walked up the street together, away from me. When they were out of sight, I made my move.

I approached the Walters' door with my lock pick in my hand. The thing with picking a lock in broad daylight is to look like you have a key, focus on the lock, and not look around or over your shoulder. Amateurs look around.

BAD BLOOD

I was through the door in ten seconds.

Harry's Cleopatra painting had been replaced by a series of portraits of Fran Walter's sons.

In the lounge—the same thing. Portraits of her sons decorated the walls now, and an oil painting of a man I assumed was Fran Walter's father or grandfather by the similarities in the eyes, nose and mouth. Harry's sketches were gone, all of them. Fran hadn't wasted time scrubbing out her existence.

I went into Edwin's office. The room had been searched. The bookcases were in disarray, and the desk was a mess. A chequebook, calendar, and ledger were opened and looked through. Joy and Fran had shifted through the obvious places but turned up empty-handed. I started looking for the less obvious. I searched the desk, bookcase, and liquor cabinet, looking for hidden compartments. There were none.

I rummaged through papers and notepads on the desk. They were filled with story ideas but told me nothing.

Edwin must have a hideaway somewhere. But it was not here.

I wanted to be sure, though. I began to search behind the scenic paintings and surveyed the fireplace. It was hopeless. I walked through the lounge, dining room, and kitchen. Nothing. Upstairs, I searched the master bedroom—nothing there either.

Back in Edwin's office, I circled the room. I knew I couldn't hang around much longer. I moved behind Edwin's desk, scanning around. His antler chairs were ridiculous. I sat in his kingly desk chair and looked up at the mounted antlers above. Where the hell did he keep the shit?

I spun around in the chair and looked down at the wallpaper by the skirting board behind the desk. Something caught my eye. I knelt down—the paper had a tiny ruffle in it, and I found a thin, nearly invisible crack, one a blade might make. I removed my pocket knife, inserted it into the gap, and pressed it down. A small secret compartment swung open, and behind it was a narrow dial safe.

Got it.

I started fiddling with the dial and feeling the clicks. One of the numbers I got. The sound of heated voices caught my attention. Then, a key rattled in the front door. I shot up. The door opened. I shut the hidden compartment and stood against the wall by the door.

"Where are my paintings?" It was Harry. She was furious. "My goodness, you got rid of them?"

"Stop acting like an entitled child, Harriet."

"This is about Edwin and me, isn't it?" Harry said. "You threw everything of mine out on purpose."

"To Edwin, you were a means to fill the void left by our sons. Nothing else. Everything about you, your art, your body, it was all a pathetic distraction for a pathetic man. He replaced all our sons' photographs with your paintings and sketches as if that made it all better. Together, you erased all signs of my boys—so yes, I'll erase you.

"Would you keep a constant reminder that your spouse abandoned the memory of your dead children? Because that's what he did—day after day, you reminded me that he'd found some pretty young thing to distract himself with and take their place. I have had to keep our sons' memories alive alone."

"Why didn't you get divorced? That would've made us happy!"

"You stupid child, we didn't need one. Edwin was never going to leave me for you. We had a workable situation long before you came into the picture. That's right, you're far from the first plaything he had..."

"You didn't love each other," Harry cried.

"He didn't love you either. Love. Oh, lord. Marriage is so rarely about love. It's survival, status, business."

"Well, if I had the choice, I'd rather survive with someone I loved than survive with someone for their money."

"Good for you, Harriet. I like that you believe that. So hopeful, so naive. Now, tell me, was it love that took you to Mr Bishop's hotel room? Or a free place to sleep?"

"You cow!"

"Get out of my house!" Fran roared.

"Not without my sketches."

BAD BLOOD

The feet moved out of the lounge and down the corridor. Then climbed upstairs.

"You get back down here!" Fran called.

I looked over at the hidden safe. There was no time for me to get inside it now. I'd have to come back.

I raced for the front door and slipped outside unnoticed.

Harry rushed through the door, tears streaming down her face a moment later.

"If you come here again, I'll call the police," Fran shouted at her. "You won't get a damn thing! I'll make sure of it." Fran saw me. "Take your whore, Mr Bishop." The front door slammed shut. Harry rushed up the street, and I ran after her.

"What was that?"

"This was a bad idea, Logan."

She wiped her face dry with her hands.

"What happened?"

Harry composed herself. "I asked her to have a coffee with me to discuss things. Told her I didn't like how things ended. I poured my heart out to her, Logan, and she just turned and started accusing me of nonsense. Saying I was out to get her, out to get Edwin's money and his publishing rights. I told her she was hysterical and asked her where she got this idea. She said Edwin's lawyers. Then she said she threw out all my paintings, and I lost it. I stormed back to the house to find them."

"That was damned reckless, Harry. I found a hidden safe but didn't have time to crack it because you two came back squabbling like a couple of teenagers. In case you forgot, I'm trying to help you out."

Harry stopped walking: "You don't have to be a pig, Logan. I had to see if any of my art was salvageable!"

"Dammit. Let's go somewhere to rethink this," I said.

We went to a small Italian café on Rose Street called Rizza. The old Italian man waiting on us, doted over Harry: "Ah, you are such a beauty, much too pretty for this man. You are a very lucky man, you know that?" An older woman behind the counter smiled and shook her head at him. The other patrons, a man with a newspaper and two middle-aged women with tea and cake watched us. He said, "For you two, I will give you the best table in the house—the most romantic spot for the lovely lady and her lover-man." He directed us to a two-seater table in front of the window. He brought us two decent cups of coffee and a slice of vanilla cake to share. Harry wore a fake smile throughout the whole thing, which fell when the man wandered off to be with his wife behind the counter.

She picked at the cake and said: "We're never getting the materials, Logan. Joy's going to ruin me."

"We will. Besides, we have our own ammunition."

"What?" Harry asked.

"I discovered something about Joy and Fran when I visited the Wrights. They were at the party together, and they were seen kissing. The two of them argued about Edwin, and then Joy stormed out." I retrieved the guest book page I took from the Wrights from my wallet. "They were there together."

"What? Why didn't you tell me? Joy must've killed Edwin."

"I don't know—I wasn't sold on that at first, but he could've. He has a motive. And his eagerness to get these documents tells me Edwin has something on him."

"But Joy wasn't in his memoir."

"Then it was something Edwin hadn't written about yet."

"Christ."

"Look, you lived there for years, what's her schedule? When does she go to bed?"

"Uh, I don't know, around eleven."

"Okay. I'll sneak in when she's asleep and pick the safe. I can do it in ten or fifteen minutes. I know I can."

50

Harry and I went back to the hotel. I opened the door and saw a note on the floor that someone had slid under.

"What is it?" Harry asked as I read the handwritten message:

We have Greta. Give up the ring. Bring it to Roxburgh Court at midnight for an exchange. Or we kill her.

Spatty and Grey Man never left the city. They did what I had failed to do: find Greta. My stomach knotted, and my head spun. Greta's life—my answers—hung in the balance.

"Logan? Logan, what is it?"

I went and perched on the desk. I had to push McLean, Joy, Harry—all that—to the back of my mind. I had let them all get in my way and crowd my thinking. Greta needed me. My whole reason for being here was to avoid this situation, and here I was, right where I didn't want to be. I had let myself become distracted by Harry and her problems—and for what?

"We have to do the safe another day," I said. I handed her the note.

The look in her eyes said she wanted to be mad, to snap at me, but that little death threat in her hands kept me safe.

"We'll talk later," I said.

I knew exactly what I needed to do.

After two pawnbrokers and three jewellers, I remembered the second-hand clothing shop on St Mary's Wynd, near Darius Lanka's office. I hurried over, worried the shop would be shut. I pulled the door, and it didn't budge—a sign read: *Closed For Lunch*. The ring was there, in the window. The only thing in my way was a locked door and a sheet of glass. Both I could get past if I wanted to.

I banged on the door—it wobbled so hard I could've knocked it off its hinges. I pounded until a little old man showed his face and yelled through the glass that he was having his lunch and could I not read the sign.

"I need that ring!" He looked at where my finger pointed. "I'll pay you double if you let me buy it now."

He didn't hesitate to open the door.

After I bought it, I went back to the North British Hotel. I needed something from the kitchen.

Gabriel locked eyes with me.

"I need to speak with you," I said.

We stepped outside the service entrance. A sweet and sour stench crept under my nose from the waste bins.

"I said I was done, Bishop." Gabriel ignited a roll-up—there was a sense of déjà vu.

"What time do you finish your shift?" I asked.

"Nine, why?"

"Good. I need backup on a job tonight. I'll pay you fifty pounds."

"Ha. No thank you, Bishop." He shook his head and couldn't stop smiling. Even when he went to suck on the roll-up, the edges of his mouth remained curled.

"Greta's in danger…"

The smile turned off—the roll-up burned between his lips.

"You found her?"

"No. The bad guys have."

I showed him the note. His eyes narrowed, and his face turned a shade of red. He flicked the half-smoked roll-up on the ground and cursed before he looked at me and said: "Do you have what they want?"

"Yes. I don't doubt they'll kill her if I don't do this. But I need someone who can provide practical support."

"Handle a gun, you mean."

"Yes, I do." I removed twenty-five pounds from my wallet. "You can have this as an advance. I'll give you another twenty-five after. You in?"

"It'll do it for Greta, no' for money."

***

At 9.15pm, I met Gabriel waiting outside the North British with a roll-up between his lips and wrapped up in a tatty grey coat and a dark flat cap. I spent the rest of the day alone. When I returned to the hotel earlier, Harry was gone, and I had no clue where she was. I opened the safe and took the emerald ring out. I held both the blue ring box and the red one in my hands and contemplated what to do.

Gabriel and I sat in a dim pub on Fleshmarket Close. He ate steak pie and chips with a cup of water. He declined alcohol, saying he didn't drink anymore. I sipped a Black Label and discussed the plan.

I told him to find a place to conceal himself in or near Roxburgh Court. Stay low, stay quiet, stay in the shadows. I would enter the court from Roxburgh Close, wait under the gaslight, and face Writers' Court. I passed him my Colt under the table and talked him through how to use it. He admitted he was familiar with the make.

"Havnae fired a shot since '18," Gabriel confirmed with a heavy voice. There wasn't excitement in his eyes, just uncertainty and sorrow. He didn't enjoy the idea of being violent again.

"Let's hope you don't have to tonight. Unless the men get violent, don't pull the trigger. And if you do, wound, don't kill if you can."

"I may have a good twenty years on you, Bishop, but ah can still hit a target."

"Just don't try to be a hero for Greta, yeah?"

"Aye."

***

It was time. The gas lamp flickered in the corner of Roxburgh Close, creating long, deep shadows. The stone buildings towered above. A few amber lights were on inside some of the windows. Gabriel hid somewhere in the darkness.

The clap of shoes came from the direction of Writers' Close. A figure emerged wearing a long coat and fedora. The light spilt across his face—the Grey Man. Where Spatty or the young buck was, I didn't know. The Grey Man aimed a pistol at my belly.

"Logan Bishop." The Grey Man's voice was growly—the accent

distinctly Chicagoan.

"That's right."

"Keep still, yeah."

He came within a few feet of me. A whiff of rum and bay leaf floated over.

"You have the ring?"

"Greta first," I said.

The man put two fingers in his mouth and whistled. Spatty came into view—he lugged a woman with him. It was too dark to get a clear look at Greta's face. She didn't wear a jacket, only a blue cardigan and a dress. She had to be freezing. Her arms were pinned to her sides, bound by a rope, and her mouth gagged. Her body looked unstable, and her head bobbed like she was half-conscious. I suspected their third man was somewhere with a clear shot at me. A bead of sweat dripped down the side of my face.

"What've you done to her?" Gabriel shouted, emerging from the darkness and pointing the gun at the thugs.

The Grey Man and Spatty aimed their guns. Grey Man pointed at me and Spatty pressed his gun to Greta's head.

"Keep it cool," I said.

"Take another step, pal, and you're all dead," the Grey Man said. "The bitch is fine. It's a little sedative."

"Gabriel, listen to me. Lower the gun," I ordered.

The gun in his hand shook. He was ready to die to save Greta. But all he was going to do was get us killed.

"Gabriel!"

He broke his concentration on Spatty and Greta, and he looked at me. He nodded.

"Get it over with, Bishop," he said.

"The ring. Now," the Grey Man demanded.

"Fine, fine," I said. "Just answer me this. I assume you're the guys who trashed my flat and strangled Daniel Bishop."

"That's safe to assume." He chuckled. "Now, pally, the ring or we kill you both."

"Prove she's alive," Gabriel said, nodding at Greta.

"Your friend's got a big mouth," the Grey Man said.

"No, he's right. Prove it," I said.

The Grey Man huffed and then nodded. He walked over to Spatty and wafted smelling salts under her nose. Gaslight splashed on Greta's face as the salts startled her. I sunk inside. Greta was blonde, the woman in Spatty's arms wasn't. It was Mary Palvienė. Her boy flashed in my mind—where was he? What had happened to him?

"See, she's alive," the Grey Man said.

"That's not Greta!" Gabriel's gun went up.

The Grey Man said, "We had to get your attention somehow. We had a little look around your hotel room and found the bear and the note... course, we couldn't get into that damn safe."

"Fuck you!" I took a step forward.

"Watch it!" Spatty said as he held his gun to Mary's side. "Give us what we want."

The gun in the Grey Man's hand was cocked and aimed at my forehead.

"All right! All right!" I surrendered. "Take the ring. Just don't hurt her."

I removed the blue ring box from my left coat pocket and set it in my open palm. The Grey Man snatched it and examined the ring under the flickering gaslight. The lump of green and white glinted. He glared at me, and then a sickly grin crossed his face. The Grey Man chuckled to himself and stuffed the ring into his pocket. He started to back up, with the gun still aimed at me, until he was next to Spatty, holding Mary. She swayed and gurgled, and her knees kept bending. Spatty continued to force her to remain upright.

Mary was thrown to the pavement. A shot was fired. I dove to the ground. The gas lamp burst and then everything went dark.

"Bishop?" Gabriel called.

"I'm here." I got to my hands and knees. My eyes adjusted to the darkness, and I crawled to Mary. Gabriel was at my side.

"I'm sorry! I bloody blew it all."

"Don't beat yourself up. Help me."

We untied Mary's arms and removed the gag. Her body trembled, and her hands and face were cold as ice. I pushed her hair out of her face. She groaned like a child who didn't want to be woken up. But she was alive—that's what mattered to me.

"Mary, can you hear me?" I tried to get her eyes to focus on me, but they rolled, and her head continued to bob. She started to mumble. "Mary? Mary?"

"You know this lassie?" Gabriel asked.

"I do. Hold her up."

Gabriel held her with his meaty hands. I got a bottle of Winslow's and poured some down her throat. It roused her and brought her back to life. Despite the darkness, I could see her eyes had opened.

Gabriel said: "Bishop, where is Greta?"

"No idea. But first things first, we need to get Mary home now, and make sure her boy is safe."

51

Mary sat between Gabriel and me in a cab. The driver didn't seem to care that two men had a doped-up woman with them. She rested on my shoulder and continued to fall in and out of consciousness.

"They never had Greta?" Gabriel whispers.

"No."

"Now they've got that ring."

"They don't."

"How d'you figure that?"

"Because I gave them a decoy ring. The actual ring is still in my hotel room. I swapped the boxes and gave them a glass ring that looked similar."

"Fuckin' hell, if you've done that it might piss them off enough tae kill you. Christ, Bishop."

"I'm not done with them, Gabriel. They'll regret hurting Mary… and if they've harmed her children, I'll gut them all."

When we arrived, Gabriel and I led Mary to the front door. I told Gabriel to hold her while I picked the lock and got us inside. I then ran in, leaving her with Gabriel.

"Son? Son, where are you?" I called.

I swung the bedroom door open. My heart stopped. The boy was in bed, sound asleep. It didn't make sense—they'd had Mary for hours.

"Bishop!" Gabriel shouted.

Mary rested on the sofa in the lounge, and Gabriel stood with a round-faced old woman with grey hair. "This is," Gabriel stopped, "what was your name?"

"Jane Buchan, from next door."

"Tell Bishop what you told me."

"Well, must have been about eleven thirty yesterday morn' when this man came poundin' on the door. Said the foreign lass what stayed here was going tae the hospital an' the boy were left alone. He didn't even wait for me to come over. I found the wee lad in the doorway. Then you two come rushin' in here with Mary."

"Thank you for looking after him," I said.

"Aye," Gabriel added.

Mary began to stir on the sofa. Her eyes opened, and she began to recognise our faces. She tried to jump up—whatever they doped her with had done a number on her. I knelt beside her. She muttered about her son.

"He's safe, Mary. He's safe." Her face contorted, and she began to cry. "I'll take you somewhere safe, Mary." I turned to Gabriel. "We need to pack their things."

***

I beat on Mrs Mears's door for ten minutes before a light came on, and she answered. She wore a pink robe and blue nightcap.

"What the devil is this now? Comin' at all inappropriate hours. Is it Henrikas again?" She looked at Mary and the kids behind me.

"No, it's not him. I'm sorry, Mrs Mears. Mary and her son need a place to stay for a while. Mary was dragged into something that had nothing to do with her. Stuff that concerns Greta. Someone abducted her tonight. She needs to be somewhere safe. Here." I took what was left of Edwin Walter's money and handed it to Mrs Mears.

"Youse must be freezing. Let's get inside," she said to Mary and her son. I nodded at her, and she smiled.

We helped Mary settle into a room. Her arrival meant another tenant needed to bunk with someone else so Mary and her son could use the space.

Mrs Mears pulled me out into the hall after bringing in fresh bedsheets. "Will that man be stayin' with her?" Mrs Mears asked with a long face.

"Gabriel? No."

"Aye. Okay."

Gabriel stuck his head out: "Mary wants tae see you, Bishop."

I went to her room. The experience had shocked her. I hoped she would recover from what happened.

I sat next to Mary on her bed. Gabriel stood over us. Mary's eyes were red and puffy, and she looked beyond tired.

"I am so sorry about all this," I said. "None of this should've happened to you."

BAD BLOOD

She nodded and wiped her nose with a hanky.

"Can you tell me what happened?" I asked.

"They say I am Greta," Mary started. "I say I not her, that I am Mary." She sniffed. "They want a ring. I do not have it, but they no believe me. They take me… in a car to somewhere…" She started to cry. "I tell then about you… your hotel… Forgive me."

I wrapped Mary in my arms and held her tight.

"No, you're fine. You're fine. You did nothing wrong."

I released her and wiped the tears from her face. She said: "Will they find me here? My boy!"

"No, they won't," I assured. I wrapped my arm around her, and she melted into me. "It's okay. You're both safe." Mary nodded. "Where'd they take you?"

"My eyes uh covered with cloth. But I hear boats. Very loud doors."

"A warehouse? Somewhere near the docks?" Gabriel asked. "No way tae know where though."

"It cold and smell like oil," Mary said.

I glanced at Gabriel, and our eyes said that was a hopeless lead.

"Do you remember anything else?" I asked.

Mary thought for a moment with watery eyes. "A name."

"What?" I pushed.

"Colman's Lodge."

"Colman's?" Gabriel said. "That's in Canongate."

I stood up. "Are you sure?"

"Aye. It's in the Speaking House, next tae a pub me and the lads drink in sometimes. There's cheap rooms tae rent above it."

"We need to get over there." I turned to Mary. "I promise you, when I find them, I'll make them pay for what they've done to you and your kids."

"You sure this is a good idea?" Gabriel asked.

"I've been avoiding these guys for too long."

Mary stood up. "Please be safe, Mr Bishop. If I don't see you," she hugged me and pecked me on the cheek, "thank you."

***

It was 6am when Gabriel and I arrived at Colman's Lodge. The

LUKE DECKARD

building looked barely habitable. Chipped plaster exposed shoddy brickwork, and the roof tiles were bowed and dislodged.

The inside was a dive. Gabriel said the building was up for sale and figured the site would be demolished. At the top of the stairs, he pointed to a door. "The porter. He'll know if they're here." Gabriel knocked.

A chubby man in his early forties and fully dressed with bright, wide-awake eyes opened the door to us.

"What the devil? What are ye doin here, Gabe?"

"I'm sorry, Chuck," Gabriel said. "My friend here is looking for some Americans. We think they're stayin' here."

"Americans? Yeah, we have three of them here. Sharing a room," Chuck, the porter, said, pointing his eyes up the next floor. "No' too friendly a bunch, I must say."

"You got a key to the room?" I asked.

Chuck's eyes bounced between Gabriel and me. "They're bad people, Chuck," Gabriel said.

"I don't want no trouble," Chuck said.

"Too late for that," I said. "The key?"

"Now, wait a moment, do I need tae get the police?"

"Oh, forget this…" I said.

I went upstairs. The porter shouted 'oi' after me. Gabriel followed up behind. My Colt was in my hand. I tried the door handle—it wasn't locked. I swung it open. The room was empty.

Chuck rushed up behind Gabriel and me and looked in. "They were up an' down the stairs around one this morning, sounded like a herd a coos."

"Cause they're gone," I said. I pointed my gun at the bed. The room key was left.

Gabriel and I went outside.

"Thanks for your help," I said.

He nodded and looked sad to disappoint us.

"I wanted them," I said, "I wanted to hurt them for hurting Mary."

"You might still get the chance, Bishop, when they realise you duped them with a fake ring. Or hell, you never know, Bishop, maybe whoever they're takin' that ring back tae will kill them for the muck-up."

"Maybe."

"Bishop, I gotta go," Gabriel said. "I got work in a few hours."

"Thanks for the help," I said.

"Some night," he replied.

I shrugged.

"You never left the war, did you, laddie?"

I shook my head.

"Well, take care of yourself. I'll see you around, huh?"

"Yeah."

I went back to the hotel. It was after 7am, and I was beat. The light was on in the room, and a fashion magazine lay on the bed. The stench of Woodbines lingered in the hotel room. Two butts were in the ashtray—Harry had finished off Petras's cigarettes. Her suitcases and bags weren't there—she was gone, and a note had been propped on the desk.

Logan,

I knew if I discussed this with you, you would have stopped me. Convinced me that you can fix everything, but I don't believe you can. No one can. I'm scared to death of Inspector Joy; I don't trust that even if we do find what he wants, he will return the photograph to me. And the truth is, I feel I need to get away from you. I don't feel safe with you. Too much danger follows you.

I won't tell you where I'm going because I don't want you or anyone else to find me. My life here is over. If I were to stay, it would be an existence of constant fear of Joy and what he might do to me. We cannot stop him or control him. Go back to London, go back to America, just get far away from here and from Joy.

Harry

52

I don't know why, but I threw the note down and ran to Waverley Station.

Princes Street was starting to get busy with morning traffic. I dodged and sidestepped people in my way. She couldn't have been gone long—the stink of cigarettes and perfume was too fresh. I wanted to stop her.

At Waverley Station, I scanned departure times. I had no idea where she would go. I darted into the ticket hall and I ran around the ticket office, but she wasn't there. One of the tellers was free, and I asked him if he'd seen a woman with red hair, maybe wearing a leopard-print coat.

"Yes, I served her," he said. "Very pretty lassie."

"What train did she take?"

"Erm, the 7.25 tae Manchester."

I looked at the clock on the wall—it was 7.23.

"What platform?"

"Th-thirteen," he said. "Oi! Ye need a ticket!"

I hustled through the station, following the platform numbers to thirteen.

I was too late. The train was out of the station when I ran onto the platform.

Harry was gone.

It felt strange to me, Harry leaving like that. Maybe it was all too much for her—Edwin's death, Fran scrapping all her work, Joy's threats, my condemnation. As the back of the train disappeared, I resigned myself to her wishes. I'd let her go, let her run. The problem was that Joy was still going to expose Harry and me. She could run, but I couldn't. I had to beat Joy—I wasn't ready for my secrets to come out. And if I didn't get Edwin's docs, they would. Even if Harry never found out, I wanted to get that photograph back and burn it if I could.

Walking back through the station, I dug into my pocket and grabbed the Winslow's—I hesitated before I took a drink.

BAD BLOOD

McLean's warning rang in my mind. I have control, I thought, and drank it.

Putting the bottle in my pocket, I realised I had Greta's photograph in my wallet. I took it first to the ticket office. No one there recognised her. Next, I went to the different platforms, asking inspectors, guards and conductors. No one remembered Greta. I sat on a bench watching travellers go this way and that, feeling hopeless. The gangsters might be gone, Greta might be safe from them, but I still had questions that needed answering. I didn't want to give up on my search for her or Petras, my half-brother.

I was tired and hungry, and the morning was half-spent. I went to a café on Princes Street and gobbled up bacon, eggs, beans, and a slice of dry toast. I chased it with coffee and a glass of orange juice. Afterwards, my eyes were heavy. I told myself I would break into Fran Walter's house tonight and see what was in the safe. I just hoped it was what I needed to get Joy off my back. Once that was taken care of, I would go back to Davies Colliery to find Liepsnelė and hopefully Petras and Greta.

I made my way towards the hotel. Ahead, a man walked directly towards me, intentionally blocking my way. I stopped as he approached me, the hairs on my neck standing. I glanced over my shoulder, and a man came up behind me.

"Was it Lady Clark or Inspector Joy who sent you?" I asked.

The man didn't reply. The one behind me put his arm around me and pressed a blade into my side. The one in front took my Colt and hid it in his coat.

A car screeched up next to us, and the door opened. The blade pressed harder into me—its sharp tip stung through my clothes. "Get in," I was told, and I did.

53

Inside the car, the penny dropped. I sat in the back, between the guy with the blade and Spatty. I buckled when his fist plunged into my gut. Crippled and out of breath, the two men rummaged through my pockets. My wallet, ID, pocket knife, lighter, and hotel room key were taken.

Spatty said to Grey Man, who sat in the front: "It ain't here, boss."

"Fellas, let's talk?" I said through coughs.

Another fist smashed into my gut.

"Don't say another fucking word, Bishop."

We pulled into a dark warehouse down by the docks. I was yanked out and thrown in front of the car, the headlights beaming in my face.

"Sit down," the man in grey snarled.

A wooden chair was placed behind me. Five men formed a half-circle around me. Spatty, Grey Man, the young buck, and the two new faces who stopped me on the street. A couple of hired hands I assumed. The headlights behind them made it hard to see their faces.

A fist swiped my face—I tasted blood in my mouth and felt it drain from my nose. My body was hot and cold.

"We gave you a chance to give us the ring, Bishop," Grey Man said, "and you gave us this fake shit?" The decoy ring was shoved in my face. "Cheap glass!" He pressed the ring deep into my cheek, then scraped it down, cutting my face. He threw it at me, and it pinged when it hit the ground.

"Now, where's the real deal, Bishop?"

"I don't have it!" I said.

Grey Man said, "Do it."

A bucket of water was in front of me, and the two men who'd abducted me threw me onto the floor—pain shot through my knees. They plunged my head into the water and held me down. I jerked and twisted, desperate for air. The cut on my face seared as saltwater got into it. My chest ached, and my lungs strained—I gulped in saltwater. It burnt my eyes and sinuses.

I was pulled out, and spat up water. I hacked and sucked in the air.

"Where've you got it?" Grey Man asked.

"What's it worth to you?" I said.

"What's your life worth to you?" I heard as my head went back into the salty water. I tried to inhale before they pushed me down; I didn't get enough air. A firm hand pressed down on me—my head pounded, and I jostled and thrashed, starved for air. It wasn't coming. I was growing weak. I started to fade into blackness.

I was pulled back out. My vision was blurry. My head spun.

A smack whipped my face to the right and jolted me.

Grey Man grabbed my face and made me look him in the eyes. He pressed a gun to my temple.

The gun remained pressed there, and Spatty took my hand and pried my fingers open. I tried to fight but had little strength. The cold barrel against my head said resistance was futile.

Spatty held cold metal pliers. He gripped my index fingernail with them.

"This is for fucking with us, Bishop," Spatty said.

"No don't! Don't! DON'T! Gah!" The nail was slowly ripped clean off, taking flesh with it. I was dizzy with pain, and my finger throbbed. "Jesus Christ! Are you fucking mad?" They didn't stop there. Spatty started on my second finger—I bellowed in pain. The nail didn't want to give as easily as the first. I begged him to stop as he jerked my nail back little by little. My face scrunched, and I wailed. Tears streamed down my cheeks. I bit so hard on my lower lip that I drew blood. Finally, the nail was gone. The pliers gripped my third nail. I pleaded: "Stop. Stop! For fuck sake, stop! God, no! NO! NO!" My third nail was ripped off. "You sick motherfuckers!" My bloody fingers felt like they were on fire. Each pulse in my fingers was amplified. The man in grey grabbed my bloody fingertips and squeezed as hard as he could. I gritted my teeth and growled.

"Where's the ring?" he demanded.

"If I give it to you, will you leave Greta alone?" I begged.

Spatty slapped me in the face, and the Grey Man laughed and said: "Give us the ring and we won't kill her when we find her."

Spatty grabbed my nostril with the pliers and squeezed.

"It's in my fucking hotel!" My panicked voice bounced off the walls.

He let go.

"It's in the room safe," I said, exhausted and in pain. And I gave up the code.

I was struck over the head, and the world went black, and I fell into a warm dream...

I awoke, standing in the middle of a field. The grass came up to my shins. The sun was bright and warm, and the sky was the most vivid blue I had ever seen. To my right were four beat-up armchairs and a rickety table. I began to cry. Tim was sitting with a bottle of wine in one hand and a tin cup in the other. He wore civilian clothes: a cream shirt unbuttoned at the top, tan slacks, and black shoes.

I felt calm and at peace—a peace I hadn't felt since I was a boy, before a life of nastiness. All my pain was gone, and my body felt light. A gentle breeze washed over me.

Tim saw me. He leapt from his chair and ran over, leaving the wine and tin cup on the ground.

"Logan!"

We embraced.

"Why are you crying, my friend?" he asked me.

"Are you really here?" I said.

"Of course I am, pally!" He slapped my arm. "We're all here."

"All?"

Tim just smiled.

"I'm so sorry, Tim," I said. "I'm sorry I couldn't save you."

"Hey, Logan, don't. You beat yourself up too much. I'm at peace."

"Is this heaven?"

"If it is, what the hell are you doing here?"

We laughed.

BAD BLOOD

"Seriously, though, what I mean is... is this it? Am I... are we..."
"Buddy," Tim said, "we're just here for a moment."
"Moment?" I stepped back.
"There are people who need you right now."
"Tim, man, I'm done. I want to be done. I'm so tired of walking in the darkness. I want to stay with you."
"Like I said, we're all here... and we're waiting." He smiled assuredly like he had some sort of divine knowledge. "What I want you to know, man, is you're forgiven. You can let me go."
"Let you go?"
He smiled and put a hand on my shoulder.
"Logan, you're a good man, okay? The best damn guy I ever knew."
"But I..."
"You didn't fail me. You never did. And there are others who still need you. Save them for me."
We hugged. It was firm and warm. Tears ran down my smiling face.
"I gotta go, buddy, but I'm glad we had this moment."
"No. Tim, wait."
"Goodbye, Logan."

I jolted awake. I was on the cold and wet cement floor. The warm dream had faded, and my body shook. As I came to I could hear Tim's voice say: *'you're a good man.'*

Then a man's voice said: "I'm going to take a piss. Keep an eye on him."

Another man replied: "Yeah, okay."

My head throbbed, and my hand stung. My fingers were sticky with blood. Each movement of them was unbearable. The rope dug into my wrists. As I came to, I noticed the car was gone. I must've been out for five or ten minutes.

A shaft of daylight spilt in from an opening door, and someone went outside.

My eyes adjusted to the darkness—I spotted the bucket of water a few feet away.

"Keep still!" I was ordered.

"Who are you guys?" I asked, moving my head to find the man. He tutted a laugh.

"Just tell me what he did?" I asked. "What did Daniel Bishop do? That's what this is about, right? What's the story with him and that emerald ring?"

The man moved around from behind me and stood next to the bucket of water. It was Spatty. I pushed myself to sit upright and looked up at him. His square jaw chewed, like a grazing cow, on a piece of gum, and he grinned.

"Danny and that ring." He shook his head. "He took it from someone he shouldn't."

"Who?" I asked.

"No one you'll know. You've been outta the Chicago game a long time. One of your papa's pals ratted him out—said he was goin' to London for the ring. Implied he might not come back. Well, you don't steal from us and get away with it."

"You weren't going after Greta for the ring?" I said. "You just wanted to hurt my dad by hurting her. You figured I had the ring and that I would lead you to her?"

"That's right." Spatty stepped closer. "We came to collect... and make a point. Your dad got rough in the hotel room... wouldn't answer my questions... well, you know what happened next."

I pictured Spatty and his gang rushing Dad's hotel room. A towel stuffed in his mouth. Ripping off his fingernails as they did to me. Bashing his knee. Strangling him for information until they thought he was dead. Now he was dead, and now they'd got the ring—and still, I had no Greta, but she *was* alive.

Spatty started to chuckle to himself.

I moved and swiped his feet out from under him.

He fell on his side—something in his body cracked.

I got to my feet and clubbed my tied hands, and hit Spatty in the face as he rose, knocking him back. I slammed my foot into his side until I felt ribs break, and then I dragged him to the bucket of water and plunged his head in.

Water bubbled as he writhed. I growled as the saltwater set my bloody fingertips alight with burning pain. I pushed through it and forced him down—my forearms shook. I held him under until he stopped moving.

Just then, the door opened.

"What the hell's going on?" another American voice called. The piss-taker was back. He saw me standing over his dead friend and went for his gun. I reached for my Colt in Spatty's jacket and dropped to the floor. The piss-taker fired twice. One hit Spatty, the other hit the bucket of water, making it bleed onto the floor. I fired one shot—the piss-taker fell dead.

Inside Spatty's coat pockets were my things: wallet, ID, and pocket knife. I cut the rope and freed my hands.

A car engine caught my attention. I hid in the dark as it pulled into the warehouse. The man in grey shouted as he jumped out: "Where the fuck is Bishop? What the hell's happened here?"

I fired two shots, killing the other two and leaving the man in grey.

"Throw your gun and get on your knees," I shouted.

He looked around, unable to see me. I fired a shot. He ducked.

He obeyed, and I approached.

"You make any sudden moves, you're dead."

"I ain't moving, Bishop."

I came up behind him and put my Colt in the back of his head.

"Tell whoever it is you work for this is over. You fuck with anyone I know again, it'll be the last thing you do."

"Fuck you, Bishop."

"Maybe I didn't make myself clear."

I held the gun an inch from the left side of his face and fired it, burning his skin and, likely, deafening him. I left him wailing on the floor, surrounded by his dead friends.

I jumped in the car and took it back to New Town, where I ditched it somewhere on George Street. I went to the drug store, bought medication and bandages, and returned to my hotel.

54

It was early afternoon when I returned to the Palace Hotel. I hid my ruined hand inside my pocket. I couldn't hide my bruised and cut face and ruffled hair. I got a few odd looks. I had to ask the clerk for a new room key since I'd lost mine. She said it would cost me, and I said I didn't give a damn. I went to my room, cleaned myself up, packed my things, returned downstairs thirty minutes later, and checked out. Then I went to the Caledonian Hotel and checked in. I was tired and in pain, I didn't remember anything once I got to the new room.

I woke at around seven—my head was groggy, and I had the shakes. I had a fever, but I ignored it the best I could and downed painkillers and Winslow's.

I was in a comfortable bed. It was twice the size and twice the price of the one in the Palace. I didn't care, though. No one was likely to find me here. Not Joy nor the Grey Man—if they had the balls to come at me again.

Petras's wallet was on the floor and was open. I had rummaged through it in my tired state. I leaned over the side of the bed and picked it up. There was a flap I had missed when at Mary Palvienė's house. It was a hidden compartment. I opened it and out fell a picture. The black and white image was a face I recognised: Robin Rankin, Donald Yonge's secretary at the colliery. On the back, *Liepsnelė* was written.

"Fuck."

Robin and Liepsnelė were the same person.

I misunderstood Mary. Liepsnelė, a girlfriend of Petras's, a bird, a redbreast: it's a damn robin. That's why Robin was so prickly when Yonge had her take me to Petras's lodgings. It explains why she was pale as a ghost when I told her why I was there.

I rummaged further into the wallet, and in the same compartment, I found a folded note written in Lithuanian.

Atsiprašau, kad nepaaiškinau prieš išvykdamas. Pažadu

BAD BLOOD

pasakoti kiekvieną detalę, kai čia pateksite. Viskas įvyko per greitai, ir man reikėjo būti slaptai ir saugiai. Tikiuosi, jūs nesijaučiate, kad jus apleidau. Aš niekada to nedaryčiau.

Petras, miestas jaudina, o mes turime namą sau. Tai puiki vieta mums pradėti iš naujo. Prašome atvykti. Mes galime jums gauti geresnį, saugesnį darbą.

Su meile, Motina.

I hadn't a clue what it said. I showered and shaved. My fingers hurt like hell, and my body was sore. My thoughts bounced from Harry to Petras on the run, to Liepsnelė/Robin, and what nasty things Dad said in the letters to Greta. I needed to return to Davies Colliery and speak to Robin—she would know how to reach Petras. But Joy came to the forefront of my mind. His threats. I had one more full day to get Edwin's documents before he smeared Harry and me.

What I needed to do was speak to McLean without Joy knowing. For him and I to work together against Joy.

I made my way up Lothian Road to the phone booth—a couple of squares of Cadbury's melted in my mouth.

I scanned the directory and then used the payphone.

"DCI McLean speaking."

"This is Bishop."

"Bishop, I'm sitting down to dinner with my family." He sounded agitated. "This better be important."

"We need to talk, but not at the station and not over the phone," I said down the line. "I have the information I think you want."

"What do you have for me, Bishop?" he whispered anxiously.

"A strong lead on the document, but Joy is gunning for them too."

McLean went silent. Crackles filled the void. He huffed over the line.

"Meet me on the castle esplanade at 9pm, Bishop."

"I'll be there," I said. "And McLean, you're compromised. Don't tell anyone where you're going or what you're doing. Got it?"

"Fine."

The line went dead.

***

At 9pm, I waited on the windy esplanade. It was deserted and eerie. From this height, the trams and cars below looked like miniatures in a toy store window. I wondered how Harry was doing and if I'd ever see her again. I didn't think I would, but I never say never.

McLean marched towards me.

"What happened to your hand?" McLean eyed my wrapped fingers.

"Occupational hazard," I said. "Were you followed?"

"No. Now, what's all this about, Bishop? How am I compromised, and what's this about Joy?"

"Joy wants Edwin Walter's materials. He tried to blackmail Harry and me to get them. I'm risking everything by telling you—he warned me not to. Harry's been spooked, and she's left the city."

McLean's chewing came to a halt. "What's he got on you?"

"Somehow, he knows about my blue ticket, and he'll smear my reputation with it if I don't do what he wants. He's a monster that needs to be stopped, McLean."

"How'd you get a blue ticket?" he asked.

"It doesn't matter—what matters is that he knows, and I don't want it coming out. What the record says versus what really happened are two different things. But the official record could ruin me. Do you know how many boys with blue tickets have difficulty getting work? Lots. It's why I never went back to the States. The Pinkertons wouldn't take me back. If it comes out here, it could destroy what I've built. I can't have that. Not now. It's all I have."

McLean put his hand on my shoulder. "We'll make sure that doesn't happen. We just need to get the documents before Joy can." He paused. "What did he have on Miss Napier, by the way?"

"A smutty image of Harry. He threatened to leak them and humiliate her. And Joy said if we talk, he'll leak everything."

"Christ in the tomb. The little git."

"The expression is Christ on a cross, but yeah."

McLean did a 360 with his head down, thinking before he stopped, putting his back to New Town.

"There's more you're not saying, Bishop."

I was hesitant, but then I said: "I think Joy might've killed Edwin Walter."

"What?"

"I got a good hunch."

"I need more than a hunch, Bishop."

"Well, I got something on him."

McLean straightened his shoulders. "What?" He folded his lips in and spiked his beard.

"Fran Walter and Inspector Joy are involved romantically. They were at a party the night of the murder. A witness saw them in each other's arms. The two argued about Edwin, and Joy stormed out not long before Edwin was killed."

"Joy and Fran are together?"

"I also took the page from the guest book. Both signed it. It puts him in the area and sounds like he had the motive."

"Christ's sake," McLean shook his head. Then Edwin must have known, and Joy wanted it covered up. He goes to argue with Edwin, things get heated, and he kills him. I'm glad you brought this to me. Once we get those documents, I'll make sure Joy can't do you or anyone else more harm. Where are they?"

"There's a safe in Edwin Walter's office… Harry didn't know about it. And Fran and Joy have been looking. They've not found it."

"His office was checked…" McLean protested.

"It's built into the wall. Very well hidden. I'm not surprised you missed it."

"How'd you find it?"

"I went looking for it. But unless you're good at picking locks, you'll need me."

"You can pick it?"

"Absolutely."

"Let's go."

55

Yellow, warm light spilt from the house when Fran Walter opened the door to McLean and me. She wore casual tan trousers, a white blouse, and a green cardigan. There was a look of surprise followed by a flash of worry on her face. She then tried to soften her eyes and smiled at us.

"Mr McLean, Mr Bishop, what's this?" she asked and pulled the door to a bit.

"Mrs Walter, our apologies for the late hour, but may we come inside?" McLean asked.

Her face flushed. "Is this about Edwin?" Her voice cracked.

"Let's talk inside," said McLean.

She stepped aside, and we entered.

Fran sat on the sofa in the pastel-blue lounge, and McLean and I put ourselves in the two armchairs facing her. The fireplace roared.

I laid the facts before her: a witness caught her and Joy in each other's arms and overheard them fight about Edwin. Then Joy stormed out. I produced the guest book page with their signatures.

"Is that all?" Mrs Walter said—a smile formed on her face. "Edwin and I were open about our... other partners. We just didn't parade them around in public."

"He knew?" I pushed.

"Of course." She laughed.

"Harry didn't."

"Why would I tell her? Is this why you're here? I, well, I thought you finally had done your job, Mr McLean and caught the man who killed my husband."

"If you will," McLean stated, "I have some questions. Why were you and Inspector Joy arguing?"

"David knew I was upset with Edwin that night. I had found a letter from Edwin's solicitor—he had purchased a flat and put it in Harriet's name. I confronted Edwin about it and told him to stop wasting money on his whore. It's one thing to take her on trips and buy her clothes and jewellery. I never imagined Edwin would buy her a house."

"What made Joy storm out?" I asked.

She looked embarrassed. "David always wanted me to leave Edwin—in the same way Harriet wanted Edwin to leave me—so that we could be together publicly. Neither Edwin nor I cared to put ourselves through that sort of scandal. David said to choose between him or Edwin, and I refused. So he stormed out."

"Do you know where he went?" McLean asked.

She shrugged. "I can't say where he went after, and I didn't see him until he and you, Mr McLean, arrived at the house after Harriet found Edwin's body."

"Mrs Walter, why didn't you tell me about this that night?"

"It was irrelevant."

"Irrelevant?" I muttered. Fran gave me a side-eyed look.

"Why are you here, Mr Bishop?" she snapped.

"Because I got pulled into this, and I'm going to finish it."

"Meaning what?"

"Mrs Walter, I need to look inside your husband's office," McLean said. "Do I have your permission, or must I procure a warrant?"

Mrs Walter sat still. She would've been a dream model for a painter. A few lines formed around her mouth and brow, belying the stoic front.

"Mrs Walter," McLean pushed.

"Go on."

McLean asked her to wait out in the lounge, and we went inside.

I went behind the desk and whipped out my pocket knife. McLean watched as I pried open the secret door and revealed the safe.

"My God," he whispered.

I gripped the dial with my uninjured hand and started to twist it. My bare fingertips rested against the metal door. I felt each vibration from the clicks.

"How's it coming, Bishop?"

"Better if you'd be quiet," I said.

McLean lingered behind me, his heavy breathing strangled my concentration.

"McLean, stop huffing like an aroused ox!"

"Sorry." He stepped back. "She's awfully quiet."

"Yeah? Go check on her then. Make sure she's not calling Joy."

He peered into the lounge. "Damn. Shout when you open the safe."

"Yeah, yeah. Now shush."

I got my concentration back. The last number in the combination came first. Next, I worked my way through two more numbers.

Footsteps thudded through the house.

A moment later, I got the final number. I spun the dial, entering the combination code—*click*. The door swung open, and inside was a thick yellow folder sealed with string. I took it out and laid it on Edwin's desk.

I heard McLean going upstairs, calling for Fran. She didn't respond. I thought about calling him in, but I wanted to know what was in there. What did Edwin have on Joy?

I leafed through the alphabetised folder. I jumped to J—it didn't make sense. There wasn't a file for Joy. I flipped back and forth, thinking I'd missed it. No, there wasn't a file on him in here. So, where was it? Misplaced? Stolen? Incorrectly categorised?

I started to flip through.

There were discarded newspaper clippings from gossip columns, a love letter from a Scott Barker to another man, Chris Jones, and a woman's birth certificate.

My hands felt dirty the deeper I went.

E, F, G—Nothing.

…K, L—

"Mrs Walter? Who is that you're talking to?" McLean roared. His thick fists pounded on a door. "Mrs Walter. Mrs Walter! Open up."

My blood turned to ice. There was a file labelled *McLean, F.*

56

My palms sweated. Inside was a card for 15b Leith Street, and attached was a partially charred photograph. I removed the half-burnt image. McLean was in profile. His body was halfway seared from fire damage. Also in view was a naked woman on the bed. Her hands were bound, and her mouth was gagged. Her face was aimed at the camera. She squinted in pain as McLean's hand smashed her face down into the bed.

My heart was racing. I looked at the pained woman's face and felt sick. This wasn't a woman; it was a girl, maybe twelve or thirteen.

"Bishop?"

The voice sent a jolt of fear through me.

McLean was in the doorway. His eyes were wide and fiery. Three deep and bloody scratch marks went down the right side of his face, from just above his eye down to his beard. Mrs Walter had dragged her nails across his pre-existing scar. Blood soaked into his beard.

"You son of a bitch," I said.

McLean, mad as hell, charged.

I couldn't get my Colt out before he was on me. His thick hands went for my throat. I smashed my heel on his foot and pushed him off. McLean picked up an ashtray from the desk and threw it at me. It hit me in the head, and ash covered me. I stumbled back. My head ached. Ash was in my eyes. He rugby-tackled me into the wall.

His hands wrapped around my neck and squeezed. I punched him in the ribs and gagged, desperate to breathe. He wasn't letting up. He headbutted me, and I saw stars. I was going to die. With what little consciousness I had left, I reached down and grabbed his balls and crushed them. He yelped, released me, and leapt back.

McLean was bent over, recovering. I held myself up on the wall, coughing.

I went for the document, and he rushed me again. I grabbed him by the lapels and swiped his leg. He stumbled back and fell over one of the antler chairs.

He screamed. There was a tear, a wet crunch, and a gulp.

One of the antler points pierced through his leg, blood dripped onto the floor, and he groaned and wagged his head, delirious with pain.

I grabbed the image of McLean from under the desk and reached for the file. Another file with the name Yonge, D, was sticking out of the folder. Donald Yonge, from the coal mine?

McLean groaned and gurgled on the floor. I felt no remorse, leaving him impaled on the chair, his trouser leg soaked with blood, while I looked in the file. I found a photograph of Donald Yonge and a dark-haired man I didn't recognise. The two were standing outside—it was at the coal mine. The framing was close, showing them from head to torso. Yonge, who was half in profile, sucked on a pipe. I spotted a chain laced with gems which hung from Yonge's waistcoat. The other man was thin with sunken cheeks, had a thick moustache and wore a straw hat. On the back of the image, I read the names Donald Yonge and Tommy Clackman, the latter being the man Petras supposedly murdered.

The file had pages from a coal-weight ledger with dates. Each page highlighted discrepancies in the weight logged and the miner's payment. Sign-offs from Clackman and Yonge. Among the examples highlighted, many of them were of Peter Mathew's reduced income due to 'rock' in the cart. There were figures showing how much Yonge was pocking by skimming wages.

Someone from the mine had leaked information to Edwin Walter. Was it Petras? Could that be why Clackman went to Petras's that night... he confronted him?

My mind went back to Petras's clothes. The bloodstains. Who else was in the room with Petras and Clackman? I was none the wiser yet.

"N'aww." McLean groaned and rocked his head back and forth—he dipped in and out of consciousness.

My mind flashed to McLean, showing Mrs Walter and me a broken gold chain with red gems found in Edwin's hand. I stared at the picture of Yonge and Clackman, the chain Yonge wore—it was the same.

I got that wrong.

It wasn't Joy. Joy must've suspected McLean. That's why he wanted the documents. Then it hit me. Donald Yonge murdered Edwin Walter. I recalled Yonge saying he was going into Edinburgh when I paid a visit to the mine. I needed to confirm he was in town the night of the murder.

I took Yonge's file and shoved it into my coat pocket.

I squatted next to McLean and smacked his sweaty, sticky face. The three cuts on his face had started to congeal. His head wobbled, and his eyes shot open. He moved his body and gritted his teeth from the pain. A stink of blood and shit hung around him.

"Let's have it," I ordered. "Edwin had nothing on Joy, did he? It was you."

"I need help..." he said, eyes rolling.

I grabbed his face and jerked it to look at me. I squeezed his jaw—his beard felt scratchy and wet.

"I don't give a shit what you need. Joy suspected, didn't he? That's why he wanted this shit—you wanted to beat him to it. That's why you asked me to press Harry for it secretly." McLean stared at me. I let go of his face and grabbed his impaled leg. He howled.

"Christ, yes, yes, you're right! Oh Jesus, stop." I let go. "You're a cunt, Bishop."

"I'd rather be a cunt than a child fucker."

I smashed my fist into his face and broke his nose.

I stood and removed the Colt, and aimed it at him. McLean squirmed and stared at the gun, blood oozing from his nose—mixing with the sweat and slobber in his beard.

His skin was pale, almost grey. "Bishop... wait, wait, wait... don't. Come on... now..."

On the other hand, I held up the image of him and the girl.

"Did she beg? Did she plead?" He crushed his eyes shut and shook his head. "Look at her!"

He peeled his eyes open and moved them to the image. He cried unrepentant tears.

My grip tightened on the Colt.

"Kill me, you coward!" he shouted.

My grip firmed around the handle of the gun, and my finger trembled. I moved it closer to the trigger. Bloodlust raged through me. He needed to pay for what he'd done. I could be his judge, jury, and executioner. I stared into McLean's wild and frantic eyes.

"No." I put the gun away. "There's no justice in a bullet."

I started for the door.

"Is that it, Bishop? You think you can turn me in and walk away from all this?"

I ignored him and kept walking; otherwise, the police would've found a corpse.

Standing in the lounge was Fran Walter. Her hair was a mess, and her eyes were red.

"What's happened?" she asked, keeping her distance from me.

"He's in there—he won't hurt you. Did you call the police?"

She nodded. I glanced at a photograph on the sideboard. It was Fran when she was younger. Standing next to her was a much younger Edwin and also Donald Yonge.

"That's Donald Yonge; he manages a colliery," I said. "How do you know him?"

"Don?" Fran Walter was taken aback by the question. She couldn't think why I was asking. "Don's my cousin."

"When did you see him last?" I asked.

"What an odd question."

"Please."

Fran thought. "The night at the Wright's party."

***

After McLean was taken away, I sat in the dining room, where Joy first interviewed me. The folders were open, and Joy looked through McLean's with disgust.

"That's what you wanted, isn't it?" I said.

Joy's V's sharpened. "Aye."

"Then we're even?"

BAD BLOOD

It was close to midnight and the police were walking through the house. Fran Walter was lingering in the corridors.

Joy looked at me. "Let's step outside, Bishop."

We stepped out front into the night, and he walked me around the corner, out of sight. It was quiet. Most of the houses were dark. Smoke rose from the chimneys. We stood under a glowing street lamp. It was snowing again.

Before Joy spoke, I said: "Look pal, I don't really care how you sort this mess. I don't care what you make public or not. All I want is the image of Harry and your word that you'll keep your mouth shut about my service record. But I swear to God, if you don't stop, neither will I."

Joy pursed his lips and deepened the V's on his face.

His right eye twitched.

"You are a bastard, aren't you?" he said.

"Maybe I am," I admitted.

We stared at each other for an uncomfortable few seconds. We understood each other for a moment, standing there in the falling snow.

Joy reached into his pocket and withdrew the photograph of Edwin, Harry, and the other woman. He handed it to me, and I took my lighter out and lit it up. When the fire had a good hold, I let it fall to the ground. It continued to burn, boil, pop, and curl until it was gone.

I looked at Joy and said, "I know who killed Edwin."

"That so?" Joy folded his arms.

"Donald Yonge. Fran's cousin. He manages that coal mine south of Edinburgh."

"I know who he is, Bishop."

"He was at the party at the Wrights'—you might've seen him."

"You don't know what you're talking about. The man who murdered Edwin is impaled on a chair in that house."

"I get why you'd think that. But McLean found a gold chain with little gems in it, remember? It belonged to Yonge."

"Planted, no doubt."

"I'm certain." I went to reach for the papers in my pocket but stopped.

"Listen, Bishop." He got in my face, and his hot breath beat against me. "You're done. No more fuckin' with my investigations. Next time I will arrest you. Get out of my city. I never want to see you again."

Talking with him was hopeless. There wasn't any humanity to appeal to in Joy. I clipped his shoulder as I stormed off.

Aimless, I walked through the night. The snowfall became heavier and piled quickly—a cold wind bit at my cheeks. My feet crunched on the snowy pavement. I walked past lavish New Town houses with golden lights inside and private, gated gardens. The bandages on my fingers needed to be replaced. My hand ached from punching McLean, and my bound fingers throbbed. The fight had soiled the bandages, and blood had soaked through.

I swallowed some Winslow's and tossed an empty bottle into the gutter.

All I could think about now was Petras. Yonge was at the party, and his watch chain was in Edwin's death grip. I thought about Petras's bloody clothes in my hotel room. What the fuck did it matter? Harry came to mind. She knew about the house Edwin bought for her. Perhaps she was there and happier than she was. A fresh start for her while I was stuck in this mess. Maybe she would know I took care of Joy for her and that image, one day.

Then I thought about my dad. All he wanted was to bury the past. Escape responsibility for his actions. No different to McLean. Dad wanted to deny Greta motherhood, refuse his son's life, and reject his fatherhood. He got everything he wanted. Why do evil men always win? He didn't send me here to find family, but I could've. He sent me here to bury his secrets, but the past, like the dead, never stays buried. The forgetful snow melts. It had melted. I wasn't sure if I had done good or if there was a chance of doing good in this city.

I was in Old Town when my feet stopped outside *Žmonių Balsas*.

57

It was after midnight when I opened the door to the tiny, dank office.

Lanka looked up from the typewriter. "Mr Bishop, what are you doing here?"

"I don't know. I saw your light on. Can we talk?"

My Lithuanian friend rose and repositioned his pince-nez on his face.

"What in the world happened to you?"

"The job," I said.

"Where did you go the other day?"

"Is Mr Blue angry?"

"He was less than thrilled. Do you have his chocolates?"

"What?"

"He wants his chocolates back."

I laughed. "Seriously? Tell him to bill me."

"I don't think you can afford these chocolates."

"Whatever. You could've given him my hotel."

"Rūta nearly did."

"Are you angry with me?"

Lanka's body eased: "Me? No."

"Rūta?"

"I don't believe she would do you any more favours."

"Suppose not. Not that I have any to ask."

"Sit down, son," Lanka said.

Son hit me like a truck. He said the word so naturally, with casualness and honesty. It meant nothing to him, but no one had ever called me son in that way. Maybe it was the day's events making me emotional? Hell if I knew.

I said: "Do you have anything strong to drink?"

We sat at the cluttered table with a glass of cheap, piss-yellow whisky.

"I want you to translate this." I handed him the letter written in Lithuanian that I found in Petras's wallet.

LUKE DECKARD

Lanka took it. "What do we have here?" Lanka skimmed it. "It says: 'I'm sorry I didn't explain before I left. I promise to tell you every detail when you get here. It all happened too fast and I needed to be stealthy and safe. I hope you don't feel that I have abandoned you. I would never do that. Petras, the city is exciting, and we have a house to ourselves. It's a great place for us to start over. Please come. We can get you a better, safer job. With love, Mother'."

"Nothing else?" I questioned. "It doesn't say where she is?"

"I'm afraid not. I presume you aren't any closer to finding Mrs Matienė?"

"No. After Mr Blue made her forged papers, she hopped on a train at Waverley, and that was it. But there's this Ian Clark fella who Greta was involved with. His mom caught them sleeping together and, to avoid a scandal, had Greta fired from the hotel. He apparently wanted to pay her off, too. I spoke to Mrs Clark—she claims she had nothing to do with Greta's disappearing act. I could go back to London and question Ian Clark—but why bother now? She's long gone, and so is Petras... I'm fed up with this shit."

"Where is the boy?"

I filled Lanka in on Petras's story. The murder at the mine, the lack of blood on his clothes, finding him at Mary Palvienė's, him fleeing, and his connection to Robin Rankin and the documents I found at Edwin Walter's.

I threw back the whisky—it gave me the chills as it went down.

"You say you don't think he committed this crime. Why?"

I explained what I knew about Petras—that the weigher, Clackman, was found axed to death in his lodging. The two argued the day before over wages, which Clackman was skimming. Petras knew and threatened him. Perfect motive, really, to kill someone. However, the clothes and the bloodstains didn't make sense. The axe Petras used was tossed into the fire, handle first.

"Why would he do that?" Lanka asked.

"Who knows? Threw the axe away, and it happened to land in the fire? Or someone wanted to burn fingerprints off the handle.

Pick whatever reason you want. Of course, then he tried to whack me with an iron poker before he was arrested. So maybe I am reading too much into things. Maybe he is a killer, and I just don't want it to be true because I don't want my..." The word 'brother' wouldn't come out—it was too personal.

Lanka waved his hands to catch up: "He hit you? Was it to kill?"

"He didn't intend to tickle me."

"Do you think he was trying to kill you?"

"Honestly? I think he was just scared. Fighting his way out. But if he's innocent, why run like this?"

"You are a smart man, Mr Bishop. But it is late, and you look like hell, so I will assume that is why you cannot see it."

"See what?" I asked.

"Men, women, we do extreme things when we are cornered," Lanka said. "We are animals, after all, Mr Bishop. There are primal instincts in us. You don't understand why he ran from the mine? Why did he not rely on the justice system? I can tell you."

Darius collected a stack of newspapers: copies of the *Bellshill Speaker* and *The Scotsman*.

"Read the articles I've circled."

DRUNKEN POLE IN COURT
Joseph Williams, a Pole, was fined ten shillings for being drunken disorderly.

BELLSHILL MURDER. POLISH MINER CHARGED. PLEA OF CULPABLE HOMICIDE
Ten years Penal Servitude and Deportation upon Completion.

POLE PLEADS GUILTY TO BEING DISORDERLY
Sentenced to 14 Days Imprisonment with Deportation to Russia. Bryce Hope Found Guilty of being Disorderly. Fined Ten Shillings.

CARFIN TRAGEDY
Pole Died After A Punch. Michael Miller – Charged Carfin

Blacksmith – Not Proven. A Popular Verdict.

"Now look at this," Lanka said. In small letters, the headline about a Scotsman read:

THE COATBRIDGE TRAGEDY
Young lad charged. Plea of Culpable Homicide. Accused lad's story: Verdict Not Guilty. Popular Finding.

Lanka, leaning back in his chair, swirling his pissy whisky, continued: "None of them were Polish, Mr Bishop; they are Lithuanians. Do you see? Do you think the law is on Petras's side?"
"No."
"That is the story of our people, not just here but wherever we go. Why fight a hopeless battle, Mr Bishop, for equality when running is easier?"
I rose and finished off the whisky. "So what hope is there?" I crossed the room to the door. "Thanks for the drink and the translation." I opened the door.
"Mr Bishop, try to consider Petras's life, his war… his hell."
I nodded, and I left hell on my mind.

58

I wandered back out into the cold, snowy night. It was nearly two in the morning, and I walked the dark mean streets of Old Town. Ghosts seemed to linger in the shadows.

Darius Lanka's talk hadn't helped. The headlines he showed me and the contradictions made me feel hopeless. Fourteen days imprisonment and deportation to Russia for a damn disorderly? A guy punches someone, and he dies, and the popular verdict is 'not proven'. Englishmen, Scotsmen, I know why they get off.

I'm no fool. Life is easier for a guy like me in many ways, but I felt stranded. I was isolated on an island of lamentation. Petras didn't stand a chance against someone like Yonge or Clackman. Who cares what I think I know about Petras's involvement? Facts don't matter against powerful people. People stomach fiction because reality feels like swallowing sawdust. Not five years since the war ended, what did we have to show? Homelessness, joblessness, destitution, overrun slums.

I thought about Mary Palvenė. I hoped Mary and those kids would have a better life back in Lithuania. I can't imagine what it must feel like to live in a country and be so despised by its people that they are willing to cover the costs just to get you out. She was a sweet woman. How many more were there just like her?

Maybe Rūta is right. Perhaps I wasn't immigrant enough to understand.

I diverted from my hotel and found myself now on the esplanade, trawling through several inches of untouched snow. Most of Princes Street Gardens was blanketed in white. A few dark figures moved over the snow. The wind was strong, and I flipped my coat collar up.

The clock face of the North British shone like a disc of yellow fire. A train pulled out of Waverley, with a trail of smoke coming from the stack. Lights from ships moved across the harbour in the far distance.

Time pulsed on, leaving the past further and further behind. The game was over—I don't know who won. No sermon could make me feel better, feel hopeful. At my feet were washed up bones on the dank shoreline of my mind.

The world is a damn hellscape. Murder, extortion, scams, eviction, lies, prejudice, segregation, it's not how people should behave. It's not what humanity should do, but we don't stop it. We go to war over and over again. We pretended that the last war ended future ones—that's a lie. Some places are still at war. And more wars will come. As a race, we continue to fail. We are nothing but a disillusioned species. And that's what we'll continue to be. Idiots playing chess and burying the dead over and over so that in the spring, we're reminded that all those bodies are feeding the earth, and we just continue it, continue on and on, over and over until we're that corpse and someone else's guilt.

I reached into my coat pocket and balled my hand around another bottle of Winslow's.

Guilt weighed my body down. I thought about the war. The time Tim, me and a few others raided a German trench. Enemy soldiers sat against the muddy wall. One Jerry was drenched in his own blood. His jaw was blown off, and his eyes rolled. But he was conscious… somewhat.

'We should piss on 'em,' one soldier said.

'No, we shouldn't,' Tim said.

'Get off me,' the soldier said. He was trying to undo his trousers and Tim was stopping him.

'Look out!' I shouted. Tim and the soldier turned. A hidden Jerry leapt out of a dark room swinging a club riddled with metal spikes. Tim ran and tripped. The crazed Jerry slashed at the other soldier. The spiked club took his helmet clean off before plunging into the side of his face. There was a wet crack as the Jerry yanked the club from the man's broken skull. I went to shoot as the wild-eyed soldier charged at me. The rifle jammed. I had to move quickly. The spiked club swung at me. The blow was blocked with my gun. I kicked the man in the gut, pushing him backwards.

The rifle was bent from the force of the club and unusable. He swung at me again. This time, the rifle was ripped out of my hands,

BAD BLOOD

and I fell over.

Bang! Bang! Two shots hit him. One in the arm, making him lose hold on the deadly club. The second in his leg. The Jerry fell over and writhed in pain.

Tim had got him with his pistol.

The club sat beside my enemy—his chest beat. I stood over him, and he looked up at me. It was like he had woken from a trance. His body trembled, and he started to sob. Tommy stood next to me and pointed his gun at the German. He begged with hands up: 'Nicht schießen, nicht schießen. Ich will nicht sterben…'

'Lower it,' I ordered Tim.

'Bishop?'

'I said, lower it.'

Tim did.

'Look at us,' I said. 'Look at what they turned us into…'

I saved a German, a so-called enemy. He didn't die. He became a POW.

I saved him, but I couldn't save Tim when that explosion tore him to shreds, or Petras, or Harry, or Dad. How was I a good man?

I was back in the present, standing on the esplanade in the snow. The cap on the Winslow's was off, and I stared at the bottle.

'*You have to let us go,*' Tim said in my mind.

No, I don't deserve to, I told myself. I deserve to be with you. Why do I get to roam the Earth while your corpse feeds it? What good am I doing here?

I removed the Colt from the holster and kept it at my side. I brought the bottle of Winslow's closer to my face and stared at it in silence.

What more can I do at this point? I'm so deep in this fucking labyrinth where there's nothing but bad memories and dead bodies. I wanted to leave the body count back in Europe. I didn't want it to follow me for this long, let alone grow like it has.

Tim was in the corner of my eye. A cold wetness streamed over my cheeks. He wasn't like he normally was, it was like the dream. He wasn't dead.

I thought about those cold trenches. The violence. The men who put bullets in their brains just to escape it all.

I raised the Colt and considered putting it in my mouth. My other hand, holding the Winslow's, shook. McLean's voice was in my head… that dirty bastard. But his advice… not letting this stuff control me, ruin me. I didn't know if I could escape.

I lifted the Colt and stared down the barrel into its blackness. I wanted the blackness to take me.

My mind flashed back to the dream I had with Tim. I wanted to go back there, and finally escape this hell I seemed trapped in. I wanted, no, I needed it. I was sick and tired of being here, being addicted to Winslow's, and being so fucked in the head. I needed to feel the peace that place could bring me.

I looked at the gun in one hand, the Winslow's in the other. This shit wasn't working for me anymore. My body trembled. "Goddammit, my nerves are shot to hell!"

As I stared into the black pit of the gun Tim's voice rang in my head: *'There are people who need you.'*

I dropped the Colt into the snow and then lopped the bottle of Winslow's over the side of the esplanade wall.

59

At 6.30am, I stared at my packed luggage. I had barely slept a wink. I hadn't killed myself; that was a relief, but I felt done and ready to go home. What good could I really do for Petras now? What chance was there of ever finding Greta? Dad was dead, I still needed to deal with that, and the gangsters after him and Greta were gone. I wanted to get out of this two-faced city. I had a cold shower and I realised then that I couldn't just go home. As I packed I found the page I took from the Wright's guestbook. I saw Fran and Joy's names. Turning it over, I saw Donald Yonge's.

It was late morning when I left the hotel. I didn't go to the train station. Instead, I went to the Royal Infirmary, where the Clairvoyant, otherwise known as Clive Roberts, was laid up in bed recovering from the gunshot wound I inflicted on him.

After I packed, I told myself I might not find Greta or do anything for Petras, but I could find out what Petras was involved in and maybe even solve a murder or two. Joy didn't want to listen to what I had to say about Yonge—he was done with me—but I wasn't done with him.

The Royal Infirmary stunk of antiseptic. Nurses and doctors darted up and down the corridors and in and out of rooms like chaotic bees looking for flowers.

I reached the men's ward and spotted Clive resting on a narrow spring bed. His arm was in a sling, and he looked a little pale and dehydrated.

"Wake up," I said, sitting beside his bed. On the table next to him were a half-drunk glass of water and a photograph of the leathery woman.

He opened his eyes, and a jolt of fear surged through him.

"You!" He looked around the room for help.

"It's good to see you," I said.

"What do you want?"

"For you to look at a photograph and tell me if you recognise the men."

LUKE DECKARD

I held up the photograph of Yonge and Clackman.

He refused to look and said: "You shattered my shoulder bone, and you killed Maud."

"No, dummy, you brought that on yourself. When you lied, scammed, and robbed people. Now before you get all self-righteous-criminal on me, I have an olive branch you'll want to take."

"Why should I believe you?"

"Because if you do, it might help you avoid a harsher jail sentence. So stop being a little punk and look."

I shook the picture of Donald Yonge and Thomas Clackman. "Do you recognise these men?"

He moved his eyes over the image and squirmed in his bed. Pain scrunched his face as he adjusted.

"Aye. That man," he pointed to Donald Yonge, "is the man I met at the party—he wanted Maud and me to pretend to channel Edwin Walter's son."

"And the other man?"

He studied the photo. "Aye. Aye, I do! He's the man who hired me tae steal the manuscript. He gave me the key tae the locker at the station."

"Are you certain?"

"Positive. That's him!"

"Okay."

I stood up and put the photograph into my pocket.

"How are you going tae help me?" Clive's eyes begged for reassurance.

"You got a lawyer?"

"Aye."

"Get him in here, make a statement. The men are Donald Yonge and Thomas Clackman." With that, I stood.

"I need that photograph. Where you going?"

"To catch a murderer."

60

I found a public telephone in the hospital and asked the operator to connect me to the Davies Colliery. The line was scratchy while I waited. I wanted to be sure Yonge was at the mine before I trekked out there to confront him. I was doing what Inspector Joy didn't want me to do, but I wasn't leaving Edinburgh with loose ends. He didn't believe me that Yonge killed Walter, and I was going to prove it.

"Hello, Davies Colliery."

It was a voice I knew. Robin Rankin. My other loose end sounded bright and chipper over the line.

"Hello, Robin," I said. "It's Logan Bishop. Is Yonge there?"

"Naw. I can take a message."

"No messages. Where is he?"

"No' here."

"I need you to tell me where he is."

There was silence down the line.

"Robin, it's urgent. I know Yonge and Clackman were skimming wages, and you gave information to Edwin Walter. I also know you lied when you said you didn't know Petras. You do. You know each other very well."

"I don't know him," she said unconvincingly.

"*Lispsnelè*, there's no sense in denying it. I have proof. I have the picture of you, the one you gave Petras."

"What do you want?" Robin's voice was shaken.

"Yonge is a dangerous man, Robin. I'll make sure he pays for his crimes. Just tell me, where is he?"

"I want nae part of… whatever this is! Goodbye."

"Robin, I can make things better for you and Petras if you tell me where Yonge is. I know Petras isn't a murderer, and I know you love him. No one will know you told me, and no one will know about you and Petras."

I stood there, silent, pressing the phone firmly to my ear. Robin wasn't speaking, nor had she hung up.

"You promise you can help Petras?"

"I promise."

"Mr Yonge is attendin' a dinner party tonight, at the castle."

"He's in Edinburgh?"

"Aye."

"What's the dinner for?"

"Tae discuss the future of the coal industry with Scottish Party leaders. But you cannae get in there."

"Why?"

"It's invitation only."

"Where is Yonge staying in Edinburgh? A hotel? Does he have a house?"

"I don't know. I just know that he'll be at the dinner."

"Fine. Oh, one more thing, Robin. Yonge had a pocket watch with a gold chain with gems; he broke it a few days ago, didn't he?"

"Aye. The chain fell off. He had me take it tae the watchmakers in the village tae have the chain replaced. Ah collected it for him yesterday."

"You have proof? Receipts?"

"Aye."

"Keep them safe. I'll be in touch."

I hung up. I was going to dinner at Edinburgh Castle.

BAD BLOOD

61

It was 7pm when I walked across the snowy esplanade towards Edinburgh Castle. There was a welcome reception at 7.30pm with dinner at 8pm. Torches blazed outside the castle entrance, throwing long, dark shadows against the Gothic fortress. Taxis and cars were funnelling in and dropping people off at the door. I had three ideas—wait and spot Donald Yonge before he goes inside, try to bribe the man at the door checking invites, or swipe an invite off someone. I couldn't find out if Donald Yonge was inside without giving myself away, which meant I could be waiting out in the cold for a hell of a long time. And I didn't care to do that. I wanted a confession from Yonge and to throw him down at Inspector Joy's feet. Ever since my dad arrived in London, I had done nothing but watch poor people suffer injustice at the hands of greedy, rich asses.

A short queue had formed at the castle entrance. I stood in line, trying to decide how to get inside and find Yonge. Ahead of me was an older man with large grey sideburns and a thick moustache, fiddling with a gold cigarette case in one hand and his invitation in the other. As he clumsily tried to open the case it slipped and landed on the ground. "Dammit!" he shouted and stuffed his invite into his coat pocket.

I shot down and picked up the heavy case, which shone in the firelight. The man turned towards me with a grateful look in his eye.

"Here you are," I said.

"Thank you," he replied. He took it and shook my hand. As we shook, I quickly lifted the invitation from the man's pocket. Smiling, he said: "I'm positively gagging for a smoke. Care for a fag?"

"No, thank you."

When we reached the entrance, the man at the door asked for an invitation. The man patted himself down and twisted and turned. "I bloody had it a few minutes ago. Can you just let me in?"

LUKE DECKARD

"I need to see the invitation, sir," the doorman said.

The old man looked at me and asked: "Did you see it?"

"Sorry, no. Maybe you dropped it back there?"

"Dammit."

While he stormed back to where he dropped his cigarette case, I flashed the invite and got inside. Dinner was being held in the Great Hall. I didn't care to sit around a bunch of slimy businessmen and greasy politicians and pretend to be someone I wasn't. I followed the crowd around the castle grounds. The stone paths were lit with lanterns. There were many dark corners.

I found the Great Hall. Three rows of tables went longways down the elaborate and royal room. A head table was in front of a large stone fireplace on the far side. The walls were covered in fine wood panelling, and suits of armour stood guard around the room. A violinist and harpist were in one corner playing sweet melodies while fat old men drank, chit-chatted, and laughed.

I scanned faces for Donald Yonge. A waiter offered me a glass of wine from his tray. I took it and had a little sip as I circled the hall, looking for my target.

Donald Yonge's ginger beard stood out. I spotted him near the entrance, talking to a group of men. His suit looked a little big on his hefty frame. I slithered through the crowd towards him.

"Good evening, Mr Yonge..." I said, interrupting the conversation.

"Yes, hullo, uh, don't I know you?" His mouth was a little black hole in his ginger-bearded face.

"Logan Bishop. We spoke about Petras."

"Oh. Aye, the private detective." He glanced at my bandaged hand and the scabbed scratches on my face. "What happened to you?"

"Occupational hazard," I said.

Yonge smiled. The men around us looked at each other, confused.

"You have a perfectly adequate memory, Mr Yonge." I looked at the other men. "If you gentlemen don't mind, would you excuse us just a moment? I need to borrow Mr Yonge." Before Yonge could protest, I put my arm around him and led him outside into the cold courtyard. Torches whipped in the wind.

"What's the meaning of this, Mr Bishop?"

I glanced at his shiny new golden watch chain. "Did you break your watch?"

"What?" He reached for it. "No."

"Yeah, that's not your normal chain, Donny. You put a new chain on it since I saw you last."

"Ah… aye, well, uh, the last one came loose."

"How'd that happen?"

"It, uh, just did. Why are you here?" Agitation grew in his voice.

"First, let me give you my condolences."

"I beg your pardon?"

"Your cousin is Fran Walter, correct?"

"She is."

"Her husband was murdered. Stabbed in the throat."

Donald Yonge hesitated. "Yes. It's a tragedy."

"Well, I'm sorry for your loss."

"Thank you. But that's not why you're here… is this to do with Peter Mathews?"

"His name is Petras. And, actually, *Edwin* is why I'm here."

He cocked his head. "I don't understand."

I leaned in and whispered into his ear: "You killed him."

"I beg your pardon?" He took a dramatic step back.

"Your watch chain was found in his hand, Donny."

"M-my what?"

"The golden chain with the little gems."

Yonge looked over his shoulder towards the entrance to the Great Hall. A few people stood by the door smoking. Yonge's eyes met mine. The yellowish-orange light from the fires danced across his face. "Let's go somewhere private to talk, huh?"

I waved my hand. "After you."

Yonge led, and I followed him across the courtyard into the darkness.

62

The noise of the dinner party began to fade as we walked deeper into the dark areas of the castle. We left the courtyard through a pinch between two buildings. There were no torches, no electric lights, just blackness, the crunch of feet on white snow, and the whistle of the wind. In the distance, the sky over New Town glowed yellow in the hazy fog. Ahead was a structure with a short, chunky, cylindrical tower. Between it and an elevated platform, I caught a glimpse of the city lights below.

"I understand why you'd want to kill him…" I said.

Donald Yonge faced me. He was breathing heavily. "Mr Bishop, this intimidation tactic won't work. You understand?"

"I know Edwin Walter hoarded incriminating information, including stuff on how you and Thomas Clackman skimmed wages from your miners."

"There's no proof of any of that!" he scoffed.

"I also know you arranged to have Edwin's manuscript stolen."

Yonge laughed. "Preposterous."

"I have a witness. I can also place you in Edinburgh the night of the murder at the Wrights' house party. Your watch chain was found in his dead hand, which I've linked back to you."

Donald Yonge shook his head.

"Then where are the police?" he asked.

"I wanted you first. Then they can have you."

He licked his lips nervously and nodded.

He swung a right hook. I ducked, feeling the wind of it hit my face.

I pulled out my gun. As I did, Donald Yonge grabbed my wrist, twisting it until I lost hold. My gun smacked on the ground. He moved quickly and growled with fury. I painfully clenched my hand with the bandaged fingers and swung. I clipped Yonge in the head. It had no effect. His meaty hand grabbed me by the collar and heaved me forward. My face skidded across the rough, snowy cobbles. My cheek burned. He picked me up and threw me on my back, then grabbed my bandaged fingers and squeezed. A pulsing pain surged through me and I shouted. He slugged me in the gut, knocking the wind out of me and shutting me up.

My head spun as he dragged me several feet across the ground. I didn't have the coordination to do anything.

Suddenly, Yonge hoisted me up, and I found myself tumbling down a hill over frozen earth and rock. A lamp-post broke my fall. I looked up—Yonge had thrown me over the edge of a short, nasty drop. I lay there, aching and bleeding. I spat blood. Pure luck meant my body fell down the smoothest route, missing the sharp drop and most jagged rock.

I crawled towards the battery of cannons and propped myself against the stone wall. A moment later, I heard footsteps. Donald Yonge came into view. He scanned the area, looking for my body.

Every inch of me ached, but if he found me, I knew I was a dead man. I crawled towards the One O'Clock Gun as quickly and quietly as possible. There was a crack of a gunshot, and a piece of the stone wall exploded in front of me.

"On your feet." Donald Yonge approached me. I painfully stood up. Behind me, just over the wall, was a steep drop. "I did what had to be done." My Colt was in his hand. "Do you have any idea how many lives that man ruined? How many other people out there hated him and feared what he knew? I had to get that book when I found out he had written a tell-all memoir."

"Who told you?"

"Fran! I had to know what he wrote about me. The bastard had put it all in there. And *she* knew. She knew and didn't care. I told her I wanted that book. She said to deal with Edwin myself. She wouldn't get involved."

"So, hired Clive to get Harry out of the house the same night Fran was at the party so that you could murder him!"

"I did the world a favour. You have to understand. Edwin's book would've ruined so many people."

"Killing does no favours, even when they are scum, Donald."

Donald Yonge looked over New Town. My gun waved in his hand. "I gave him a chance. I told him I had his book and that I wanted his carbon copies. I told him I knew Tommy had been leaking information to him. And if he would hand over whatever else he had and promised to leave me alone, I'd leave him alone. He wouldn't do it."

"Wait, so it was you. You killed Thomas Clackman," I said. "And Petras, the argument he and Clackman had over the wages. You sorry son of a bitch, you framed Petras."

"That damn Pole had been running his mouth for months. I had had enough of it."

"Christ."

"Tommy and the Pole had it coming…"

"Only you didn't expect Petras to get away."

"The fucking Pole doesn't matter now. Let him rot in the wilderness. No one would believe him if he told the truth."

"Do you still have Edwin's manuscript and carbon copy?"

"You'll never get it."

Yonge extended his arm, and I dove just as he fired my Colt. I jumped behind the cannon. Bullets exploded pieces off the stone wall and ricocheted off the cannon's surface.

The gun clicked. It was out of bullets. He threw the gun and growled.

I felt a sting in my left arm. Yonge had clipped me, and I was bleeding.

He stormed around the cannon, his face red with fury. He picked me up and hauled me to the wall. I grabbed his hands and tried to gain purchase with my feet—nothing.

Yonge pushed me up and onto the parapet. Below was a steep drop over sharp rocks. I grabbed the wall. Yonge pressed harder. My grip slipped.

"What's the meaning of this?" shouted a new voice.

Yonge jolted. He let go of me and turned around. I pulled myself back from the abyss.

The gunshots had brought a crowd. They surrounded us.

"What's the meaning of this, Yonge?" a voice said.

"This man… he, he tried to kill me," Yonge said.

I laughed. It surprised me. It also surprised Yonge. He glared at me. I sat on the ground, my face cut, my arm bloody, aching from the pounding and the fall.

"Donald Yonge is responsible for the murder of Edwin Walter," I said, pulling myself up and limping away from Yonge, towards the crowd.

"Shut your mouth!" he said.

"He's also responsible for murdering Thomas Clackman and trying to frame it on one of his miners."

"You shut up!"

"It's over," I said.

"Is it?"

Yonge was stuck, like an animal in a trap. The crowd of his peers stared him down. The information was out. His secrets were busted. "You don't understand!"

A couple of palace guards stepped forward. One helped me stand. Another moved towards Yonge.

"Stay back!" Yonge shouted. He was frantic. He inched away.

"Come with me, sir," the guard said.

Yonge climbed onto the parapet. The crowd gasped, and the guard ordered him down. Yonge looked over his shoulder. His body trembled.

"I'm not sorry," Yonge said. "I did the world a favour!" And he stepped back, and his body fell into the abyss below.

My head spun.

"I could really use a doctor now," I said before I fell unconscious.

63

I spent the night in a hospital. The gunshot wound was stitched, my hand was cleaned and bandaged, and my ribs were wrapped. Thankfully, none were broken, only bruised. I even had a peaceful, dreamless sleep.

In the morning, the Devil was at my bedside. Inspector Joy stood over me with arms crossed and the V features of his face sharpened.

"Donald Yonge is dead," he said.

"I figured," I replied, sitting up in bed.

Inspector Joy removed a thick folder from under his arm. He placed it on my lap. "Open it," he said. I did. Inside was a manuscript, and on the first page I read:

THEY LIE
by Edwin Walter

"The manuscript?" I said.

"Aye. A carbon copy, too."

"Where did you find it?" I asked.

"I went to Yonge's house this morning and looked around." Joy's tense body eased, and he walked over to the window and looked out. He continued with his back to me: "I didn't want to hear it when you told me Yonge was responsible, but I should've listened to you." Turning back to me he added: "I also should've known you wouldn't drop it and leave Edinburgh. Anyway, there's a full investigation into Yonge."

"He killed Thomas Clackman, Joy. Petras didn't."

Joy leaned back with his arms crossed. "Maybe."

"No 'maybe' about it. Yonge told me he set the whole thing up. He wanted to frame Clackman's death on Petras. I think Yonge would've killed Petras, made it look like they did it to themselves, but he got away."

"I'm inclined to believe you, but I need the kid to corroborate that and explain why he ran."

"Because who would believe him?" I said.

Joy nodded.

Then he asked: "Any idea where he is?"

"None."

"Truthfully?"

I nodded. "But I'll look for him. More than anyone here, I want to see him cleared."

"Why's that, Bishop?"

"I just do," I said.

"Well, if you ever find him, send him my way." Joy paused. "We got McLean to talk. We shut down the brothel where he... well, we rescued some kids."

"Good."

Joy approached my bed. He extended his hand. I lifted my good arm and we shook hands. We didn't need to say anything more. Joy didn't suddenly like me, but there was a new-found respect—and it was mutual, or so I felt.

Joy took Edwin Walter's manuscript and went to the door. He said, "I don't think you deserved that blue ticket," and left before I could reply.

I lay there, moved. Had I actually done some good? Maybe, but there was still more that needed to be done. There was one person who still might know where Petras was, and bruised and stitched, I wanted to tie up that last loose end.

64

The next morning, I travelled to Davies Colliery. My arm was in a sling, and the bandages around my ribs were tight, which forced me to keep a near-perfect posture when all I wanted was to slouch. Despite the pain, I knew I had to come here. I had to get the answers I needed.

The sky was dark. A few inches of snow clung to the frozen earth: the grind and whirl of machinery rumbled like thunder from inside the coal mine. The sulphuric and oily smell made my throat itch.

I went to the main office and found Robin Rankin sat at her desk, twirling her hair and talking on the telephone. The acne on her face looked more vivid than the last I saw her. She saw me and hung up the phone.

"What happened tae you?" she said.

"I ran into a door," I said, smiling.

I grabbed one of the waiting chairs, dragged it over to the desk, and sat facing her. I huffed and said, "Donald Yonge is dead."

Robin locked eyes on me: "I heard. Did you?"

I didn't reply. I took out the photograph of her and the letter she gave Petras and laid them on her desk. "Listen, I'm on your side," I said. "I get it. You were protecting Petras, but you don't need to anymore. Yonge admitted to killing Clackman and wanting to frame Petras. But you knew this already, didn't you?"

"Aye." Her eyes welled up, and her face turned pale. Robin's shoulders began to shake, and in her eyes, I could see the look of horror that lingers beneath the surface of every soldier who's witnessed too much death.

"You were there when it happened."

The tears were now running down Robin's cheeks. She buried her face in her hands and sobbed. I went around and placed my hand in the middle of her back.

When she finished crying, she said she needed a smoke, and we went outside. She lit a cigarette and inhaled.

"We shouldnae have done it—run, I mean." She took another hit of her cigarette. "On the day it happened, after work, I told Mr Yonge I was headin' home but instead went tae Petras's. We've been together for some time. He said the rota worked out that he had the lodgin' tae himself for the evenin', so... When I was there, there was this loud bangin' on the door. Petras told me tae hide in the closet.

"He answered, and it was Mr Clackman. He was ragin', sayin' somethin' about Yonge wantin' him tae get rid of him. Then there was another knock, and it was Mr Yonge. Petras was terrified. The men were shouting. Then I heard the... the commotion. I heard Mr Yonge hit Clackman with the axe. Petra yelled. There was a thud. Yonge said he'd blame Petras for this if he didnae do what he said. That's when I heard the door open—that's when Petras ran.

"I waited for Mr Yonge tae leave before I came out. That's when I saw Mr Clackman. There was so much blood."

Robin finished off her cigarette.

"When I got home," Robin continued, "Petras was waitin' for me. Said he didnae know what else tae do and asked me tae run away with him. But we needed money. He was goin' tae see if anyone in Edinburgh could help him, and he asked me tae write tae his mum for money."

"Greta? Grace?" I corrected.

"Aye."

"Where is Petras now?"

"He wrote tae me. He made it tae London. He's with his mam."

"London?" I said. "What's the address?"

"Ivy House, The Boltons, Kensington."

"She's in been in London this whole time..."

I started to laugh to myself.

"What's so funny?" Robin asked.

"I just can't believe it." I pushed my hat up and rubbed my brow.

"You said you could help us?" Robin said.

"I did, and I will. There will be an investigation, but Petras won't be blamed. For once, the law will be on his side. I want you to write to Petras... tell him everything is okay, and I'm going to see him and his mother."

65

Two days later, after several interviews with Edinburgh police, I handed over Edwin Walter's documents, and Robin and Clive the Clairvoyant gave statements to back up everything. I sat on the train waiting to depart Waverley with 400 miles of track to reconquer. When I returned to London, I knew I needed to make arrangements for my dad. I also needed to write to my family and tell them about why Dad came to see me and how he died. I needed to figure out how to tell them that his death was the result of foolish greed and infidelity. But other things were pressing on my mind.

I had to get back to London and speak with Greta, and tell my brother everything would be okay. I needed to get to The Boltons.

I knew The Boltons. It was a fancy address in Kensington. How Greta ended up there was just one of the last remaining mysteries I needed to clear up.

Guilt rose in me as the train rocked onwards. I craved the last Winslow's in my pocket. I balled my fist and refused to fetch it. Instead, I reached into my pocket, and took out one of the chocolates I'd nabbed from Mr Blue and tossed it into my mouth. I bit down on something hard—for a split second, I worried my tooth had broken. I spat the saliva-drenched, soft-centred chocolate into my hanky. My finger dove into my mouth—no broken teeth.

I looked at the partly chewed chocolate. In the middle of it were two white diamonds. I broke open the other chocolates and found two more diamonds, a ruby and a sapphire. Mr Blue was smuggling precious stones in chocolates. No wonder he wanted them back. I thought about the emerald ring and the gangster with the scarred face who I let take it, and I laughed.

66

Percy Street was a sight for sore eyes. London, unlike Edinburgh, wasn't covered in snow. I was glad to be back home and nearly done. There was excitement in the air, and I realised I'd returned the day before Christmas Eve. I went home, tidied my flat from when Spatty and his pals broke in, and slept.

The following morning, I set out for Greta for the last time. I exited Gloucester Road station and headed to The Boltons, walking between imposing elegant Kensington houses.

Ivy House was a two-storey terraced mansion with a balcony on the first floor. A glass awning led from the front gate to the door. In the first-floor window, I saw the face of a young man—it was Petras. He ducked out of view as I went under the awning and pressed the doorbell.

A beautiful blonde woman answered. Her long hair was parted at the side and framed her face. She wore a yellow blouse with an electric-blue vest over the top and an earthy green skirt, and maroon shoes. Her crystal-blue eyes stared at me with frightened recognition.

I removed my hat.

"Hello, Miss Grace," I said like I was a child, and she was still my Sunday school teacher.

"Little Logan?" I recognised her voice all these years later—a hint of Eastern European with a bit of American.

"Not so little anymore."

"No, I suppose you're not. What happened to you?" She reached out a kind hand and laid it on my shoulder. I must've been a sight. My left arm was in a sling, the fingers on my left hand bandaged from my fingernails being torn off, the right side of my face scratched and bruised.

"It's a long story. I brought your suitcase."

I lifted the battered case and she took it.

"Oh my."

"Can we talk?"

"I think we should." She placed the case down.

"Grace? Who's at the door?" a man's voice came from inside.

I looked past Greta to see him. He was either a few years younger than I or well-preserved. He wore brown and tan plaid trousers and a beige sweater vest over a white shirt.

"Ian Clark?" I asked Greta.

She nodded.

"Grace, darling, what's going on?" Ian Clark came up behind her and was staring at me. I was confused all over again. He put his arm around her, and that's when I spotted the wedding rings. The son of a bitch married her? He ditched his engagement.

"Ian, this is my... old friend, Logan Bishop. I used to teach him in Sunday school when I lived in America."

"Is that right?" he said with a smile. Logan Bishop? I know that name."

"Yeah, your mother isn't my biggest fan," I said.

"Good lord, you're the PI who was snooping around the hotel? Yes, my lawyers told me my mother sent her lawyers to scare you off."

"She tried, but it didn't work. Sorry, but I think someone needs to explain a thing or two. You were engaged?" I said to Ian Clark.

"I was. But that wasn't what I wanted. Grace is." He looked at Greta... Grace... and smiled.

It was nice to see a couple who married for love, not anything else. Especially after Harry, Edwin, Fran, and every other fucked up love story I'd encountered in Edinburgh.

"I'm so sorry, chap. Would you like to come in for tea or coffee?" Ian Clark asked. "Better than standing in the cold. I'm sure we have some cake too."

"Ian," Greta turned to him. "I would like to go for a walk with Little Logan. Is that okay?"

Ian melted at her sweet smile.

"By all means," he said. "I have work to see to."

Greta grabbed a thick brown coat, a chocolate cloche hat, and gloves, and we left. We walked up the road, her shoes clapping on the pavement, my gumshoes less so.

"Miss Grace—"

"It's just Grace, Logan."

"How did it happen, you and Ian Clark?"

"It just did. His family often came to the hotel, and he was always very kind to me, unlike some other guests. He would flirt with me. I never thought much of it until one time we kissed. We had a secret relationship for a few months; then his parents forced an engagement on him—it was something he never wanted. The last time Ian was at the hotel, his mother walked in on us, and I lost my job."

"That's when you went to your communist pals for work?"

"I needed money, Logan. I kept waiting for your father, who promised me money, but it never came."

"It was inside the bear," I said.

"What?"

"There was an emerald ring sewn inside."

"I had no idea," Grace said.

"I know. But Rūta Kanaitė, though, she got you a nice job as a nanny."

"I don't know if you can understand this, but I just got it in my head that I wanted to go to America. I wanted to confront your father. I thought the bear was a joke, and I knew Marsh Travel could get me there. Everything was in place for me to travel to America when Ian contacted me. He said he wanted to be with me and didn't care what it meant to his family. I told him what I planned, but he said just come to London."

"Henrikas saw you at Waverley, at the lockers."

"Yes. He caught me. I didn't know what I was going to do. I collected the documents and just made the choice. Ian had a ticket for me at the office, but I still wanted to confront your father. But I threw the fake papers in the trash and came to London to meet him instead of fetching a boat from Glasgow to America. I chose Ian over revenge. He married me the day my train arrived. His mother won't be too pleased when she finds out."

"Did Petras take it well?" I asked.

"He's come around, yes."

"You two had an argument—Mary Palvienė walked in on it. Was it about Ian?"

"Goodness, no. I told him about my wanting to go to America. He was angry that I considered working for Marsh. Petras and I have had some difficulties these last few years. He doesn't approve of my politics. But we spoke before I left. He encouraged me to go to London to be with Ian. We can be family here, Ian, Petras and I. Would you like to meet Petras properly?"

"I'd like that," I said. "But the boy needs help."

"Ian will help him. He's promised me."

I told Grace about Donald Yonge, Clackman, Edwin Walter, and Robin. I promised I would help in any way I could and told her Inspector Joy believed Petras's story too. Then I said: "Grace. I read Dad's letters to you. What went on?" We turned up Old Brompton Road. "Why, after all these years, did you contact him?"

"Desperation. I was angry, Logan, at my circumstances and what your father did. Your father and I were together for two years. I loved him. It was wrong, I know all that, but I thought he loved me too until I became pregnant. He did what men do best and panicked. My father barely made enough at the meat factory for the two of us, let alone a baby, so it was decided I would go to Edinburgh, where I had family. Your father paid, and he promised me an allowance. All I had was the money he gave me when I got on the train to New York. I never saw another penny. I was angry that I was forced to struggle to make ends meet for all these years. I finally wrote to your father and demanded he helped us. After all, Petras is his son too." She paused for thought. "Logan, if someone told me what my life would be like right now two months ago I never would've believed them. I never would've written to your father. But I had no money, and Petras was not doing well at the mine either."

We entered Brompton Cemetery. It felt right, digging up the past as we walked amongst the tombstones and mausoleums.

"I'm sorry," Grace continued, "about what happened between your father and me and what that did to you. I can't say it was all down to me being young, ignorant, and impressionable. I knew I shouldn't have gotten involved with a married man."

"The way I see it, my dad was great at one thing—manipulating and using people. He did it to you. He did it to me. Right up till the very end."

"The end?"

"He's dead."

"How?"

I told her what had happened. We walked several loops around Brompton Cemetery as I told her Dad came with a ring he'd taken from some dangerous people who followed him to London. That he wanted my help to bring it to her, but they got to him first, and his lies put her in their sights. That I thought they were going to kill her, so I went up with the ring to make sure they didn't, and to find out who they were and what her connection was to my dad. I told her how it had spun out of control, and I ended up looking for Petras and investigating the murder at the coal mine, which led me to believe he didn't do it, but which also led to her address in London. I told Grace what Mary, Mrs Mears, Henrikas, Rūta Kanaitė and Gabriel went through for her, for Petras. "If you'd just told one of them what was happening, a lot of pain could've been avoided."

"I couldn't tell anyone," Grace said. "I couldn't risk it."

"Because of the fake papers made for you at Marsh Travel?"

"I knew they would come after me. I didn't want them to find me." We came to the other end of the cemetery, and Grace took my hand. "I know I hurt you as a boy, and now you've gone to such lengths to find me... to help me, to help Petras. It's more than I deserve."

"I'm just glad you're safe and alive."

She smiled. "You are an impressive young man."

"I'm a private investigator, Grace. It's what I do."

"I remember when you wanted to be a cowboy."

We laughed. It felt nice. But the smiles faded.

"Logan?"

"Yes?"

"Can you find it in your heart to forgive me?"

We stopped, and I placed a hand on her arm: "I never had any resentment towards you, just Dad."

A partial smile formed on her broken, sad face. "Little Logan. If you can, try to forgive your father."

I walked Grace back home and hugged her goodbye at the front door.

"What are you doing for Christmas?" Grace asked.

"Nothing."

"Why don't you come over tomorrow for dinner, and you can see Petras. After the holidays all the serious talk can resume."

"I'd like that."

***

I found my way back to Gloucester Road station. I still had work to do. I needed to arrange to have my father's body sent back to the States and write to the family. But I felt something I hadn't in years: relief. Like maybe there was a way forward? Maybe I could leave the war, my war, behind.

From my pocket, I removed the last bottle of Winslow's. I finally understood what it represented. It was never an escape. It was a prison. Greta had managed to free herself from her prison. Just like Greta, I was no longer walking in the darkness of the past, and I didn't have to either.

I could never forget what Dad had done to me, Petras, and Grace, but in time, I could forgive him. The bad blood between us was gone. Perhaps after everything, there is peace in this life?

As I approached the underground station, I tossed my last, full bottle of Winslow's into the gutter where it belonged. I could that that go too.

Entering the underground, I flipped up my coat collar and didn't look back.

BAD BLOOD

Acknowledgements

Many thanks to Dr Adam Baron and Dr James Miller at Kingston University who supervised *Bad Blood* throughout my PhD; Claire, my lovely and beautiful wife, for your endless encouragement and support; Bonnie MacBird, James Benmore, and James Pierson for giving up your time to read the different iterations of this novel over the years and always believing in this project; Special shout out to Ian Skewis, Kate Griffin, Jamie West, my family in the States, and of course, you, the reader.

Get In Touch
Luke is on X, Threads, and Instagram **@lukewritescrime**
Listen to **Mean Streets - The Film Noir Podcast**, Luke's weekly show with cohost and author Matthew Booth, on Spotify, Apple Podcasts or wherever you listen.
Contact him via lukedeckard.com

Printed in Great Britain
by Amazon